NINE LADIES
A PRIDE AND PREJUDICE VARIATION

HEATHER MOLL

EXCESSIVELY
DIVERTED
PRESS

Copyright © 2021 by Heather Moll

Excessively Diverted Press

All rights reserved.

No part of this book may be reproduced in any form or by any electronic or mechanical means, including information storage and retrieval systems, without written permission from the author, except for the use of brief quotations in a book review.

This is a work of fiction. Names, characters, businesses, places, events, locales, and incidents are either the product of the author's imagination or used in a fictitious manner. Any resemblance to actual persons, living or dead, or actual events, is purely coincidental.

Edited by Lopt & Cropt Editing Services

Proofread by Regency Proofreading LLC

Cover by Carpe Librum Book Design www.carpelibrumbookdesign.com

ISBN: 978-1-7351866-1-0 [ebook] and 978-1-7351866-2-7 [paperback]

For Sarah

For the acrostic jewelry, for going to the real Nine Ladies with me, and for everything in between and since

PROLOGUE

Thursday, March 21, 1811
Vernal equinox
Stanton Moor, Derbyshire

A black rain cloud menaced as Pemberley's gamekeeper rode across the moor. Nothing would prevent Hank Roland from fulfilling his responsibility to the Darcy family, but he could no longer avoid the consequence of time on one's body. It was past due that he bring his grandson with him on this important, furtive task. He could not ride out here every spring and autumn forever.

"Grandfather?" Young Henry's voice cracked. "What are we doing here?"

"I told you we must see to the stones." Roland dismounted and gestured for him to leave his horse and cart.

He heard an adolescent huff. "Aye, but you did not tell me why."

"We neither of us need a reason. If you want to be in the employ of the Darcys, you will do as you are bid. That it was old Mr. Darcy's wish is enough."

"Does the present Mr. Darcy know we are here?"

"Aye, he doesn't like it, but he knows." They penetrated the wood on foot toward the stone circle. "And you will not tell another human being about our being here."

"I won't! If this is what Pemberley's gamekeeper must do, I shall do it without reservation." Young Henry was a good lad. Ambitious, but he was loyal to Pemberley.

They arrived at the clearing with a rough ring of nine upright rocks each about three feet high. Roland pulled out his pocket watch, a gift from his late master, and squinted; his grandson lifted the lantern higher.

"'Tis well after sunset. If anything were to happen, it would have by now." Roland relaxed his shoulders and turned around.

Instead of following, Young Henry took several paces into the clearing, holding the lantern aloft. "Grandfather! I see something!"

"You cannot let your imagination take a flight o' fancy."

Young Henry sprinted toward the stones, and now, with his lantern swinging, casting beams of light off and on the circle, Roland saw what had caught his attention, and he, too, ran.

"I'll be damned!"

"What do we do? Is he hurt?"

"I don't think 'tis a he," Roland whispered.

"But looka' what he's wearing!"

Roland grabbed the lantern and stepped into the circle to get a better view. No, it was not a boy, in spite of the clothes. The young woman wore blue trousers that fit her legs as tight as buckskin. Roland was distracted by the improper sight of the lady's loose brown tresses. The gamekeeper shook his head, still marveling that this shocking occurrence could truly happen.

"Has she struck her head?" Young Henry's voice cracked.

This roused him; he hurried to the woman's side. There was no visible wound, but her eyes were closed, and although she breathed, she appeared lifeless. "Take my horse and ride ahead! Speak only to Mrs. Reynolds, do you hear? Tell no one else. I shall bring her in the cart."

"'Tis four miles to Pemberley, but Haddon Hall is only two, and there might—"

"Do you understand nothing?" The gamekeeper took the lady in his arms, no longer feeling old now that he had an urgent purpose. "Go directly to Reynolds and tell her it has happened again!"

Young Henry ran through the birch woods. Although Roland had come to the stone circle every spring and autumn at sunset for over twenty-five years, only a few times had he found anyone.

A troubled feeling settled in his stomach. He knew after he consigned the woman to Reynolds, he must speak with the master. Mr. Darcy would not be pleased.

CHAPTER ONE

Thursday, March 17, 2011
Beech Hill Rehabilitation Unit
Sheffield, South Yorkshire

Disposing of the flowers was the easiest way to begin. Their petals drooped, and brown leaves floated in the water. The contents of the en suite went into the trash. She had taken her father's clothes to the launderette the day before he died so the wardrobe was nearly empty.

Elizabeth Bennet took a calming breath before she put the picture frames in a box, which produced a brief coughing fit. One had a picture of her and Jane as children, and the other was from Jane's graduation. She thought her father might be interested since he had only seen his daughters twice during those years. She had not displayed any that included his ex-wife. *Why distress a frustrated man recovering from a stroke?*

The books were the hardest to pack. The expressive aphasia had left her father isolated and discouraged, but it did not affect his thinking. From two to four, she had read to him, every single day. For someone whose profession involved physics and subatomic particles, her father had had a strange fondness for poetry like Wordsworth and Cowper, and the works of Shakespeare.

Elizabeth coughed again as she packed the books. She was a reader too. It was a shame she never had the opportunity to share that interest with her father.

Then again, that was entirely his fault.

"Good morning." Elizabeth turned as she heard the unit matron's voice. "The ward sister would've done this for you."

"It was no trouble." Her father was interred, without ceremony, yesterday. She preferred to do something useful rather than sit in her rented house in Bakewell wondering what to do next with her life.

"I wanted to say, on behalf of the entire team, how sorry I am for your loss. Mr. Bennet's passing was unexpected." They had been planning how her father could live independently after he was discharged when she got the call he had suffered a fatal heart attack.

"Thank you. Is Dr. Lucas making ward calls today?"

The unit matron nodded and, after empty words about bereavement and time, finally left.

Elizabeth looked over the empty room, and heard the voice of the general practitioner she'd met soon after she arrived in England ask, "How are you holding up?" Charlotte was a gentle, sensible woman, several years older than herself. *So much like Jane.*

"I'm all right." Disappointment of having lost the chance to know her father still struck her, but Elizabeth thought she was coping well enough. Her regrets were easier to manage when she remembered his long-standing disinterest in his daughters, save for twice-yearly checks.

"You aren't going back to the States yet, are you?"

She shook her head. "My family visitor visa is good for months still, and I have the flat in Bakewell for the year. My father had a three-bedroom semi-detached in Alvaston and I'll stay in England until it sells, then send Jane a check."

"After what you told me about your sister, will she accept it?"

Elizabeth cleared her throat as she remembered Jane's parting words. *"I can't believe you're abandoning your MBA to take care of him! After he left us?"* Her mother expressed the same sentiment, using more expletives, adding that if Elizabeth took care of "that man," she would never speak to her again. She had never replied to Elizabeth's text that her children's father had died. "Jane will accept the money. Her equal share of a hundred and fifty thousand pounds would go a long way to repaying her med school loans."

"It's a shame your sister can't see your point of view."

"She's not one to hold a grudge like my mother. Jane's the peacemaker." Elizabeth was used to being a disappointment to her mother; Jane's rejection, though temporary, was harder to bear. She changed the subject. "How's your sister? You said she got the internship she wanted, working with old newspapers?"

"How about I come to Bakewell this weekend and stay with you?" Charlotte's voice was soft, and the kindness from the only friend Elizabeth had made since she arrived in England felt overwhelming. "We'll do some sightseeing."

"I'm fine." It had been lonely spending every day in the sole company of an ill man she hardly knew, who could scarcely communicate.

"You may've been born in England, but all you've seen of it is Manchester airport and hospital rooms. My sister and some friends can join us too. You don't mind houseguests and a little walking?"

The prospect of a weekend with friends was cheering, but another cough interrupted her answer.

"I don't like that cough." Charlotte put her stethoscope to her ears. "How long have you had it?"

"A week."

"Any fever, sore throat, or runny nose? Asthma?"

"No, just a cough."

Charlotte removed the stethoscope. "You look like you've lost weight."

"Why, thank you." Elizabeth flashed a smile, but Charlotte's stern expression drove it away. "I haven't been eating or sleeping well. My mother hates me, my sister is disappointed in me, and the father I wanted to connect with died four days ago. A cold and stress, that's all."

"I'd suggest paracetamol, and rest and fluids for a cold, but since you've spent so much time among the patients, I can't rule out hospital-acquired pneumonia. You may need a chest X-ray."

"I have a *cold*!"

"Bacterial pneumonia is common among patients." When Elizabeth shook her head, Charlotte sighed. "You have ordinarily resident status, right, on the NHS? Do you have kidney problems, liver disease? Are you taking other drugs?" Charlotte pulled out her script pad, scribbled, and tore off a sheet. "Erythromycin, 250 mg, every six hours. I'll give you two weeks' worth in case you develop a fever and it's a bacterial infection. If you have a fever or chest pain when I come to Bakewell, we are going straight to surgery for an X-ray."

Elizabeth shifted the box to her other hip to take the prescription. "I have to run to make the bus. Do you remember how to get to my place?"

"Yes, and we'll come Saturday morning instead to give you more time to rest. But you do need some fun—doctor's orders."

ELIZABETH ARRIVED AT HER RENTED HOUSE ON BATH STREET IN BAKEWELL, after stopping to fill her prescription. Her academic advisor back in the States, Professor Gardiner, had passed her childhood here, and she offered Elizabeth use of her Grade II-listed furnished house at a discount while she took time off her degree to care for her father.

Of course, my advisor believes I'm going to finish my MBA. That would not be happening. It was time to stop the impossible task of trying to please her mother. Mrs. Bennet would only help pay for a "marketable" degree, and Elizabeth chose accounting since she was good at it. At least she had managed a minor in history so not every college course was boring.

She dropped the box on the floor by the fireplace next to a large pillow that read "God Save the Queen," then went into the galley kitchen and filled a glass to take one of the tablets. Deciding she would have that Indian place on Bridge Street deliver rather than cook, she climbed the stairs to lie on her bed and stare at the ceiling. How many evenings after leaving the hospital had she passed this way, entirely drained of energy?

Since when do I stay at home, eating takeaway? I used to be active, lively. She had spent too much time being a caregiver for someone who had never taken care of her beyond child support payments.

THERE WERE FOUR PEOPLE ON HER DOORSTEP WHEN ELIZABETH ANSWERED the bell on Saturday morning. After Charlotte was satisfied Elizabeth was in good health and Elizabeth lied about taking the rest of the antibiotics, they walked to breakfast. Charlotte's nineteen-year-old sister Maria looked just like her, but she seemed to think speaking was out of the question. Charlotte had also brought a garrulous colleague and a dull man who only talked about himself or quoted from one of the guidebooks on his phone.

Missy King was a nurse who had married a man more interested in her family's money than in her beauty or intelligence. She readily acknowledged this defect in her husband, but did not recognize any deficiency in herself for marrying him in the first place. Willie Collins claimed to be an artist and felt having two paintings on the wall of a pub in Sheffield equal to an installation at the Tate.

"Lizzy," Missy asked in between bites of fried egg, "Char tells me your dad, like, just died?"

Missy winced, and Elizabeth was certain Charlotte had kicked her under the table.

"I prefer Elizabeth, but yes, he suffered a stroke in January, and had a heart attack last week."

"I'm sorry for your loss," Maria whispered, before returning her attention to her teacup.

"Thank you. We weren't close since my parents' divorce. This is my first time back to England since I was two."

"You're English?" Missy exclaimed. "You have *such* an American accent."

"My father was British, but my mother is American, and when my dad walked out, my mother brought us back to Illinois after their divorce was final. I'm British, but I have a certificate of American citizenship too."

Willie cleared his throat. "I would neglect my duties as a person of rank if I didn't tell you that it's a mark of distinction to be able to say that one is a British subject."

They looked at him in bewildered surprise. After a long moment, Charlotte asked, "What rank? Your dad's a machinist from the Torbay area in Devon."

"My mother's uncle was a baronet." Elizabeth couldn't claim a thorough understanding of the British aristocracy, but Willie's pretensions were definitely ridiculous.

They agreed to visit nearby Haddon Hall. The bus ride took only ten minutes, but Elizabeth felt it was hours since she was trapped between the window and Willie.

"Haddon is the best example of a fortified medieval manor house in existence. Being an artist, I am particularly knowledgeable about such things." He turned his screen so she could see the pictures.

"I'd rather see it for—"

"In 1593, the heiress, Dorothy Vernon, eloped with John Manners, a young man her father disapproved of. She was torn between her love and her father, but she chose her lover, and the Hall has been in the hands of the Manners family ever since. Isn't that romantic?"

Elizabeth did not care for the tone Willie used as he drawled the word "romantic." "They must've reconciled if she still inherited."

Willie patted her knee, then rested his hand there. "The Manners family became earls and then dukes, and moved their main seat to Belvoir Castle, using the Hall little in the eighteenth and nineteenth centuries. You and I should go to Leicestershire to see Belvoir. We can make a weekend of it." He squeezed her knee.

Elizabeth looked at Willie's hand, then back to meet his eye. "Whatever part of you is touching me by the time I count to three will be returned to you in pieces. Very small pieces."

Willie forced a laugh. "You are charming!" He did not remove his hand. "Here are pics of my latest series. I call this one 'Flattery with Delicacy'."

"One."

He hastily moved across the aisle, but Elizabeth's solitude was interrupted when Missy leapt from her seat and plopped beside her.

"You're staying in England a while, Lizzy?"

"I prefer Elizabeth. Yes, it's the best plan I have at the present." To avoid any questions about her own career, she asked, "Where are you a nurse?"

"I'm a mental health nurse at a day hospital. Not that I *need* to work, but I like being needed. I don't get that from my husband!" Missy nudged her shoulder and asked, "So, you gotta boyfriend?"

"Not lately."

"Me neither." She winked. "Maybe we can find you one. Don't American girls swoon over an English accent?"

Elizabeth refrained from rolling her eyes. "I aim a little higher than basing my choice on how a guy pronounces his words."

"Yeah, otherwise you'd have gone out with Willie. Kidding! He asks out every girl within five minutes of knowing her name."

After Elizabeth got off the bus, she tried to draw Charlotte aside to talk about Willie, but Missy collected them to pay for admission tickets for everyone.

"No, I got it! My trust fund is what my husband loves most about me. Ha!"

At Haddon, Elizabeth felt like she had been forcibly thrown back to the Middle Ages. She could appreciate its conservation and restoration, but fifteenth-century tapestries and somber Tudor styling were not to her taste. She was happy to escape the dark paneling to go outside even though nothing was in bloom. After the others completed their tour, she finally had an opportunity to speak to Charlotte.

"What is up with your friend? He was ready to whisk me away for a romantic weekend."

"Yeah, he's an odd duck. We've known each other since we were teenagers. Now that he's hit on you and was shot down, he won't bother you again."

"Why are you friends with him?"

Charlotte drew back, and Elizabeth realized her rudeness. "He's a good person. Haven't you been friends with someone for so long that the only reason you're still friends is because you've been friends for so long?"

"Of course," Elizabeth said, more out of a desire to be agreeable than from actual agreement. They met the others, and to dispel any further awkwardness, she said, "Let's take some pictures."

While Elizabeth took a few of the manor, she heard the others discuss what to do with the rest of their day. As they talked, Elizabeth considered the new personalities she had met.

Maria: Shy, but good-humored.

Missy: Foolish, has boundary issues, and married a gold digger.

Willie: No idea how to interact with women; pretends to be humble, but thinks his art makes him superior.

Their chatter became more animated, and it drew Elizabeth's attention.

"Let's take Lizzy to Stanton Moor to see the stone circle."

"They're just nine rocks in a field, Missy."

"Lizzy, do you want to see a Bronze Age stone circle?"

"Sure, but I prefer to go by Eliz—"

"See, Liz wants to be outside. No more mansions!"

"We might go to Sheffield to see my paintings. Two are on display at the Wortley Arms. Most of the patrons view them, as they are conveniently located in the corridor that leads to the loo."

The women decidedly did not hear him.

"But there's *nothing* on Stanton Moor. If you've seen Stonehenge, Nine Ladies is a disappointment."

Elizabeth, having not seen Stonehenge, said she would be interested in Nine Ladies if the others were willing. Charlotte shrugged her shoulders, Willie pulled up one of his paintings inspired by nature, and Maria said nothing.

Missy rolled her eyes. "If no one wants to go to Nine Ladies, why don't we go to Pemberley? That way we can walk outside, but there's more to see."

This pleased the others, although Elizabeth had been curious to see the stone circle. When the next bus arrived, Elizabeth took a seat next to Missy to avoid hearing about Willie's art.

"What's Pemberley?" she asked.

"It was a stately Georgian home. Now it's a derelict shell."

CHAPTER TWO

Thursday, March 21, 1811
Vernal equinox
Pemberley House

Darcy walked with quick steps across the library, his thoughts fixed on how to manage the catastrophe. Not once since he learned of the truth at his father's death had he believed anyone would appear on Stanton Moor again. Never witnessing an event himself, he could willfully disbelieve it possible. And yet, against all reason, Roland brought someone from Nine Ladies who was out of her time.

It could be the ruin of the Darcy family!

His tenants would flee; no servant would work in the house, and his reputation would be in tatters. It did not matter if the secret was believed or disbelieved; the rumors and fear would be enough. The hint that one might slip through time—and that the family at Pemberley had concealed it—would forbear his family's movement in decent society.

The damage to my good name will be irreparable. My sister will not marry anyone worthy of her. The influence of Pemberley House will be devastated, and I will have failed the legacy of my family.

His fortune would suffer, but that did not distress him so far as it would prevent him from giving his money freely. The loss of his family's consequence was distressing, but the loss of his respectability as a gentleman was the most painful contemplation. Darcy paced, clenching and unclenching his hand as if he might grasp his legacy and reputation to keep them from slipping through his fingers.

There was a brisk knock, and the housekeeper entered. *She alone would remain should everything fall to ruin.* Only a slight frown betrayed her annoyance. He could not forget that the appearance of such a stranger would affect Reynolds too.

"I do not often see you wanting in self-possession, sir."

This drew Darcy up to his full height, and he stopped pacing. Only from a loyal retainer, who had known him since he was four years old, could he allow the liberty of a private admonition. Darcy calmly walked to the mantle and rested his arm on it, then leveled his gaze at her. She did not allow a smile, but Darcy could see satisfaction in her eyes.

"Have you seen this . . . person?"

"Yes, sir. She is in the oak parlor. None have seen her but myself and Mr. Roland. And Young Henry," she added.

"Why is she not in one of the outbuildings in the courtyard? Or one of the park buildings?"

"She is not a dog to be kept in the kennels."

"But she cannot remain *here* for three months. How could we credit her presence in the house? As I understand it, the old man who appeared years ago was content to remain in the office rooms in the stable before he . . . returned."

"Your father did suggest the man remain in the stables. However, he was elderly and confused from age before he ever appeared on the moor. By the time your father had him brought to Nine Ladies on the solstice, that visitor no longer remembered where he came from. This woman has *not* lost her senses from old age, and I do not think she will be obliging."

Reynolds's tone had changed. "Is this . . . visitor not agreeable? She must comprehend how fortunate she is that she was found unharmed and is now under my protection." Unfortunately, this woman *was* under his protection, his authority, and his kindness, as far as it went.

The frown lines around her lips returned. "She is not biddable as those other young ladies you are accustomed to; Miss Darcy for example. This woman may not be content to live in isolation for three months after she comes to reason."

Reason? What has reason to do with any of this? "We can disguise her presence by taking her on as a servant." Darcy did hate deceit, but this was a desperate circumstance.

"Yes, sir."

Reynolds had a way of assenting and yet expressing her disagreement. "Speak your concern."

"Her voice and manner will call attention to her strangeness. None would credit that the Darcy family would employ such a peculiar woman."

"If her behavior is peculiar, then I must isolate her until summer. We must preserve every person associated with Pemberley from scrutiny."

"Whatever you decide will be for the best, sir. She demands to speak with whoever is responsible for her imprisonment."

"Imprisonment! It is for her sake as well as ours that she remains out of sight. I need not speak with her." The idea appalled him. "You may speak for me."

"She does not comprehend my position. In her mind, the housekeeper is some manner of scullery maid and cook." Reynolds's frown lines reappeared.

He was never one to shirk responsibility, however distasteful. "Very well. If she asks for me tomorrow, I will see her. I shall disclose how we shall conceal her presence and return her home. There are too many servants on the top floor; put her in one of the secondary bedrooms on the first floor when no one is about."

"Shall I lock her in?"

Darcy nodded. He could not imagine the uproar that would follow if a young lady with unbound hair wearing blue trousers was seen roaming his corridors at night. She and Roland had been caught in the rain, but the woman had refused to allow Reynolds to find her appropriate, dry clothes.

He recalled something Roland said. "She was unconscious when Roland found her. Does she require an apothecary? A physician?" He did not know how to explain her presence to a doctor, but he would not deny her proper care.

"Mr. Roland says she only fainted. She appears to have suffered no ill effects from her . . . travels."

Darcy was well aware that his relief at not needing to send for a doctor was more for selfish reasons than out of concern for her health.

Reynolds was at the door when Darcy was struck by a fearful thought. "You were in my father's confidence from the beginning. You are *certain* the old man all those years ago was returned to . . . whenever he came from?"

"I have no doubt that if our visitor is at Nine Ladies at sunset in June, she will be sent back to where she belongs."

MARCH 19, 2011
BAKEWELL, DERBYSHIRE

Booked your flight yet?

> No, I'm staying until the house sells

An agent can do that. Come home and get a job

> I'm going to let some Englishman be my sugar daddy

Funny

> I need to figure out what to do with my life.
> Taking care of Dad took a lot out of me

DAD?! WTF Since when is he DAD?

> Don't start. I got enough of that from Mom

I have rounds
Don't text me until you're home

When they'd learned of their father's stroke, Elizabeth had dropped everything to care for him, but Jane had taken to heart their mother's loathing of him. As a result of her ex-husband's desertion, Mrs. Bennet had a near-manic desire to be certain her daughters were independent.

"I barely had a high school diploma, no career, and I was abandoned by my husband. You two will be doctors or lawyers! You WILL support yourselves."

Elizabeth was startled out of her reverie when Missy stood; the bus had stopped. Her mind was too full for conversation with the others. Her regrets about falling out with Jane, and doubts about her future, distracted her. They crossed a bridge over a swelled stream and walked up a gradual hill. Elizabeth outstripped the others and reached the top first. Her whole attention was captured by Pemberley House. It had once been a large, handsome stone building, standing on the rising ground and backed by a ridge of high woody hills.

Now it's a ruinous shell.

Pemberley was entirely devoid of warmth, and its beauty was haunting, not majestic. The exterior walls still stood at their full height, but the house was completely open to the elements. Rows of empty windows stared out like dead, unseeing eyes. She walked one side of the massively columned, blemished exterior until she came to a doorway. Grass grew within. Walking through the frame, she stopped short at the sight of the exposed interior brick. It seemed immodest, somehow, to be able to see what ought to have been concealed.

Elizabeth craned her neck to the sky. The roof was entirely gone, as were the intermediary floors. The original ornamental stonework remained on the exterior, but within, it was more like an archeological dig than a home. Most of the interior walls, like all of the exterior ones, still stood at their full height. Elizabeth took a few pictures of the ceiling-less brick rooms with their glassless windows and unadorned fireplaces.

She went outside and tried to enjoy the views of the valley, but her attention was continually drawn to the imposing structure. She pulled out her phone to snap a few more pictures.

"Elizabeth!" Charlotte jumped down through one of the ground floor's glassless windows. "What do you think?"

"It's depressing to see a place like this in ruins." Elizabeth shook her head, dispelling the building's gloomy aura. "I'm having a great time, though. What happened here?"

Charlotte shrugged. "Willie could tell you from one of his guidebooks."

They walked around the façade to where the others had gathered. Willie clapped his hands with glee when Charlotte told him Elizabeth was curious about Pemberley's history.

"There had been a house on the grounds of Pemberley's ruins for a thousand years. Until the nineteenth century, it was held by the Darcy family. The home featured oak ornamental panels and stucco plasterwork by Italian masters, as well as Adam fireplaces in marble and an ornate mahogany staircase."

"What happened?" Elizabeth asked.

"In 1811, the owner died without issue. His sister inherited, but her husband was an extravagant spender. She died young, and the husband died later deeply in debt. They had no children, and Pemberley was sold several times over for the next one hundred years, falling into disrepair with more of its land parceled off."

"But what happened to the house? Why is the roof gone?" Missy interjected.

"Pemberley was sold in 1919 at auction to be demolished for building materials. The roof was stripped of lead, the massive wooden joists removed, and some of the finely decorated rooms sold as architectural salvage. The remaining structure is under the care of English Heritage."

"Why? Tear it down and build something else here!" Elizabeth's stomach dropped at Missy's idea. "I could go for a pudding! My treat."

Elizabeth took a final look over her shoulder at the imposing shell. She suspected Pemberley only retained a small sense of the dignity and grandeur of its former life.

March 20, 2011
Vernal equinox

After a late evening at the Queen's Arms with live music, pool, and too many pints, the group rose late on Sunday.

"Thank you for letting us stay the night," Maria said to Elizabeth's shoes. Willie's leave-taking was a long speech that ended with the promise of a viewing of his paintings whenever she wished.

"Nice to meet you, Lizzy!" Elizabeth had given up correcting Missy. "Next time you want to have some fun, give me a call. We'll find you a hot man with an English accent!"

Elizabeth gave Charlotte a hug. "Thank you for coming. I needed this."

"I hope you'll stay in England so we can do this again."

"I plan to. I need to figure out what to do with my life, and Bakewell is a beautiful place to do that."

"I'll be out of hours for the next few weekends, but when I'm free, you should come to Sheffield. We can go to the Winter Garden or the Millennium Gallery."

"As long as we don't have to look at Willie's paintings."

"I promise!"

After a full day in company, the quiet of the house was welcome, but for only a short time. *A nice, long walk would be good.* The stone circle Charlotte's friends mentioned might be the distraction she needed from thinking about her father and her life. She found English Heritage's listing for Nine Ladies:

> *A small early Bronze Age stone circle traditionally believed to depict nine ladies turned to stone as a penalty for dancing on Sunday. It is part of a complex of prehistoric circles and standing stones on Stanton Moor.*

At Pemberley, there was a hint of majesty behind its crumbling brick and plaster, whereas Nine Ladies was, as Charlotte put it, nine rocks in a field. Still, Stanton Moor had a picturesque quality, and if she was going to stay in England, she may as well enjoy the beauties in her backyard instead of staring at her ceiling and worrying about the future.

She grabbed her coat and phone to go to the Visitor Centre for a local's directions. The clerk gave her a disbelieving look when she told him where she intended to walk.

"Gerraway wi' yer. You can take the bus to Stanton-in-Peak instead; it's a twenty-minute walk from there."

"I don't mean to avoid a walk." She strove to be polite in the face of his disbelief.

"You have a decent sense of direction?"

"I can tell left from right."

He jotted directions as he muttered. "Footpath to Haddon Fields, through the orchard and then the woods. Walk to the Alport Road, past the quarry, up the other side of the valley." He looked up. "Still wi' me?" She nodded. "That'll take you to Stanton-in-Peak. Go past Flying Childers Pub down Lees Road 'til you see a sign for the moor. The stone circle is in a clearing. With any luck, you won't find a bunch of women doing a pagan virility ceremony."

"I'm sorry?"

"You know, druids and celebrating the sun, portals, magical auras. Don't put any stock in it m'self, but the pagans think it's uncanny there. You're not headed for a druid gathering, are you?"

Elizabeth laughed. "My interest is purely as a tourist. I left my pointed witch hat in the States."

"You might see others walking the moor, but it's the solstice when the druids flock there by the hundreds."

"How long do you think it will take me to walk there?"

"If it's dark by the time you get to Nine Ladies, get a bus in Stanton-in-Peak to come back to Bakewell. You best get started. Sunset is . . ."—he paused to tap on his phone—"at 6:12."

The English are serious walkers.

The climb to Haddon Fields was steep. She was grateful her cough wasn't anything more serious than a cold. The landscape beyond the apple orchard included dense, tall brambles. Elizabeth rested against a stone wall in Stanton-in-Peak to read online about Nine Ladies:

- *In the early 1780s, Major Hayman Rooke surveyed and recorded some of the major monuments and excavated a number of sites on Stanton Moor.*
- *Nine Ladies is one of the few stone circles in Britain to have survived from the Bronze Age relatively intact. Its construction — based on large-scale earth removal rather than deposition — appears unusual in a national context.*
- *For several decades, the Nine Ladies stone circle has acted as a popular focus for various forms of observance and celebration.*

She passed no one on the moor and paused only long enough to take pictures of the heather and the gorse. The path led her to a sparse woods that had an eerie quality and opened to a clearing. It was a tranquil setting, ringed with silver birch, but the fading light lent it a gloomy air. She supposed she could understand how a woodland stone circle would appeal to those believing in energy flows, spiritual connections with the sun, and other nonsense.

These are the stones that have stood for four thousand years. Pemberley had only been in ruins for a hundred years. Elizabeth saw nine gritstone blocks, each about a yard tall, embedded into the grass. The circle was no more than forty feet around; she walked the perimeter before stepping inside.

She stood in the center and felt tired after her hike. The sun was nearly set and throwing long shadows across the ground as she looked at her watch. *I am definitely taking the bus back to Bakewell.*

CHAPTER THREE

MARCH 22, 1811
PEMBERLEY

After her father died, the rehabilitation facility's unit matron had handed Elizabeth a pamphlet on the five stages of grief: denial, anger, bargaining, depression, and acceptance. She supposed herself to be moving through similar stages now as she attempted to comprehend what happened last night at Nine Ladies. One moment she was looking at the shadows cast by the setting sun, and the next she was in a horse cart, raindrops falling on her face.

"It is not 1811!" denials faded into angry "Let me go!" pleas. Bargaining went on all night: "When I wake up, I promise to figure out what to do with my life." But when she awoke after a fitful sleep still in a locked room with curtains around the bed, no light switches, and a cupboard with a pot in it, Elizabeth burst into tears.

She was still sniffling when she heard a key turning in the lock.

"I see you are awake. Shall I bring you something to eat?"

The housekeeper, Mrs. Reynolds, gave no notice that she was on the floor, arms wrapped around her knees, with tears on her cheeks.

Elizabeth was able to look on her with more calm than last night.

What little of her hair that peeked out from beneath her cap was all black. Her face was chiseled with sharp angles, but it was the fine lines around her eyes, mouth, and throat that gave away her age. She appeared to be in her fifties. Reynolds was the sort of woman who looked young until seated near a twenty-year-old.

"I don't want food. Let me go!"

"Are we to have the same discussion we had last evening? You are under Mr. Darcy's protection, and until you can behave in a ladylike manner, you shall not quit this room."

Elizabeth rose and looked to the door. The last time she tried to force her way out, the man who brought her from the moor overpowered her. Maybe calm and reason would work better. "If this is 1811, why did you kidnap me through time?"

Her eyes widened. "None here have done anything but ensure your safety, and I assure you we did not take you from your time. You arrived here by accident, and I recommend you show gratitude toward Mr. Darcy's generosity."

"Generosity? As far as I can tell, he's a heartless man who told you to lock me up!"

"None here will tolerate your disrespect to the master. If you will refrain from raising your voice, I will explain what happened."

Elizabeth exhaled loudly. "Fine."

"We do not know how, nor do we know why, but at sunset on the vernal and autumnal equinoxes, any who stand in the center of the Nine Ladies stone circle go through time two hundred years. From our perspective, they come from the future, and from their perspective, they drop into the past."

"I've lost my mind," Elizabeth muttered.

"You are not the first traveler through time. An elderly man appeared in the year eighty-two, an infant appeared in the year ninety-six, and here you are in 1811."

"Where are they now?"

"As far as we know, they returned to where they belong."

"'As far as you know'?" She gave an exasperated shriek. "What does that even mean? Tell me how to get home now!"

"I am not accustomed to being spoken to in such a manner."

Reynolds turned to leave.

Elizabeth ran around her to the door, gripping the locked knob. "No! I want answers. I want to know how to get back, and I want to know *now*!"

"If you continue to lose your temper, I will tell you nothing. You may stay alone in this room, and it will make my life simpler. It is for your benefit as well as everyone at Pemberley that none learn from whence you have come, in any event."

"Pemberley?" Elizabeth slackened and leaned against the door. "Pemberley is in ruins."

Reynolds raised an eyebrow and looked around the room. "I assure you it is not."

"I want to talk to this Mr. Darcy." If this insanity was real, then he was the one running the show. If it was *not*, maybe the more people she interacted with, the more likely one of them would commit her to the psych ward for her own good.

"He does not wish to know *you*. Our world is—"

"I'm going to scream."

"I beg your pardon?"

"You tell that old man who lords over this place he *will* answer my questions. Get him in here, or I start screaming."

"I am the only one to hold the key, and none shall break the door to free you, I can assure you of that. We are all loyal to Mr. Darcy."

Elizabeth gave her a cold smirk. "If this is real, you don't want anyone to know someone from the future is here. If Mr. Darcy's not here in one hour, I scream, and everyone will know. And if your oppressive dictator doesn't get in here after *that*, I'll start screaming about what's going to happen in your future. I always loved history class. Should I break the glass and yell out the window if Napoleon wins or not?"

Reynolds's face paled. "You would not dare."

Elizabeth inhaled a large, noisy breath.

"Stop! I shall send in the master. But first I must bring you suitable attire. A woman of this time does not wear trousers. Mr. Darcy will be shocked at the sight of you."

"I refuse to put on a dress to be ogled by some lecherous old man!

You have an hour, so move quickly." Elizabeth stepped aside and gestured to the door.

Reynolds's frown lines settled in before she went through the door and slammed it behind her.

DARCY STARED AT THE DOOR WHILE REYNOLDS SEARCHED THROUGH THE keys on her chatelaine. The pause was nearly enough to break his resolve to acknowledge the woman from the future. Her existence defied reason, and it felt as though by seeing her with his own eyes he validated this madness. *But a gentleman discharges any duty required of him.*

The door was thrown open, and Darcy settled his features into indifference. Reynolds announced him and was then gone, closing the door firmly behind her.

The woman was looking out the window she had threatened to break. When she turned, her eyes widened, and she stared at him in a forward manner. *As though she has just cause to be alarmed by my appearance.*

"Madam." He bowed. The woman did not acknowledge him with a curtsey. *Such rudeness.* She was indecent, her legs fitted in indigo buckskin with thick, strange laced half-boots. She wore a lilac gentleman's shirt with buttons down the front that stopped at her hips. Darcy could think of no respectable reason a woman would be dressed that way.

"So you're the ruler of Pemberley. I thought you'd be older."

The woman's strange voice brought his attention from her clothes to her face and person. She was of average height and thinner than was becoming in a woman. Her nose wanted character, her mouth only tolerable, her cheekbones high, and her eyes wide-set. Her air was arrogant, angry, and she looked into his eyes with total attention. It alarmed him.

"You have me at a disadvantage, madam." She stared as though she did not understand him. *Is she a simpleton?* "I do not know how to address you."

"I'm Elizabeth Bennet, but let's get right to it. I'm either crazy, or I've traveled through time. Either way, *you* have no right to lock me up.

I don't want to be here, and you don't want me here, so what will you do to get me home?"

Darcy strained to catch her meaning through her strange inflection and language. "Miss Bennet, you are here for your own safety and for the safety of those under my protection. Any person of sense could not fail to comprehend the confusion and chaos that would result were it known one might pass through time."

"Time traveling doesn't surprise you?" She gave a disappointed sigh.

"Simply because it has been known to happen, it does not follow that I am not surprised. I am astounded that I live in a world where such a thing is possible."

"That makes two of us. But why are you keeping me here? Send me back!"

"It is not as simple as putting you in my carriage and telling the coachman to walk on." For some reason, this made her laugh, and it fueled Darcy's indignation. "Do not you comprehend the danger you pose to me? I am not given to hyperbole, but let me assure you I will not allow you to ruin my family's reputation or safety. Cannot you imagine what might become of Pemberley if it is known I concealed such a thing? And there is considerable danger to yourself, and any who shelter you, if others learn from whence you came."

Her eyes narrowed. "What, are your serfs going to burn me at the stake if they find out I'm from the future?"

Darcy flinched. "What manner of people do you take us for?"

"The type that kidnaps women through time and keeps them under lock and key!"

"We did not abduct you!"

They glared at one another, only a few feet stood between them. The woman took a deep breath and closed her eyes. "Let's say time traveling is real. You don't want anyone to know I'm from 2011, and I don't want to be here in the dark ages. I don't want to cause you any problems, really I don't. I won't tell anyone the truth, I promise—just let me go home."

"As far as our limited understanding of these strange events go, it is impossible to send you back until the summer solstice. One can stand in the center of the stone circle and go forward in time on the solstice, and one comes here—back in time, according to you—on the equinox."

"I have to stay *three months*?" Her shoulders dropped, and she appeared overwrought. "Why?"

He gestured toward the chair at the dressing table, and she fell into it. "Miss Bennet, you are laboring under the impression this is under my control. But you are the first person I have seen with my own eyes appear from the stone circle."

"Your housekeeper said it happened before."

"Yes, but Pemberley then belonged to my father, and he kept his silence on the matter until I was one-and-twenty. The first person appeared in 1782, two years before I was born. My father told me the first visitor was an elderly man seen wandering the moor by Hank Roland, Pemberley's gamekeeper. It was thought he lost his senses from old age. My father, a benevolent man, saw he was cared for, and indulged him."

"Indulged him?"

"The man thought he would return to where he belonged by that same method he arrived. He appeared here at sundown, and every evening he wished to go to Nine Ladies. As weeks went by, he became more confused and agitated, but, at my father's request, Roland always brought him at sunset until one evening, the solstice, the man was in the center of the circle, and then the next moment he was not."

"He disappeared at sunset from the middle of the stone circle? Okay. And the other one?"

"I beg your pardon?"

"Mrs. Reynolds mentioned another person."

Darcy took his time answering. "There was a child who appeared many years later, at the autumnal equinox."

"And?"

"I was told the child was brought to the stone circle at the winter solstice." He did not wish to speak about this.

"But you have no idea where they went! For all we know, they went back in time another two hundred years. Or ceased to exist! Or maybe I'm crazy!" Miss Bennet dropped her forehead to the table.

Darcy stood in uncomfortable silence. The idea of offering her comfort was intolerable. He was about to have Reynolds bring her some wine when she suddenly sat up.

"Okay, if this is real, and two others appeared here from exactly two hundred years in the future at sunset on the equinox, then disappeared from here at sunset on the solstice, let's assume it will work for me."

"I am pleased you accepted my supposition."

She made an unladylike sound of derision. "It's not because *you* said so. It either will work or it won't, and until I step into Nine Ladies on the solstice, we won't know. Right now, both outcomes are possible. I'm choosing to believe in the one that might get me home."

Darcy felt exquisite relief. Miss Bennet was not unreasonable, no matter how strange her manners or appearance. "I shall tell Reynolds to find you suitable accommodation on the grounds, and on the solstice, Roland will take you to Nine Ladies. Good day."

"Hold on! What does 'on the grounds' mean?"

This woman and her abrasive manner! Darcy strove to speak evenly. "You will be hidden in one of the work buildings on the land that I own. Mrs. Reynolds will see you are fed and provided books or work for your amusement."

"No, I refuse to hide alone for three months. With nothing to do and no one to talk to? No way."

"I do not presume to know what is appropriate behavior in the twenty-first century, but a woman such as you is in no position to dictate terms to me."

"A woman such as . . . Yeah, it really is the nineteenth century. Let's get one thing straight: You want me to keep quiet about time traveling? Well, I refuse to stay alone in one of your far-flung, miserable hovels until June."

Such an intentional and injurious affront is not to be born. Darcy's words came out slowly, in a low, harsh tone. "This is one of the noblest estates in England. I assure you that nowhere in all of Pemberley's five thousand acres, thirty farms, over sixty dwellings and cottages will you find anything deserving of the term *hovel*."

"Good for you! But I'm staying *here*, in this house. Not alone!"

"I fail to comprehend why you insist on remaining in *my* house!"

"I can't spend months alone again. Not after—" Her expression showed a frantic panic. "If I'm not crazy now, I will be by the end of three months all alone."

"Believe me when I say you are not of unsound mind. That I am desirous of you being of my own time is certain, but such a thing is not influenced by my hopes or fears. You have indeed fallen backwards through time."

The woman stood and stared him in the face. *She is so bold.*

"If I promise I won't tell anyone where I'm from, will you let me stay in the house and come and go as I please? Would you want to be kept in solitary confinement, like a criminal?" The anger had slipped from her voice, and her plaintive tone caught his sympathy.

"Indeed not, but unless you are a guest, a servant, or a member of the family, there is no respectable reason for a young woman to remain in a single man's home. None could believe you are my relation, and I am certain you would refuse to be put to work in the washhouse."

"That leaves guest. Just tell everyone your friend is visiting."

Darcy laughed. "Pardon me for being direct, but you would cause a scandal." She wrinkled her eyebrows. "All and sundry would assume you are my mistress were you to remain here alone. To install a mistress in my own home is beyond the pale."

"What does—Oh! An unmarried woman in your house automatically means you're sleeping with her? And that idea insults you? Then bring someone else in on the secret and have them be my *chaperone*." The woman bent and straightened her first two fingers on each hand in an incomprehensible gesture. Darcy shook his head. "Do you have a cousin, or sisters? Would a female relative have friends sleep over?"

Automatically? Sleep over? Parsing her language was taxing. "I am the guardian of one sister, but she lives in London with a woman who superintends her education. She is fifteen, and only an older or married woman can protect the vulnerability of an unmarried young lady."

"So, *she* has a chaperone?"

He saw a small smile at the corner of Miss Bennet's lips as she tilted her head and raised an eyebrow.

"My sister knows nothing about Nine Ladies, and no, I shall not divulge it to her or her companion!"

"You don't have to. Ask her to host your poor relation, or ward, or whatever you want to call me. Say I have nowhere else to go for some reason and I need to stay at Pemberley until June because you're too kind to throw me on the street. Then tell the companion to make sure I don't get seduced because I'm a defenseless female." Miss Bennet laughed, although Darcy found nothing amusing.

"Even if I agreed, you have neglected the most incriminatory aspect of your outlandish plan."

"What? It's perfect." She held out her fingers to count on them. "I get a proper chaperone, I get to interact with people, no one learns the truth, no one will accuse you of having a mistress, and I can stay in a house rather than in a shed alone."

Darcy kept his gaze fixed on the top of her head. "None who see you would credit the notion that you are a woman of this time."

She looked down at herself. "I'll wear skirts if it means I don't have to be isolated and lonely."

"It is more appalling than that. In your voice, your words, your manner, there is nothing suitable about you as a woman." She was odd, argumentative. She was not pretty, not elegant, not amiable, not well-informed.

"If that's the way you talk to women, it's no wonder you're single."

"I beg your—"

"Just arrange for your sister and her keeper to come, and I'll do what I have to do to be the model of a perfect woman in 1811. How long can I stay here without someone to make sure I don't get seduced?"

He was losing control of this situation. "If Reynolds will vouch for your credibility, perhaps a fortnight if it is understood my sister and her companion are on their way."

"Then you and Reynolds get the fun job of turning me into a submissive, powerless nineteenth-century woman before they get here."

Darcy shrugged and rolled his eyes. She was willful, and she would certainly not hide quietly for three months. If he forced her to remain isolated, he would be faced with her outbursts and attempts to escape. Perhaps keeping her under close watch would be the lesser of two evils.

"Let us assume it were possible to present you as a lady of my own time. My remaining reservation is this: I have no guarantee that you would act in the manner of a genteel woman at all times and tell no one the truth of your origins."

Miss Bennet walked toward him with a hand outstretched. "I promise to fit in if you don't lock me up."

Darcy was distressed by her forwardness and clasped his hands behind his back. "I know nothing of your character or even the general character of a twenty-first century woman."

"There is such a thing as integrity and honor, even in the twenty-first century," she said softly. She reached her hand out again with an earnest smile. "Please?"

Her circumstance provoked his pity. She did not, at this moment, appear to be trying to anger him. Darcy slowly raised his hand to clasp hers. He was surprised by her firm grip, and he marveled at the sensation of touching an unrelated woman's hand without a layer of gloves between them.

"What's first? A dress?"

It took Darcy a moment to realize she meant a gown and not her manner of speaking. "I must speak with Reynolds and decide how to announce your presence at Pemberley. If you pass yourself off credibly, I will write to my sister to come."

"You, Reynolds, and the gamekeeper are the only ones who know the truth? I don't want to ask for help from the wrong people. See, I want to hold up my end of the deal."

Darcy paused with his hand on the knob. "There is one other who I hope will aid us. I will write to him at once and beg him to come. Good day."

Her reply to his courtesies was to say "bye."

This will not be easy.

CHAPTER FOUR

MARCH 24, 1811

"Damn it!" Elizabeth brought her needle-pricked finger to her lips. *When was store-bought clothing invented anyway?*

The housekeeper's eyes narrowed before returning to her own sewing. For two days, Elizabeth had helped Mrs. Reynolds assemble a credible wardrobe for her. Reynolds radiated silent resentment at being put to a purpose beneath her dignity. Apparently, in great houses like Pemberley, the housekeeper wielded considerable power and responsibility, and that didn't include sewing clothes for time travelers.

Not a word unrelated to measuring Elizabeth or explaining clothing crossed the housekeeper's lips. It reminded her of weeks spent at the side of the silent, ill father she scarcely knew. She needed her moments of solitude and reflection, but she was desperate for conversation by now. *I'd even talk to that jerk Mr. Darcy. I could tell him about third-wave feminism. Or just women's suffrage.*

She was taken aback when she first saw the master of the house. Elizabeth remembered what Willie Collins had said about Pemberley: the owner died without issue in 1811. She assumed Mr. Darcy would be an old bachelor with one foot in the grave. Instead, he appeared healthy and said he was born in 1784.

She did not like him, but she did not want to watch him die. *Let's hope I'm gone before he does.*

Too many hours of monotony made her amuse herself by forcing Reynolds to speak with her. "I don't think I'll need all those layers of whatever you're making, if you want a break."

"Yes, ma'am." Reynolds did not stop.

Elizabeth stared at the older woman until she looked up. "Is there a problem? I would like to save you from doing extra work."

"Should you not wear a chemise, the gown will be transparent, and when the gown clings to your body instead of draping over the petticoat, you will expose yourself to ridicule when it reveals parts of your body that none but your husband ought to see." Reynolds paused. "You ought not to voice peculiar notions."

"Maybe you should talk to me instead of sitting in miserable silence," Elizabeth muttered as she tried to thread her needle.

"You might oblige yourself to speak with me."

"Me?" Elizabeth dropped her needle. "I'm the one trying to talk to *you*!"

"I was not admonishing you; I corrected you. Your speech is, although understandable to the patient listener, peculiar and informal for this time. You must pass yourself off as a lady of quality."

"I need to talk more formally?"

"Your language is appallingly abrupt and not rich enough to pass yourself as one with an education and equal to being a guest of Miss Darcy."

"So, what do you suggest?" Reynolds only stared. Elizabeth suppressed a sigh. "May I ask what you recommend I do?"

A ghost of a smile floated across the housekeeper's lips. "Model your speech on Mr. Darcy's, and his cousin's after he arrives."

"I don't expect to see much of Mr. Darcy once I'm dressed like a doll and free to come and go." The only thing good about Mr. Darcy was he was easy on the eyes. *". . . there is nothing suitable about you as a woman." Unforgivable jerk!*

"Do not use so many contractions. You would do well to remember that Mr. Darcy is a generous master and friend. There is not one of his tenants or servants but what will give him a good name."

"I won't talk trash about him." Elizabeth squinted to thread her needle; she felt Reynolds's glare. "I shall not speak against Mr. Darcy. Is that better?" The needle finally threaded. "How long have you worked at Pemberley?"

"Since the present Mr. Darcy was four years old." The warmth in Reynolds's voice surprised her. "I began as a housemaid in the year eighty-eight, was then maid to Lady Anne Darcy, Mr. Darcy's mother, and then I became the housekeeper."

"Your master likes to have his own way. Was Mr. Darcy like that as a child?" She imagined an imperious little boy ordering and scolding everyone in sight.

Reynolds expressed her disapproval by the appearance of a few lines near her mouth and eyes.

"If I was to go through all the world and time, I could not meet with a better young man. Mr. Darcy was the sweetest-tempered, most generous-hearted boy in the world."

Elizabeth kept her opinion that he was a bad-tempered man who needed to update his attitude on women to herself.

"Mr. Darcy asked us to arrange your history for the purpose of convincing Miss Darcy and the neighborhood of why you are at Pemberley. He suggests we create a connection between us, to both explain what brings you here and so it would not seem out of place for us to be in conversation together."

"A cover story? Okay." Reynolds stared that now-familiar disapproving stare that meant Elizabeth had said something wrong. "Relax, I'm not going to talk that way in front of anyone not in on the time-traveling secret!" She took a breath and settled her shoulders. "What do you recommend?"

"That you are a relation to my husband, left alone in the world through some calamity and have come to Pemberley until other arrangements can be made. It will allow us to speak without raising attention, and explain why we are not familiar with one another. A distant relationship, through marriage, will explain why you are gentry and I am not."

"Is your husband a servant at Pemberley?"

"No, he is dead."

"I'm sor—"

Reynolds stood. "You and Mr. Darcy may arrange the particulars; it is sufficient for me that you are a cousin by marriage and none but me in all of England know you. Tomorrow Young Henry will take you to Lambton, and Mr. Roland will fetch you as if you had traveled on the mail coach. If you do nothing else correct, remember to curtsey properly." The housekeeper gathered her work bag and left.

"And who is supposed to teach me how to curtsey?" she called to the empty room.

EARLY THE NEXT MORNING, ELIZABETH WAS TRUSSED UP IN HER STRANGE clothes and snuck out to the courtyard where she had been told to walk some ways to meet Young Henry.

I'm in a handmade dress with no underwear. I have to trudge in the dark to play this charade so no one assumes the master is sleeping around. She tried to convince herself she hadn't lost her mind as she stepped through the darkness down the hill, swinging her reticule over her wrist.

What a stupid name for a purse. When Reynolds's back was turned, Elizabeth hid her iPhone in it. The battery was at 65%, and she obviously couldn't connect to a cell tower, but she felt calmer for having something from her own time with her.

Elizabeth heard a low whistle. She turned to see a teenager standing by a cart where a small trunk was stored. He was ungainly in that way all adolescent boys tended to be. He touched his hat, and Elizabeth realized she had no idea how to behave.

"Good morning," she said breathlessly. "Am I supposed to curtsey to you?"

Even in the dim morning light, she saw him turn crimson. "No, ma'am. Is that what the gentry do in the future?" She smiled at his curiosity. "Pardon me. I am not to ask you about what is to come."

When they were seated and Elizabeth untangled her skirt, she said,

"You must be the Young Henry I've heard about. You can ask me about the future, if you like."

"I would never go against Mr. Darcy."

"He would throw you out of his kingdom if he knew you were curious?" *Maybe everyone will be better off when he dies.*

"I want to be gamekeeper when my grandfather is no longer able. If Mr. Darcy cannot trust me, he won't give me an important position, but he is too liberal a master to throw me off forever."

"Your grandfather is the man who brought me from Nine Ladies?"

"Aye, ma'am."

Elizabeth heard in his tone a desire to say more. "We *can* talk. I mean, you are welcome to speak freely with me. I need the practice."

"If you insist. My grandfather is Hank Roland, the gamekeeper, and I am Young Henry. Although my father has been dead twelve years, and since I am fifteen, I would prefer dropping the 'young.'"

Spoken like a true teenager. "Why do you want to be Pemberley's gamekeeper?"

"Pemberley is a fine estate!"

"England is full of large estates. Many of them are still standing when I'm from." She pushed aside the unsettling memory of visiting Pemberley's ruins.

"Pemberley earns a clear ten thousand per annum." Given the pride in Henry's voice, Elizabeth supposed this was impressive. *Mr. Darcy's wealthy and not in debt, so I guess he's not a deadbeat.* "The gamekeeper has his own cottage on the estate. I have lived there since my parents died from a fever."

People die from just fevers here? "What does the gamekeeper do?"

"He breeds and feeds the game." A hint of incredulity at her ignorance crept into his voice. "My grandfather arranges the hunts and does a fair amount of the hunting himself. You won't find anyone who knows more about poaching and game laws than him. I am learning too. Old Mr. Darcy always took my grandfather's advice when they went out to shoot, and someday the present Mr. Darcy is going to attend to my advice."

Her young companion was eager and ambitious. *And loyal to that sexist jerk.* She would have to show Mr. Darcy the same respect everyone else thought he deserved if she was going to live at Pemberley until summer. *I wonder if I have enough money in my bank account for three months of direct payments. The rent was taken care of in advance, but what about the other bills?*

"Here we are. Lambton is an estate village of Pemberley." Young Henry said this as though she ought to know what an estate village was. "If you walk through the mews, you will arrive at the posting inn. Mrs. Reynolds instructed me to tell you that if anyone asks, you walked from Rowsley, where you arrived on the mail coach. Someone from Pemberley will bring you to the house."

"Wait! Who do I curtsey to? And how do I do it?"

Young Henry shifted his feet. "A gentleman makes a slight bow, and a lady makes a reserved curtsey when they meet. You won't meet anyone at the Pemberley Arms or at the house who needs to be shown more respect than that."

"Like this?" she asked, staring him in the face and bobbing up and down.

Young Henry folded his arms over his chest and projected disgust and embarrassment as well as any modern teenager would. "No, ma'am. You must put one foot behind the other." She tried again, earning a huff of exasperation. "No, bend your knees and slower. No, you cannot lean. The lady looks down whilst she curtsies." Her next attempt earned a small nod. "That is better."

"You people do this all day long, with every person you interact with?"

"Intimate friends and family are not always curtseying and bowing when they enter and leave the room." He emphatically touched his hat and scrambled into the cart.

Elizabeth arrived at the Pemberley Arms amid other bleary-eyed travelers from a night coach. She sat near to them and repressed the compulsion to pull out her phone. One of them cast aside a magazine, and Elizabeth surreptitiously picked it up and passed the hours with *Repository of Arts, Literature, Commerce, Manufacturers, Fashion, and Politics.*

She was appalled the magazine had to defend a chemist's experiments against those who thought her pursuits were unseemly for women. *This is definitely not the century for me. Note to self: Google Mrs. Fulhame someday.*

There were music reviews, fashion and furniture plates, and a physician's report outlining the types of cases he had seen in the last month and the number of patients suffering from each. *What is scrofula? Or a furred tongue? Why would a patient with a typhoid-like fever need his head shaved and blistered?* If this was the medical care expected in 1811, no wonder a healthy, twenty-seven-year-old man like Mr. Darcy could just die.

"Miss Bennet?"

She gave a shriek of surprise. Mr. Roland stood before her. "Um, hi! I mean, good day!" She started a curtsey, before she remembered she wasn't supposed to curtsey to a servant. He gave her an odd look and silently led her to the cart.

"Have you been told to not speak with me too?" she asked after they were on their way.

"I would not refuse to acknowledge a lady, but a lady of quality does not chat with a servant."

"I mean, did Mr. Darcy tell you to not ask me about the future—never mind. Why don't you tell me about the grounds? Your grandson is proud of Pemberley."

They traveled through a well-timbered deer park that was gone in Elizabeth's time. Roland mentioned wood plantations, an ice house, a fish pond, a kennel, and a home farm. It was bucolic, and she suspected the gardens would be beautiful in the summer. *How many parcels of land were sold over time as Pemberley went bankrupt?* All those tenants forced off their land, many to end up in a workhouse, unemployed, separated from their homes and community.

Roland brought the cart past the front façade, and Elizabeth saw the four giant classical columns topped by a pediment. The rich plaster shone in the sun, the windows sported clear glass, and, unlike the last time she saw Pemberley in the daylight, it was resplendent. They stopped near to where an impressive, four-wheeled vehicle was being led into the stable yard.

"Is that Mr. Darcy's carriage?" It looked expensive even to her untrained eye.

"A chaise and four, and it does not belong to the master. You can tell by the crest it belongs to Mr. Darcy's uncle, Lord Fitzwilliam. He is one of the wealthiest landowners in England."

"Mr. Darcy's uncle is an earl?"

"Aye. It is likely his lordship is not here, but his younger son, who is a favorite of Mr. Darcy's."

Mr. Darcy mentioned someone else who knew the truth would come to help. *Great, another snob to think there is "nothing suitable about me as a woman."*

Roland led the way past a food storage room, pointing out the steward's room, the servants' hall, and the passage to the kitchen before he took her to the housekeeper's room. It was part office, part living room, part storeroom.

Elizabeth took off her hat and gloves, tossing them on to the table as she went to the window. The last time she was here, Pemberley's glassless windows looked unseeing and dead. She gently tapped on one of the panes.

I couldn't have ever imagined these details. I'm really in 1811.

"You must be Miss Bennet, my late husband's distant cousin."

Elizabeth saw Mrs. Reynolds in the doorway, her expression as inscrutable as ever. The door remained open, and Elizabeth heard footsteps and voices carrying down the passageway. *I should have joined the drama club.* "It's a pleasure to meet you."

"I was saddened to read in your letter that you traveled all this way only to learn the death of your remaining family preceded your arrival."

Nothing in the housekeeper's tone displayed any emotion, let alone sadness. "It is good of you to allow me to stay."

"It is Mr. Darcy who allows you to stay."

Elizabeth heard footsteps approaching. *Keep up the performance.* "Yes, he must be a . . . generous man." A maid appeared with a tea tray.

"Polly, this is Elizabeth Bennet; her mother was my husband's cousin. Her mother improved her station by marrying well. Now that her parents are dead, Miss Bennet has traveled a long way only to find her relations here have predeceased her. Mr. Darcy has allowed her to remain for the present. I suspect she may have the pleasure of meeting Miss Darcy."

The maid, who hung on every word, curtsied and left, closing the door behind her.

"That was a thorough introduction."

"Polly Brooks is a diligent maid; her fault is she is inclined to chat. She will tell the servants what she knows of you, and I can be free of their questions."

She smiled. "Gossip hasn't changed in two hundred years, I see."

"Remember that neither of us knows what gossip is like two hundred years in the future."

Elizabeth heaved a sigh. "Would the servants be curious about any visitor of yours?"

"No."

"Do you often have visitors?"

"No."

Reynolds poured the tea, but did not drink. And did not speak. Elizabeth decided to wait her out. Two full minutes passed. *This is painful.* "Is there a bed you have to make?"

"I beg your pardon?"

"It is clear you resent me and have no desire to speak to me. You can go back to work."

The housekeeper let out a small sigh. "I shall not be accused of being uncivil to my guest, or a guest of Mr. Darcy's. I do not resent you, nor do I, as you say, make the beds."

"What *do* you do?"

"I oversee the care of the furniture and linens, the grocery and stores, I have charge of the still room, I make the remedies and preserves, and I am in charge of the china and the tea. Pemberley has fifteen servants, and I oversee their duties. As there is no mistress, the management of the household is deputed to me."

"The housekeeper is a skilled professional?"

"It is the highest respectable position a woman may reach."

"When I'm from, women can do, and are expected to do, much more than that."

"As far as any here know, you are from the same time as the rest of us."

It beats being a trophy wife with nothing to do but pet a lap dog. "The wife of someone like Mr. Darcy would have nothing to do?"

"On the contrary, the future Mrs. Darcy would fix her eye continually upon me. Negligence on her part would throw the whole house into confusion. Although, I do not know when Mr. Darcy would marry. I do not know who is good enough for him."

Elizabeth resisted the impulse to tell her he would never marry; he would be dead before the year was out.

Reynolds offered to show her the house. Elizabeth grudgingly admired Mr. Darcy's taste, but the lofty and handsome rooms reminded her of the crumbling brick pile she had seen. Even the beauties from every window served to remind her of its sad state in 2011. Here in 1811, it burst with energy, activity, and potential.

This all falls to nothing. Mr. Darcy will die, his estate is squandered, and in a hundred years, it's torn to pieces for scrap.

Reynolds led the way to the picture gallery where Elizabeth noticed bright landscape pencil drawings.

"Those were done by Miss Darcy. She is only fifteen, but she is a talented lady."

"What is she like?"

"She appears older than her age, but is the handsomest young lady that ever was seen. Her drawings are excellent, but it is in music her talents are most readily seen. She plays and sings all day long."

"But what is she *like*?"

"Did I not just say? To add, she is intelligent, but shy. She is less sure of herself than her brother, but gentle-tempered, and with age will come confidence. A lovely girl in every respect."

Reynolds really cares about the Darcy siblings. Elizabeth then saw a familiar face. There was a large portrait of Mr. Darcy, painted perhaps within the last five years. He was painted with an arresting gaze and a smile. *The portraitist must have had a good imagination.* Mr. Darcy was an ass, but knowing about his impending death made it impossible to hate him entirely.

"I do not expect to be available to you during the day." Reynolds's voice made Elizabeth jump, and she hurried to catch up. They strode through the picture gallery to see a few of the principal bedrooms. "I will have time for you in the evenings. I suspect you shall need advice and have questions."

"What about after I become a guest of Miss Darcy?" Her life was becoming an upstairs-downstairs drama.

"As you are my relation"—her mouth twisted at that—"you would always be welcomed. However, if you are to be the daughter of a gentleman, and a guest of Miss Darcy of Pemberley, you ought not to be always in the housekeeper's room."

"I won't cramp your style." A blank stare was her response. "Do not worry, I will not interfere with your position here. Why don't you return to whatever it is you need to do? I'll go for a walk."

"Wear a bonnet and gloves, and tell a footman or gardener where you intend to walk. A young unmarried lady does not speak to one she has not been introduced to. The library is available to you, and any of the rooms I have shown you. Join me at five o'clock in my sitting room."

Elizabeth raised her left hand and turned her wrist, but, of course, she had removed her watch to blend in. Reynolds reached for the small watch that hung from a gold chain around her neck. "It is past midday. There is a Chippendale clock in the hall by the main staircase, and the library has a clock on the mantle." With only a nod in parting, she was gone.

Elizabeth could not be sure who was more relieved when they parted.

CHAPTER FIVE

MARCH 25, 1811

"It is in every way horrible!"

"You are not about to cry, are you, Darcy? I do not love you enough to console you should you cry like a little girl."

"When a gentleman's livelihood and respectability are threatened by fractures in time and a strange being that can scarcely be credited as a member of her sex, he has every right to be on the verge of weeping!"

Darcy slumped in a chair, his cousin seated across from him.

"This woman must be a terror to behold." Colonel Fitzwilliam rose to warm himself before the fire. "If it is impossible for her to be viewed as a woman, let alone a woman of our time, why am I here?"

Darcy raised his head from his hands. "To share the burden with me. Would you deny me that?"

"You are my closest friend; I would deny you nothing in my power to give."

Darcy smiled, grateful for his loyalty. "This woman is not a terror. Were she any other stranger forced upon my notice, she would merely be a nuisance. But her presence might cost me dearly should the truth come out."

"The previous visitors did not cause your father distress. Why would one woman ruin you?"

Darcy hauled himself from his chair with a sigh. "A man easily led and infirm from old age appeared at Nine Ladies before I was born, and the infant when I was teenaged. Neither one had the remotest influence on Pemberley. But with her, I must justify her presence and be vigilant that her behavior does not reflect negatively on my reputation. Let us not forget the catastrophic possibility that she admits to someone from whence she came."

"Did she not give her word to participate in the deception? I thought this was partly her scheme."

Darcy cleared his throat, embarrassed by how he was swayed when she proclaimed that twenty-first century women could be honorable. "She gave me a feeling of being able to trust her, and that, combined with my pity for her, provoked me to agree. Of course, any stranger among the family at Pemberley would be a destruction of all my comfort."

"When shall my formidable introduction take place?"

"If anyone were to ask, she only today arrived on the mail coach. You ought to prepare yourself for something dreadful when she speaks."

His cousin laughed. "You are too fastidious! How do you mean?"

"Miss Bennet's voice is peculiar. She uses an astonishing number of contracted words for an educated woman. When she says *don't* and *want*, the t disappears. With other words, the *t* is pronounced like a *d*. And I cannot begin to describe the words she used that do not exist."

"Is English not her primary language? Where did she say she was from?"

Darcy stared. "Two thousand and eleven."

Fitzwilliam laughed again. "I must meet this fearsome creature! Will Reynolds bring her to the drawing room this evening?"

"I ought to not meet with her too soon. She may be represented here as a daughter of a gentleman, but she is beneath me in consequence, and poor and unconnected."

"It would be at odds with your sense of generosity to treat her as an interloper for three months. I can stay with you a week without raising my father's suspicions; he expects me at Easter. If you want my assistance to acquaint her with what is expected, we ought to begin immediately."

The door opened, and both gentlemen turned, surprised upon seeing a woman, simply but tastefully dressed, enter. She wore a bonnet and pelisse, and held her gloves. Upon seeing them, the woman stopped short, but she neither spoke nor moved. *Reynolds must be giving a tour and lost one of her charges.* "A tourist?" Darcy whispered before turning away.

"May I help you, madam?" Fitzwilliam asked.

"I, yes, um, sorry for interrupting. I wanted to see the clock in the library, but I entered the wrong room."

Darcy spun from the window and looked at her in amazement. "Miss *Bennet*?"

Fitzwilliam's pocket watch slipped through his fingers as he stared, and she gave an inelegant curtsey. "Hel—good afternoon. Like I said, I only wished to know the time, but I am interrupting. I'm just, um, going to . . . go now."

"You are not a tourist? You, *you* are the visitor from Nine Ladies?" Fitzwilliam looked at Darcy with a question on his lips, but thought better of it and gave Miss Bennet a charismatic grin.

Miss Bennet bestowed upon his cousin a smile nothing short of luminous as she removed her bonnet. "You might say I am a tourist after all."

Darcy stared in shock; his cousin joined in her laughter. "I daresay you have traveled farther than anyone in all of England! Darcy, will you not introduce me to your witty guest?"

How was *this* the bold woman in trousers who had assaulted his sensibilities three days ago?

"Since Mr. Darcy has lost his tongue, do I introduce myself?"

Her admonishment roused Darcy, and ingrained proper behavior asserted itself enough to introduce them.

"Colonel, I would shake your hand, but the last time I offered my hand to Mr. Darcy, he looked as though I insulted his mother. Since you know my secret, would you tell me how to properly greet someone in this situation?"

"With a curtsey and a smile, you would win the heart of any gentleman fortunate enough to make your acquaintance."

"Gallantry is usually a mockery in my time, but here and now, I'm *almost* inclined to believe you."

Darcy stood in silent confusion as he watched them banter and smile. Fitzwilliam helped to remove her pelisse, led her to sit by the fire, and asked how she liked Pemberley. Her voice held its strange tones, but other than that, she bore little resemblance to the creature he had first met. The flattering gown and her less aggressive posture made him realize there was a woman there after all.

Maybe our scheme will succeed.

She was not beautiful, fractionally above average height, only a slight figure to speak of. Yet there was a liveliness in her that might otherwise draw him had she been of his own time. Her dark hair was appropriately pinned back, and it allowed him a better view of her fine eyes.

"Does he always stand around like an idiot?"

"An idiot? No, he is not incapable of ordinary reasoning. Darcy is, in fact, a clever man. I think, however, I comprehend you. He does look dull at the moment. You might instead ask me if he often stands about in that stupid manner."

"Does your cousin often stand about in that stupid manner?"

"No, he is livelier at home than anywhere else. I cannot account for him."

Darcy's hopeful feelings effervesced, replaced by indignation and apprehension.

"I am lively when I have reason to be! Miss Bennet, we may as well make use of this time and arrange the particulars of your history so I can write to my sister to begin this strange performance. What have you and Reynolds agreed upon?"

Large brown eyes fixed on his and narrowed. "Reynolds hates me."

Darcy's jaw dropped, and Fitzwilliam gave an uncomfortable laugh before answering. "Miss Bennet, that is rude."

"Well, she does. I have been cooperative, but she wants nothing to do with me." *I do not blame Reynolds's feelings.* "She said to be a distant cousin to her deceased husband, that I was left alone in the world except for her, and to leave the details to us."

"I have not written a play or a story to entertain the family since I was a child. Darcy, will not this be amusing?" Fitzwilliam clapped his hands once and ran his palms together. "What sad, sensational history ought we to create?"

"Amusing?" Darcy was appalled. "Miss Bennet does not even sound as though she speaks the same language as us, and you are worried about creating a gothic drama?"

"Her voice may be hard to account for, but once her address is improved—"

"You're worried about my accent? Why?"

"Miss Bennet, anything that appears out of the ordinary will attract undue attention," Darcy said. "I cannot have you stay amongst us if you appear to be anything but a genteel English lady of this time."

"I'm not English. Well, technically I am, but I'm an American. I was only in England to . . . to visit my father."

Darcy exchanged a fearful look with Fitzwilliam.

"Is that a problem?" And *there* it was, that edge in her voice that reminded Darcy of the furious woman in trousers who had antagonized him.

Fitzwilliam cleared his throat. "In general, we English are convinced of our own superiority, rightfully so since ours is the most stable nation on earth. The reputation of Americans is that they are often . . . uncivilized."

"Uncivilized? You and Mr. Darcy have no idea how uncivilized this world is to *me*. I can't wear pants! You have no indoor plumbing! I can't walk outside without a hat! This place is unsophisticated and unenlightened, and you *dare* to talk to me about the stereotype of uncouth Americans?"

Darcy and his cousin could make no reply to this vulgar outburst. Miss Bennet's eyes flashed, her fists clenched at her sides, and Fitzwilliam leaned back in his chair. However, before violence or hysteria ensued, she sighed and calmed. "I apologize, it's not your fault you're ignorant and backward. It's not fair to blame you for your antiquated world view and for being misogynistic when you're incapable of knowing better."

Darcy recalled his classical language tutor. "You think we hate women? How did we progress from unrefined colonists to us hating women?"

"The twenty-first century treats women a little better than you do. Can you comprehend the idea that women can vote and hold public office?" She closed her eyes. "But I made a promise; I will play the role I've been cast in: the ignorant little woman. But between us, in my time, America is the richest, most prosperous, and most promising nation in the world."

Fitzwilliam smiled. "You are teasing! And next you will tell me your navy is the most powerful."

Miss Bennet also smiled, but it was a chilling smirk. "Wait and see what your naval blockade of the United States next year gets you."

Fitzwilliam's humor disappeared. "Are you telling me the tensions with America regarding trade will lead to another conflict?"

"For what it's worth to either of our nations, at the end of the War of 1812, your country will be out-sailed, outgunned, and—"

"Stop!" Darcy cried. "Say nothing. I shall not be accused of using your knowledge for my own gain, and your presence is already a disruption to the natural order of things. You must not make it worse by telling us what will come!"

There was a long pause before she answered. "You're *certain* you don't want to know about your—about the future?"

"Not one thing."

She surprised him by giving him a pitying look and quietly said, "If you're sure. Well, if no one will believe I'm English, then what if I was a loyalist whose family went to Canada after the revolution?"

Fitzwilliam found his voice and turned to Darcy. "Thousands of settlers loyal to England left America after the Paris Treaty. What if her father was a commissioned officer who fled to Lower Canada? Do you know that area, Miss Bennet, in the event anyone asks you about it?"

"I went to Niagara Falls once."

"Upper Canada, then. Let us say your English father received a land grant for his loyalty, and you live in the capital."

"I could be from Toronto?"

"Where?"

"Biggest city in Canada? The capital of Ontario, or Upper Canada is what you call it now? I think it's on a lake."

Darcy placed his head on the mantle. Forcefully. "York! She must mean Fort York. This will never work!"

"It will, Darcy! What about this: Her mother was Reynolds's husband's distant cousin. She was a merchant's daughter who traveled to America and married an English army officer, a gentleman's younger son. After the conflict, he brings his wife to the Canadas and was granted his two hundred acres of land. Miss Bennet's parents are now dead, and she has returned to England to be with her mother's family."

Darcy raised his head from the mantle, but did not turn. He felt ill to his stomach. "And where is that family now?"

"Any relations near enough to claim her have died, and no one else will take her on in charity. Perhaps her father's family never approved of her mother's relations in trade, and the only family she found is the wife of her mother's cousin, who is the housekeeper in this home."

"You like this storytelling, don'cha?" Darcy cringed; Miss Bennet caught his gaze in the reflection in the mirror, cleared her throat, and spoke again, without the sarcastic tone. "You enjoy creating stories, do you not?"

Darcy turned to face the room, and Fitzwilliam gave them both a wide smile. "Indeed! If you are from the other side of the world, it will explain your ignorance, and if your parents were English and your father a gentleman, you shall be accepted well enough if Darcy will vouchsafe for you."

"She must have been in British North America at the right time. How old are you, Miss Bennet?"

"I was born in 1987. Can you do the math without a calculator?"

Since he did not understand it, Darcy let the implied insult pass. "You were born after the war to an English officer, in the Canadas, in 1787. Your parents are dead, and with what resources you had, you came home to England to find your mother's family. You arrived to find any who would claim you are dead, and your father's family does not acknowledge you out of resentment that your mother came from trade. Since you are Reynolds's relation and a genteel young lady"—he glared to emphasize the point—"I will allow you to stay at Pemberley with my sister until you can be put on a ship back to your friends."

"Got it. Poor, lonely Canadian girl. From York, not Toronto. Embarrassingly grateful to everyone at Pemberley. I'm ready for my close-up." She smirked from some private amusement, but her expression fell when she saw their confused faces. Darcy was surprised by the pink on her cheeks. "I'm sorry. I made you a promise, and I intend to keep it. I will be pleasant and keep my sarcastic quips to myself. But I hope you understand how strange, frightening, and downright regressive I find this. Can you imagine how you might feel if you woke up in 1611? In a country that isn't even your own?"

"The terror you must be feeling, I would not wish upon anyone." Fitzwilliam spoke gently. "While I am at Pemberley, you may speak freely with me when opportunity and propriety permit. You will undoubtedly feel the need to unburden yourself, to in essence be yourself. Darcy will fulfill that role after I must leave, will not you, Darcy?"

The devil could not prescribe a worse punishment. "Your servant, madam."

YEAH, RIGHT. MR. DARCY IS JUST TOO POLITE TO TELL ME TO GO TO HELL. Still, she would behave and not antagonize Mr. Darcy for her own amusement. Colonel Fitzwilliam was friendly and patient, and other than a similarity in height and the shape of the eyes, the cousins had nothing in common. She would be hard-pressed to find someone to talk to after the outgoing colonel left.

The two men pored over a travel book, putting together the last pieces of her backstory. It was a striking display of their disparate but complementary characters. Mr. Darcy focused on practicality; Colonel Fitzwilliam cared more about creating an entertaining story.

"Who did she sail with, and when did she realize none in London would meet her? When and how did she find Reynolds?"

"It does not matter." Elizabeth heard pages turn. "Anyone of good breeding is too polite to ask, and she will not be among us for long enough for anyone to invite her confidence. Leave your imagination out of this."

"People would be interested in how she found Reynolds, not how many miles per hour she made from Nottingham to Matlock."

"These are the facts someone might ask about." She heard Mr. Darcy tap the page. "She will only need to answer the polite inquiry as to how her journey was."

"Guys!" They turned, but had that now-familiar look as though she had grown another head. "I'll say I don't want to talk about the details because of my disappointment when I realized no one in England wanted me. It's close enough to the truth, so you can put away your *Paterson's British Itinerary* and move on."

"Miss Bennet, you appear distressed. Would you like to sit?"

Because remembering my dead father who walked out, and how lost I am, will make me too weak to stand? Just because she had been neglected, abandoned, didn't mean that she couldn't pretend to be without any family in 1811 without breaking down. Those poor underestimated nineteenth-century women. "No, Colonel, I'm fine."

"If I may, fine means expertly fashioned or skillfully made. Or a blade's sharp edge."

She suppressed the compulsion to say "okey-dokey." "I am not about to faint in a fit of vapors. Shall we go over some things I need to know before Georgiana arrives?"

Mr. Darcy's dark eyes twitched, as if he wanted to roll them, but his force of will held them in place. "Her Christian name is Georgiana; however, as scarcely an acquaintance, she would not permit you to use it."

"I gathered *that*. That's why I didn't ask you to call me Elizabeth. I didn't want you to spontaneously combust from shock."

Colonel Fitzwilliam paled. "That does not happen in the future . . . does it?"

Mr. Darcy and Elizabeth shared a look, and slowly shared a smile. *Hey, there's a sense of humor there after all.* "I know Mr. Darcy said not to discuss the future, but I think he will forgive me when I say spontaneous human combustion is not a problem facing the twenty-first century."

"Can we turn our attention to more urgent matters? We can explain some of Miss Bennet's ignorance by saying she is from York, but a genteel woman of this time ought to know French, play an instrument, sing, draw, dance, and move and speak with elegance."

"I can't do any of those things. I took Spanish in high school, I suck at art, and, trust me, what I consider dancing would make you faint. Those so-called skills have nothing to do with being a woman."

"I am far from agreeing that that is what makes a woman truly accomplished. Netting a purse and singing in Italian does not make a woman inherently admirable. It does, however, mean you are respectable."

Mr. Darcy's reply surprised her; she expected more of an argument. "What about education making a woman respectable?" She didn't expect women of this time to have college degrees and careers, but they must be taught more than drawing and singing.

Colonel Fitzwilliam laughed. "The point of educating girls is to ensure they are useful and pleasing companions to their husbands. No gentleman is in need of a wife who knows as much as he does; she might demonstrate such in front of his friends!"

Elizabeth's mind reeled. This well-spoken, engaging man was appalled at the idea of educating women. This world was even less enlightened than she thought. Now she *did* feel faint. "I have a degree in accounting. I keep abreast of what's happening in the world. A man in my time, a man with any sense, would hardly want an ignorant wife."

Mr. Darcy stared at her in silence. She was used to that. Colonel Fitzwilliam answered patronizingly, "A man of this time, and likely in yours as well, wants a sweet wife, all gratitude and devotion. There is no reason to educate women beyond the schoolroom since they are destined to become wives and mothers."

"But not every woman receives an offer of marriage, and she can't do the asking now, and a woman shouldn't settle for a bad marriage to not end up on the streets. Why not educate women on equal terms with men—"

Colonel Fitzwilliam laughed. "I am glad we discussed this before we threw you into society. I agree an intelligent man would not want a silly wife. She needs to manage a home and be a decent hostess, after all. More to what you are saying, a proper lady should appear to think well of books, not speak well and at length of them. That is the crucial difference."

Elizabeth breathed faster and felt terrified. Her throat felt raw, and tears stung at her eyes. *What if I can't go home? How could I live in this ignorant world, assumed to be less than any man?* It would be unbearable. She tried to control her breathing, already feeling her fingers and lips tingle from hyperventilating.

When Mr. Darcy appeared at her side, holding out a glass of wine, she started. This hardly seemed like a moment to share a friendly drink, but his compassionate look compelled her to at least take it and thank him. The smug confidence in Colonel Fitzwilliam's replies struck her cold, and her panic drove her to ask, "Do you agree with him?" She was ashamed of her own fear of living among such people, possibly forever.

"I am not opposed to a woman who engages in serious reading and intellectual conversation, but most you will encounter here are opposed to educating women the way you suggest." He sat beside her and spoke in a low tone. "You do not strike me as a woman who can be dictated to, but allow me to reason with you. All people, not just men, will be uncomfortable around a clever, well-read, opinionated woman. You must be careful about how you present yourself."

"Afraid for your reputation? You don't want the crazy lady from the future trying to campaign for women's rights? I told you, I won't cause any problems." Her fingers shook, and the wine sloshed in its glass.

"You mistake me. You will remain in constant anxiety if you hold us to your own standards. I would not wish for your time at Pemberley to be ridden with hopelessness. I fear for your safety if you are outspoken, but I also fear for your state of mind. Three months is a long time to be miserably unhappy and afraid."

His voice had a degree of concern she hadn't heard from him before. He gave her a small serious smile. She felt herself smiling back, then the corners of his mouth turned up further and the warmth spread to his eyes. For the first time since she arrived, she did feel some gratitude toward Mr. Darcy. When her uneven breathing began to have less to do with fear, and more to do with the desire to push back the dark lock of hair that had fallen forward on his head, she set her glass down and stood.

Both men rose, and Elizabeth took a deep breath, blinked, and adjusted her smile. "This discussion has been too much for me." She brought a hand to her chest and dropped her shoulders, fluttering her eyelashes.

She heard Mr. Darcy scoff, and she saw his smile before he turned away, but Colonel Fitzwilliam spoke with sincerity. "Of course it has. Reynolds will bring you to the drawing room after dinner. Darcy, what ought we to teach our friend about English life at the beginning of the nineteenth century?"

"We can start with whist. What card games do you play in 2011?"

"Card games have been replaced by—" She stopped when she saw the apprehension on Mr. Darcy's face. "I do not know how to play whist. My grandparents used to make us play a game called bridge. Perhaps there are similarities." She gave the best curtsey she could, and left.

DARCY WATCHED MISS BENNET LEAVE, SHAKING HIS HEAD AT THE MEMORY of staring into those dark and worried eyes. She looked strained, but the essential passion and intelligence in her face was heightened. There was something more elemental in her than in most women. He hoped that returning to Nine Ladies on the solstice worked, because Miss Bennet would be miserable if she was forced to live here forever.

"Your pretty traveler from the future has caught my fancy," Fitzwilliam said and then laughed.

"You cannot have formed a tender attachment. And do not call her mine."

"I just enjoy speaking with her. She is satirical, and her ideas are peculiar, but from how you described her, I thought she would have a gorgon's face and a serpent's tongue!"

Darcy repressed his impulse to recant his former opinion. "It is worse than that," he said with forced hostility. "I have an outspoken

Yankee Doodle from the future living in my house for the next three months."

Fitzwilliam waved his hand. "She has an accent, is all." He laughed. "Can you imagine! Two hundred years from now, women are expected to attend university. What is the point of educating a woman when all she will do is become a wife and mother?"

"A generation of young men raised by educated mothers could not be bad for England." Upon seeing his cousin's incredulous stare, Darcy went on in a different manner. "She has good sense and showed she has agreeable manners. There is little to be done, however, to correct her ignorance of current events and culture."

"We shall teach her to play whist, and perhaps teach her to often remain silent."

Darcy suspected teaching Elizabeth Bennet the former would be easy. He had serious reservations about the latter.

CHAPTER SIX

April 1, 1811

Elizabeth stood in the beautiful music room staring at the pianoforte and remembering the cheap used piano shoved into the dining room in her childhood home. There was another pianoforte in the best drawing room for entertaining in the evenings. *I guess you do need someone who can play if there's no TV to watch.* She looked through the music books until a title page caught her attention.

"*Sonata Quasi una fantasia*, Op. 27 No. 2."

It turned out six years of unwanted piano lessons did not help her to play the pianoforte well. Instead of pedals, there were knee levers that operated the sustain and damper. The keys fell only half the depth of a modern piano, and she kept crashing them too hard. Having only five octaves threw her off. This instrument had less sustaining power than she remembered a piano having. Also, she had never been good at the piano in the first place.

When she finished, she saw Mrs. Reynolds standing in the doorway like a statue.

"Is this where you tell me I do not play half so well as Miss Darcy?"

The housekeeper's lips twitched. "You do not strike me as one who seeks compliments. Although, that I recognize those notes as *Moonlight Sonata* could be taken as a compliment."

A backhanded one. "This is a little different than the instrument I know."

"You might gainfully take the trouble to practice. To be proficient in music would speak to your credibility and make your time here pass a little easier."

"Thank you for the suggestion." Elizabeth smiled, but the housekeeper seemed to remember her dislike and left.

A walk would suit her mood better than sitting at the piano, since she couldn't go for a run. While she sprinted up Pemberley's main staircase to her room, Elizabeth imagined the shock on everyone's faces if she were to jog in a sports bra. Suddenly, her long skirts tangled between her legs, and she caught the hem underneath her slipper as she climbed a step. Her foot came down hard on her skirt, and the force pulled her forward.

Before she banged her face into the stairs, two hands caught her shoulders to steady her. Elizabeth turned to see Mr. Darcy bending over her. She felt the heat in her cheeks and looked away. He straightened and held out one hand, raising her up while keeping the other on her shoulder, as though afraid she might tip over without his help.

"Attending university has not helped you with more mundane tasks." He was two steps below her and spoke low into her ear so only she could hear. When she was upright, he swiftly pulled his hands away.

"I'm not used to long skirts." She tried to smile through her embarrassment.

"Are hem lengths shorter in—" He stopped, maybe regretting his curiosity.

"They are. And, if you recall what I wore when I first arrived, you could see why I have trouble."

"I did not imagine that stair climbing would be something you needed to practice." His lips never quite made it to a full smile.

"The stairs I can handle. Apparently, I am better off practicing the pianoforte. Reynolds told me my *Moonlight Sonata* was not going to earn me any compliments."

"What is a moonlight sonata?"

"A Beethoven sonata, but my shortcomings frustrated me, so I was about to go for a walk instead."

"It is a lovely morning." He bowed and descended the stairs.

"Would you like to come?" Mr. Darcy stopped and turned. She added, "Maybe you could show me new places to walk?"

"As much as I may like to, I must meet with my steward."

Elizabeth couldn't tell if Mr. Darcy wanted to join her or not. This society had such strict conventions of decorum that she often had no idea what was sincere and what was only polite. "I thought *you* were in charge. If you want to go for a walk, can you not meet him later?" From what she understood, the steward had his own cottage and was like an accountant, a secretary, and a manager all in one.

"Philip Willers said he has concerns about an investment, and I agreed to meet him at one o'clock."

The dutiful Mr. Darcy said he would do something, and nothing will change that. "Another time. I will try not to get lost in the massive expanse you call a park."

"Fitzwilliam knows the park; he would be happy to guide you."

Elizabeth had tried her best to keep Colonel Fitzwilliam's outdated opinions from offending her. In general, he was the sort of guy you would invite to your party: friendly and ready to speak to anyone on any subject. She could practice keeping her patience while he discussed how women ought to be meek and modest, and only men were ambitious. After all, she had no one else to talk to.

"So, the larger the park around the estate, the higher up the social ladder you are?"

"I would not simplify it to such a degree," Colonel Fitzwilliam said. "Every park has its beauty and prospects, no matter the fortune of the proprietor."

"How tactful of you."

"I am not impolitic. However, in confidence, the grounds of Pemberley are the most beautiful I have seen."

"You will get no argument from me. I have never seen anything like it."

"You had no park at your father's home? Perhaps it is done in a different style where, and when, you are from?"

"The park" meant the apartment playground with creaky swings, and it was nowhere near her father's home because he had walked out on them. She twirled her reticule around her wrist before deflecting his question. "Your cousin said Pemberley has over five thousand acres? How big is the park?"

"Perhaps ten miles around."

"All I have seen is this circuit. I can't comprehend how large that is." A thought crossed her mind. "I have been to Haddon Hall. Do you know how much land is there?"

Colonel Fitzwilliam inhaled and tilted his head as he pursed his lips. The gesture struck her; two hundred years separated them, but he was, of course, thinking. "I have been there once. Less than three thousand, perhaps."

Now that she had a frame of reference, the sheer size of Pemberley staggered her.

"If I may, what brought you to Haddon? That house is dormant now since Lord Manners is at Belvoir Castle."

"It's open for tours. It was restored in the early twentieth century after it spent a few hundred years in disrepair. The same family still owns it and lives there."

"You say that as though in your time homes are not inherited and lived in!" Elizabeth said nothing. "You must tell me how you found it."

Elizabeth began to pull out her iPhone before she remembered herself. She sighed at her own stupidity.

"Are you well?"

"I was about to show you pictures, but that would not be appropriate."

"How could drawings be inappropriate?"

"It's not the pictures that are inappropriate, but the device—the tool with which I would show them to you." Elizabeth exhaled a shaky breath. "They are not drawings."

"How could you have pictures if you did not draw or paint them?"

"Mr. Darcy would not approve of my answering."

"You pique my curiosity! I told you to speak freely when none could hear us."

"If someone from my time asked me about Haddon, I would take out this"—she opened the bag—"and show them."

"What is that little box with a black lid?"

"That's not a lid; it's a screen."

"Like those used for magic lantern shows?"

"Sort of," she hedged. She was almost out of battery, but she should be able to show a few pictures.

Colonel Fitzwilliam stared in wide-eyed silence as she brought them up. She stood next to him and held up the phone, scrolling through. She laughed when he swore under his breath.

"These images are incredible!" He looked around, and then back at the photos. "The colors . . . I have never in my life seen any painting so realistic. Is that the entrance courtyard?"

"Yes, it is very medieval, almost frozen in time."

"May I?" The colonel's fingers stretched toward it. Elizabeth handed it to him.

"Take your finger like this to scroll, to look through the pictures." She lifted his hand, tugging on his pointer finger to demonstrate.

Colonel Fitzwilliam brought the phone within inches of his eyes. He scrolled in silence for another minute, before crying out, "What are those costumes?"

Elizabeth peered at the phone, which he still held in front of his face. "Those are my friends. I promise, they're dressed appropriately for the time and for the activity."

"The ladies are wearing trousers. Their clothing must be the strangest thing I ever laid eyes on."

Elizabeth laughed. "I'm not sure what to tell you."

After a few swipes, he asked, "What is this structure? Good God!" He dropped the phone, and it clattered on the gravel. Elizabeth picked it up and was about to explain its fragility when she saw his white face.

"Are you all right?" Elizabeth looked at her screen. "Oh no!" There, in rich, saturated color, was Pemberley's east façade as it looked in

2011. Chipped plaster, glassless windows, exposed brick; its dirty columns and pediment a depressing crown on its ruins. "Colonel, I am *so* sorry! I forgot, I would never—"

"Does Darcy know?" He choked on the words as though they were glass.

"Of course not! He doesn't want to know the future, and besides, it'd be cruel to—"

"You must not tell him!"

"I won't—"

"To know his life's work, his family's legacy, his livelihood, and his future children and grandchildren's livelihood, the lives of everyone connected to Pemberley, his *home* . . . he would be devastated." The colonel was furious, or frightened. Or both.

"I won't tell him, I promise!"

His tension was replaced by gloom. "'Tis a sad business. I have unknowingly sucked down a poison. How do I look him in the eye knowing what is to come?"

"Remember, two hundred years is a long time."

"I suspect you do not comprehend the societal, the financial, the emotional value of a gentleman's estate, and what it means for his family and future generations. What it means to all who rent land and who are employed here, what it means to their children, what it means to those who live in the village, those who depend on what is produced here."

"If it's any comfort, Pemberley is not in actual ruins until—"

"No! If I do not know the details, then I cannot tell Darcy." The colonel took in a large breath. After collecting himself, he spoke calmly. "I daresay it is time to turn back. I shall be here for only a few more days, and if you are to learn any dancing at all, it must be done before I leave to join my family at Easter."

His tone was lighter, and she strove to answer him in the same style. "Are you so good a dancer that you are the only man in 1811 who could instruct me?"

"I am competent enough, especially when I have a pretty partner. If I am gone, the task will fall to Darcy, and he hates dancing. He will have you believe gentlemen stand about at a ball and ladies love to sit down for want of a partner. Heaven knows how that good man will find a wife when he only dances with women he has no intention of marrying."

Mr. Darcy wouldn't marry, but she suspected knowing about his own death would upset him less than knowing about the destruction of his home. If the colonel was this upset, how would Mr. Darcy feel if he knew?

April 12, 1811

The colonel had left Pemberley a few days ago, and today was the day Mr. Darcy's sister arrived and Elizabeth's playacting began in earnest. For a woman normally staid and, in Elizabeth's opinion, cold, Mrs. Reynolds moved with anticipation. She wished to be in the hall when Miss Darcy arrived, and could not remain at her breakfast table with them another moment.

The butler went with her and Mr. Darcy's valet soon left; Philip Willers, the steward, was the only one who remained with Elizabeth.

"I understand you are to be a houseguest of Miss Darcy rather than Mrs. Reynolds's visitor," he said pleasantly. "I am not often at her table, but I suppose this is the last meal you will share with us here?"

"I was not brought up so high as to be unable to share a meal here with those who provide me with good company." There, she had been practicing.

"Your manners do you credit anywhere, I am sure. You must be relieved that you found Mrs. Reynolds. I cannot imagine crossing an ocean seeking your family only to learn you are still alone in the world. You could not have found a woman who works for a more generous master."

Elizabeth kept from rolling her eyes. "Mr. Darcy and Reynolds have been good to me."

"Do you know what ship you intend to take your return voyage on? It is soon to be the best time of year to cross the Atlantic."

"I do not. What brings you to the house so early that you can have breakfast with us? You cannot have been willing to leave your wife so soon."

Elizabeth listened while Mr. Willers extolled the virtues of the new Mrs. Willers. It was easier to allow others to talk than come up with replies to questions she had no idea how to answer. He soon left to review some matter on behalf of Mr. Darcy, and Reynolds returned.

"Are you prepared to be introduced to Miss Darcy?" There was something different about the housekeeper.

"Doesn't she want to relax before she meets a stranger? Take a shower, touch up her lipstick, check her messages?" Reynolds inhaled loudly and exhaled slowly. "I am willing to wait if she wishes to spend time with her brother first."

"Mr. Darcy prefers it to be over with as soon as possible."

Elizabeth rose and clapped her hands once, loudly. "Let's do this!"

"Miss Darcy is shy, so do not be offended if she does not speak to you. She is, in truth, as agreeable as her brother." As they walked, Elizabeth realized what was wrong with Reynolds's face: she was smiling. "It is good to have her home. She has been a lonely child and has not had many friends."

"If she's done with school and only has a chaperone for company, she might want me here so she has a girl near her age to spend time with." Elizabeth liked the idea of being a friend to Georgiana Darcy. She had been lonely at Pemberley herself.

Reynolds stopped to look her in the eye, the smile gone. A muscle in her jaw twitched. "Do not forget, Miss Bennet, that as good-natured as Miss Darcy is, as generous as the master is, we none of us *want* you here."

Elizabeth gritted her teeth as Reynolds continued walking. "Got it, Mrs. Danvers."

The housekeeper spun on her heels to face her. "How da—" She sighed. "I cannot believe you forgot my name."

I need to keep my temper. "Forgive me. You reminded me of someone I knew from home."

Reynolds reclaimed her grasp on her self-control and left Elizabeth in the drawing room.

Mr. Darcy sat on the sofa, holding his sister's hand. He stood, pulling Georgiana with him, and the warm smile he had been giving his sister remained on his face while he looked at Elizabeth. *He's a handsome man when he relaxes long enough to smile.*

"Georgiana, may I present Reynolds's cousin and our houseguest for the spring, Miss Elizabeth Bennet. Miss Bennet, I have the pleasure of making Miss Darcy known to you. This is her companion, Mrs. Younge."

Elizabeth's arm twitched as she repressed the habit to shake hands. Georgiana was tall and looked older than she was. Mrs. Younge gave her a cursory glance and nodded. *She* was younger and prettier than expected.

"It is a pleasure to make your acquaintance," the girl whispered. She acted more like a shy child dragged in to talk to the grown-ups rather than someone considered, in this time, to be an adult.

"I understand you have come from London. It seemed an exciting city, so much larger than York." Georgiana finally made eye contact, but did not reply. "I appreciate you leaving London to be your brother's hostess on my behalf."

Mrs. Younge's not-so-subtle swat on Georgiana's arm provoked her to answer. "You are welcome."

Now they were seated, and the anticipatory silence became uncomfortable, then awkward. Elizabeth did not know what topics were fit for conversation, and Georgiana stared at the embroidery on her own skirt. Mrs. Younge looked bored to the point of pain, and when Elizabeth thought she might have been better off in one of Mr. Darcy's outbuildings for three months, he tried to save their flagging conversation.

"Georgiana, Miss Bennet has pleasure in music. Not long ago, she played a Beethoven sonata of yours. She might like to hear what new music you have."

Georgiana opened her mouth, but did not speak. Mr. Darcy gave her a pointed but patient smile. "I, I did not purchase anything recently."

Mr. Darcy closed his eyes, but kept his pleasant smile in place. Not that his sister could see it, since she resumed her inspection of her own fingernails. The companion's eyes glazed over, and she did nothing to help. "Georgiana, Miss Bennet may not be as fond of music as you are, but she would enjoy hearing about whatever you have. I daresay the Canadas is not as up to date with new music as London is."

Another long pause. "I, I cannot remember."

Mr. Darcy shifted his weight. "Miss Bennet has no knowledge of the harp. She might enjoy hearing you play. You might amuse your new acquaintance if you allow her to listen to you."

"As you wish." Georgiana blanched.

This is painful. Mr. Darcy was trying but failing, the companion was useless, and Georgiana looked like she might throw up. Elizabeth had to get this shy girl to relax.

"Whenever your name is mentioned, the speaker mentions what a talented musician you are." She was told not to compliment, but something had to be done.

Mrs. Younge cleared her throat before Georgiana whispered, "You are very kind."

"My own performance on the pianoforte is mediocre. And that is being generous; anyone who hears me says worse."

Georgiana raised her eyes in surprise. "I . . . none at Pemberley has said such a thing to you, have they?"

"No, your brother's manners are too generous to be so honest. But when *you* hear me, you and I will know the truth." She leaned forward and gave a conspiratorial smile.

Silence. Elizabeth kept smiling. "We should decide together how you will describe my playing to others. We both know I will be bad, so we may as well choose the polite phrases now." Georgiana looked at her in curiosity. *At least she's not staring at her own hands.* "Will you say I at least have good taste in selecting music, or at least I try hard?"

Georgiana looked at her brother, but Elizabeth's pointed look regained her attention. "I could only speak the truth, I suppose."

"I admire your honesty. We are decided: you must say I am terrible!" Georgiana looked shocked, but when Elizabeth laughed, a smile graced the younger girl's lips. "Could you say that your houseguest plays terribly? It is the truth, after all; I wouldn't—I would not mind."

"I do not think I could be so . . . no, I could not."

Elizabeth turned to Mr. Darcy, who followed their conversation with an inquiring expression. "Your sister is too good. Do you have a suggestion for how she could describe my talents that would be less blunt?"

"I have not heard you myself, but perhaps Georgiana could say you play just good enough to be praised."

Elizabeth laughed when she saw his teasing smile. "Your sister's talents are beyond mine. Could I listen to you, Miss Darcy? I have been lonely at Pemberley." Elizabeth felt Mr. Darcy's attention shift toward her, but he said nothing.

Georgiana's tentative smile fell. "I am not accustomed to performing before others..."

The girl was just starting to relax. "I will not judge, I will not compare, I will not applaud. I won't even enjoy it if you tell me not to." This earned her a small laugh, and Georgiana's fidgeting hands rested on her lap. "I will only happily listen."

"Very well."

Mrs. Younge lifted her watch noisily, but Georgiana did not understand the message. Mr. Darcy mouthed "stand up" to Elizabeth. Introductions were meant to be short. *So many rules.* "Perhaps this evening we can talk about music? Or think of synonyms for untalented?"

Georgiana stood, but only nodded. Mrs. Younge sighed, and rose also. "Miss Darcy and I are pleased to have met you, and we look forward to furthering our acquaintance whilst you remain with us." She said the right things, but without a shred of inflection.

Elizabeth caught Mr. Darcy's eye, since he was staring at her, and he walked her to the door. He was a half-step behind her, and when she stopped and he reached for the handle, he murmured, "Thank you." She felt his breath across the hair on the top of her head; she shivered as she left.

Georgiana Darcy was tall and curvy, and one would think she was eighteen, rather than on the verge of sixteen, until she opened her mouth. She was tall like her brother, but that was where the similarity ended. *And where did her bashfulness come from?* Mr. Darcy was nothing but patient and kind with her.

Maybe her companion is mean to her? Elizabeth expected a matronly woman, but Mrs. Younge had a figure her mother would have politely called "busty." *"Porn star" is more like it.* She had large blue eyes, glossy black hair, a rich voice, and she moved like she knew men watched her hips with every step. She was probably thirty and seemed bored out of her mind.

Elizabeth doubted the responsible Mr. Darcy would have hired just anyone to shepherd his sister, so Mrs. Younge probably had been a companion to other girls before they married and she had to move to a new position. How many times had Mrs. Younge paraded around some young thing until they got a husband while she stayed single?

A physically mature but emotionally insecure girl being led by a jaded woman who could have landed a husband of her own had her circumstances been different.

Yeah, this is not going to end well for Georgiana Darcy.

CHAPTER SEVEN

APRIL 19, 1811

In church, Pemberley's neighbors had their first look at Elizabeth, and every morning that week, curious ladies called to see the Darcys' charity case. Miss Ferris, the local clergyman's sister, was the only lady out of a dozen who seemed genuinely interested in her or Georgiana. After days of pointless chatter, Elizabeth was as sick of it as Mrs. Younge was and Georgiana was emotionally exhausted.

At least she no longer trembles when I speak to her.

After the final caller left, Elizabeth went to visit Reynolds to keep up appearances that they were long-lost family. She heard Mr. Darcy's and Mr. Willers's voices carrying down the corridor.

"Help me to understand why you cannot endorse my uncle's recommendation if you agree it is best to diversify."

"Mining *is* in Pemberley's best interest, sir; however, I cannot duplicate values his lordship's steward suggested you ought to earn if you allow the same mining here as he does."

Elizabeth hovered between the housekeeper's room and the steward's office. *There's probably a rule against eavesdropping. Or more likely, men can eavesdrop, but women can't.* She decided to remain.

"Either you or his lordship's steward has made an error. I shall not assume the mistake is yours." Mr. Darcy said. "However, mining will ruin that land for generations, and Pemberley's future is not to be taken lightly."

"I shall review it again until you are confident. The scheme cannot go forward otherwise." There was a pause. "I could, if you wish, write to his lordship's steward and ask him to lay plain how he arrived at those numbers." Elizabeth realized she ought to leave. She didn't want to embarrass Mr. Willers.

"I have faith in your abilities, and we both know if one of us is to make sense of it, it will be you. Why not take another day before admitting defeat?"

"I appreciate your confidence, sir, even if I do not currently share it. Miss Bennet, is that you?"

Busted. "I did not mean to interrupt; I am looking for Mrs. Reynolds."

"She is still in Lambton. If there is nothing else?" He directed the last to Mr. Darcy, who shook his head, and Mr. Willers bowed and left.

Elizabeth said, "So . . . mining at Pemberley?"

Mr. Darcy set his jaw. "You are fortunate not to suffer the listener's proverbial fate."

"For you to say anything against me would force you to admit when I'm from. I'm not afraid of you."

His small smile and lowered eyes told her he conceded. "Yes, I am considering allowing a mining interest on Pemberley's grounds. There is a significant amount of lead to be had."

"You *do* know by now lead is poisonous, right?"

He sighed at her condescending tone. "They will not be washing their ore in my trout stream. It is only the immediate area that would be unusable for future farming and that land has been uncultivated."

"The land is worth more if it can be mined?" *How 'industrial revolution' of him.* "Then what is the problem?" The long look Mr. Darcy gave her made her angry. "If you won't explain because I'm a woman, I'm going to pretend to faint right here on Mr. Willers's desk. I studied accounting, remember? I can handle a little financial analysis." After another stretch of silence, Elizabeth fanned her face and closed her eyes. She swayed until an inarticulate grumbling sound came from Mr. Darcy's throat.

"As landlord, I would receive greater income on those acres than I could from produce, labor, or rent, and the proprietor should receive significant profits. My uncle partakes in a similar venture, on a larger scale, and both his agent and Mr. Willers believe one-fifth the profit is an appropriate rent for a ten-year lease."

"So what is the problem?"

"The *challenge* is that the future value does not approach what my uncle's steward suggested I ought to earn. Until I understand why, I refuse to commit ten years of use on my family's land."

"May I see?" Elizabeth gestured to the ledgers and letters on Mr. Willers's desk.

"You may not."

"Oh, come on! No one will see the ignorant lady reading those complicated, masculine numbers."

"It is not that I cannot comprehend a woman being talented at accounts. That is far from the truth. It is not the place of my guest to review the calculations my agent is employed to do."

Elizabeth saw his point. It wasn't her job, and neither Mr. Willers nor Mr. Darcy had asked for help. "I'm bored. Is that a word you have yet? I am suffering from a state of boredom. I have no friends to talk with, I can't paint, or draw, or sew pretty things. I may not love accounting, but I am good at it. I want to help Pemberley."

To her surprise, he agreed and pulled out the chair for her. She rifled through Mr. Willers's ledgers and sheets of calculations and read the loping script of the letters. Mr. Darcy had the good grace not to hover while she worked.

"Mr. Willers compounded the interest quarterly instead of monthly like your uncle's steward. That's why their future values never coincide, no matter the rent or the term of the lease."

Mr. Darcy came closer to look at her equation. His hand came to rest on the chair back, but his fingertips grazed her shoulder as he leaned closer. "The interest should be compounded monthly. Can you calculate what the future value will be in ten years if the initial rent paid is five hundred pounds and the interest rate is four percent? How many years from now will the value be ten thousand pounds?"

"The first I can do; that's an exponential equation. But solving an exponential equation with different bases means I have to use logarithms." Now that she turned to look at him, their faces were inches apart. After looking into her eyes, a heartbeat later he stepped back, pulling his hand from the chair. She wondered if her cheeks looked pink; they felt warm. "Calculating logarithms is time-consuming. When I'm from, we have computing machines to do it for you. Do you even have slide rules in these backward times?"

Mr. Darcy narrowed his eyes, and gestured for her to stand from the desk. He lifted papers and ledger books, returning each exactly where it was, until he held out what he had been searching for. The Latin title held no meaning for her, but the subtitle was in English: *Mathematical Tables. Contrived after a most comprehensive method. A table of logarithms from 1-10,000.*

Elizabeth smirked and handed it back. "I stand corrected. I guess it's too much to ask that you tell Mr. Willers your lady houseguest solved his math problem?"

"I could never tell him you corrected his error." Something in her look made him add, "You are generous for wishing to be of use."

"Whatever. My mother would be pleased her insistence I study something that would earn me a well-paying job proved *useful*. If I end up stuck here, I could dress like a man and get a job as a steward."

"Your mother?"

Mr. Darcy's voice held a tone of marvel that Elizabeth couldn't explain. "Yes, my *mother*. We still procreate in the same way in 2011."

He blushed. "I had not considered any family you left behind, and how they might worry for you."

"You were too busy thinking about yourself."

Mr. Darcy's expression turned haughty. "My primary concern has always been Pemberley, above my own interests. How can you claim that I think of nothing but myself?"

Well, he asked. "You're generous to those who work for you, you adore your shy sister, you love your cousin although he teases you. But I don't think you give a damn for anyone outside your little circle. If they're not connected to this estate, a Darcy by blood or marriage, or one of your wealthy friends, you don't care. You either disdain the feelings of those who aren't close to you, or you're just so selfish that you don't even realize they have feelings."

As she pronounced these words, Mr. Darcy changed color, but he did not interrupt her.

"This is your opinion of me?" His voice was less tranquil than it had been. "After all I have done to assist you?"

"Look, you're not as much of a jerk as I thought you were. An obnoxious person," she corrected when she saw that crease between Mr. Darcy's eyes. "But I've been here nearly a month, and it never occurred to you I have a life I was ripped away from?" *My mother hates me right now and might not even know I'm missing, but he doesn't need to know that.*

When it seemed he had nothing to say, she gave a curtsey and turned.

"Wait, I . . . Thank you for your help."

Elizabeth looked at him, but said nothing.

"If we present you as a lady from Upper Canada, lacking the typical accomplishments, then I cannot justify how you are expert at financial analysis. I will tell Mr. Willers you said something about interest that made me consider how it was compounded, and with that prompt, he will arrive at the same conclusion as you. You comprehend why I cannot raise anyone's suspicions, for your sake as well as my own?"

"I can understand. I didn't help you for the credit." *She* could be considerate of his feelings, even if Mr. Darcy sucked at empathy.

He looked at her with total attention. It was disconcerting. "I am a walk in your debt. Perhaps you might tell me about your mother. Shall we?"

Until now he had never shown concern in who she was, only what she had to pretend to be to survive in 1811. But, he decided to learn about her and intended to begin right now? *Why not?* Walking was the only thing she was allowed to do, other than music. *And I'm terrible at that.*

. . .

"I WALK THIS CIRCUIT EVERY DAY AND COULD DO IT BLINDFOLDED," MISS Bennet said tersely. "Since you were so good as to join me, make yourself useful and show me somewhere new to walk."

Darcy led them off the gravel and through the woods where they could ascend to higher ground away from the river. They walked in silence, but her harsh words in Mr. Willers's office repeated in his head.

"You either disdain the feelings of those who aren't close to you, or you're just so selfish that you don't even realize they have feelings."

He was now accustomed to her outbursts, and had been able to dismiss them as a symptom of her life in the future. Yet these words stayed with him, ringing in his ears and settling in his heart.

She is not wrong.

He *had* been struck, at that moment, by who she truly was. Yes, he pitied her circumstances; yes, he did not want her to be unhappy here, but he had not once considered her as someone with a full life, family who doted on her, friends who admired her.

He treated everyone with the same general courtesy, did he not? A guilty feeling twisted in his stomach.

How have I behaved towards Miss Bennet, as a woman, as an equal? Consistently critical, almost offensive. She would be at Pemberley two more months, ostensibly his sister and his housekeeper's visitor, but in actuality *his* responsibility, and perhaps with him as her only genuine acquaintance and possible friend.

I am the only person with whom she could have some semblance of honesty.

"Since you're not talking, draw me a map and be done with me."

"I beg your pardon?"

"You speak politely to your servants; with your family, I have seen your considerable powers of conversation on topics that interest you. And from my experience, I know you are capable of arguing, rationalizing, and sharing your opinion. If you didn't come here to combine the best of those abilities, to talk with me and apologize, then go away."

Darcy looked at her. She was in general a lively and witty young lady. Comely enough to look at, but not beautiful, apart from those large brown eyes that were often filled with laughter and intelligence. And at this moment, they were upbraiding him.

"You said nothing that I did not deserve. I was unjust to you, and I would like to be better acquainted. Not with the orphaned Miss Bennet, home from British North America, but with Elizabeth Bennet, born in 1987, from . . . I do not even know where you are from or why you were in England."

"I'm certain some things haven't changed, so let me help you. 'I am sorry for . . .'"

Darcy tried to remember the last time he had to make amends to anyone. "I am sorry for neglecting your feelings and for being too preoccupied with my own concerns to consider yours."

"I think, Mr. Darcy, that you're a good man after all. A little proud, maybe, but not as selfish as I thought. I'm sorry I was harsh. If it means anything to you, I forgive you."

The rock in the bottom of his stomach, that he had not known was there, disappeared. "Where are you from and what brought you to England?"

"I'm from a tiny town in Illinois. It's known for its dairy festival, and what every pretty girl wants to be is the Milk Queen. My mother was Milk Queen, but she told us to spend our time studying for something that would earn us more than a cheap tiara."

He only understood half of her words. "You said you were born in England. Will you tell me, or do I ask too much, to know why you left and what brought you back?"

"It's not appropriate for you to explicitly ask about me, is it? And it's not appropriate for me to answer?"

"I think your unfathomable tumbling backwards through time allows us a few social liberties so we can communicate."

His wry response earned him a sincere laugh. "My mother was out of high school, pretty, and she went to a party where she met a graduate student from England. They married quickly, and when my father's studies in the States were done, they went to England where my sister was born and I came four years later."

Miss Bennet stopped walking now that they crested the hill. He suspected she was gathering her thoughts. "I was two years old. My mother was ironing my father's shirts when he said he was leaving. My mother thought he was going to the store, so she said, 'See you soon.' Jane, my sister, remembers more of what followed. My father was tired of his pretty but not smart wife, and left a copy of the divorce petition on the ironing board before he walked out."

"Good God!" Darcy's mind whirled over the callousness of abandoning one's wife for anything less than adultery.

"My mother was in a foreign country with no husband, no money, no education, and two little girls. She had never even balanced a checkbook! After she got her decree, she borrowed enough money for our tickets home and spent the next twenty years teaching us to be independent."

"I cannot comprehend a world in which one can easily divorce his wife"—Miss Bennet scoffed—"but did your father not support you? How could your mother be expected to maintain his children?"

"Hence the need to educate *everyone*, and allow men *and* women to be employed. My father mailed us a check every December and June until I was eighteen. It was never enough."

Darcy suspected she was not talking about the money. "Did you see him again?"

"In twenty years, he saw us twice. Jane and I didn't realize it at the time, but the visits coincided with a conference at the University of Chicago where he presented a paper."

"I suspect, then, that your return to England had nothing to do with your father."

"A reasonable person would assume that." Her voice was brittle. "In January, he suffered a stroke, and someone called my mother. Jane and Mom weren't going to arrange for his care, let alone participate in it. But he was still my *father*, and he needed someone to help with his recovery, and I . . ."

Darcy realized she held back some strong feeling he was not ready to have a stake in. She was lost in a distressing memory; he needed to return her to the present. "What is a stroke?"

She took a calming breath. "A blood clot blocked one of the vessels carrying blood to his brain, depriving it of oxygen. His speech and balance were affected. It happened while he was at work; they said his face drooped, his speech slurred, and he complained of being dizzy before he fell."

"That might be what we call an apoplectic seizure. Those few who survive are often thought to be mad."

"Killed brain cells don't mean you need to be in an asylum. My father needed medicine to dissolve the blood clot, and months of monitoring and rehabilitation."

"The twenty-first century has physicians who can restore someone who suffered an apoplexy to their original state?"

"Sometimes. No one deserves to be left alone and vulnerable. He needed a support system and . . . I thought if I was there for him, I might learn why he was never there for us." Miss Bennet blinked furiously. "He needed me, but I needed answers. Maybe I'm selfish too."

"No!" Darcy's fierce response surprised himself more than her. "No, I think you are a compassionate woman. Regardless of his prior behavior, Mr. Bennet must be exceedingly worried for you."

"He's dead." Miss Bennet's eyes were fixed on a rooftop in the distance. "He suffered a heart attack. Another blood clot, this time damaging the muscles of his heart. He died a week before I visited Nine Ladies and wound up here."

"Miss Bennet! I had no notion you were in mourn—"

"Where are your parents?" Miss Bennet began to walk briskly. After several paces, it became clear she had no idea which way to go, and with a shuddering breath she paused, her eyes anywhere but on him. He gestured with one hand, and left guiding fingertips on her spine longer than he ought to have. "Have your parents retired to warmer climates and left Pemberley to you?"

He accepted her obvious attempt to deflect him, although it took him, as it often did, a moment to comprehend her meaning. "They have not gone to sleep nor have they withdrawn into seclusion. My sister would be with my mother were she alive, and I could not inherit Pemberley if my father was alive."

Miss Bennet's mouth formed an 'o' of shock. "I'm so sorry, I didn't realize! I would never—"

"I know." She looked as though she might cry anew. He wondered if causing him pain distressed her more than remembering her own.

"My father has been dead five years. He died of dropsy. He was swollen from fluid in his chest and had a weak heart."

"I wonder if that's congestive heart failure. Jane is a medical student, and my friend Charlotte is a physician; they would know."

"Your sister wishes to become a physician, and your friend, a woman, is a physician?"

"If you believe you can travel through time by being in a certain place, at a certain time, depending on the position of the earth to the sun, can't you believe in a future where women are respected physicians?" Her voice rose while her eyes narrowed. *She is too quick to judge.*

"I am now to learn that you live in a world where marriage is not a permanent union. If your mother was uneducated and cast off by her husband, of course she would insist you learn to support yourself with dignity. It is no leap to comprehend that in such a world you might learn to be an accountant or your sister a physician. You need not presume the worst of me."

She lowered her head. "I'll work on that." After several moments, she spoke again. "My mother's worst fear for her daughters was probably your mother's best hope for Miss Darcy." Darcy silently asked the question with a look. "Don't spend much time in the classroom, and find some wealthy man to take care of you."

"You forget that despite the expansive cultural differences and variant societal expectations, your mother and mine held one important thing in common: They both wanted their daughters to be secure and free from want."

"Maybe I'm not so sharp a judge of character as I thought. You care a great deal about this place and its people. I thought estates like Pemberley were ostentatious shows of wealth to proclaim the status of a lazy owner."

"Some gentlemen are content to display their wealth and allow others to manage that wealth for them. I, however, make the best use of my assets and talents and am involved in every critical decision. I have an obligation to preserve the prosperity that has fallen to me for my children and for future generations."

There was an inexplicable flash of sadness in Miss Bennet's eyes. "I never understood until now. Pemberley is a home, a source of income, and it's your family's legacy. It's not just the Darcys' future at stake with your decisions, but it's for the sake of the servants and tenants and laborers and the villagers who live in a symbiotic relationship. Pemberley is who you are."

They gradually descended the valley toward the house when she asked, in a hesitant voice, "When did your mother pass away?"

"Time passes away. People do not."

"In 2011, it's an acceptable phrase."

"Nearly twelve years ago; Georgiana scarcely remembers her. Perhaps there is a blessing in that, because it took my mother a long time to die. It was thought to be a pulmonic disease made worse by a catarrh, but as months passed, she developed hemoptoe that worsened until . . . she was carried off."

Miss Bennet looked as though she wished to ask a question, and he braced himself for her curiosity. But she simply laid a hand on his arm, gave it a pat that from anyone else would have been a patronizing indignity, and whispered her condolences.

"I hope I can get home. The lack of medical knowledge now frightens me. Young Henry told me his family died when a fever went through the village!"

While Darcy was often content with silence, these distressing topics compelled him to distract her.

"It was by chance that I was at Pemberley when you appeared. I am usually in town until I go to Kent at Easter to visit my aunt. This year I wished to consult with Mr. Willers in person, and it delayed my trip."

"I was fortunate you were at home. Otherwise, Reynolds might have locked me in the kennel." Before he could refute this, she asked, "If you are not at Pemberley, where would you be?"

"A month here or there at the homes of friends or family. I pass the Season at my house in town and return to Pemberley in the summer months. I am not so often at Pemberley, although it is the place where I am the happiest."

"You have a home in London too?"

"I keep a house in town. Pemberley is *home*."

CHAPTER EIGHT

MAY 1, 1811

Elizabeth was held captive by Georgiana Darcy's stirring playing. She was dedicated to her art, and her playing was flawless. Her commitment came across in her performance; it sent shivers down Elizabeth's spine.

While Elizabeth sighed in enjoyment at the end, Mrs. Younge barked, "Again." The sagged shoulders of the young performer did not go unnoticed. "A lady's attitude should never engender disgust, Miss Darcy. Keep your displeasure to yourself! Again."

One heavy wet drop clung to Georgiana's bottom lashes, but she did not so much as blink. *Must be that Darcy family self-control.* Or maybe this society's strict rules against displaying emotions. If the companion wouldn't encourage Georgiana, then Elizabeth decided that she would.

"I thought that sounded lovely. Mrs. Younge, what could possibly be lacking?"

The companion, whose face, hair, and body reminded Elizabeth of a tall Kardashian, raised her cold blue eyes from her needlework. Elizabeth played her ignorant outsider card. "Would you humor a girl who has grown up so far from London?"

Mrs. Younge glowered. "A young lady must be easy and graceful. Miss Darcy is at a disadvantage by preferring the pianoforte to the harp. That instrument does not exhibit a lady's form with as much elegance as the harp since she must sit square and upright; it is not an attractive position. If she does not play with that *ne plus ultra* of grace, she may as well stop wasting my time."

Georgiana stared at her intertwined hands on her lap.

"And her timidity and downcast eyes will earn her no suitors! False modesty is unbecoming."

You are a bitch. She really is devastatingly shy. "I think Miss Darcy played splendidly. Let's call it a day? I mean, this is a good time to pause; it is nearly time for breakfast."

Elizabeth hoped Georgiana would stand up for herself, or at least say she wanted to eat before she was drilled again. She looked at Elizabeth long enough to give a subtle shake of her head, pulled herself up, and brought her fingers above the keys.

"Again, Miss Darcy."

Elizabeth barely remembered to curtsey before she stormed from the room. The girl was browbeaten into practicing a song she performed beautifully just to make sure her body looked pretty while doing it. *I could never live here.*

She went to ask Reynolds a question that had been on her mind since her first walk with Mr. Darcy last week. She found her in the servants' hall overseeing her minions. With a discreet wave, she indicated from the door that she wished to speak to her, and went to the housekeeper's room to wait.

"Good morning, cousin Elizabeth," Reynolds said as she entered. "I trust you are in good health?" Elizabeth noted that Polly Brooks, the maid, was walking past the housekeeper. As soon as Reynolds closed the door, her false cheer dropped. "Did I not tell you I would not be at liberty to speak with you during the day?"

"*Did* you? I forgot! I have been *so* busy watching Miss Darcy play, reading, and, let us not forget, that scintillating activity, walking."

Reynolds's crow's feet deepened, and the frown lines around her lips appeared. "Do you find joy in wasting my time?"

"I do. While I'm at it, tell me how Lady Anne Darcy died."

A sadness filled Reynolds's eyes so quickly that, had she been a kinder woman, Elizabeth would have pitied her. "The poor woman has been dead over a decade. What does it matter *how* she died?"

"Mr. Darcy told me how his parents died, but I didn't understand what happened to his mother. It would be heartless of me to ask him to explain."

"I am surprised Mr. Darcy confided in you; he is a private man. Lady Anne was a reserved woman, more so than her amiable husband, but with her children, she was different. She taught them, played with them, and listened to all their serious and innocent concerns and stories." Her wistful tone was replaced by her usual brusque manner. "Lady Anne developed a cough that never improved. Later, during an outbreak of epidemic catarrh—"

"What is that?"

"The fl—it was likely influenza. However, months passed, and although the catarrh symptoms resolved, she had trouble breathing, the dry cough remained, and she tired easily."

"Mr. Darcy mentioned hemo—hemp-something."

"You ought to study classical languages to define the word, since you have time."

"Would you just tell me?"

"She coughed up blood."

"Oh my God!" Elizabeth's stomach turned over.

"Lady Anne coughed up blood for months, filling basins' worth each day by the end. I left to empty the basin, and old Mr. Darcy left the sick room to pray and gather his emotions for the imminent death of his wife; and Master Fitzwilliam, unbeknownst to anyone and no older than his sister is now, comforted his mother while she choked, and she died in his arms. When his father returned, Lady Anne's body was propped against their son, her blood covering both of them."

Through her tears, Elizabeth watched Reynolds take a deep breath. "Make yourself presentable for the breakfast table. I have better things to do than chatter about the demise of a respectable woman and the mother of those dear children." She left without another word.

They thought Lady Anne had the flu, but she spit up buckets of blood until she choked to death! Her stomach rolled. And poor Mr. Darcy! A teenage boy alone with his mother as she drowned in her own blood? Elizabeth gave a violent shudder. The sooner the solstice came, the better. People died so easily here. It was depressing to only know Mr. Darcy would be dead by the end of the year. How could she stand to watch it happen?

"Are you well? Forgive me, but you appear a little pale."

Georgiana was so shy she rarely initiated conversation. *I must look like a disaster.* Elizabeth forced herself to smile.

"Nothing that a long walk could not remedy." She looked at Mr. Darcy; he met her gaze and gave a slight nod before returning to his paper. Since he apologized, they had begun walking together nearly every day. "I enjoyed listening to you play this morning. I thought you performed admirably." She picked up that phrase from Colonel Fitzwilliam; too bad none of them appreciated how hard she tried to sound like them.

"Miss Darcy is a true adherent to her music, sir," said Mrs. Younge. "She is prepared to perform after dinner at Sir Wesley Clarke's home this week. She was sharing her opinion with me about being ready to spend more time in company, and I heartily agree with her."

Elizabeth felt few fifteen-year-old girls could be less called upon to speak their own opinion than Georgiana Darcy.

"Is this true, Georgiana? You told Mrs. Younge you wish not only to dine out but to exhibit?" He gave her an encouraging smile.

Georgiana looked between her companion and her brother, paled, and began breathing faster.

Mr. Darcy said, "We all were included in Sir Wesley's invitation, and it is to be a small gathering. I am proud that you are inclined to play."

Elizabeth thought Georgiana might vomit on the table, but instead she gave her brother a shaky smile. *She is desperate for her brother's approval.*

Mrs. Younge simpered. "She will be sixteen this winter. These past two months with your sister have shown me that she is intelligent, graceful, and ready to be out in company." Georgiana dropped her teacup, which clattered in its saucer and splashed tea across the table. Mr. Darcy ignored her error as Mrs. Young went on. "Dining out with a close neighbor and performing before friends is such like being out that, I daresay, she is almost out as it now stands. Such a poised and self-possessed young lady."

Elizabeth snorted into her napkin, disguising it as a cough.

"I disagree," Mr. Darcy said in his straightforward way. Georgiana let out a relieved sigh. "Georgiana may dine with a few neighbors amid a small party, but she is too shy, at the present, to be out."

"Girls pass in little time from reserve to the opposite, to confidence. I have much experience in these matters."

"Yes, madam, you came highly recommended, but I insist she not be out. Georgiana, I am pleased that you wish to attend and will play a few songs. You must comprehend that, until you are more comfortable with conversation, you cannot be out. You are not disappointed, my dear?"

Mr. Darcy's tone suggested he would brook no opposition. Not that any opposition was forthcoming, as his sister tripped over her tongue to agree.

Mrs. Younge pursed her bee-stung lips and leaned forward to recapture her employer's attention. Elizabeth feared for the safety of the glass that came close to being knocked over by Mrs. Younge's assets.

"Sir Wesley's son Robert must be of age. A gentleman likes a lady who is as ready to listen as to talk, and you cannot disagree, sir, that Miss Darcy has gentle manners."

"She is dining out with the neighbors she has known since childhood, but until she is more comfortable speaking at length, I say she ought not to be out, and Georgiana has not said to me that she is ready." He gave Mrs. Younge a long look for emphasis. "If you will excuse me, ladies?" After his exit, Mrs. Young heaved an exasperated sigh.

"Miss Darcy, how am I to see you wed if you do not help me on! Why would you be content to remain the demure little sister, for all your looks and wealth? You could be married before summer."

"Fitzwilliam sees no reason for me to be in a hurry . . ."

"Robert Clarke will inherit his father's baronetcy, and Stadler Hall is ten miles from Pemberley. It is the perfect situation for you. I fail to comprehend why you are not doing all you are able to secure him!"

Georgiana's fingers shook and she mumbled about not being well acquainted with him.

"What? I could not hear you, with you trembling like a leaf! You cannot enter a room without fancying all eyes upon you or be spoken to without stammering. You are sure to become conspicuous through these faults, your faults will intensify, and you will become an object of ridicule. The sooner you marry, the better!"

"Mrs. Younge!" Elizabeth cried. "You have said enough."

"She throws restraint over an entire group with her shyness and silence, and I suspect at Stadler, she will make even the most sparkling conversation flag. Miss Darcy, you have a champion in this poor, peculiar colonist. It is unfortunate that your reticence and awkwardness will make it impossible for Miss Bennet to befriend you." She rose, saying, "Find me when you have finished, and we will continue your lessons."

While Elizabeth seethed, Georgiana cried, silently and stoically. This sad young woman was more like a lonely little girl.

"Don't let that bi—monster make you feel bad about yourself. You're fifteen! No one, not even your brother, expects you to marry now. Mrs. Younge places undue pressure on you."

Georgiana gathered her composure, and her tears stopped. She had been hanging on Elizabeth's words. "I thank you for your consideration, but I would like to be alone."

"Miss Darcy, you don't *have* to be alone. We haven't known each other long, but I want to be your friend. Mrs. Younge is cruel, and for some reason she's manipulating you to get you married. I don't think Mr. Darcy sees her for what she is. I can speak with him about Mrs.

Younge. She works for him, so he might be able to convince her to change her attitude, or maybe replace her."

Georgiana bit her lip in lieu of replying.

Elizabeth touched her hand. "You deserve to be treated better."

"Mrs. Younge has launched many well-connected girls into society. Now that I am removed from school, she is all I have." The note of finality in her voice reminded Elizabeth of Mr. Darcy.

"You have your brother, and you will find other friends. And until you do, you have me."

Georgiana smiled, but pulled her hand out from under Elizabeth's. "I must prepare for my lessons. I will bear it as best I can. Thank you, but I cannot tolerate your pity now, forgive me."

She hardly looked like her brother, but they had a similar sense of duty. "Does more than one lady play at parties?"

Georgiana looked as though this were a stupid question; Elizabeth was well-accustomed to that look. "Of course. However, Lady Clarke has given up playing, and I do not think Dr. Ferris's sister plays, although she sings. I shall be the only performer. All eyes will be turned to me alone." She picked at her fingernails.

"Then I shall play too." Georgiana's expression was skeptical. Elizabeth did not bother to hold back her laugh. "I *know* I am not any good! We have a few days to practice so I can be just good enough to be praised, like your brother said. Will you help me?"

"I—you, you want *me* to help you?"

"Yes, I need you to help me learn one song. Who better than the best performer I have met?" *In this century.* "And maybe you can show me how to look elegant while I am doing it. We would not want Mrs. Younge to berate me too." She tried to make Georgiana smile.

"She would not do that to you. It is only me—" Georgiana's cut-off sentence spoke volumes. "I am certain you will not need my help. We are not so dissimilar in talent."

Elizabeth barked a dry laugh. "You are trying to be kind, but let's call it like—let us speak the truth. That is what friends do. If my playing is a lamp, yours is the sunshine."

Georgiana blushed, and she twisted her fingers in her lap, muttering a soft "thank you." When Elizabeth rose to leave, she asked,

"If you have no talent or interest, no desire to find a husband while you are with us, why put yourself on display?"

"I will play first so you can show off your superior performance to an appreciative crowd."

Had she been in 2011, Elizabeth would have run to her side and hugged her while tears of gratitude fell from the young girl's eyes. But Georgiana had her pride, and she was a product of her time, so Elizabeth smiled, curtsied, and gave Georgiana her privacy to cry.

May 8, 1811

Although the evening at Stadler Hall had been late, Miss Bennet still appeared at the edge of the garden after breakfast. He had become accustomed to walking with her every day when the weather was fair. Darcy did not think long on how much his spirits were in a state of enjoyment during his walks with Miss Bennet.

He recognized her lilac muslin walking gown as one his sister had worn last year, recut at the bodice, and now fitted over a white cambric slip. Given how he had seen his sister and Miss Bennet more often in conversation, he suspected Georgiana had thought to present it to her. It made him happy to know that his timid sister had taken the effort to engage with his houseguest. She was peculiar, but a good-natured and amiable woman.

"That storm on Sunday evening was fierce," she said by way of greeting. "I have seen nothing like it since I've been in England—in the future or now."

These strange turns of phrase no longer sounded as odd as they once did. Darcy was more comfortable with the notion of Miss Bennet being out of her time. *Perhaps I am more at ease with her in general.*

"The days of rain did not prevent us from going to Stadler, though I feared for the coach's wheels over the muddy lanes. How did you enjoy your first evening party?"

"Sir Wesley seemed like an oily car salesman." Darcy raised an eyebrow. "The sort of man who could talk himself out of any trouble, and Lady Clarke had as much personality as that sleeping pug she held on her lap."

"It is uncharitable of you to speak against your hosts. They were gracious enough to include you because you are my sister's guest."

"I notice you didn't say I was wrong." She punctuated this with a tilt of her head, a raised eyebrow, and an amused grin. "I suspect you accepted their invitation because you need to keep up connections in this 'who knows who' world of yours, not because you like them."

She was a clever woman. "It is also proper to be hospitable and amiable to one's neighbors."

"Your rules are a lot of false pretenses over trifles."

"Consideration for the rights and feelings of one's acquaintances is not merely a rule for behavior in public, but the foundation upon which our social life is built. And, as you well know, I am attempting to be more generous to those beyond my closest circle."

"You mean you normally wouldn't let that clergyman, Dr. Ferris, spend twenty minutes talking at you about glebes? I am proud of you. I could scarcely keep from rolling my eyes whenever Sir Wesley opened his mouth."

"Ought I to thank you for keeping silent rather than being your more . . . modern self?"

"No, I'm just venting. They were kind enough to invite me, so at the least I can be kind to them in their own home." They walked in silence until they passed the wall of the home garden and strolled toward the stream. "I guess my snarky comments make you think I'm awful."

"Underneath your blunt manner, you have a warm heart. You showed my sister a kindness last night. The others could not comprehend the true value in your performance; by playing first and displaying yourself at a disadvantage, you made it possible for Georgiana to perform with confidence."

"I was glad to do it. I would love for her to feel better about herself before I leave. And are you saying I didn't play well? I practiced that piece for three days! Even Reynolds-Who-Hates-Me said I was 'tolerable.'" There was an arch look in her pretty eyes. They held much knowledge, wit, and assurance for a single woman of only four-and-twenty.

For the first time on their walks, Darcy offered his arm, and she did not hesitate to take it. "There was goodness in what you did for my sister, and you well know it. Your playing, you also know, *is* only just good enough to be applauded by polite company."

Her laugh was a rich, throaty sound, rippling with delight. "Your manner is as dry and blunt as mine, you know; you just hide it better."

"For one who said she wanted to attend, Georgiana was reluctant to speak with Sir Wesley Clarke's son. They knew each other as children; I thought she might have been at ease with him."

Miss Bennet made that snorting sound she did when she thought him stupid. "Everyone saw he had the hots for that clergyman's sister."

It was not difficult to discern what she meant. "Flora Ferris? She is a gentleman's daughter who keeps her brother's house, has no connections, is five years Robert Clarke's senior, and she has no dowry to speak of. She would need several thousand pounds settled on her for his parents to agree."

"I don't know how you missed it, but even Georgiana knew there was no point in talking to Mr. Clarke when Miss Ferris was in the room. You know Mrs. Younge wants Sir Wesley's son for Georgiana, right?"

"I doubt Mrs. Younge had any designs other than to give Georgiana the opportunity to be more comfortable in conversation."

"Your sister's shyness is exacerbated by Mrs. Younge. Haven't you noticed your sister stammers, bumps things off the table, and stumbles over footstools? Those things follow when pressure has been put on her by Mrs. Younge. I've seen her reduced to tears."

"Georgiana was too often left by herself, and it has made her bashful. There are twelve years between us, and she was orphaned at a much younger age than I. It was regrettable, but after our father's death, I had to send her to school. A companion to superintend her education and readiness to be out is in Georgiana's best interest."

"Having a companion, in this time, is not the problem. Georgiana is shy, has few friends, and has latched onto Mrs. Younge because she's lonely. But she'll never have confidence in herself under Mrs. Younge. I think you hired the wrong woman for the job."

Miss Bennet had no authority for opposing his decisions. "A woman of this time would not pry into an unrelated man's concerns."

"Then you know a lot of oppressed women, and you know *me* better. And it's *Georgiana's* concern. I like her. And I'm worried about her."

He must argue her into a little more rationality. "Mrs. Younge has come to us highly recommended. She has seen wed in a brilliant match three girls in the last ten years. There is nothing in her interest to treat Georgiana unkindly."

"She's jaded, and it has made her cruel. I think she wants Georgiana married so she can find a different situation where it's more likely she'll be in a position to land a husband herself."

"You are assuming a great deal."

"She is not the same woman with your sister as she is with you. Georgiana needs someone gentler and more thoughtful to boost her self-esteem."

He supposed boost meant to improve something. "Self-esteem? Are you talking about phrenology?"

"*What?* I swear, it's like we don't even speak the same language. I mean how she values herself."

"You think Georgiana needs a companion with more delicate sympathy to improve her own sense of worth?" The idea had never before occurred to him.

"Yes! Remember, I'm not busy here. I spend a lot of time listening to the way Mrs. Younge loses patience with your sister."

"I cannot dismiss a respectable woman because my secret, liberal traveler from the twenty-first century thinks she is harsh." Miss Bennet's jaw clenched, her pretty eyes narrowed, and he suspected a tirade was forthcoming. "You judge me quickly, *again*. You think because I will not do what you suggest that I do not believe your concern is valid? You tell me that women are educated and employed equally as men in two hundred years. Would it be justified in your time to sever one woman's employment based on the hearsay of another?"

Miss Bennet grumbled, "No."

"I will observe her closely. If what you say is true, I will replace her.

Perhaps Mrs. Younge is out of sorts since they are removed from town. Country life may not suit her. When they go on to Ramsgate at the end of the summer, her manner may improve."

"I told Georgiana you aren't in any hurry for her to marry. Is that true?"

"Of course; she is fifteen. Mrs. Younge, if she is not unjust and unkind as you suggest, will be with us for another three years, at least. Besides, I have a fri—" *Have I lost all reserve around this woman?*

"A . . . friend? Who likes your sister?"

"I have said too much."

"Who do you think I'm going to discuss your matchmaking schemes with here?"

He bristled at the idea of his slight preference being akin to cunning. "I am not concerned with your speaking out of turn. My friend Bingley is seven years older than Georgiana. He is good-humored and considered to be handsome. His liveliness would be a credit to her reticent nature. And he is sensible, though not secure in his own judgment. I wonder, as she grows older and has the occasion to meet my friend on more intimate footing, if I could forward their match."

"You're hoping your young, wealthy, good-looking, nice friend will stay single long enough to see Georgiana as a love interest? Good luck. Maybe instead of getting her married to one of your buddies, you should worry about your future."

"How do you mean?"

Her arm tensed under his, but her reply was lighthearted. "I mean, get yourself married first. You're older than your friend Bingley. Don't you need a son to inherit Pemberley? Better go to a few dances and meet some ladies."

"I am not in a hurry to settle."

"Colonel Fitzwilliam made it sound as though you didn't ever want to."

"I am not easily taken in and do not form new acquaintances impulsively. I always take care to know what I am about and who I have to deal with."

"That's good for what mining company you're allowing on

Pemberley's land, but I hardly think it's necessary for everyone you meet."

"You do not comprehend our social structure. Acquaintance leads to connections that cannot be easily undone, and I do not know what motivations single ladies have in seeking me out. They are not all young girls who only want to be seen dancing with me." Darcy did his best to keep his bitterness from forming a hard edge to his voice, but Miss Bennet looked as though she heard it.

He expected a caustic rebuttal, but instead she threw her shoulder into his arm in a playful gesture. "Does that include time-traveling girls too? I promise I'm not after your money."

"I never suspected you of appearing in Nine Ladies in the rain two hundred years out of your time because you were hatefully mercenary." Her amused giggle was unguarded, not a flirtatious ploy. It charmed him, and he smiled at her.

"But ladies sitting down and unable to dance because no man has asked them"—she shrugged in disapproval—"do you think they all want your house and your money? What's the harm with dancing and talking?"

"A gentleman should not be too assiduous in his attentions toward a single lady. Most every girl is willing to accept attentions that are offered, even if she intends at some future time to check them, but a sensible man would never depend on that. It would not do to raise expectations I have no intention of fulfilling."

"Isn't that out of the norm for this time and place? And it leaves you without a child to inherit Pemberley. Not to mention it leaves you a little, well, lonely?"

"To be married would mean I would have little privacy; I could not decorate a room as I wished or travel according to my whim."

"I don't believe that reason for a second."

What was it about this woman who did not belong that invited his confidence, to make him admit his failings and fears? "The truth is that the great emotional commitment to spend the rest of my life with another person, to tolerate her weaknesses, her temper, to tend to her needs, her illnesses, her emotional wounds, would be more than I believe I am capable of."

"But she would do the same for you." Her voice held a low warmth he had not before heard from her. "You would do those things for one another." Miss Bennet dropped his arm and met his eye.

"If I am so fortunate in my choice, then we would have the deepest of friendships, one that shared every success and failure with equal loyalty." *I would have someone to tell me the truth. To love me.* How many times had he danced or talked with an accomplished, wealthy lady and still felt desperately, soul-achingly lonely? "But that is rarely how marriages come to pass, and I would sooner remain single than commit myself unequally." He wondered how well he disguised the pain in his voice; it sounded like a razor's edge to his own ears.

"Do you ever go into Lambton?" Miss Bennet mercifully changed the subject after the silence stretched too long. He appreciated that she understood when not to press him. "I hardly saw any of it while I waited for Mr. Roland."

"I am liberal to the poor, and to the families of my servants who live there, but there is no person or business to draw me." Miss Bennet looked at Lambton's rooftops with curiosity. "Would you like to visit the village? I can take you in the curricle when the ground is dryer. There are few shops to speak of. I have no acquaintances there to call upon, but after being confined to the house by rain, you might enjoy a small excursion."

"Ah, but I'm trapped no matter where I go, aren't I?" She gave him a rueful smile.

"Your time with us is now half over. It has not passed dreadfully, I trust?" His voice lowered on its own accord.

"It has gotten much easier since those difficult first weeks." Darcy exhaled the breath he had not realized he was holding. "If I didn't have these walks, these moments to stop pretending to be someone I'm not, to stop trying so hard not to give myself away, I would be miserable. Thank you." She gave him an affectionate smile, and Darcy's heart beat quickly. When he realized he was admiring her and returning her smile, he turned away. He heard Miss Bennet clear her throat.

"Yes, I would like to go to Lambton. But what is a curricle?"

It was a liberating release to laugh. "It is a two-wheeled carriage pulled by a pair of horses abreast. It is lighter and faster than the coach we took to Stadler Hall, more fashionable, and it is open. There is no coachman; I shall drive us."

"You're not going to understand me, but I am excited to go for a ride in your fancy convertible sports car."

She was right; he did not comprehend her words, but he was very aware of her amused laughter and beaming smile.

CHAPTER NINE

May 22, 1811

Elizabeth would never admit it to Mr. Darcy, but Lambton was boring and would collapse without Pemberley and its tenants. There were a few large houses on High Street, but the rest were nothing to speak of. St. Anne's, the parish church, with its imposing spire, was the only significant building, and there was no one of Mr. Darcy's social status to call upon.

And he drives me here anyway to entertain me.

Riding in the curricle was the best part of these outings. Today, they stopped at a shop so she could buy a present for Georgiana. Of course, it was with Mr. Darcy's money, and he said it was nothing to what could be found in London; but once inside, he was gracious to the shopkeeper, and she selected a fan for his sister.

Unlike in Lambton, during the ride home they were able to speak freely, and Mr. Darcy enjoyed driving fast. They only drove about fifteen miles an hour, but the way Mr. Darcy had dryly promised he would not 'upset them today,' tipping over must be a possibility. She wondered if a carriage accident would be what killed him.

I like him.

Far from perfect and still a product of his less-than-enlightened time, her moments with Mr. Darcy were the happiest she passed while stuck in 1811. *Please let him stay alive until after the solstice.* Once she was home, she could more easily accept his death; by then, in 2011, he and everyone she met here would be long dead anyway. At least, she hoped it would be easier.

Elizabeth was enjoying the gleam of excitement in his eye as they sped along when he saw a familiar man, who raised his hat in greeting. Mr. Darcy, ready to approach the lodge in any event, slowed to acknowledge his tenant. "Have you finished shearing Hill Close's sheep, Davy Tasker?"

"Not yet, sir, I am later in my time than I might have liked. My shepherd boy, as well as his father, has taken ill, and at this rate, I shall be late to begin harvesting the hay."

They talked, Mr. Darcy in authoritative, but encouraging, tones, and Davy Tasker's voice relaxed. Elizabeth was not listening closely, and instead admired her host's sharp, confident profile. He held himself with an assurance that came from years of both privilege and responsibility. Mr. Darcy caught her staring, and she suspected that calling attention to his hastily pinked cheeks would make them both more self-conscious.

Mr. Darcy passed on his good wishes to his tenant's wife, and they left. He did not look at her, embarrassed, perhaps, at being admired, and Elizabeth covered her own embarrassment by teasing him.

"Mr. Tasker is enamored of his new wife. Why haven't you taken my suggestion to go to a ball to find Mrs. Darcy?"

"Because I will not encounter anyone between the ages of eighteen and thirty worthy of me," he said with a smile.

"Way to keep that pride under good regulation. You might meet someone worthy of you if you tried to get to know them. Pretend you're interested if you have to."

"I am not in the habit of performing to strangers."

"I know you can do it. You had no problem talking with your tenant, someone who is, in your world, of less consequence. You just need practice at being friendly and curious about strangers. You might enjoy what they have to say, and even like them, if you try."

"I do not enjoy senseless talk with strangers in a crowded room when I have no intention of continuing any new acquaintance."

"Poor you. These hostesses treat you so horribly when they send you invitations."

"That is the most sensible thing you have said yet."

She grinned and leaned toward him, peeking up at him from under the stupid bonnet she had to wear. *How many people see his humorous side?* He gave her a wry, amused smile in return, but said nothing. It was enough.

Were it not for the fact that she did not belong here, Darcy knew he should be in danger of being bewitched by Elizabeth Bennet. He enjoyed their private walks and curricle rides more as every day passed. However, by the time he reached the library he decided his fascination with a unique individual was natural and did not imply any stronger attachment.

He was in the library with the purpose of observing Mrs. Younge and his sister. Darcy took an opportunity every day to watch their interactions after Miss Bennet raised her concern. So far, he observed nothing to support Miss Bennet's dismal interpretation of her behavior. Mrs. Younge was abrupt and campaigned for his sister to be out, but he had not heard any cutting remarks.

Is Miss Bennet mistaken, or is Mrs. Younge behaving differently because I am in attendance?

Currently, Mrs. Younge provided moral instruction, and Georgiana had only to listen. Miss Bennet read on the other side of the room by the window while Darcy attempted to read a letter from his friend.

Charles Bingley was a steady friend and loyal correspondent, but he was not a *legible* correspondent. He left out half of his words, blotted the rest, and seemed ignorant of the purpose of stops. It took a quarter of an hour, but by the end, he was confident his friend and his sisters wished to come to Pemberley in June rather than August. Bingley intended to find an estate to lease for the autumn in August and preferred to visit Pemberley sooner.

Darcy turned the question over in his mind, with a glance at his singular houseguest. When the morality lesson finished, Mrs. Younge departed, and Darcy watched with curiosity as Georgiana tentatively crossed the room to sit nearer to Miss Bennet.

"Are you still reading *Lady of the Lake*?"

Miss Bennet smiled and tossed her volume aside. "Yes, but I am not making progress."

Georgiana bit her lip, then opened and closed her lips twice before she spoke. "Perhaps, perhaps you might enjoy *Marmion* better?"

Darcy kept his eyes on his letter, but listened to his sister's attempt to forward a conversation with a father's pride. Perhaps Mrs. Younge's guidance would be to Georgiana's credit, despite Miss Bennet's misgivings. He needed to observe his sister's companion more closely before making a decision.

"Long narrative poems aren't my—I do not care for them. It is not the author; I enjoyed *Ivanhoe*."

"What is i-van-hoe?"

"A novel by the same author as this." She tapped the volume.

"I did not know Scott wrote novels; I only know his poetry."

Darcy dropped his letter and watched the ladies in enough time to see the color drain from Miss Bennet's face as she glanced at him with the panicked look of a drowning woman. *She knows she made a mistake.*

"I think, Miss Bennet, perhaps you are mistaken with the name of the author." His heavy-handed tone made his implication clear.

Miss Bennet composed her features into a more relaxed expression, but her color had not returned. "Yes, my mistake. Sir Walter Scott is of course a poet, not a novelist." The situation went from bad to worse. *Apparently, in addition to writing novels, Walter Scott earns himself a baronetcy. I do not wish to know what is to come!*

Darcy tried to speak calmly. "I know not with whom you have confused the author of *Marmion* and *Lady of the Lake*, but *Walter* Scott attained his well-deserved celebrity through his poetry."

It took a moment for Miss Bennet to realize her second mistake. Her composure surprised him; after a grimace, she smiled and asked Georgiana to describe *Marmion*. If his sister thought her behavior strange, she did not show it and recounted *Marmion* with an enthusiasm that made him believe she would buy every copy lest it fall into unworthy hands.

Georgiana would not correct someone who claimed the sky was green. But if Bingley and his sisters came, Miss Bennet would be under greater scrutiny. Bingley would be kind; perhaps the worst he would do is describe her as peculiar when the ladies were absent. But Miss Bingley and Mrs. Hurst, Bingley's sisters, would be scathing in their disapproval. They would mock her privately, or even be rude to her publicly.

And when Miss Bennet knew what they thought of her, from their sly or ridiculing manner, she might not hold back her own disapproving rejoinders. She might give herself away in her anger, and their preparation and caution would be for naught. His dignity, his reputation, his very home could be lost forever if the truth came out.

To not know Walter Scott's poetry would be inconceivable even for a woman born in the Canadas in 1787. He could not in good conscience tell his closest friend *not* to come. And he could not hide Miss Bennet without raising his sister's suspicions or his guest's ire. He pushed aside the truth that he would miss her company if he sent her off.

His thoughts were interrupted by the ladies' voices; their conversation had moved on while he considered the matter.

"She wishes us to go to Ramsgate. I will meet with school friends, but to be forced into *their* wide range of acquaintances every day . . . "

"Is there nothing good about going to Ramsgate in August?"

"Ramsgate shall be more full than my taste allows, but I should enjoy walking the pier, and I am curious about the bathing machines."

"And you are able to go, even though you are not out?"

"Mrs. Younge will be with me, of course. Fitzwilliam might even join me if we stay through September." There was a stretch of silence. "Mrs. Younge will have me receive callers every morning and go out every night. I will be forced into constant exertion."

Darcy remained still, but attentive; the ladies appeared to have forgotten he was on the other side of the room.

"You just need to be encouraged to talk, but gently, and by someone who respects you."

"Mrs. Younge . . . I do not think—I do not think she holds me in particular regard."

Darcy's heart seized at the sorrow in Georgiana's voice.

"Well, who needs her! I think you're worthy of regard. You will see friends in Ramsgate, and none of their friends will think meanly of you."

"I never know what to say; and at Ramsgate, every night will have its engagement if Mrs. Younge has her way. She will force me to mix more in the world . . ."

"A little social friction is necessary for you to become polished, but there is no hurry. Remember this: No one is thinking about you as much as you think they are."

"I worry they are, and I become uneasy and—"

"First, work on sitting still. Mrs. Younge scolds you about it, but she does not help you. Don't fidget with your hands or your skirt. Here, hold the fan I gave you. Just watch the conversation with a smile. Look at each person who speaks, not at the floor. Now, you can focus on the conversation, even if you are not ready to join it. Anyone who is your friend will try to draw you out if you seem attentive."

"Do you think I can go to Ramsgate and not be made uneasy by being in a crowded room?"

"Miss Darcy, I have no doubt you can, and *will*, do anything you set your mind to."

Darcy slipped from the room. Of Miss Bennet's sense and goodness, there could be no doubt. He could not deny she was a suitable friend to his sister, far more earnest and benevolent than Bingley's sisters. Miss Bennet was no reason not to allow his friends to come to Pemberley.

He ought to have rung for Reynolds, but instead went to her room. When he was bid to enter, she nearly upset her inkwell in her hurry to stand. His coming shocked her, but by the time she completed a respectful curtsey, her face was its implacable and familiar self.

"Did you ring for me, sir?"

He shook his head. "The last time I entered your room, I was given more cake than was good for me." The room looked smaller than he remembered, but familiar in its cheerful coziness.

A fond smile appeared on her face. "It was the best way to keep you in good order, if I recall. What did you need of me?"

"Bingley, Miss Bingley, and the Hursts shall arrive the first week in June to spend four weeks at Pemberley."

He saw the range of acknowledgment, resignation, and lastly, a trace of fear in her eyes.

"Have you considered, sir, what is best to be done in regards to Miss Bennet if you host your friends?"

"Our neighbors are familiar with Georgiana's houseguest, and her connection to you is well-known. We shall say her return voyage is planned for the end of June, and be cautious about removing her from the house on the solstice."

"Are you concerned about Miss Bennet revealing her true history?"

"No," he answered truthfully. "Upon the whole, she has done well. She would not betray us on purpose, and we shall help her to not raise any suspicions by accident."

"And what of Miss Bingley's temper, after she realizes a single young lady is also in residence, with you?"

Only with Reynolds could he allow such an impertinent observation, even if it was true. "We shall bear Miss Bingley the best we can." He allowed himself a resigned smile in recognition of the secret that was not a secret: Miss Bingley was a termagant to the servants and had aspirations of being Pemberley's mistress.

There was a knock, and a maid entered. Darcy struggled to recall her name, as he was distracted by her red-rimmed eyes and quivering lips. Upon realizing the master was there, she apologized and was gone by the time he remembered she was Polly Brooks. He looked the question to Reynolds.

"Polly is distressed because her young brother in Lambton is very ill."

"She may go home if she wishes to help nurse him."

"I already have a maid-of-all-work who has gone home to tend to a sibling with a fever; I cannot spare Polly with us about to have guests. When the other girl returns, if her brother is still ill, she may go."

"Davy Tasker says his shepherd's boy and the boy's father have a fever as well. They are behind in shearing and suspect it will set back the haymaking."

"All children are prone to have colds and make everyone around them ill as well."

"All children except for Georgiana, if I recall."

Reynolds smiled. "Yes, sir. She had the occasional cold, but never the whooping cough, nor the measles, not like you."

Darcy left, his mind lingering over memories of his parents sitting at his bedside, of eating round cakes that Reynolds brought him while he was ill, and playing with toy soldiers in bed.

JUNE 5, 1811
17 DAYS UNTIL SUMMER SOLSTICE

Elizabeth was in the library after dinner, having found Samuel Johnson's *Dictionary of the English Language*. She pulled both volumes from the shelf and brought them near the candle on the table.

"Whirl" was in use, but she could not find "dervish." She could not describe Caroline Bingley as a whirling dervish, but her arrival at Pemberley was like a whirlwind. She made more demands of the servants than Mr. Darcy and Georgiana together. The maids cringed at the sound of her voice, the footmen shrugged when her back was turned, and Reynolds's lips disappeared entirely instead of remaining in their usual thin line.

Reynolds has someone she hates more than me! At least Mrs. Younge has toned down her harshness towards Georgiana with so many guests to observe her.

Miss Bingley strutted around Pemberley like she owned it. She looked at Elizabeth as though she would as soon step on her as speak to her since she was poor and therefore was not worth knowing. However, that was preferable to the obsessive attention Miss Bingley showed Mr. Darcy.

She interrupted Mr. Darcy's letter-writing to praise his penmanship. She was enraptured by whatever book he *held*, since her prattling prevented him from reading. She expressed a passion for walking if he mentioned going outside. *If she focused that ambition on a career rather than pursuing a man, Miss Bingley could be Prime Minister, even in this time.*

The entertaining part was that all her ploys, all her flattery, all her fake curiosity in his interests, were all hopeless. Mr. Darcy's complete disinterest may as well have been spelled in ten-foot-tall burning letters on Pemberley's lawn. And *still* Miss Bingley hovered at his side, admiring how evenly he wrote his lines, admiring his books, his carriages, his sister's accomplishments.

"I can't even," Elizabeth muttered, turning the pages of the dictionary to avoid returning to the drawing room. She was more than happy to escape Miss Bingley on the pretense of finding a book.

Mrs. Hurst was a ventriloquist's dummy controlled by her sister, and Mr. Hurst lived purely for eating, drinking, and beating people at cards. As for Mr. Darcy's friend, the reason behind this invasion, Elizabeth could say nothing against him. Charles Bingley was friendly, quick enough to tease his friend, the first to say something kind, and wanted everyone to get along. He was one of those nice guys you couldn't help but like.

"Miss Bennet? Have not you yet found a book?"

Elizabeth jumped at the sound of Mr. Darcy's low voice. "A whirlwind. Miss Bingley has descended upon Pemberley as a whirlwind. A violent gust of ambition and superciliousness that knocks us over in her wake."

"Your lack of manners is appalling; she is the sister of my closest friend as well as my guest." He did not sound angry in the slightest.

"Did you hear the way she snapped at Reynolds after she told her she would have to wait all of ten minutes for another maid? Miss Bingley didn't care that your maid's brother *died* and she's gone home in mourning."

"I know her brother died and she was gone, but as to Miss Bingley and the maid, such matters are beneath my notice unless Reynolds sees fit to mention them to me."

"What are you doing here, anyway?" She put the dictionary volumes back. "You know I left to keep my patience. I can only listen to Miss Bingley go on about her accomplishments and my lack of them for so long."

Mr. Darcy set his candlestick on the mantle and stoked the dying embers of the fire. "I wanted to be certain my guest found a means of passing the evening."

"I suspect you got tired of Miss Bingley praising every idea that crosses your brain. Tell me this: Have you ever tried to get her to state an opinion, then professed the opposite opinion just to watch her trip over her words to contradict herself and agree with you?"

He laughed. *Mr. Darcy actually laughed!* She did love these unguarded moments with him. He rubbed his hand across his mouth and shook his head, his laughter fading, but his amusement stayed in his eyes as he looked at her. "I would not admit to an ungentlemanly scheme."

"Your big secret is safe with me." She walked closer; it was hard to see him in the dim light of only two candles.

"Right now, you and your origins are my greatest secret."

"That secret is safe too. I made you a promise."

"I have not forgotten. And I have no reason to doubt you."

Their silence and lingering eye contact stretched out a moment too long. In less than three weeks, these moments would end. "Hence why I'm here taking a mental health break rather than doing what I would do in 2011, which is tell Miss Bingley where she can shove it."

"She has not been rude to you, not in my presence. I thought your indignation was on my behalf."

"It mostly is. She is shamelessly throwing herself at you, and it's painful to watch. I'll bet she's ordered the monogrammed towels, so watch out. I think the nineteenth-century words to describe Miss Bingley's behavior toward me are 'civil disdain.' If she's the sort of woman you meet at dances, I can understand why you haven't married."

"Perhaps instead I remain single because I am . . . what was your word for an obnoxious person?"

"A jerk?" She laughed. "I told you, you weren't as much of a jerk as I originally thought." Although he teased, he sounded defensive at being thought of as a jerk. "Don't be so offended; you didn't even think I was a woman when you first saw me."

Darcy turned quickly and walked to the table where she previously set *Marmion* aside. With his back still to her, he said quietly, "Yes, but that was when I first knew you. It has been many weeks now that I—I realized how mistaken I was." He handed her the book, but not before her heart turned over in her chest. After staring into her eyes a heartbeat too long, he said, "We ought to return to the others."

She nodded and hastily remembered to grab the candlestick from the table. It guttered and went out, and she spilled the wax, hissing in pain as some splashed on her hand and she dropped the book. Mr. Darcy was instantly at her side, taking the holder from her and laying both of their candles aside before scraping off the hardening wax from her hand.

"Good heavens! I shall have to teach you how to carry a candle upright."

She had no witty rejoinder. Elizabeth was engrossed in looking at his long-fingered, smooth hands and noticing how warm they felt around her own. The hot wax was nothing.

"Do you only use oil lamps in the future? I saw gas lights for the first time in Pall Mall in the year nine. Is that how homes are illuminated in 2011?" The hand that had been brushing off the wax now rested on top of hers.

He asked about the future, but he wouldn't have a future. He wouldn't live to see gas lights become widespread. He wouldn't marry and have children. At least he'd be dead before he saw Pemberley sold for scraps, all its people and possessions long displaced.

Mr. Darcy's death, sometime within the next six months, became immediately, painfully, agonizingly real to Elizabeth. A man full of emotion, clever, serious but capable of laughter and warmth, would be dead. And everything he loved and lived for would fall into literal ruins.

"Miss Bennet, you are not burned badly, are you?" He must have realized he still held her hand and dropped it. Elizabeth snatched his hand back less gently than he had been cradling hers.

"If you're going to ask about the future, are you sure you want to talk about candles?" Her voice rose on its own accord, and she tightened her grip. "Ask me about what happens to *you*, to Pemberley."

He shook his head and gently pulled his hand from her clutches. "Whatever you know of what is to come, say nothing to me about it."

"The solstice is a few weeks away. You won't have another chance to—"

"Please, *please* do not tempt me."

The uneven tone of his voice nearly broke her resolve to give him the choice to know. She wanted to shout at him that he'd die this year, to tell him to listen to whatever his doctors told him, to warn him to be careful in case his future could be changed after all. Elizabeth felt tears welling in her eyes. "Please, ask me."

"Whatever you tell me, it may not make any difference. Or it could make all the difference in the world. I am not entitled to know my future." He pulled a handkerchief from his pocket and, instead of handing it to her, dried her eyes for her. He picked up his candlestick, and took her fingers and wrapped them around it. "I will tell the others you have gone to bed. I daresay you are not of a mind to be in company this evening." Mr. Darcy opened his mouth to say more but, in the end, bowed and made his way back to the drawing room in the dark.

Elizabeth stood in the library with her solitary candle for a long time, tears rolling down her face. He was going to die from accident or disease, Georgiana would die young without children, her husband would bankrupt all that they had, and Pemberley was doomed to be a derelict shell. And there was nothing she could do about it.

CHAPTER TEN

June 10, 1811
12 days until summer solstice

Elizabeth had missed her daily walk with Mr. Darcy because he needed to call at the homes of a few of his tenants along with Mr. Willers. After spending hours reading outside in the summer house, the June sun eventually became too much for her fair complexion and long skirts. Elizabeth returned to the house and went to the library to check the time, where she found Mr. Bingley.

"Miss Bennet!" He jumped from his chair and gave an eager bow. "Join me, or were you looking for my sisters?"

Elizabeth used all she learned in 1811 to not roll her eyes. "I was reading outdoors, but I grew hot."

At her words, Mr. Bingley rang the bell. A maid Elizabeth did not recognize entered, and he asked for refreshments for her. *What a thoughtful guy. I think he's like this with everyone.*

"You have made good use of Darcy's library, I understand." Mr. Bingley waved an arm toward the shelves. "I am an idle fellow myself, and have more books than I ever look into." He gave a self-deprecating smile.

"I have only skimmed the surface of all Mr. Darcy's library affords."

"And that fellow is always buying books. You would not get ahead were you to remain a year at Pemberley. Or ten years!"

Where will this impressive collection be in ten years? Would they still be the neglected property of Georgiana's wasteful husband, whoever he is? Could he be Mr. Bingley? She could not imagine him being so foolish and destructive. Or might Pemberley be sold by then to the first in a line of indifferent owners?

Elizabeth forced herself to match Mr. Bingley's cheerfulness. "Pemberley's library, as the rest of this home, is beautiful, and ten years wouldn't be long enough to enjoy all it has to offer. My own visit will soon come to an end."

"I know nothing about Upper Canada and am not likely to see it myself. I am certain you have stories to share of York and its society. Your voyage to England must have been an adventure all on its own!" His open expression showed genuine curiosity.

Redirect! "My voyage was nothing to speak of. I spent five weeks below deck, ill to my stomach." She spoke the words calmly, without betraying her inward tremble.

She was saved from coming up with a subject by the most unwelcome of sources. Miss Bingley and Mrs. Hurst entered, followed by Reynolds bearing a cart with lemonade along with cold meat, cake, and fruit.

"Set those there, then go," Miss Bingley demanded. Elizabeth looked to see how Reynolds bore being told what to do by her, but her face was inscrutable. Miss Bingley approached the table, but Reynolds looked at Elizabeth and asked if anything else was needed.

Elizabeth took in Miss Bingley's huff of indignation without understanding. Reynolds looked at the cake, back at Elizabeth, and made a gesture toward the others. *I'm supposed to be the hostess and serve the food, because Georgiana isn't here.* But Miss Bingley was already in the process of taking charge, so why not just let her finish?

Reynolds hates Caroline too. Elizabeth gave her unlikely ally a wink, then walked to the table to slice the cake, and asked the others what they might like. She thanked Reynolds kindly before telling her they needed nothing else.

"What a lovely selection," Miss Bingley cried. "Grapes, nectarines, peaches. Mr. Darcy has an impressive—"

"Save your breath, Caroline. He is not even here," Mr. Bingley cut off his sister and poured Elizabeth a glass. She could not contain a snort of amusement. Mr. Bingley pretended not to hear; Mrs. Hurst looked down her nose in distaste; and Miss Bingley's eyes burned with a fury that contained all the blazes of hell.

"Of course he is not here; he has responsibilities toward his tenants. I understand he is speaking to several families today in that little village about aiding the Sunday school. I only mentioned the fruit so Miss Bennet could appreciate such things as a conservatory. Her home in the Canadas could hardly be so progressive."

"That is an absurd pretension. Darcy has a fine one, 'tis true, but it is still just a glass room."

"I only hope Miss Bennet appreciates her good fortune in finding herself among those who have the means to show a poor woman charity."

"Darcy is generous, but he is still not here, so you may as well talk on other things." Mr. Bingley was oblivious to the undercurrent of dislike between them. "Miss Bennet is from the other side of the world and has never been to England. You know nothing of Upper Canada; there can be no want of subject."

"That is right." Miss Bingley turned to her. "You are returning since none in England would claim you. What a waste of resources you do not have to spare."

"It was an adventure. I regret nothing."

"And who is to pay for your passage since you have nothing to your name?"

"Mr. Darcy is willing to equip me for my return to Canada. I have made a great friend in Miss Darcy." Elizabeth tried to change the subject. "Does she not play beautifully?"

"Perhaps one of your friends can instead equip you for the East Indies? It is not as common as it once was, but it might be your last, best option for your maintenance."

Elizabeth had no idea what this meant, but it would be unwise to smile and nod. She turned to her tormentor's brother, who took pity on her ignorance.

"She is suggesting you consider seeking your fortune in India. It is sometimes necessary for a woman to embrace the only possibility of maintenance offered to her. However, Caroline, there is no reason to suppose that is the truth in Miss Bennet's case."

She means to ship me off to India to find a husband! "That is against my inclination. I would prefer servitude."

Miss Bingley and her sister shared a laugh; their brother shifted uncomfortably. "I understood," said Miss Bingley when she composed herself, "that given your lack of friends, fortune, and accomplishments, going to the East Indies was the best possibility that offered you an establishment of your own. You must recognize you cannot remain *here.*"

Was she so jealous of her friendship with Mr. Darcy that she actually wanted her on the next boat to India? *That still won't make Mr. Darcy marry you.* "You raise an interesting point about my future. Perhaps I ought to remain in England. My personal attractions might gain me a husband."

"Let me recommend that you not assume that whatever passes for accomplished in Little York will gain you recognition in any respectable society in England. Even you could not arrive in India without attracting the notice of some manner of man willing to have you."

"I would never sell myself to the highest bidder and settle for a husband who is not entirely devoted to me."

"Yes, we all have reason to thank Providence that we might make our own choices as to what will make our own situations agreeable!" Mr. Bingley poured a glass of lemonade and thrust it into his sister's hand. "Louisa, is that a new bracelet?"

Mr. Bingley did not enjoy a dispute as much as his youngest sister did, and Elizabeth was pleased to put him at ease by quitting the room. By the time she reached Reynolds's room, her temper was under control.

"I wanted to thank you for what you did in the library. Miss

Bingley needed to be put in her place." *Preferably in a ditch filling with dirty water, but a metaphorical place is sufficient.*

"I do not know what you mean. You have been in residence some time and could act as hostess."

"Thanks all the same. I've had enough of her flattering Mr. Darcy. He hates it! You've known him since he was a child; I know you can tell when he's scarcely holding his patience. 'I admire your generosity, Mr. Darcy, even though I'm not kind.' 'I admire your sister, even though I don't know a damn thing about her.' 'I admire your books, even though I won't shut up so you can read.' She's a broken record!"

A ghost of a smile and a small escape of air from Reynolds's nose was the only indication of her amusement. Elizabeth turned to go, but then remembered the maid who answered when Mr. Bingley pulled the bell. "I didn't recognize the maid who came into the library. Where is Polly Brooks?"

"Mr. Darcy allowed her to spend a week with her mother. Her younger brother has died."

"How awful. Another maid had a sibling die not long ago."

"The death of a child is always, always tragic. I suspect it is more common now than when you are from."

JUNE 12, 1811
10 DAYS TO SUMMER SOLSTICE

Darcy spent breakfast reading his letters, one infuriating him to such a degree that he wrenched it in two. He felt the others' curious looks and he studiously avoided Miss Bennet's eye. His attention often turned to her without his realizing it. Darcy did his best to pay no notice to Miss Bingley's and Mrs. Younge's prattle about a small dance after dinner. Miss Bennet was uncharacteristically silent, and Darcy's eyes stayed on his post instead of trying to read her expressions.

The opportunity to know her mind came later when he walked to the summer house where he knew Miss Bennet now came to read. He stopped short at the sight of her; her head was down and she stood in the center, her back to the arched doorway, shuffling her feet and hopping about and humming.

"What *are* you doing?"

Miss Bennet gave a shriek. "I'm . . . waiting for you so we can go for our walk." Darcy stared, raising one eyebrow. "Okay! I'm trying to remember what Colonel Fitzwilliam taught me about dancing."

"Why?"

"Did you not listen at breakfast? Miss Bingley, her puppet sister, and Mrs. Younge have arranged for a dance after dinner." The degree of indignation in her voice seemed disproportionate for the activity.

"Informal dances at home are common. You need not dance. I suspect Georgiana will prefer to play so you—"

"You have no idea what is going on?" Miss Bennet's voice was now on the verge of panic.

He stared in confused silence.

"Busty Mrs. Younge and scheming Miss Bingley have united in a common cause, and your sister will suffer for it. Mrs. Younge wants your sister married so she can leave, and Mr. Bingley is here, single, and has a pulse. Mrs. Younge has promised to play so your sister can dance with her friends." Miss Bennet did that strange gesture with the first two fingers of both hands.

"My hopes and wishes for an alliance between my friend and sister are years in the future, and I have shared them with none but you. Even if what you say about Mrs. Younge is accurate, what purpose does Miss Bingley have in promoting the match? She knows she is but fifteen and shy."

"For a smart guy, you can be oblivious." Miss Bennet approached, her arms akimbo. She now spoke as though he were a slow child. "Miss Bingley is anxious to get her brother for Georgiana because if there is *one* Darcy-Bingley marriage, she might achieve another. That would be ingenious if you liked her, which we all know you don't."

It would be ungentlemanly to acknowledge that, as he could not honestly refute it. "You still suspect Mrs. Younge is unhappy and wishes Georgiana to marry so she can sooner find another position?"

"Yes! The idea of dancing terrifies Georgiana. She's timid, not stupid. She's just not ready to be put on display like that. She knows her friends are planning romantic dancing to get her to flirt with Mr.

Bingley, your closest friend. And she and I know she can't do it. She's afraid of disappointing *everyone*."

The scheme was now clear, except for Miss Bennet's practicing something she had done but twice with Fitzwilliam two months ago. "I will tell her no one expects her to be wed in the near term and to think of the evening as an opportunity to show you dancing. There are three gentlemen and three other ladies, if Mrs. Younge only plays. You need not dance at all."

"Of *course* I have to. The three harpies will contrive it so you dance with Miss Bingley, Mrs. Hurst dances with her husband, and your sister dances with Mr. Bingley. I remember you saying you don't dance with one person all night, but Mrs. Younge and Miss Bingley have a common goal. Georgiana will be stuck dancing with Mr. Bingley. I need to remember what your cousin showed me so I don't make a fool of myself."

"And *your* dancing will accomplish . . .?"

"The only way Georgiana gets out of being forced to dance all night with Mr. Bingley is if I say I want to dance. Mr. Hurst won't think to ask me, but your friend is a sweetheart. If I say I want to dance, *he'll* ask me, and then Georgiana gets to sit out. She can't talk to anyone for half an hour, let alone dance and talk all night with the man her friends picked out for her. I would rather Caroline Bingley laugh at my mistakes than have Georgiana suffer all night. I'll muddle through the best I can."

The realization of her thoughtfulness struck Darcy's heart. It began to beat quickly, and the depths of her kindness to his sister moved him. He bent his head to hide the emotions in his eyes. "Miss Bennet, you have—you have a heart unrivaled in all the women of my acquaintance."

"I care about Georgiana, and she deserves not to feel anxious in her own home. If she feels confident about herself, maybe I can save her from . . ." She hesitated. "Maybe someday she'll choose a husband who is worthy of her. Besides, if I dance with Mr. Bingley, and you ask Georgiana, then Miss Bingley has to sit out and *you'll* be spared her flattery. I can help both Darcy siblings."

His heart, still beating wildly, now resided somewhere in his throat.

"Will you do me the honor of dancing with me?" Never before had he cared about the answer to this polite supplication.

She blushed. "Are you sure you want to? Mr. Bingley would take my mistakes in his stride, but you strike me as one to take it more seriously."

"I know not what a lady's expected response is in the twenty-first century, but unless you intend on not dancing or are promised to another, when a—"

"Yes, I would love to dance with you. As long as you promise not to laugh at me in front of Miss Bingley." She was a curious mixture of strength and femininity. She was determined to protect his sister—and him—and yet the thought of being laughed at caused her to blush.

"I dare not laugh at you. I will do all I can to see you are prepared. We will practice without the others learning of it, and I shall instruct Mrs. Younge to play tunes for the dances you know. If she calls a dance that is modern and we have not practiced it, we can claim it has not yet come to British North America."

Her eyes widened in surprise then softened, and a gentle smile graced her lips. Miss Bennet then shocked him. She abandoned all restraint and threw her arms around his neck. It was impulsive, improper. But even as his senses and thoughts were in turmoil, Darcy tightened his arms around her in return and bent his head to her cheek. It was the most natural, and the most unsuitable, response. And it was marvelous.

"You think I can do this?" She removed her hands from around his neck, but still stood closer than was appropriate. Darcy acknowledged to himself that he did not mind this at all. It took him a moment to find his voice.

"All you need do is recall the few steps Fitzwilliam practiced with you. A lively step is critical."

"I suspect a *precise* one is more critical."

"Remember to not walk, give the impression of lightness and keep your posture upright, and point your toes down and turned out as much as you can manage. Smile and look at your partner, and he will be less inclined to notice if you misstep."

"Thank you. Teaching time travelers how to dance goes beyond keeping me safe until the solstice. You've more than held up your end of the bargain when you let me stay as long as I behaved correctly. I judged you too quickly. You're a good man, Mr. Darcy."

"*Until the solstice.*" Darcy could hardly keep his countenance. *She is leaving, and I will never see her again.* It was inevitable, it was necessary, and it wounded him. He was far too familiar with her. He took a step back and cleared his throat. It was raw, and it hurt to swallow.

"Do you remember the Boulanger, the brisk round dance? We ought to practice something fast and lively, without any fancy footwork to challenge you."

His brusqueness hurt her, he saw, but it was short-lived. Miss Bennet, for all her temper and forwardness, was not by nature one to be melancholy. He spent a happy afternoon leading a pretty woman from two hundred years in the future through longways country dances, enjoying her laugh and creating memories he suspected he would hold private and extraordinary for years to come.

JUNE 14, 1811
8 DAYS UNTIL SUMMER SOLSTICE

On such a fine summer evening, Darcy acquiesced to his sister's request that they sit out of doors after dinner. The ladies, save Miss Bennet, were seated beneath their parasols in front of the summer house, while the gentlemen were several feet away, seated on the grass. He felt hot, but the others appeared relaxed and comfortable.

Miss Bingley, unable to make her way into his two-person game of piquet with Bingley, spent time at Georgiana's side, lauding her work on a decorative vase while Mrs. Younge admonished it. Mr. Hurst was asleep on the grass.

"May I pick some flowers to put in your sister's lovely vase?" Miss Bennet soon asked him.

Darcy immediately set aside his cards and asked Tom the gardener to bring a basket and shears. Miss Bennet gave him a curtsey along with an impertinent grin. He knew she found the custom of bowing and curtseying strange and she sought to do it whenever she could. He returned her smile before picking up his cards.

"May I join you?" Miss Bingley asked with the tone of command rather than supplication. "You must allow me to advise you; it would not do for you to fill Miss Darcy's vase with only roses." She laughed as though this possibility were a crime against nature.

"I can handle gathering flowers, but join me if you want."

"Why, I simply must." Darcy saw Miss Bingley watching him. "It would not do for you to select flowers that do not compliment Miss Darcy's precise design. I suspect I am more talented in such domestic matters."

"I am usually indifferent to flowers. I just wanted to go for a walk and pick a few pretty ones for my friend." Miss Bennet gave Georgiana a small wave. It was an informal gesture, but to Darcy it looked to be one of friendship. He saw his sister's expression soften into a smile as she returned the gesture.

"I am all astonishment!" Miss Bingley's loud voice caught their attention. "A knowledge of and a taste for flowers is desirable in the fairer sex. You must learn if you manage to find yourself a suitor. Your dancing, after all, could hardly be called elegant."

Miss Bennet heaved a great sigh, as though drawing strength for either patience or to unleash a torrent of fury. Darcy forced himself to remain where he was. Bingley, affable, courteous, and disliking an argument, said to his sister, "You are mistaken, Caroline. Miss Bennet, you were an able partner. If you were to remain in London, I would ask you to dance at the next ball."

"Thank you, but I do not need you to defend me. I am aware of my talents and defects, and I know my dancing was only tolerable. But I did dance more often with Mr. Darcy than with you, so perhaps, Miss Bingley, we shall let *him* share his opinion of my dancing."

She is going to further provoke Miss Bingley's jealousy. Darcy felt warm, as though he had a fever.

"Miss Bennet, you ought not to speak against my brother. To contradict a gentleman is not done amongst good society. Why, if you were to be here longer, I think I might become ashamed of you." She gave a false laugh Darcy supposed was intended to be playful. "Thank heavens you are soon to return to those more of your own manner and character."

"I *do* wish to remain longer; I have become good friends with the Darcys. But you have not asked Mr. Darcy his opinion on my dancing. I noticed you watched us while you were sitting down. Mr. Darcy, what do you have to say?"

Darcy knew she was nettling Miss Bingley in return, but to not answer might make the situation worse. "You executed the simple steps with elegance and without any errors."

"Well, that is high praise." She changed her tone to a more sincere one. "I had an excellent instructor." She smiled that warm, intimate smile she often gave him, and he returned it. Miss Bingley gripped her parasol handle tightly. "Shall we gather some flowers for Miss Darcy?"

"You were rude to both my brother and Mr. Darcy." Her voice rose. "I insist you apologize for your forwardness."

Darcy cast a look at Bingley, who shook his head, perplexed. Darcy rose, but Miss Bennet answered before he could intervene.

"If they feel offended, they may speak for themselves and I will apologize. I doubt your brother needs you to defend him, and Mr. Darcy is nothing to you. Now, are we picking these fu—are we gathering flowers or not?"

"You ought to know a man wants a woman who is agreeable and easily pleased. Not one who is critical, like you. It is no wonder you are not married, and it is no wonder your father's family would not know you after you returned to England."

Miss Bennet threw down her basket and shears, and Darcy saw a muscle twitch in her jaw. The uncomfortable heat in Darcy's forehead now felt like a full-fledged fever. His throat was painfully dry.

Miss Bennet said quietly, "I am sure your advice about my getting married was kindly meant, though I wonder, as another single lady, that you are in the best position to offer it."

"No gentleman wants a woman who presumes to be his equal. Let me tell you something, no man will ever love you. You"—she pointed into Miss Bennet's face—"are poor, friendless, and peculiar. Does anyone love you? I doubt it."

"Miss Bingley!" Darcy crossed the grass and stood behind Miss Bennet, allowing Miss Bingley to see and hear the full force of his anger. "You are lashing out in anger, and speaking about that which you know nothing. You have no grounds and no right to insult my guest. There are many kinds of men, and many kinds of love. Miss Bennet may be loved, very deeply, indeed."

He saw Miss Bennet give a brief tremble out of the corner of his eye; he dared not look away from Miss Bingley. If the full realization of what her outburst had done to damage his opinion of her was not imminent, it soon would be. "If you offer Miss Bennet an apology, I am certain she would accept it."

Darcy walked toward the house, without looking back. If he did, he might look into Miss Bennet's eyes and make a commitment, an error, he could never redeem.

CHAPTER ELEVEN

JUNE 15, 1811
7 DAYS UNTIL SUMMER SOLSTICE

Elizabeth decided to breakfast with Reynolds and the upper servants rather than share a table with Miss Bingley so soon after their fight last evening. The idea of putting on a polite face for that bitch was more than Elizabeth could stomach. *One more week with Miss Bingley. I can last one more week without giving myself away.*

The door opened, and a footman brought in a letter for Mr. Willers. The steward read it, changed color, and heaved a weary sigh.

"Not bad news, I hope?" she asked quietly.

"I am afraid it is. Davy Tasker's shepherd is dead, as is the shepherd's little boy." Mr. Willers gave Reynolds a woeful look. "As I told Mrs. Reynolds yesterday, three other children in Lambton have died, not to mention Polly Brooks's youngest brother, and now she herself is too ill to return to Pemberley. One of the gardeners is now in bed with a fever."

"What do the doctors say?"

Reynolds kicked her under the table. "The apothecary has seen to the children; there is no need to send for a physician for a cold."

Mr. Willers's pallor waned, slightly. "Yes, perhaps it is a cold that a few of the children were not strong enough to fight. It is still distressing." He rose slowly. "I must meet with Mr. Darcy before the family has breakfast."

The others trickled from the room, leaving only Elizabeth and Reynolds.

"People don't die of colds, even now!"

"Keep your voice down. You will distress Mr. Willers; he may still be in his office. His wife has had a fever and a sore throat for a week. She now has difficulty breathing."

Elizabeth sighed sadly. "Five children are dead, and one adult. Now Polly, the gardener, and Mrs. Willers are ill."

Reynolds's frown lines around her lips appeared. "Tenants at Pemberley and people in Lambton have complained of a sore throat and a fever. I, their families, and the apothecary can tend to them."

"We need a real doctor."

"There is no need for a physician. They need nursing, not a physician to prescribe useless medicines and recommend leeching. It is not done, except in a dire case."

"It was dire for those dead children! And children aren't the only ones getting sick now."

"None who live in the house are ill. Mrs. Willers lives in a house on the estate, and Polly Brooks got sick while at home in Lambton. The Bingleys and Hursts will be off in a fright if a physician comes to Pemberley."

"You are so concerned with appearances." Elizabeth's voice shook. "People are *dying*! It's contagious." A horrible thought struck her. "Do you even know what 'contagious' means?"

Reynolds took a deep breath with her eyes closed. "The harsh reality of this time and place is that a physician would likely not help."

"How do you know that?"

Reynolds's self-control slipped. "In a week, it will no longer be any concern of yours!"

The thought of leaving Pemberley forever, of leaving her friend Georgiana, of leaving Mr. Darcy and never seeing him—*them*—again tore at her heart. The knowledge that Mr. Darcy would die hurt her deeply. "Is that what you think of me?"

"I hardly think of you at all. If you want to make yourself useful, sit with Miss Darcy and spare her from Miss Bingley's flattery or Mrs. Younge's admonitions."

It was a furious, hopeless feeling that burned in her chest when she entered the music room. Miss Bingley and Mrs. Hurst listened to Georgiana while sewing something useless. Mrs. Younge was seated near the door, writing a letter.

As Elizabeth strode by her table, Mrs. Younge's papers rustled and one of the sheets fluttered to the floor. Mrs. Younge snatched it, but not before Elizabeth read the salutation: *My dearest George*. Elizabeth stifled a laugh. *First-name basis.* Mrs. Younge had a secret boyfriend.

"Miss Bennet, I missed you at breakfast." Georgiana ceased playing and rose to greet her. Elizabeth smiled at the genuine concern in her voice. "I wondered if you were unwell."

Elizabeth's eyes hurt as she forced them to remain on Georgiana and not turn a hateful glare toward Miss Bingley. "I needed to sleep in. How is Derbyshire's most accomplished musician today? I admire your dress, Miss Darcy. That shade is becoming on you."

Miss Bingley muttered, "So rude; must not compliment." Elizabeth ignored her. She was not so fortunate in return. "You cannot imagine Miss Darcy needs to be flattered. She has no vanity to be gratified."

"In that case, you must think Mr. Darcy is a vain man."

Miss Bingley drew back. "How could you make that assumption?"

"Since you compliment his home, his manners, his interests, his taste, and his opinions all day long, I assumed you thought Mr. Darcy vain. Or maybe you think he is insecure and is in need of encouragement?"

The collective gasps and stares of the others made her realize she went too far, and she left them. *I was doing so well before Miss Bingley showed up!* Elizabeth remembered how Reynolds had smirked when she called Miss Bingley a broken record with her constant admiration and deference to Mr. Darcy. *Even the housekeeper thinks Miss Bingley is a joke.*

Her stomach dropped to the floor as a dreadful comprehension dawned. She held out her hand to the wall to balance herself, closing her eyes as her thoughts passed over her months of conversations with the housekeeper. Elizabeth took a shaky breath and returned to the housekeeper's room without knocking.

Reynolds sat at the desk with her ledger book and actually rolled her eyes. "I do not know what the etiquette is when you are from, but one does not enter others' rooms without asking."

Elizabeth struggled to find her voice, and saw Reynolds's attitude toward her in a different light.

"You laughed."

"I beg your pardon?"

She took a breath and tried again. "You laughed, as much as you ever do, when I made fun of Miss Bingley's constant admiration of Mr. Darcy."

"You—as well as anyone—ought to know that sometimes one does not act as properly as one ought. You diverted me against my conscience."

"You smiled after I called Miss Bingley a broken record."

Reynolds knocked over her inkwell, and Elizabeth watched ink dribble along the desk and drip into a puddle on the floor. Elizabeth leaned against her desk, more certain now that her guess was correct. "I'd say we're a long way from even Thomas Edison's phonograph."

"I—your general meaning was understandable. I need not comprehend every strange turn of phrase to take your true meaning, or even find humor in it."

Reynolds was white as a sheet and hadn't noticed the ink dripping to the floor. "You also got mad when I called you Mrs. Danvers."

"You forgot my name; I had every right to be insulted."

"Or maybe you read *Rebecca* and didn't like my comparison."

"I do not know what you are implying."

"When I turn my wrist to look for a watch that isn't there, you tell me the time, but I haven't seen anyone wear a wristwatch. Mr. Darcy didn't recognize the name *Moonlight Sonata*, a Beethoven piece his sister plays. But you called it that, even though I play terribly. I'm guessing that moniker doesn't come about until later."

Reynolds realized her tipped inkwell was ruining her desk and carpet, and righted it. Elizabeth watched her tend to the spill before she asked her question.

"In what year were you born?"

Reynolds rose from the floor, tossing the blackened rag away in frustration. "That is an impertinent question, Miss Bennet, but you are an impertinent girl. I was born in fifty-seven."

They eyed one another. Elizabeth broke the silence with a whisper. "*Nineteen* fifty-seven?"

A long pause passed before Mrs. Reynolds hissed a furious "yes."

Elizabeth felt dizzy, and blindly groped for the chair before falling into it. "All that crap about the solstice was a lie? I'm never getting home!" *I'll have to watch Mr. Darcy die.*

"You presume I am not here by choice?"

She raised her head, her vision swimming before settling on the housekeeper's stern gaze. "You're here, now, because, because you *want* to be? Wait, Mr. Darcy said before me there was only an infant and an old man from the future."

"Mr. Roland knows the truth, as did the late Mr. Darcy and Lady Anne; the young master does not." Reynolds's whispers grew louder. "And I will do all in my power to keep it that way. It is distressing enough to him that time travel is possible. To know his most loyal retainer, who has known him since childhood, is not who she claims, would be a cruel blow. That dear boy has suffered enough. And I dare not put my position in jeopardy."

"Bullshit! I can say that now because I know you won't drop dead from shock. Mr. Darcy would never throw you out. You know how well he takes care of everyone and everything at Pemberley." Another realization struck her. "You've known Mr. Darcy since he was *four*. You've been living in the past for twenty-three years?"

"I have; and happily, upon the whole."

Elizabeth's headache moved from a dull nuisance to a painful throb. "Why?"

"I owe you no explanations."

She clenched her fists but repressed the desire to scream. "It doesn't matter why you gave up equal rights and clean running water to be a servant in the nineteenth century. But I want to know how you're certain *I'm* going to get back when you've been stuck here!"

Reynolds slowly sat across from Elizabeth. "I know you will be able to go home because I have done it. I traveled backwards through time by accident on the equinox and returned on the solstice. And later I decided to return to Pemberley, on an equinox at sunset, and made my home here."

Elizabeth looked at the housekeeper's pressed lips, her tightly entwined fingers, and furrowed brow. Whatever emotions she felt, she held a vise-like grip on them.

"I was born in 1957, in Bredbury, outside of Manchester. I got a job at a shop when I was eighteen. I met my husband coming in to buy confectioneries for his mother. He was older, born in 1936. He smoked like a chimney, we didn't have a car, and he was a shift worker at Bredbury Steel Works. No one understood why I married a divorced man twenty years older than me; it caused a rift in my family. But he was kind, and funny, and he thought I walked on water. I was his second wife, his second chance at a family. I was going to work at the sweet shop until I got pregnant and then stay home with our children."

Elizabeth was shocked to see tears shining in Reynolds's eyes.

"We had a stillborn son. In those days, they didn't let you see the baby. I never even got to hold him. I don't know where he is buried. The senior sister said, 'Out of sight, out of mind.' Eight more years and no other children came, but we were happy in our own way. Things were hard—there was a recession, and the factory was often on strike, inflation was high—but it was the two of us against the world.

"And then Donald started to forget things. He couldn't remember the way to the shop I'd worked in for years, or how to play bridge when we played with friends every Friday. He often lost track of how much time passed, what day it was. He couldn't keep his manufacturing job, and his incapacity pension hardly bought us anything."

Reynolds stopped, and for the first time met Elizabeth's eye. Her grief was unmistakable. "How old was your husband?"

"Forty-seven. They said he had a young-onset type of dementia called Alzheimer's disease. It was progressive and incurable. We decided to take a trip to the Peaks while we still could, and that's how we came to be walking along Stanton Moor in the spring of eighty-three."

A new understanding dawned on Elizabeth. "Your husband was the old man?"

"Yes. Poor Donald wasn't even fifty, but in this time and with his dementia, they presumed he was older."

"So Roland found you wandering the moor and brought you to Pemberley, where Mr. Darcy's father hid you?"

"My husband was too confused to socialize, but I said I would work as a maid to earn our keep. Lady Anne looked after me, and old Mr. Darcy made certain Donald was taken care of, in isolation. My husband grew distrustful, anxious, but one thing that calmed him was going to the stone circle. Mr. Roland brought us back most evenings at sunset to appease Donald; he couldn't sleep until he had been to the circle. One evening in June, we walked in the circle together, and in an instant left 1783 and returned to June 1983."

"What happened in the years after you returned?"

"My husband had language problems, more hallucinations. He wandered more, became suspicious, angry. He was no longer the cheerful man I met in Sercombe's when I was eighteen. He would have needed more care than I could have managed alone had he lived longer. He was in hospital for a while, where he died of pneumonia in 1988."

"I'm so sorry."

A few of Reynolds's tears had permission to fall. "Have—have doctors found a way to cure this terrible disease?"

All of Elizabeth's dislike vanished at her raw pleading. "They have drugs that can slow Alzheimer's progress a bit, but there's still no cure."

Reynolds blinked twice and regained her implacable composure. "I lost my job after disappearing for three months, and unemployment was still high. I had no job, no family, no husband, and no children. But I was happy at Pemberley. It seemed the best place for me to go. Old Mr. Darcy was kind, Lady Anne patient, and I knew I could have a life here after Donald. Lady Anne had confided in me that she expected to have a child. I knew she wanted children as much as I had."

"Mr. Darcy?"

The housekeeper nodded. "Lady Anne was brought to bed in February 1784. By the time Donald was gone, it was the summer of eighty-eight when I returned." Reynolds smiled to herself, lost in old memories. "He was a beloved little boy, such big brown eyes and a warm heart and a sweet temper. Clever, curious, too serious. He still is, dear boy."

Elizabeth was quiet for a long moment. "You love him like a son." *Like the one you lost.*

"I make no presumptions that he is mine. Lady Anne and Mr. Darcy were devoted parents."

"I don't think that changes the fact that you love and protect him like a parent." Elizabeth could tell from Reynolds's face, unusually expressive in this moment, that she was right. "And you don't want to disappoint him or hurt him because, after all this time, how could you tell him you've deceived him his whole life? That's why you hate me. You were good enough to convince everyone you belong, but you were afraid I'd figure it out and tell Mr. Darcy."

"I do not hate you."

"You're afraid of what I could do."

"That . . . is closer to the truth."

Elizabeth rose. "Your secret isn't mine to tell. I promised Mr. Darcy I wouldn't tell anyone where *I* came from. I won't tell your secret, either."

Reynolds looked at the table, biting her lip, and gave a nod of acknowledgment.

"Do you . . . do you *know*?"

Reynolds's expression did not change. "Do I know what?"

"Do you know what Pemberley is like in the twentieth century?"

"No, England is filled with fine old houses. After I decided to return, I could never bring myself to find out any details. I wanted to throw my lot in entirely with the Darcys."

There came a knock at the door, and Mr. Darcy's valet entered.

"Yes, Mr. Easton?"

Mr. Darcy's valet sighed. "Two more estate children complain of sore throats and difficulty breathing, and Willers told me as I came through the passage that Tom the gardener just died."

Elizabeth covered her mouth with her hands. Reynolds rose, not at all appearing as though she had lived in an age with antiseptic, X-rays, and medical boards.

"What a tragedy. So many children stricken in such a short time. And Tom's death is a blow; I know Mr. Roland was fond of him. But why are you here to tell me this yourself?"

"I was already on my way to see you. I need some James's powder for the master and anything else you might recommend." Mr. Easton looked as though the words he spoke brought him physical pain. "He complained of a fever last evening and now says his throat is sore."

Elizabeth felt as though the air had been sucked out of the room. There was a long, grave silence.

"I—Cook and I will prepare something for him. What an odd time of year to be brought low by a cold." Reynolds went to the cabinet on the far wall to look through bottles. Elizabeth saw her fingers shake as she selected one.

Mr. Easton stepped closer to the cabinets. "Is it true that Mrs. Willers is very ill? Davy Tasker's shepherd is dead, and with the gardener dead and Polly ill, we cannot presume this is a children's disease any longer. Ought I to send for Mr. Boyle?"

"How was Mr. Darcy last night?"

"He passed a restless and feverish night. He persisted in rising, but has now confessed himself unable to remain up and returned voluntarily to his bed."

Mr. Easton and Reynolds stared at one another for a long moment. Elizabeth felt something shift in the room, the tension elevated again.

"I am ready to adopt your advice of sending for Mr. Boyle. The apothecary will be preoccupied with the estate children, but Mr. Darcy's physician ought to see to Mrs. Willers, and he may as well examine Mr. Darcy whilst he is at Pemberley. I will go to Cook directly and send for you when I have something to ease him."

Elizabeth's hands were shaking, and she felt dizzy again. This couldn't be *it*. Not some cold-like infection. She thought it would be an accident, a curricle tipping over or a fall from a horse.

"Do you *know* what this is?" Elizabeth shrieked as soon as the valet was gone.

"Maintain your composure."

"It isn't a cold or the flu! This place is so backwards. What can the doctors even do?" She felt on the verge of a full-blown panic attack.

"A physician could do nothing that a member of our own household could not. There is no reason to suppose the master is going to die."

"I can't believe you gave up a life with modern medicine to stay *here*!"

A cold fury overtook Reynolds's countenance. "And how advanced is medical care in two hundred years? My child was stillborn. My husband suffered from dementia and died from pneumonia. Mr. Darcy said your father had a stroke and died of a heart attack."

Elizabeth struggled against the wave of panic and fury that threatened to sink her. "When will this so-called doctor get here?"

"Tomorrow. He has ostensibly been called to tend to Mrs. Willers, so as not to distress Miss Darcy and our guests, but he will tend to Mr. Darcy. We need not raise an alarm yet."

"You mean don't tell his guests that Mr. Darcy might have a deadly infection?" Could she do anything to help him before she left on the solstice? "I want to hear *exactly* what the doctor says to Mr. Darcy."

"You are a single, unrelated woman. It would not be proper—"

"I need to know what the doctor says and make sure Mr. Darcy follows the right advice. Maybe I can convince him to listen to the doctor when he otherwise might have . . ." She had no reason to assume she could change the future, but she had to try. "You need to tell Colonel Fitzwilliam to come. I told him, by accident, some things about the future. He can convince Mr. Darcy to follow the doctor's advice, or ours, whatever is best."

"You still believe the physician will be able to care for him better than we can? Do you know what this illness is?"

"I only know we have to take this seriously."

June 17, 1811
5 days until summer solstice

Darcy had spent the previous day in bed, with a raw throat, a fever, and chills. His willfulness overrode his body's complaints this morning, however, and he decided one day of rest was enough to overcome a cold. He rose at his usual time, to every inquiry replied he was better, and tried to prove himself so, by engaging in his customary employments. After breakfast, the party dispersed, and he went to his study to prepare to meet with Mr. Willers to review the week's accounts.

He either dozed, or lost focus, because he did not know how much time passed when he sensed someone near his desk.

"Mr. Darcy?" Miss Bennet gave him a sympathetic look. "Are you certain you ought to be out of bed? Come sit over here."

His inclination was to tell her in no uncertain terms that it was not her concern. But one look at Miss Bennet's face, one moment to remember what their strange friendship meant to him, to remember that impulsive embrace in the summer house, and he decided against it.

He gestured toward a seat by the fire, where a maid had removed the screen and built it high despite the time of year. The seat by the fire was the most honored position, and he offered it to Miss Bennet. She shook her head, and instead stepped aside, tugged on his arm, and pushed him into it. In truth, she hardly applied any pressure at all.

"You need that warm fire and comfortable seat more than I do."

"A woman, a guest, does not tell her host, a gentleman, what he ought to do." His heart was not in this admonition, and Miss Bennet knew it. She picked up a footstool and dropped it in front of him.

"Where I come from, a good friend will tell you when you are sick and need to rest, regardless of status and gender. And—and we are friends, are we not?"

Darcy shivered. It was entirely due to his feeling ill. "Yes, we are very good friends."

"Friends take care of one another when one is sick. And an even better friend will tell you to shut up and rest. Don't worry, everyone is out. And as far as they know, I'm writing letters to arrange my transatlantic crossing. I'm really keeping an eye on you."

He coughed before he spoke. "To what purpose?"

Before she replied, Reynolds entered, bearing a tray with tea, and another concoction that, by the smell, reminded him of childhood ailments. The two ladies shared a glance, and Darcy knew he was the victim of their scheming.

"Sir, if you do not drink that cordial, Mr. Easton has been instructed to force you to do so."

"I am not ten, Reynolds."

"Then you do not need the promise of a round cake to convince you to take it?"

Darcy swallowed roughly before speaking. "I could not eat one now, even if you put in extra sugar." He drank the bitter draught, and Reynolds left.

"Have you appointed yourself my nurse rather than pass the afternoon with Miss Bingley?"

She smiled and poured his tea. Miss Bennet was better at these domestic undertakings than she had been when she first arrived.

"It's a shame Jane didn't wander into Nine Ladies instead of me. You'll have to settle for a well-intentioned accountant who isn't so much in awe of your position to tell you to rest."

"Settle . . . for you?" Did she mean marry, to settle in to a domestic life with her? In his feverish state he might allow himself to entertain the idea.

"Is that another word whose definition has changed? I mean since you didn't get my sister-physician from the future, you'll have to be content with less, namely me."

"No one who has the pleasure of your company could find anything wanting." His eyelids were heavy, and he found it difficult to swallow.

"No more talking. Mr. Boyle is checking on Mrs. Willers, and then you get a turn. Let's do this." Darcy watched, both appalled and grateful, as Miss Bennet shoved forward the sofa until it was near to the fireplace, and took his hands and pulled him to his feet, turned him with surprising ease, and pushed him onto the sofa.

"I've gathered respectable gentlemen don't lie on sofas in 1811. Someone ought to tell Mr. Hurst, but then I've never thought he was a proper gentleman. Good thing I come from a place where it's acceptable to stretch out on the sofa when you're ill."

"A day lying weary and languid on the sofa will not get the weekly accounts reviewed."

Miss Bennet's voice lowered. "Mr. Willers is with his wife; he won't be meeting with you. She is very ill. I can tell your throat hurts, you're tired, and you have a fever and chills. Close your eyes and I'll read to you. I'm sick of Walter Scott and the newspapers, so you get to listen to *Self-Control*, which your little sister reads when Mrs. Younge isn't around. I gather it's a ridiculous romance."

Darcy closed his eyes as he heard a rustle of pages. A sweet, clever, sometimes satirical woman to sit by his sickbed and read to him. He shivered again. He would enjoy his good fortune, because he knew it would soon be over. One week left.

Mr. Darcy fell asleep before Montague de Courcy met Laura, and after that Elizabeth sacrificed her dignity to hide behind a heavy curtain before Mr. Boyle appeared. Apparently, the study was as good a place as any for a medical exam. She wanted to hear for herself what the doctor thought the sickness was so she could convince everyone to make sure Mr. Darcy followed the right advice, in case there was a chance to save him after all.

But all she heard was "a throat much inflamed, with a great deal of heat about the good sir, and a quick low pulse." The doctor trusted to the certainty and efficacy of sleep, and felt no alarm. Mr. Boyle promised to return the next day and left. Elizabeth remained behind the curtain, listening to Mr. Easton help a coughing Mr. Darcy to his feet and escort him to bed.

That was the fastest medical exam ever. Whatever this was, some people died and some recovered, and she knew Mr. Darcy would die this year. What could she do to save him? *Or does he die no matter what I do?*

"There you are," Georgiana said. Elizabeth started but managed to smile when Georgiana tiptoed farther into the room. "I, I wondered, if, if I may ask you something?"

Elizabeth nodded, but Georgiana paced the room in silence. She may not look like her brother, but their mannerisms were similar. Elizabeth repressed a desire to encourage her too strongly; she was shy, but in this world, Miss Darcy needed to be able to speak on her own. "You know you can say anything to me."

"I . . . I know you have begun preparations to return to the Canadas." Georgiana looked at her own hands, twisting them, and then stopped and held them behind her back, with her chin held high. Elizabeth smiled; the gesture was her brother. "However, I wondered if you might like to stay on at Pemberley."

"Stay?"

"Yes, I would be pleased for you to join me for as long as you are able. I, I value your friendship very much."

"Oh, I feel the same way." Georgiana was kind, and to help her come out of her shell and see what sort of young woman she became would be a joy. "But I am dependent upon Reynolds's and your brother's charity. My cousin cannot afford to keep me, and it would be improper to depend on Mr. Darcy." *I can't get a job here. Also, I would give my right arm for Tylenol and a real toilet.*

"Fitzwilliam is generous, and he has come to see you as a friend. He is more at ease with you than I ever expected him to be with a single woman."

"I cannot ask him to pay for my upkeep, no matter how much I enjoy being with you. Miss Darcy, I don't have two, um, two shillings to rub together. My father's family will not acknowledge me, my mother's family is dead, and I have to return to my friends in Canada."

"You have friends at Pemberley." Georgiana's eyes welled with tears.

Elizabeth put her arms around Georgiana, who stiffened in surprise, before leaning in and wrapping her arms around her waist. "I am sad to leave you too." Elizabeth squeezed the younger girl tighter. "May I call you Georgiana?" Elizabeth felt her nod. "Georgiana, I did not want to come to Pemberley. But, as it turned out, befriending you and your brother . . . honestly, it was the best thing to have happened to me."

"Miss Ben—"

"Call me Elizabeth." She gave Georgiana a playful shove, which earned a small laugh through the younger girl's silent tears.

"Elizabeth, I hoped, but I did not expect you to remain. You must promise this will not be your only voyage to England. I shall pay for your next voyage through the economy of my own private expenses, and I know my brother would not refuse you his hospitality."

A few hot tears fell on her own cheeks. How could she vow such a thing, knowing full well she would never see Georgiana again? "I would like nothing more, although it is not in my power to make you such a promise."

"You will write to me? I shall depend on your correspondence. You have given me a great deal of confidence and comfort; I shall be sad to lose it."

Elizabeth was ashamed of herself. She was so focused on leaving that she hadn't realized what she had come to mean to a lonely fifteen-year-old girl. Her throat closed, and Georgiana hugged her tighter. *What will happen to Georgiana when—if—Mr. Darcy dies? She probably marries the first man who shows her any attention.*

"Elizabeth?" Georgiana raised her head to look at her face. "Pray, write to me soon, and as often as you can."

"I will think of you often and will write when I can." Elizabeth resolved to write several letters and force Reynolds to dole them out over the next year, so Georgiana wouldn't feel abandoned.

"What will I do without someone, someone to remind me I am worthy, that although Mrs. Younge—"

"Stop! Georgiana, you are lovely, intelligent, and accomplished. You don't need me here to tell you that." Elizabeth paused; she supposed Georgiana *did* need someone to help her to believe in herself. "Promise me you won't be in a hurry to settle down. Promise me that no matter what happens, you will remember to not sacrifice your self-respect, remember that you are a worthy person, that your shyness is nothing you ought to be criticized for. That you can be strong and independent, if you choose it."

Georgiana nodded through her tears.

Elizabeth dashed away her own tears. "We must raise our spirits! I cannot spend my last days with you weeping." She looked into Georgiana's eyes as she gripped both of her hands. "We are going to laugh at Miss Bingley whenever we can, we are going to roll our eyes at Mrs. Younge when her back is turned, and we are going to sneak past Reynolds and get Cook to give us sweet cakes before we walk around the park."

Georgiana laughed. "I do not have your strength to walk the entire park. You had best wait for my brother to recover. I know he enjoys his walks with you."

Her heart skipped a beat. Those walks and curricle rides with Mr. Darcy were her saving grace in these backward times. "That is what the sweet cakes are for: to provide us with energy for a good ramble. When you are done with Mrs. Younge, we will make our escape."

While Georgiana resumed her lessons, Elizabeth went to the library's writing table and composed a letter for Georgiana, dated eight weeks in the future, as if she had just arrived in Canada.

CHAPTER TWELVE

JUNE 19, 1811
3 DAYS UNTIL SUMMER SOLSTICE

He had spent Monday and Tuesday in bed, but Darcy was determined to rise this morning. His throat was still sore, and he coughed often, but he did not feel as weak or feverish. He was not equal to his usual employments but sat in the music room to attend his sister's practice. Mrs. Younge did not praise Georgiana, but neither did she admonish her. Darcy then listened to his sister and Miss Bennet describe their rambles around the park, not understanding their private joke about the sweetmeats they found to sustain them on a vigorous walk. Not even Miss Bingley's jealous glowers could dampen his enjoyment of their genuine friendship.

But the day did not close as auspiciously as it began. Late in the evening, while playing cards in the drawing room, Darcy grew more hot, heavy, and uncomfortable than he had felt earlier.

"Darcy," Bingley whispered as he shuffled, "you need not remain for our sake. Take yourself off to bed."

"I am well."

"You are a bad liar."

Darcy cleared his throat. "My indisposition is only worsened by the fatigue of having been up all day. If I suffer the abysmal cordials prescribed, I will sleep well and be better tomorrow."

He only had a few days before Miss Bennet went through Nine Ladies to be swept forward two hundred years, never to be seen again. He was not going to allow a cold to prevent him from spending more time with her. He hoped to be improved enough so they could take a final curricle ride tomorrow. He would make the most of the time left with his friend.

"Darcy? Darcy, it is your turn."

Bingley's prompt pulled his eyes away from Miss Bennet and back to his own cards. *What was trumps?* He tried to speak, tried to swallow, and found it impossible. His cards tumbled from his hands. From the corner of his eye, before his lids closed, he saw Miss Bennet jump from her chair, calling out to Bingley to "catch him!" Darcy wondered what she was talking about before his vision went black.

JUNE 20, 1811
2 DAYS UNTIL SUMMER SOLSTICE

Elizabeth sat in the drawing room, holding Georgiana's hand. Bingley paced, having long given up offering words of encouragement. Mrs. Younge scribbled furiously, and Miss Bingley and Mrs. Hurst whispered to one another. Mr. Hurst was asleep. She found it odd that anyone other than Georgiana would be given Mr. Darcy's health information, but everyone else seemed to take it as a given.

Mr. Boyle entered to give the results of his examination. He was a thin man with sallow skin and dark lank hair who looked in need of a doctor himself.

"Miss Darcy, I am encouraged that Mr. Darcy will in a few days be restored to perfect health."

Georgiana heaved a sigh of relief. The others smiled and relaxed, but Elizabeth wasn't reassured.

"Mr. Darcy was not well last evening. Does he have the same illness as those here and at Lambton have?"

Georgiana tightened her grip on her hand and whispered, "Yes, Mr. Boyle, please tell us all you can."

The doctor shifted his feet. "There is a . . . slight fear Mr. Darcy's disorder *may* have a similar putrid tendency"—Elizabeth was the only one who did not share in the collective gasp—"but he is not a hopeless case."

"Mr. Darcy might have what killed the others?" she asked.

"I could not say definitively if this is the strangling angel of children. I do not wish to distress you—you in particular, Miss Darcy—but it *could* be a putrid infection."

The next few moments were a mixture of alarm and exclamations; Mr. Boyle promised to return tomorrow to examine the patient and left. Elizabeth watched the others' pale faces in complete confusion.

"Charles, we ought to go on to Scarborough earlier than we planned," exclaimed Miss Bingley.

"Darcy's physician said he does not assume . . . He may only have a bad sore throat."

The sisters shared a pointed glance. "If that were the case, Mr. Boyle would have said there was no infection in the complaint!" Mrs. Hurst cried.

"And the fact that a physician has been called speaks to the severity of his condition."

"I think, perhaps, we see what the physician says when he reexamines Darcy. Darcy may have a cold, and tomorrow will wonder where his friends have gone. Yes, I think it is best we remain. I understand from Mrs. Younge that a picnic has been planned. Miss Darcy, would you like to go on with the diversion?"

"But Charles—"

"I was speaking to Miss Darcy."

Georgiana opened her mouth but made no coherent sound. Elizabeth thought she might wish to stay with her brother and send the others off, but Mrs. Younge set aside her pen, walked behind her charge, and rested a firm hand on her shoulder. "A cheerful diversion is what Mr. Darcy would wish for us, and Miss Darcy looks forward to entertaining all of you—you in particular, Mr. Bingley."

Georgiana looked at Elizabeth, who gave her a weak smile. *Maybe keeping Georgiana occupied is best.* "I am sure your brother would like to hear about it when you sit with him later."

The others dispersed to change for the excursion, and Elizabeth found Reynolds crossing the lobby by the main staircase.

"Reynolds, did you hear?"

"Mr. Boyle is not without confidence that it is only an ulcerated sore throat."

"The rest of the room panicked when he said there might be a 'putrid tendency'?"

The housekeeper's frown lines appeared. "It is a general term to apply to all manner of infections with fevers. Many are fatal, but not always. It is too early to abandon hope."

"Did you write to Col—" Elizabeth stopped as a footman passed.

Reynolds lowered her voice. "I am not certain what you hope to accomplish, but I did, and referred to your vague comments. He is expected Friday afternoon."

Elizabeth hoped to say more, but the others traipsed down the stairs in their half-boots and parasols, and the servants assembled with the food and blankets. She would go along with the picnic to bolster Georgiana's spirits, and then tomorrow she would see for herself how Mr. Darcy was faring.

DARCY PASSED THE TIME AFTER MR. BOYLE LEFT WITH LITTLE OR NO alteration to his state. He knew he was feverish; his limbs felt heavy, his neck felt stiff, and he did not feel equal to being up and could not speak at length without coughing. None of this dissuaded his sister from sitting with him after dinner.

"My dear, you spent the entire evening at my side. I suspect"—he paused to cough—"I suspect the others have retired by now, and you need not avoid them."

"I am here out of sisterly regard and affection." Georgiana replaced the cold compress on his forehead.

"You are here to gain practice in being a nurse." He struggled to swallow; it took several tries.

"You jest; you do not believe that." Georgiana's smile faded.

"Fitzwilliam, you must get better. People in Lambton, and here at Pemberley . . ." She shook her head.

"I know how many children died, and Tom Gardener and the Taskers' shepherd and boy as well; and I know Polly and Mrs. Willers may not survive. A heartbreaking misfortune to those who loved them. We will help their families in any way we can."

After another coughing fit, causing him to struggle for air, Darcy saw Georgiana fighting tears.

"Why are you crying?"

"You cannot die! Miss Bingley and Mrs. Hurst fear a putrid fever and wish to be gone."

"I am not afraid of dying. Not of this illness, or ever. I am at peace with my own fate. Yet do not assume I am in immediate danger." His stern tone was lost in a rasping breath, but Georgiana composed herself. "It is late; you ought to retire."

She rose, but still hovered. Darcy knew that she would eventually come out with whatever was troubling her, so he waited. As his eyelids began to feel heavy, she said, "I invited Miss Bennet to stay for longer —for as long as she wished, in fact."

Darcy's low pulse quickened. Miss Bennet must have refused such a request; she could not continue in this time and be happy. "What was her reply?"

"She said she could not remain on our charity and must return to friends who are more obliged to maintain her. Fitzwilliam, is there anything I might say or do to influence her? I know that despite our different circumstances, she thinks of me as a true friend."

If you only knew how different those circumstances are. "I think Miss Bennet would stay if her situation allowed her more freedom. She is, however, dependent upon others. I do not expect to see her again."

"You do not oppose our friendship because she is poor and is of less consequence, do you? Or because her mother's family, however wealthy, was in trade?"

That might once have been the case. "Those truths would not deter me from welcoming her as your friend. Miss Bennet's disposition and abilities are equally worth all the friendship we may offer her."

"I desire her friendship. Do you not feel the same? You passed many hours with her when I was with Mrs. Younge."

Surely, it was the fever that made him feel so warm. "I am inclined to her company."

"She said I might call her Elizabeth." Darcy opened his eyes and saw his sister wore a smile. "I shall write to her, and she promised to write to me often."

What will she do, stand at Nine Ladies twice a year and toss letters into the center when the sun goes down? "You must not hold her to such a promise. The Canadas—" He coughed again, and closed his eyes. He felt his sister kiss his cheek, and he was asleep before the door closed behind her.

June 21, 1811
1 day until summer solstice

Elizabeth snuck into the smaller room adjacent to Mr. Darcy's bedroom. The door to his room was ajar, but she only had a view of the end of the bed. She knew it would reflect poorly on the Darcys if she were caught, but she had to know for herself what the doctor thought about Mr. Darcy's condition.

Mr. Boyle and Reynolds crossed her field of vision and disappeared. If she leaned a little farther, she could see the doctor's reflection in the mirror on the other wall. He must be standing next to the bed, at its head, looking at Mr. Darcy.

"I suspect you have cared for the good sir, Mrs. Reynolds."

"Along with his sister, we have cared for him, but given the others' illnesses, it seemed prudent to have you examine Mr. Darcy again."

Elizabeth saw in the mirror that Mr. Boyle peered over the bed, and now lifted something and held it, his wan face lost in concentration. *Taking a pulse, maybe?* Mr. Boyle moved away, and Elizabeth no longer saw his reflection. *If I can't see the doctor, he can't be examining Mr. Darcy.*

"Has the good sir slept fitfully? Were you feverish throughout the night?"

Elizabeth was too far away to hear Mr. Darcy's weak reply.

"I recommend you reduce the fever by bloodletting. Should you wish to call in a surgeon, it might reduce your overheating." Mr. Darcy's answer was lost in a cough. "Mrs. Reynolds, if *you* can convince him, releasing the excess blood may serve well in expelling the toxic substances causing his illness. Eight ounces should his fever not abate."

Elizabeth shuddered. Mr. Darcy asked something she could not hear.

"No, it is unlikely. You have some swelling of the neck, not unlike the others who were less fortunate, but you are not a hopeless case. You have been able to breathe without much trouble, despite the ulcerated throat?"

Is that just swollen lymph nodes and strep throat?

"I will return tomorrow. Remember, fresh air is fatal, and no solids after three o'clock, as a fever is generally the consequence. Please reconsider a good lance of bloodletting to keep the fever at bay."

"You cannot trust a word that comes out of that so-called doctor's mouth!" Elizabeth cried to Reynolds when she entered the dressing room after the doctor was gone. "He thinks fresh air is fatal!"

"He says it is not absolutely a putrid fever."

"I thought a doctor would know how to help Mr. Darcy." She assumed she just had to convince everyone of the seriousness of his illness and that they should follow a doctor's advice, but Mr. Boyle was useless.

"Those who live long lives tend to do so because they never took physic or saw a face of a doctor in their lives."

"These people still believe in miasma and out-of-balance humors, don't they? That doctor couldn't take an accurate pulse because your watches don't have second hands! We can't take Mr. Darcy's temperature because medical thermometers don't exist yet. That quack didn't even have a stethoscope!"

"What do you wish me to say? Of course Mr. Boyle did nothing but take his pulse, look at his neck, and suggest bloodletting. The hand washing I have encouraged is not enough to prevent an epidemic. All I can do is dissuade Mr. Darcy from bloodletting and ensure he rests. He is a strong young man who will recover."

Elizabeth wanted to scream, "He *is* going to die!" but the distressed look in Reynolds's face struck her. It would be cruel to rob her of hope. She could show Reynolds one kindness before she left.

"Of course." Elizabeth refused to give in to a sob in front of the housekeeper. "Mr. Darcy might pull through."

Elizabeth was resolved to say goodbye to him, to thank him for keeping her safe until the solstice. She was leaving tomorrow and leaving behind this society's strange etiquette and sexist rules. And the idea of not seeing Mr. Darcy one last time was unbearable.

IT WAS NOT UNTIL THAT AFTERNOON THAT ELIZABETH WAS ABLE TO SNEAK into Mr. Darcy's chamber. The bed curtains were drawn, and between the summer day, the roaring fire, and the closed windows, the room was stifling. Mr. Darcy was asleep, pale, and, despite the heat, he shivered underneath the covers. Elizabeth saw his neck was swollen, and his breathing noisy. She could hear Willie Collins's droning voice as he read, *"In 1811, the owner died without issue."*

"Mr. Darcy, I—" She sniffed and blinked her eyes. "Tomorrow is the solstice, and I'm going home. I had to see you one last—I had to say thank you." She kissed his cheek. She ached to do something more, to reach him in some way and take away his pain. "You're not that much of a jerk, you know. So, if this is just a cold, you'd better wake up so you can say goodbye."

I don't want to leave him like this.

Elizabeth wrung out a cloth from the basin and laid it on his forehead. It didn't matter to her any more if she was caught, so she stayed at his bedside. Elizabeth watched as Mr. Darcy, in his sleep, continually tried to change his position, and inarticulate sounds of complaint passed his lips. Elizabeth wondered if she should wake him from a sleep that seemed to be causing him pain when he suddenly awakened.

He started up hastily, trying to get out of the bed, as though he did not even see her.

"Stay in bed; you're not well."

With a feverish wildness, he cried out, "Has Mr. Wickham come?"

"I don't know who that is."

"He is a *liar*; spiteful and vicious. I paid him for the living years ago! All connection between us ought to be dissolved."

Elizabeth felt terror at Mr. Darcy's wild eyes. "Why don't you lie down?"

"He applied to me by letter for the preferment. Such a man ought never to be a clergyman." Mr. Darcy spoke in a desperate, hurried manner, with a rasping breath. Elizabeth finally convinced him to lie down. "He is not come to Pemberley?"

Elizabeth suppressed her alarm and tried to soothe him. "You're a little confused. Mr. Wickham isn't here, I promise." She placed a hand on his forehead, wishing for a thermometer. "You're not quite yourself."

"You are not leaving? 'Tis not the solstice yet, not for some weeks. Mr. Wickham must not come to Pemberley. I did as right by him as my conscience allowed; he is a cruel man."

Mr. Darcy rested his head against his pillow, and when he did, with his head tilted back as he tried to take in a full breath of air, Elizabeth thought she saw something. She grabbed his chin and peered closer. She could just see a gray membrane at the back of his throat. *What the hell is that?* "Mr. Wickham isn't here and he's not coming. You're dangerously ill." Her voice cracked. "I need to get Reynolds to send for Mr. Boyle." *For all the good it will do.* "I'm not leaving yet."

Mr. Darcy remained in a heavy stupor, and his fever was unabated. Mr. Boyle said he had some fresh application to try that Elizabeth did not understand. Georgiana sat silent through these discussions, and Mr. Boyle's visit concluded with assurances that reached the ears of everyone, but did not enter their hearts.

Mr. Bingley, who had been inclined to think his friend's complaint less serious than Elizabeth did, now looked grave. His sisters were now overcome with anxiety—not for the patient but for themselves.

"It is putrid sore throat, Charles! It is not prudent to remain."

Mr. Bingley sighed and covered his mouth, staring off into the distance. His sister continued, "His disorder has increased considerably. Louisa, speak sense to him!"

Mrs. Hurst looked up from fiddling with her bracelets. "Yes, there is no reason to remain if Mr. Darcy is dying."

Mr. Bingley glared at her, then looked at Georgiana, who had tears on her cheeks. "An illness, with varying degrees of danger, may last weeks."

"Did you not hear?" Miss Bingley now stood before her brother, forcing him to meet her eye. "Mr. Darcy has a bad chance of recovery. We ought to leave for our own health."

"I cannot! My closest friend is deathly ill."

"And we could be next!" Miss Bingley grabbed her brother's hand. "I insist we depart; our own health depends upon it. Mr. Darcy would not expect us to put ourselves at risk by staying in a house with infection."

"He would expect loyalty from his friends."

"What can we do for the invalid? Louisa and I ought not to be at his sickbed, and nursing does not belong to a man. You must keep *your* family safe."

Mr. Bingley considered her words. *Sweet guy, but he is easily led.*

And so, the Bingleys' and Hursts' flight from Pemberley was decided upon before Mr. Boyle's carriage passed the lodge. The ladies left to oversee their maids, and Mr. Bingley went to where Georgiana sat next to Mrs. Younge, lost in a daze.

"Miss Darcy? Would to heaven that anything could be said or done by my part that might offer consolation to your distress."

Georgiana managed to nod in acknowledgment. Mr. Bingley went on, "Would you care to join us at Scarborough? You are so young yourself; you ought not to remain where you might too become infected. Children succumb more often than adults, and you are welcome to remain with us until—well, until Darcy improves, of course."

"I will not stir from Pemberley so long as Fitzwilliam is ill."

Mrs. Younge and Mr. Bingley were taken aback by her firm refusal. Elizabeth, on the other hand, smiled. Mrs. Younge attempted to smooth over Georgiana's abrupt reply.

"Thank you, sir, but regardless of Mr. Darcy's health, our plans for the summer are fixed. We have an engagement with friends at Ramsgate. A little bracing sea air will do her good while her brother recovers. Mr. Darcy himself will wish his sister to leave a place of infection to return to her own establishment."

"Excuse me. I must see to Fitzwilliam's care."

As Georgiana left, Mrs. Younge and Mr. Bingley shook their heads in mutual confusion. Elizabeth repressed the urge to whoop, clap her hands, and yell, "Go, girl!"

Elizabeth did not learn of the extent of Mr. Darcy's decline until Colonel Fitzwilliam's arrival. He joined his young cousin in the sick chamber, and the two of them soon after came to share the news with her. Georgiana did not quit her brother's side when Bingley's party left Pemberley, but Elizabeth realized there was little she could do as Mr. Darcy passed hour after hour in sleepless pain and delirium.

The two cousins looked despondent. "I'm so sorry."

"Oh Elizabeth, I cannot even keep his fever down!"

Colonel Fitzwilliam cleared his throat before speaking. "This unexpected alteration in his state does not mean he is certain to die."

"I cannot bear it!" Georgiana cried. "I cannot sit by his side and watch him suffer when nothing I do helps him."

Elizabeth drew her arms around Georgiana and let her cry. "You do not have to. I know you love your brother and want to nurse him, but you don't have to put yourself through this." Elizabeth remembered Reynolds's story of how Lady Anne died horrifically with a fifteen-year-old Mr. Darcy at her side. She would not wish that on self-doubting Georgiana.

"I know not what to do! I have never nursed anyone, and I am so rarely sick myself."

"Georgiana." Colonel Fitzwilliam's voice was stern. "You are assuming the worst. Yes, Darcy is ill, but it is by no means certain he will die."

Elizabeth closed her eyes and held Georgiana tighter, knowing that if she looked at the colonel, she might give herself away. As such, she only heard and did not see Mrs. Younge enter.

"Mrs. Reynolds says you have not seen improvement in Mr. Darcy?" Georgiana only sniffled. Mrs. Younge pursed her full lips.

"You are not an experienced nurse; you could only prescribe him silence and quiet."

"I did try, Mrs. Younge."

"Despite your good intentions, you could not nurse a dormouse. Your brother's illness ought to be left to those whose exertions might prove some effect. And if there is the chance of a putrid infection, as one appointed to look after you, I insist we leave for your own health."

"Even if I do not nurse him, I ought to remain at Pemberley."

"Colonel Fitzwilliam, if Mr. Darcy has a putrid fever, do you not wish Miss Darcy away from a place of infection? To lose both Darcy cousins would be an insupportable loss to your family."

Elizabeth rolled her eyes. *Oh, she is good. Pull the strings and make them dance.*

Colonel Fitzwilliam nodded to himself and approached Georgiana, kneeling in front of her. "My dear, perhaps you ought to go to London. You plan to go to Ramsgate this summer, is that not correct? Your brother would wish for you to be kept healthy."

"Yes!" Mrs. Younge interjected. "Our plans for Ramsgate cannot be changed without a great deal of inconvenience to the friends we intend to meet there."

"My place is at Pemberley, is it not?"

Mrs. Younge shook her head. "We will go to London to keep you safe from infection. You must go to Ramsgate in August and September to meet your friends as I have planned. By the time you are there, your brother will be well enough to join us and complete his convalescence."

"I cannot think of sea bathing while—"

"Darcy would not risk your health for anything, my dear. You know what you mean to him; you are"—Colonel Fitzwilliam swallowed thickly—"You are his nearest relation. And if you are not able to remain in his sick chamber without sufferings that make you feel worse than helpless, why not be gone from here? Knowing you are safe from infection will be a comfort to Darcy; that is how you can best help him."

"Very well, if it will ease Fitzwilliam's mind."

Mrs. Younge declared they would be gone within the hour and left to arrange the packing of bags and order a carriage that Elizabeth suspected had already been readied.

"Elizabeth, what are his chances of recovery?"

She would not break down in front of Georgiana. "I think your brother wishes to keep you safe. He loves you above all else, even Pemberley." *Don't stay and watch him die. After watching his mother's horrific death, Mr. Darcy would wish to spare you that.*

Colonel Fitzwilliam took his cousin's hands in his own. "Go and oversee your packing like a good mistress. I promise to stay with Darcy, and I will come to London in ten days and give you a report on how he is improving."

Georgiana nodded and took a shuddering breath before leaving the room.

Elizabeth and the colonel were left to themselves, she on the sofa and he restlessly pacing. "To have such a good man cut off in the flower of his days is most melancholy. Poor Georgiana will feel his loss dreadfully."

"You just convinced Georgiana her brother might recover."

"I encouraged her to go to spare her from witnessing her brother's decline." He looked anxious.

"Miss Bennet, the images of Pemberley's ruins that you showed me are impossible to forget. Darcy is ill, and you ask Reynolds to tell me to come immediately and referenced those images. I am no fool. You comprehend more about Darcy's fate, and it cannot be good."

She shook her head and whispered, "It's not."

Colonel Fitzwilliam fell into the chair across from her, looking as though he was in pain. *Of course he's in pain; his cousin and best friend is about to die.*

"I visited the ruins and learned the owner died in 1811 without issue. Colonel, this infection will kill him. Once Mr. Darcy—" A small sob escaped her. "Once Mr. Darcy dies, Pemberley goes to Georgiana. She marries young, I don't know when or to whom, but she dies young and without children. Her husband, whoever he is, runs through her money and bankrupts Pemberley. It was in ruins for a hundred years before I ever visited it."

Colonel Fitzwilliam buried his face in his hands.

"I wanted every chance to save him to be taken, and I knew no one would listen to *me* so I had you come when he got sick. I thought there might be more to do for him and you could convince him to do what the doctor said. I'm so sorry!" Elizabeth began to cry in earnest.

After a stretch of silence, he said, "You take too much upon yourself. None of this is your doing, and you have been a comfort to Georgiana."

"We have become friends, despite her shyness. I will miss her when I go home." Tomorrow she would leave Mr. Darcy to his fate and go back through Nine Ladies. Back to Wi-Fi, indoor plumbing, refrigerators, proper health care, and the right to vote. She would have everything, but Mr. Darcy would be dead and everything he loved and cared for would be destroyed.

Health care . . .

Elizabeth stood. "I think I can save Mr. Darcy."

CHAPTER THIRTEEN

Elizabeth ran to the servants' hall as fast as her skirts would allow. Many were gathered around the table, not knowing what to do in their anxiety for their master. Reynolds looked up in dismay at the sight of her.

"Forgive me, but I must speak to you instantly somewhere." She went to the housekeeper's room to wait. Reynolds stalked into the room and shut the door, her lips set in a grim line.

"I know you are leaving tomorrow, but could you try to—"

"I think I can save Mr. Darcy's life."

"Putrid fever is not always fatal; it is more often so in children, but Mr. Darcy is a young man—"

"You know I'm from the future. Trust me when I tell you that he dies."

The housekeeper flinched as though she had been struck. Elizabeth started toward her, her hand outstretched in sympathy, but Reynolds backed away.

"I know medical care isn't perfect—we both know that—but something in 2011 could help him. He has a fever that won't lower, and now he has a gray patch at the back of his throat. How long before he gets weaker, can't breathe, and dies? That's why they call it the strangling angel of children, isn't it? Children aren't dying of putrid fever in 2011. What if penicillin can save Mr. Darcy?"

Reynolds took a long while to find her voice. "How could you know the fate of one man in one house in all the history of England? Nor can you be certain—"

"Save it. Let's talk to Colonel Fitzwilliam."

She had to convince them to agree. She was ashamed she hadn't thought of it sooner. *I can't live with myself if I do nothing.* They found Colonel Fitzwilliam pacing in the drawing room.

"Reynolds, I'll tell you what I told the colonel: I visited Pemberley before I traveled back in time, and it's in ruins. I've known all along that in 1811 Mr. Darcy dies, and soon after so does Georgiana. Her husband bankrupts you all, the land is parceled off, the house sold many times over, its contents stripped, and by the turn of the next century, Pemberley is an empty shell."

The stoic Reynolds began crying. "I do not know when I have been more shocked." Elizabeth felt a stab of guilt for so callously telling her Mr. Darcy, whom she loved as a son, was on his deathbed. Colonel Fitzwilliam handed her his handkerchief. "Do you, sir, believe her?"

The colonel held back tears. "I cannot explain how such pictures were created, nor can I explain the device that displayed them, but Pemberley, in her time, has only its exterior walls remaining. If that part of her story is true, and knowing what I know of Miss Bennet's character, how she has behaved in a manner peculiar to her simply because we asked her to, and how both Darcy and Georgiana admire her . . . yes, I believe her when she says Darcy will die."

"My poor boy," the housekeeper murmured.

"Tomorrow night is the solstice. I have antibiotics in my flat in Bakewell!" Reynolds glanced at the colonel; Elizabeth pretended to explain to both of them. "Antibiotics are medicines that fight infections. A doctor prescribed them to me when she thought I might have caught pneumonia. Mr. Darcy doesn't *have* to die."

Reynolds had stopped crying, her face resumed its usual façade. "This doorway only opens at sunset. There is no way to get medicine from Bakewell and return to Nine Ladies. You have but an instant; on the solstice you can only go forward in time, from now to the future. It is a one-way passage; you cannot come back tomorrow with the medicine."

"What if she returned on the equinox with the medicine?" Colonel Fitzwilliam stepped forward, eager hope on his face. "If there are medicines in the future that can cure him . . . Miss Bennet, I beg you to return—"

Reynolds interrupted, her voice flat with despair. "Colonel, how long do you think he has? We have all seen the course of a putrid infection if the patient's fever does not break. Mr. Darcy has a week at most. If Miss Bennet is correct, then Mr. Darcy would not live three months while we waited for her to return."

"I'm not talking about bringing medicine back for him. I'm talking about bringing Mr. Darcy *with* me."

They stared blank-faced. "All I have to do is get him home, and he can start a course of antibiotics tomorrow night. Then he just has to wait until the equinox to come back. Mr. Darcy, and those he trusted, protected me and helped me while I was trapped here. I can do the same for him in 2011."

Reynolds's expression was inscrutable as ever, but the colonel looked pensive. "How can you be certain this medicine will help him? To have him disappear forever if he goes forward in time only to die anyway . . ." He hung his head. "I would know the truth, but his friends, his family, for all they would know, he simply vanished."

"We have drugs that revolutionized medicine. And if what I have doesn't help, I'll take him to the hospital. Doctors are trained professionals who save lives." *I'll explain Mr. Darcy's presence somehow. Beg Charlotte to look the other way. Break into a pharmacy.* "I will do anything, *anything* to keep him alive!"

Colonel Fitzwilliam dragged his hand across his face. "You have no doubt that, in your time, Darcy won't die?"

"I have no doubt he will die if he stays." She gave them both a heavy stare. "I have never seen an infection like this. It has to be because in the future we have better ways of fighting infections than you have now. Not every disease can be cured, but he has a chance if he comes with me. If he stays in 1811 he will die."

"He will not wish to go," the housekeeper said without looking anyone in the eye. "He will accept it is his fate to die, and he would never use Nine Ladies for his own gain. Not when so many have died and nothing was done for *them*. You will not bring Mrs. Willers or Polly Brooks or the children into the future and give them lifesaving medicines. Mr. Darcy does not put himself before others who are under his protection."

"It's not because I don't care that I can't bring them. One person will be easier to explain than a dozen. More importantly, you know we can't divulge the truth about Nine Ladies. But Mr. Darcy already knows traveling through time is possible."

"He is not the sort of man to preserve his own life when his servants and tenants are dying, and innocent children are dying. That is not who he is." Reynolds's lips were pressed together so tightly Elizabeth wondered if they would bleed.

"He would save himself for his sister's sake," Colonel Fitzwilliam said. "Miss Bennet says Georgiana dies young, without children, and her husband is the one who leads Pemberley to destruction. She is Darcy's sole beneficiary. What if Georgiana marries someone she ought not to because her brother has died, and she is without his counsel?"

The housekeeper shook her head. "You are also her guardian, and you would never—"

"Perhaps he deceives us in his character or he is taken in by those who would lead him astray. Darcy would save himself if it would preserve his sister from an unhappy fate and protect Pemberley and all who depend upon it." The colonel's voice rose. "If Miss Bennet's time has medicines that could save him, and he has a means by which to return to us, why would we not take the chance? I would rather suffer his wrath at having chosen for him and beg his forgiveness after than bury him before the week is out. Darcy would forgive much if it saves Pemberley."

Reynolds walked to the window, covering her face with her hands. Elizabeth exchanged a glance with the colonel, then followed her. She touched her shoulder and whispered, "What is your name?"

"Sandra." Reynolds still did not look at her.

"Sandra, do you believe me when I tell you he dies and the Pemberley I know is a derelict shell?"

"Mr. Darcy would not meddle in the way things are meant to be."

Elizabeth lowered her voice. "You are the *last* person to talk about not meddling in the way things are meant to be. Why do you really not want me to bring him with me? He may have been a jerk to start out, but I misjudged him, and I *won't* let him die." Elizabeth gripped Reynolds's arm. "You love him like a son, and I'm telling you, Sandra, your boy will die if he stays here."

"What if he does not wish to come back?" Reynolds hoarsely whispered.

Elizabeth took both of Reynolds's hands in her own. "He'll come back to take care of Pemberley. And why would he want to stay in a world he won't be able to understand? Space shuttles, televisions, even cars and telephones will be mind-boggling. I can't stay here, and he won't want to be in the twenty-first century. But he's my friend," she said, choking on the word, refusing to give in to more tears. "I have to help him."

"Even if I did not approve, you would kidnap Mr. Darcy and bring him to Nine Ladies yourself."

Elizabeth smiled. There was the cold and rational Reynolds she knew. "I would rather do it with your help."

"We must be decided," Colonel Fitzwilliam cried. "Is Miss Bennet taking Darcy to where, to when she might save his life?"

"Yes, yes, I am."

SATURDAY, JUNE 22, 1811
SUMMER SOLSTICE, TWO HOURS BEFORE SUNSET

Darcy could not know for certain what was a fever dream and what was real. He knew he was hot, his body ached, and he had difficulty breathing. At times, he thought his cousin was at his bedside, prompting him to sign letters he did not remember writing. At other times, he was convinced that Miss Bennet held his hand and asked him to hang on for a little longer.

He rambled in thought and had visions that made no sense. He might have been awake or asleep when he heard his housekeeper's voice. Reynolds sounded distressed. It must be a dream; Reynolds was the most unexcitable person he knew.

"Colonel, Roland has set the fire near the stable block. We have a few moments to move him without another human being noticing."

"Has every servant gone to help? He is certain the fire will not spread? It will do Darcy no good if Pemberley burns to the ground."

"Roland has it under control. It shall hold everyone's attention for hours. We will say you took your cousin to your father's to convalesce before the fire started. Young Henry has the cart on the other side of the house. Was he alert enough to finish the letters after we stopped giving him the laudanum?"

"He managed to sign five before he fell asleep. I wrote one to Georgiana, to Mr. Willers, to Lady Catherine, to my father, and the last I leave at the bottom of a blank page for you to use as you feel necessary. We can date and post the letters over the next three months. If we can convince everyone he has gone to recover elsewhere, too weak to write, perhaps taking a cure in one place and then traveling to another, it will explain his absence for a short time."

Where am I going? I am not going anywhere, save to commit my soul to heaven.

"There could be gossip amongst his friends, and alarm amongst his family."

"Reynolds, it is either this or his death. He must go, and we shall suffer the consequence of deception. It is a small price to pay for a good man's life."

Darcy closed his eyes.

"On your feet, Darcy. I know you are ill, but you are not in a laudanum stupor any longer. Let us get you dressed and on your way." His arms were pulled and some clothes tugged off and others shoved on. He was too hot to care. "I need you to walk, because I will be damned before I carry you down all of those stairs. Rest against me; one foot in front of the other."

He leaned against his cousin and staggered down the corridor. He was struck by the comparative cold outside his stifling bedchamber. It sharpened his mind. When had Fitzwilliam come to Pemberley? Georgiana would be pleased to see him. Where was his sister? He was so hot, and by the time he collapsed on whatever hard surface he was now lying on, he mercifully fell asleep.

Now he imagined his head was in Miss Bennet's lap, her hand stroking his hair. It was no wonder he dreamed about her. She had woven herself into the threads of his life these past months. He hoped that when she left on the solstice, it would not tear him apart.

"Reynolds, I promise to keep him safe." The stroking hand ceased and rested against his cheek. "I won't let anyone know when he's from. What's this? I don't need money! You think I want *payment*?"

"I do not doubt your integrity. In two hundred years, these Georgian coins will be worth more to collectors than they are now. Cost must not be a factor in acquiring whatever treatment Mr. Darcy needs."

"I'm sorry. Thank you for everything. Will you give this to Georgiana? I wrote her a letter as if I arrived in Canada. I would hate for her to think I dropped our acquaintance. She is such a sweet girl. I wish . . ." The hand passed through his hair again.

"How will you explain your clothing? And how will you find your way from Stanton Moor to Bakewell? It must be four miles. He is barely in any condition to walk four yards."

"Costume party. Bus. I'll figure it out. Young Henry, do you have your grandfather's watch?"

"Aye, ma'am. You have five minutes. We had best get him into the circle."

The tree tops and Miss Bennet's brown hair flew out of his vision as he was pulled upright by a boy around Georgiana's age. Roland's grandson. And there was Reynolds, with red-rimmed eyes. *Why am I outside?* His throat was raw. "Reynolds, what is the matter?"

Mrs. Reynolds, who had known him since he was four and was his most devoted retainer, threw her arms around him in a brief but tight embrace. "Be careful, Master Fitzwilliam, and come back to us."

Another hallucination, naturally. He would not be outside if he were ill, and Reynolds had not hugged him since he was a child. Still, he hugged her back, and a choked sob escaped her. Fever dreams were strange.

"No, Henry, that's far enough; I don't want to risk your coming by accident. Mr. Darcy, lean on me."

His chest tightened as though he could not get enough air. After a while, the figure helping him to keep his balance stopped, and Darcy looked around. His mind imagined an uncultivated, sedge-filled vista, the sun almost below the horizon. There were sapling birch trees surrounding him and, as his eyes slowly took in what was nearer, he saw gritstone blocks a few yards away.

An arm around his waist adjusted its grip; he swayed on his feet. His arm was on Miss Bennet's shoulder. Of all the people he knew, living and dead, why imagine her?

"Miss Bennet?" *My throat hurts so much and it feels as though it is closing.*

"Don't talk. I know you're sick and weak. After we get there, you won't have far to walk until I get us a ride, I promise."

He was in no condition to travel on horseback. "Where are we going?"

"I can't even begin to answer that."

Tuesday, June 21, 2011
9:21 p.m. summer solstice
Nine Ladies

Darcy slowly realized that the pounding he heard was drumming. It was not until he brought his hand up to press against the bridge of his nose that he realized he was on his back, and he was outside. He was outside, on the ground, a chorus of nonsense thundered in his ears, and someone drummed a primal beat. When he finally rose, his vision blurring, even in the dimness he saw pockets of small fires and strange domes of varying sizes and colors dotted what little of the landscape he could make out in the darkness.

It was dark, he was burning, there were clusters of fire here and there. *Why am I in hell?*

"You got up on your own. Mr. Darcy, hey, no, no, stay up! Lean on me. We have to *go*."

He knew that assertive, female voice. An arm tugged his, and he staggered a few steps before regaining his balance. He heard a dog barking and the amused shrieks of children. He turned toward the sound and saw three people each twirling a stick alight at both ends while a small crowd watched and clapped. *Not hell, still hallucinations.* The arm around his now moved around his waist and hauled him forcefully and he staggered until he collided with someone.

"Oy, missy! Your friend have one too many?"

"No, no, he's got a headache, sorry, excuse us."

They walked farther through the blackness before Darcy realized the form next to him was Miss Bennet. She stopped and craned her neck. "Damn it, I'm all turned around in the dark. Let me get my bearings."

Darcy looked around. A man was near to one of those fabric domes with a flap door demanding an oak tree communicate with him. *Is that a tent?* The silver-white of the birch trunks behind them stretched higher than they did a moment ago. Darcy walked a few paces on his own to lean against a tree. Not far beyond him he heard a group of ladies discussing pixies and the influx of unusual energy. *What could explain such hallucinations?*

"Hiya, all right there? You shouldn't be this far from camp without a torch. If you're headed out, you ought to take this."

Darcy did not recognize this voice and was not inclined to speak to a stranger, even if it was one he conjured in his own feverish flight of fancy.

"You are absolutely right! Thank you so much. We came out here on a lark to see the sunset and we're not prepared for a camp-out."

"I can tell." The voice sounded amused. "You're dressed right smart for a druid solstice celebration."

Miss Bennet gave the falsest laugh he had ever heard from her. "We should've stayed at the, uh, costume party. Listen, my friend is—he's got a migraine, and I'm trying to get to Stanton-in-Peak. We need to catch a bus to Bakewell. Could you point me in the right direction?"

A new female voice joined the man. "Your friend doesn't look good. Does he want paracetamol? I have some in my purse."

Darcy lost the flow of the conversation as he felt a burning heat wrap itself across his body. The man talked about a "car" and leaving now that the sun had set. The woman talked of it being no trouble and they were to go on to Sheldon in any event. And then he felt a hand on his cheek; he did not open his eyes until another hand pried his lips apart.

"Take this; swallow it whole." He grimaced, but complied. He was too tired to argue with his own fantasies. "It'll lower your fever. We're going for a drive. I'm throwing away all common sense and getting into a car with strangers." She gave a frenzied laugh. "This is how horror movies start. We're going to walk a little farther and take a, um, carriage ride."

He wanted to lie down, in his own bed, and if he was to die there, then so be it.

"Look at me! Right here, that's it. A short ride, some medicine, and then you can rest. I know you're sick, but please, we have a little farther to go and I can't carry you. Hey, do not pass out!" A hand tapped roughly against his cheek. "Look at me!" He did, and saw the most terrified brown eyes he had ever seen. Miss Bennet's fine eyes. He nodded, not understanding what his imagination conjured.

At one point he was certain he was flying, and when he woke from another fever dream, he heard Miss Bennet curse at a door while she struggled with a key. *How did I get here?* He was pushed to recline on a sofa that was too short for him. He hit his head against its arm, and his cringe was rewarded with a pillow shoved under his neck. Another bitter tablet was pressed into his mouth, followed by a glass of water held to his lips.

"I'm supposed to give you one every six hours, but let's go with two pills to start."

Another pill, another drink of water. He closed his eyes, vaguely aware that through some power, not his own, his legs were shifted to dangle off the other edge of the sofa and his shoes pried from his feet.

"Sorry, but I can't get you up the stairs. I'll wake you for the next dose in six hours. I'll be right here the entire time. Try to sleep." A gentle hand ran through his hair. Sleep. That was one thing he could comprehend.

CHAPTER FOURTEEN

JUNE 22, 2011
BATH STREET, BAKEWELL

Darcy uncurled himself from a sofa and pushed himself upright, his long legs falling to the floor with a thud. He appeared to be in an incredibly small parlor with a fireplace that had been rendered useless by its being bricked over. *That is peculiar.* Darcy looked around, fixing his attention on the square pillow that was beneath him all night. A faded Union flag was painted on it, with the words "God Save the Queen" printed across it.

Damned foolish mistake to make at all, let alone to keep the finished product.

He then noticed Miss Bennet asleep on the other sofa, with her skirt hitched up displaying her bare feet. Her stockings and shoes were in a heap before her. Darcy caught his reflection in the mirror above the unserviceable fireplace. He looked wretched. He had not shaved in days and his skin was wan, his lips chapped. His wavy hair was plastered down from sweat.

Why did Miss Bennet and I sleep in a strange parlor? Her reputation would be destroyed if anyone learned of this, and his would be little better. Perhaps they had been deemed too ill to remain at Pemberley and were moved to prevent the illness from spreading. He was about to wake Miss Bennet to ask her when he caught sight of a slim rectangular box attached to the wall, slightly below his eye level. It was large, black, framed, and just shiny enough to reflect a dim image. Impossibly smooth cords came out behind it and went into the wall.

He gave the front a tap with his fingernail. It was not quite like glass. "What in the—"

"You're awake!" Miss Bennet ran her hands across her face and rose. "I woke you around six for another dose of antibiotics and acetaminophen. You were still out of it. After that your fever broke and you slept better. I guess I fell asleep too." She gave a great yawn and came closer to peer into his face. "How do you feel?"

He took a breath with only some difficulty, swallowed without great agony. "I am somewhat improved, thank you. Where—"

"I don't know how you even walked with that fever. I took your temperature while you were asleep. One hundred and four! I didn't want to wake you for another dose even though it says to take it every six hours; you were sleeping so peacefully."

She walked to the dresser beneath where the black box was suspended and selected a garishly orange vial with a white lid. She shook out a pill and held out a glass of water. "You seem better already. I think this will actually work!"

Darcy shook his head. "What to heaven is going on? I had the most peculiar fever dreams, and I now suspect I am still in one."

Miss Bennet puffed her cheeks and blew out a loud breath. "I hoped to hold off a while longer." She set them on the dresser and walked away, fiddling with her fingers. "I couldn't leave you to die once I knew I had something"—she pointed to the vial—"that could save your life."

His fever was gone, his mind once again sharp, but Darcy felt his stomach drop to the floor. "Where on God's green earth are we?"

"Bakewell." She drew out the word as would a guilty child.

"Do not try my patience!"

She rolled her eyes. "You're welcome, by the way. Here's the truth, but don't freak out. I mean, do not panic and act in an unusual—"

"I comprehend the word 'freak'!" His patience was a slowly cracking layer of ice.

She made a thoughtful sound. "Really? I always assumed 'freak' was a modern—"

"Where are we?" he cried.

Darcy watched her throat bob as she swallowed. "It's not the where that's important . . . so much as the *when*."

Darcy blinked, hard. One must be inside Nine Ladies at sunset on the solstice to move forward in time. He had been in his bed at Pemberley. No one in any sort of right mind could tell him how this was reality. Then again, he could not be certain what was real and what was a fever-driven fantasy.

"Mr. Darcy, sit down. You're weak, and I don't think you've eaten in days."

He shook off her hand and stepped away. Flashes from his feverish mental wonderings came back to him. His cousin dragging him out of the house. Reynolds embracing him. The gritstone blocks. The darkness, the drumming. Miss Bennet pressing bitter pills into his mouth. *Those hallucinations could not have been real!*

"We . . . are you telling me we *both* entered Nine Ladies?"

She nodded. "Welcome to the twenty-first century."

His indignation of being abducted against his will made him breathless with anger. "By what right did you *abduct* me from my sickbed and force me forward in time?"

"Excuse me? I believe what you're trying to say is 'thank you.' You don't realize what was at stake."

"What abominable folly compelled you to bring me with you?"

"You weren't on your sickbed, you were on your *deathbed!*"

For the sake of hearing her explanation, he contained his outrage and asked, through a clenched jaw, "Why did you presume I was to die? Not all who come down with a putrid infection are killed by it. And *if* it was through Providence that I die, what is gained by compelling me forward two hundred years to have me die *here*?"

Miss Bennet glared with all the fury her fine eyes could project. "I knew before I ever went to Nine Ladies that Pemberley's owner died in 1811."

Darcy started, and a chill went through him. The progress of his feelings about knowing the certainty of his own death was rapid. Doubt gave way to anger, and then ultimate acceptance led to confusion. "Why have you brought me here to die rather than let me die among my own people?"

Miss Bennet gave him a pitying look and held out the orange vial. "Is this what you think of me? How could I let you die and then come back to a time with antibiotics?" She shook the bottle and rattled its contents, as though the sound was to help him understand. "When I'm from, when you get an infection—most of the time—you go to the doctor and get a cheap pill that kills it. Mr. Darcy, you've had a turnaround in a *day*. I started you on a course of erythromycin in time to combat whatever putrid fever is. You didn't have to die after all."

He had a feeling of terror, and not a small amount of indignation at having lost the power of choice over his own fate. "You have shown alarming arrogance in bringing me here. It is not your place to decide who shall live and who shall die."

"You would rather have *died*? You would rather have left Pemberley without an heir, left Georgiana alone, rather than be cured here, all for the price of staying in 2011 for three months?"

"Your traveling to my time was an accident and not your choice, and your returning home was just, but your audacity in bringing me with you is beyond the pale. If, *if*, Miss Bennet, I was to die, then so be it."

"If you want to follow the divine providence argument, then maybe I was meant to go back to save you." She crossed her arms over her chest.

"Why preserve *my* life and not one of the others? I may have my pride, but I am not so arrogant as to assume that Providence would dictate *my* life be spared over another's. I would never have done as you have done."

"Do you remember your mother's death?" Her voice shook. "Wouldn't you have done anything to save her from suffering? If you *knew* that going forward in time there were medicines to save her, would you have done nothing?"

His parents' deaths were long and painful. One peaceful at its end, the other brutal, but both were drawn out enough for him to foolishly hope for some medicine, some cure, some *thing* at the last that might yet save them.

She stepped closer. "Your parents knew time travel through Nine Ladies was possible. Look me in the eye and tell me you wouldn't have brought them here if you knew it meant they didn't have to die!"

Darcy closed his eyes.

"That's what I thought. So hate me if you want, but it's going to be a miserable three months if I have to listen to your sanctimonious 'Miss Bennet, how dare you meddle' crap until you go back."

Angry tears fell from Miss Bennet's eyes. His throat was sore, but not as bad as it had been. He could not be overflowing with gratitude —he was trapped where, when he did not belong. His head pounded, and he felt unsteady on his feet. "I could never hate you. I am not ungrateful. I am"—he looked around the room—"bewildered, weak with illness, in a place I fear I cannot understand."

"Now you know how I felt when Reynolds locked me up, why I was desperate to talk to someone who could give me answers." She gave him a sad smile.

"Forgive me for judging you harshly, both then and now." Miss Bennet nodded. For all their disagreements, they had developed an easy manner between them. What sort of woman, of person, would be so generous to do what she did? He had been terrified for both his own reputation and for her safety when she appeared at Nine Ladies. "What risks have you undertaken in bringing me here, and will you come to regret it?"

"How could I have left you to die once I realized something so simple"—she held the orange vial—"could save you? I know your rules for social interactions are different than mine, but I thought we were friends."

"Your loyal efforts on my behalf amaze me. And we *are* always good friends. Do you realize the responsibility you have taken? How will you explain me to your servants?"

"First thing to learn about 2011: no one has live-in help. And no, that doesn't mean I'm poor or not equal to you. There's no one else here but you and me."

"You mean to tell me it is acceptable for a single young lady to live alone?" Another realization struck him. "You are responsible for every household task?"

"Don't worry, I'll teach you how to use the washing machine."

He had no idea what that meant and, at this moment, could not care. His body ached, and he could not remember when he had last eaten. In a conciliatory gesture, Darcy pointed to the vial and said, "How many of those am I to take to rid me of a putrid infection?"

"One, every six hours, for two weeks. Maybe your never having an antibiotic will be in our favor. You're probably hungry. No solids after three because it might cause a fever! Your doctors were morons."

Miss Bennet left the room, and Darcy swallowed the small pill. He was reconsidering the shiny black box when he heard the sound of retching. He followed the sound to a room scarcely wide enough for two people to stand next to each other. A silver cabinet stood to one side, illuminated from within and its door ajar, and Miss Bennet braced herself against a sink, her head bent over it.

"Are you well?" he asked in alarm.

Miss Bennet exhaled a long breath. "I'm fine. I mean, I am well enough. Can you shut the fridge, please?"

Darcy looked to the unadorned silver door and pushed it closed. Miss Bennet gave a shudder, then pulled a crinkled sack from a drawer and opened cabinet doors, glancing at the containers within before selecting some to remain and most to be tossed in to the sack. "What has happened?"

"Imagine if the unpreserved food in Pemberley's larder was left for three months." Miss Bennet gave the silver cabinet a glare. "That appliance is a refrigerator, like Pemberley's ice house. Here, the only edible thing I could find were crackers."

Only hunger compelled him to choke down several. He looked around the narrow room, the flat surfaces, the cupboards that allegedly held food, and the cold-keeping box. Darcy stared at the metal box on the other end of the room, with a door with a window on its front, and a twisting of raised iron on the top adjacent to a row of circular handles.

"It's the oven and a range." Miss Bennet noticed his gaze. "Charlotte tells me the English call them cookers."

Darcy looked around the room again. "This is a kitchen?"

Miss Bennet was about to pop a wafer into her mouth, but stopped and stared at him. "This is going to be so hard." She tossed the wafer onto the plate, edged past him, and left. He followed her to the parlor.

"How can I let you out of the house where you could talk to someone and they realize you don't know what room the kitchen is? You have no ID, no papers to prove that you belong, and they'll think you're crazy if you can't explain how a stove works or what a fridge does! You could end up in a mental institution, a lunatic asylum, and there's nothing I could do to get you out!"

He gave her a wry smile. "Then you can comprehend my fears and initial desire to keep you hidden when you first appeared in my time."

Her shoulders fell and she nodded knowingly. "I forgive you. At least there are no servants or family to trick this time, and until I'm sure you're not contagious, it's a good idea for you to lie low. That will buy us time to get you up to speed." In response to his raised eyebrow, she said, "I think it best you stay where no one can see you until you're healthy and know more about the twenty-first century. You ought to rest; yesterday we were certain you were going to die."

He did wish to retire; he was exhausted. Darcy glared in the direction of the small sofa on which he had passed the night. "You do have bedchambers in the year two thousand and eleven, do not you?"

"We do, but last night you were a feverish mess who outweighs me by at least seventy pounds, so be thankful I got you inside at all."

"I am," he replied honestly. While he would not have chosen to save himself, he could not deny that he was glad to be alive.

He followed Miss Bennet up the stairs, where she gestured toward a room with hideous wallpaper. "That's my room. Your chamber is across the hall, and the bathroom is there. No pots under your bed anymore." She pointed to a small room with black and white square tiles on the floor and smaller, green tiles up the wall. "I'm going to let you figure it out for yourself. You're out of your time, not stupid."

He was surprised by how tired he was by climbing one set of stairs. He breathed only slightly easier than he had yesterday and was still weak. The bedchamber was more familiar. Miss Bennet pulled down fabric to cover the window, and pointed to the lamp on the bedside table. He now saw it was not filled with oil. "We'll cover electricity later, but for now, turn this for the light to come on, turn it in the same direction to snuff the light." Darcy nodded, too tired to investigate the strange light source now.

"I'm going to take a long shower, and then I'm going out. At least I paid Professor Gardiner for six months' rent. We need food, and I need to charge my phone and make sure my bills were automatically paid, and after *that,* I have people to call to try to explain why I disappeared for three months. I guess that's one good thing about my mom and sister hating me? They may never even know I was missing."

All he understood was that Miss Bennet intended to leave her card with her acquaintances and go to the market. He found the perch on the lamp and turned it. The room fell into darkness. In a moment, he was underneath the bed clothes and fell into a deep sleep.

"THOSE CANNOT BE PROPER CLOTHING."

"You're not going *out* in them. I've never met Mr. Gardiner, but he's clearly as tall as you are, so they will fit. These will do until I can get to a store."

"I shall not wear them."

"Your clothes are gross!"

"You cannot mean vulgar, so how can there be a total profit in one's clothes?"

"You know your nineteenth-century clothes are dirty. You've sweated a fever into them, walked across a moor in them, and slept in them."

Darcy coldly withdrew his eye from Miss Bennet and glanced at the alleged clothing. "The blue shirt's sleeves stop above the elbow!" The stockings were thick and too short. And the dense cotton gray trousers were an unspeakable horror. She was dressed in a similar shirt and loose, black trousers. He attempted not to stare at Miss Bennet's legs.

"You must wear something clean and appropriate, at least until I buy you ready-made clothes that you'll like better."

It will not do to act as a petulant child. "Why does the shirt not have sleeves if there is no coat to be worn over it?"

"You'll have to get used to not having every inch of your body covered unless you want people to think you have a contagious skin condition."

Darcy silently took the strange collection and stalked past her into the room she called the bathroom and shut the door. No dressing rooms, no servants, and no hope of being decently clothed until September.

A small price to pay for my own life.

He did marvel at the water pump that brought in fresh water and the pipes that took away the used water. There must be an elaborate town-wide system of supply and drainage pipes. To bathe by which hot water poured from above like a powerful fall of rain was extraordinary.

My kingdom for my valet and a flat razor. He was not pleased with the result of the pink multi-blade razor Miss Bennet had left. His new clothes he dare not consider for long, his bare arms not fit to be seen in public. He would wear his morning coat over the shirt that had sleeves as short as a woman's evening gown.

Darcy descended the stairs and heard Miss Bennet talking; Darcy gripped the railing hard. He had not expected to encounter someone from this time so soon. Darcy hovered in indecision to enter or leave. For a strong-minded man, it was a dreadful feeling.

"You said don't talk to you until I was coming home." A short pause. "*You* sent four texts in three months! Two of which said 'hey'. I might have been dead, for all you knew."

Miss Bennet came to the doorway. She must have heard him and beckoned with one hand to follow her while she held a small black box along her jaw. She was alone. He sat and watched Miss Bennet shake her head and roll her eyes. *Her travels through time have addled her mind!* She was having a conversation with herself.

"All you've ever wanted is to please Mom. And Mom hates me for coming to England to see our father, so to stay in good with her, you had to ignore me too."

Miss Bennet paused her angry discussion with herself to point to a box on the floor. She brought the small box away from her ear and whispered, "I'll be done soon. You can find something to read in there."

She resumed. "It's not like you called *me*! Guess how many times Mom contacted me since I left the States? Zero! She said if I didn't sever all connection with *that man*, I would be a stranger to her."

The torrent of emotion coming from Miss Bennet made Darcy long to be elsewhere. If he could not afford her actual privacy, he could at least provide the appearance of it. In searching for a book, Darcy lifted out a small frame. It was the most realistic painting he had ever seen. It was of a younger Miss Bennet, and she stood next to a woman wearing a robe and cap not unlike what he had worn as a gentleman commoner at Oxford. The other woman was shorter, had fairer hair, and smaller eyes, but she was very like Miss Bennet.

He was captivated by the image behind the plate of glass. The paint was more vivid than oil and appeared to have no texture, but the artist captured Miss Bennet's likeness with perfection. He only tore his eyes away from the vivid color and realistic rendering when Miss Bennet began crying.

"I'm sorry too. I wasn't choosing our father over you. I had so many questions, but now I'll never know why—Stop crying, it's okay, Jane. I'm glad you don't hate me."

Darcy thought he heard muffled words when Miss Bennet was silent. When he realized he could be, inexplicably, eavesdropping, he set down the portrait and picked up the first book he found: *Samuel Taylor Coleridge: The Complete Poems*. He could not explain why its orange cover was thin and pliable, or why there was a penguin on it, but it was a comfort to read something familiar in this strange place.

This Lime Tree Bower My Prison. That was appropriate. *I am separated from my friends, and who can imagine what I will miss while I am trapped here*. In what ways would they move on with their lives, and how would he find Pemberley when he returned?

"No, I'm going to stay until his house sells. I'll be here through September."

He could not dwell on loneliness or what he would be deprived of in 2011. He was alive; his time here would be a prison of his own making only if he allowed it to be. Miss Bennet managed her time at Pemberley admirably, after her first difficult weeks. He would follow her example and not fall into melancholy. Darcy selected another poem.

ON TAKING LEAVE OF____1817
To know, to esteem, to love and then to part,
Makes up life's tale to many a feeling heart!
O for some dear abiding-place of Love

Darcy stopped and looked again at the title. This poem had yet to be written, as far as he was concerned. *Can I learn enough about this world to be a passable citizen, and yet not learn anything that gives me an untoward advantage when I return?* He closed the book and tossed it on top of a pile of assorted Shakespeare works.

"I love you." Darcy's breath returned when he realized Miss Bennet spoke into the box and not to him. That Miss Bennet might somehow be having a conversation with someone not present was the strangest thing he had ever laid eyes upon. "I promise we'll talk every week. I guess I was sad, and angry. Right, grief does strange things to people. Bye."

Miss Bennet lowered the box and touched it once. "Sorry, I was talking to my sister. I don't know if I should be pleased or insulted at how easy it was to explain a three-month absence." She gave a smile that could at any moment give way to tears.

"How is that possible?"

"I know! Can you imagine going three months without writing to Georgiana? We planned that for you, you know. You may not remember, but your cousin had you sign your name to letters he wrote as though you dictated them."

Darcy shook his head. "No, how is it possible to converse with your sister who is on the other side of the world?"

"Among other things, this is a telephone. Everyone carries one, and each phone has a unique identifier, a telephone number. I input my sister's number, her device rings, and she answers it, the two phones are connected, and we can speak to each other."

"How does it work?"

"It converts my voice to an electrical signal, and then it's sent over radio waves to the nearest cell tower. Those towers transmit the signal to the other person's phone, and the computer in that phone converts the signal back into sound."

"What are radio waves? Or an electrical signal, for that matter?" Darcy suspected she did not mean electrical in the sense that amber gave off electricity when it was rubbed. He hated feeling ignorant.

"Don't worry about it."

Her weary tone tried his patience. "If every person in England has one and carries it on his person, then I ought to know how it works."

She handed it to him, then sat next to him. "Technology is taken for granted. It's more important you can identify a phone or a refrigerator and know how to use it than explain how it operates."

Darcy touched the button, there was nothing else to do, and a picture reappeared with the time and date. The instructions said to "slide to unlock." Darcy touched the word "slide" and pushed the word along as though it were a tangible block on a path. When it would go no farther, he lifted his finger and the picture changed to one with a series of squares.

"You just opened the lock screen and went to the home screen," Miss Bennet explained. "Instead of going to their house to make a call in person, you're using this to speak to them."

Its brightness was an assault on his eyes. After a moment, he focused his gaze on the bottom, and saw the words phone, mail, a word he did not know, and music. He touched the curved image above the word phone, and numbers appeared. The concept was clear.

"If each person has a telephone with an identifying number, I must touch the numbers in sequence to connect this telephone with theirs? And their telephone will ring like a doorbell, and when they respond, our telephones are connected and we can converse?"

"You got it."

Miss Bennet explained how to answer a "call," how to make messages instantly appear on another person's phone, and how to capture and view images like the one in the frame. She was about to use what she called a camera to take his picture, but he refused. He cited his peculiar clothing and illness, but, in truth, he did not think there ought to be a record of his having been here.

"Mr. Darcy, now you're a passable millennial. I'll buy you an inexpensive prepaid phone."

"I have no need for one. I cannot communicate with any who might wish to speak to me."

He thought of his sister, how at best those who loved him would think he was in isolation, and at worst might assume he was dead. Miss Bennet placed a hand on his arm, giving it a gentle squeeze. None of his own time, save perhaps Georgiana, would act so familiarly, but he found it a comfort from Miss Bennet.

"I know how it feels to miss them," she said softly. "As far as the phone, if I reconnect with Charlotte, it's likely you will meet more people. Anyone could ask you to look something up and you'll be expected to pull out your phone and do it. We'll go over the internet later. Just imagine if all the knowledge in Pemberley's library and more was available at the touch of your fingertips."

Miss Bennet took a white cord and pressed it into the phone. "I need to charge the battery." Darcy knew well enough she did not mean a unit of artillery or a thrashing, but did not care enough to ask. "I bought groceries while you slept. There's soup if your throat still hurts, but I'm going to have a sandwich. Watch me so you can learn." She walked past him toward the kitchen.

"Learn what?"

"An English person would eat a cheese and pickle sandwich. Your other choice is canned soup. Or starve. Plates and bowls are in that cupboard, utensils there, cups up there." *I must purchase my own food, prepare it, and carry it to the dining table myself?* He supposed he would also have to wash the dishes and put them away.

"What do you think of tomato soup and potato chips?" she asked later as they ate in the stark dining room.

"This food is a necessary evil. It would be churlish of me to return your kindness in saving me by starving to death."

"Oh, come on!" she cried, wiping her fingers on a napkin made of paper. "Every meal in 1811 was saturated with cream, butter, or cheese, and red meat was everywhere. Your arteries are likely clogged."

"I prefer to not eat with my hands. I cannot abide not dressing for dinner. I am appalled that one must be responsible for every task related to cooking and cleaning. And none of this would constitute a proper meal for the lowest girl of all work at Pemberley."

Miss Bennet stared at him a long moment. "I spent enough time in 1811 to know insulting your host by complaining about the meal is beneath a gentleman like you." She took their dishes into the kitchen. He heard the sound of water and the noisy clatter of dishes.

Darcy sighed and rubbed his eyes. He could not allow the strangeness of this place make him forget who he was. Losing his patience with his hostess, his friend, a friend who saved his life, was against his character and good breeding. It did not matter that in 1811 a gentleman would never do what could, and ought, to be done for him.

He went into the kitchen and saw Miss Bennet placing the used dishes into a basket she rolled inside a cabinet before lifting its door closed. She did not meet his eye, and he saw the set of her jaw. Darcy would live in this small establishment for three months, and he owed it to his friend to be gracious.

I owe it to myself to remember who I am.

When she looked his way, he gave her a small bow. "Thank you for the meal. Is there anything I might do to help you?"

She looked surprised, then he saw the playful sparkle in her eyes that he admired. "I'll let you help with breakfast tomorrow. You'll be pouring cereal and loading the dishwasher like a pro before you know it."

He hardly understood her, but he knew that he was forgiven. They went to the parlor, where Miss Bennet reminded him to take another dose of the pill to cure him. His throat still bothered him, he was often breathless, and he tired sooner than he wished to admit. Miss Bennet invited him to read while she used her phone to "look something up."

"Those were my father's books. He couldn't communicate, but he understood everything. I read to him every day. I think Cowper was his favorite, and there's Shakespeare and *Paradise Lost* too."

That was why she always spoke better about books than other subjects. "All of these works are well-known at the turn of my century. How fortuitous that you recently read them to your father."

"I suppose." She did not wish to discuss her father. For his part, Darcy was content to pass the evening quietly.

At least Cowper was dead when I left. I am not going to stumble across another poem not yet written.

An hour later, he heard an oath from Miss Bennet. She looked at him with horror. Miss Bennet swung her trouser-clad legs down from her sofa and leaned forward, placing her elbows on her knees. He tried not to cringe at seeing a lady move and sit so oddly.

"I know what's wrong with you."

"Other than my brief loss of good manners this evening, I was not aware you found anything in my behavior lacking."

"I mean I know what sickness you have. What you *really* have."

"I have a putrid fever; that was never in question."

"I mean what we would call it now. It can be so hard to talk to you." Miss Bennet gave a small smile.

"Likewise, madam," Darcy replied, not unkindly.

"You, sir, have diphtheria. It's like something out of *Little House on the Prairie* or Victorian fiction."

"How are you certain I have this diphtheria?"

"Diphtheria used to be called putrid sore throat, a putrid fever, or the strangling angel of children. Sore throat, low-grade fever, chills, the cough, then difficulty breathing, difficulty swallowing, that gray membrane in your throat, and a worsening fever. The fatality rate for adults is between five and fifteen percent; that's even with antibiotics available now. If the toxins enter the bloodstream, it can lead to fatal heart damage, assuming you don't die of respiratory failure first."

"Fascinating," he said flatly.

"Sorry. The good news is there's almost no chance you could get anyone here sick. The WHO says a course of erythromycin or penicillin should work, and you need strict bed rest for two to three weeks to avoid potential complications."

"How are you certain I will not infect anyone else?" The thought that Miss Bennet brought him here to save him only to die herself was a terrifying object.

"Children are vaccinated against diphtheria. That means—"

"I know very well what you mean!" Darcy tried to keep his irritation out of his voice. "Instead of assuming I cannot understand, I shall ask you should I find your words incomprehensible."

"I didn't know that in the nineteenth century anyone was vaccinated."

"My mother insisted her children be vaccinated against contracting smallpox. Georgiana was . . . no more than four and terrified, and only after watching me did she consent to sit still for the procedure." He bore the scar on his arm. *Another reason why this short-sleeved shirt is inappropriate.*

"I could have died from *smallpox*? Oh my God!"

Miss Bennet tossed her phone aside and ran her hands through her hair. Darcy was not accustomed to seeing her hair loose. It was pretty the way it framed her face. "Why would your modern vaccination be less effective in the past?"

"We've all but eradicated smallpox. That makes sense if vaccinations began hundreds of years ago. I don't think anyone's been routinely vaccinated for smallpox since the 1970s."

Darcy raised an eyebrow and gave her a knowing look. "Perhaps we were not so 'unsophisticated and backwards' as you accused us of being."

"I choose not to acknowledge that. It might lead to an argument between us, and since you are still ill, I'll let it go. You had best finish your book and get some rest. Next time you won't get off so easily."

Darcy smiled, took her advice, and did finish his book.

CHAPTER FIFTEEN

JUNE 29, 2011

Elizabeth dropped the library books on the dining room table before continuing into the kitchen. Mr. Darcy slept late, napped often, and went to bed early and was weak from his bout with diphtheria. Elizabeth laughed at the sight of him leaning against the counter, arms crossed over his chest, head tilted. His dark eyes went round and round in their sockets as he watched the clothes tumble through the washing machine's small window.

"You don't intend to watch both the wash and the dry cycle, do you?"

Mr. Darcy, today dressed in his two-hundred-year-old shoes, flannel pajama pants and a green long-sleeved shirt, tore his eyes from the machine. He bowed and greeted her, an outdated formality she decided not to chide him on, at least not yet. Elizabeth turned on the coffee maker, filled it with water, dug out a coffee filter, and pulled two mugs from a cabinet. Given how much sleep Mr. Darcy needed, they still ate breakfast at ten as they had in the nineteenth century. She jumped when the toaster popped.

"Did you just make breakfast?" There were two plates next to the toaster and the marmalade was next to them. He had been reluctant to use anything that required electricity beyond a table lamp. At best, he placed the used dishes in the dishwasher.

"Your machine is no different in concept from a hearth toaster, and I have watched you use it. The electricity in the cord conducts heat to the metal coils inside the box and warms the bread according to the selection you set before you turn on the current. When the temperature is reached, a spring releases the grates that hold the bread in place and the tray lifts the toast out."

What was more shocking: that Mr. Darcy gave more thought to the inner workings of a toaster than anyone born after 1920, or the man who had servants bring him every meal thought to make their breakfast?

He noticed her gaping stare, placed the toast on two plates, and then found the butter and a knife. "I am not above toasting bread, now or in 1811. I will, however, leave that infernal contrivance for you alone to manage." He gestured to the coffee maker before taking the toast into the dining room. *Baby steps.* She made his coffee the way he liked and joined him.

"I need to meet with an agent to put my father's house on the market. And I'm going to see Charlotte. While you're alone and resting, I thought it might be useful to read books that have been written in the past two hundred years." Elizabeth noted the wrinkle that appeared between Mr. Darcy's eyes. "It will give you something to talk about if you can say what your favorite books are." Books were an easy way to begin acclimatizing him. He had taken to the cell phone in concept, although he did not like looking at the screen for long; she had yet to turn on the television.

She took a long drink while he sifted through the titles. Even though the antibiotics worked, Mr. Darcy still needed to recover. He was weak, but when he was awake, he had no idea what to do with himself, and giving him a reading assignment would keep him resting and occupied.

And keep him from wondering about twenty-first-century Pemberley.

Before she went out this morning, Elizabeth had wanted to learn if Pemberley survived, and English Heritage's website was the first hit. It was still roofless and abandoned, and she had to keep Mr. Darcy from seeing it.

The only difference was that "died without issue" had changed to "disappeared, and presumed dead." Georgiana had still inherited Pemberley, married a wastrel who lost everything, and died young.

Two hundred years for me and Mr. Darcy, but only a week for them. As far as those who lived their lives from 1811 onward were concerned, Mr. Darcy had disappeared. But in three months, he would return and none of that would happen. When he returned in September, he would protect Georgiana from a bad marriage, and Pemberley would be saved.

"These are all novels. Do you have no biographies or drama or historiography?"

Elizabeth was drawn back to the present. "Better watch out, these novels might corrupt your mind." For his sake, she had been wearing loose pants or a maxi skirt, but soon shorts and sundresses would take their place. Elizabeth smirked into her coffee cup, hiding her amusement in anticipation of his shock when he saw her in a short skirt and sandals.

"Is there something you find amusing?"

"Nope."

"I presume that means no, but I have had the pleasure of your acquaintance long enough to know when you are diverted."

Elizabeth redirected him. "You need something to do at breakfast. Reading is for when you're resting or when I'm not here. You used to read the newspaper, and there's no reason to talk with me *all* the time."

"I dare not suggest I would tire of your company. You appear to gain knowledge of current events from that phone rather than from a newspaper."

"What if you walk to buy a newspaper when you're feeling better? I think you can learn about this world enough to fit in and not have it impact your life when you go back. It would be good for you to get out."

His eyes widened, looked down at his plate, and then slowly rose to meet her own. It was not the steady, confident gaze she was used to.

Elizabeth leaned her elbows against the table, tilting her head toward him. "I remember when a certain gentleman sent me into the nearest village, by myself, to walk into a crowded inn to pretend I arrived on a mail coach. Young Henry had to teach me how to curtsey on the roadside."

Mr. Darcy, apparently dissatisfied with staring into his empty coffee cup, set it down. "Miss Bennet, I had no appreciation, none at all, for what you had to do to adapt. What was demanded of you was unfair—"

"I'm not trying to make you feel guilty. I'm trying to tell you that Fitzwilliam Darcy, master of Pemberley with ten thousand a year, and a confident man of the world, can walk to the store for a paper." Mr. Darcy stayed silent. "Let's just get you healthy, find a few books, and get some clothes first. I can buy the clothes today."

"How will you pay for a wardrobe? I cannot abide being indebted to you."

"You did the same for me."

"I had the financial means to be generous, in addition to my inherent obligation as a gentleman to provide for you and keep you safe. I did not do it with the expectation that you would reciprocate, which you are not in a position to do since you have no fortune and no employment."

She tried not to be nettled by his implication that she was poor. "After I sell my father's house and split the profits with my sister, I'll be in better shape. Besides, Reynolds gave us a parting gift." She left and came back, dropping the coins on the table. "She expected your medical care to cost me more, so this should take care of our expenses."

Mr. Darcy gave her a pitying look. "For one who claims to have been educated to render accounts, you cannot presume these coins have the same purchasing power they did two hundred years ago."

"Of course not. While you napped yesterday, I did a little research. This 1804 George III Bank of England silver dollar could be worth over four hundred pounds! The 1811 silver eighteen pence is flawless. It could be three hundred. The other two are older, but they're in such good condition we might get three hundred for both. Once I get these on eBay—once I sell them to the highest bidder, we could earn a thousand pounds."

"And that is sufficient to purchase clothes fit to be seen in and maintain us until I return to Nine Ladies in September?"

"We'll have more than enough for food and to keep the lights on. Reynolds showed incredible forethought in giving me coins to sell to a collector."

"She is a meticulous and considerate servant. Along with Mr. Willers, I can take comfort in knowing that matters at Pemberley are in capable hands during my absence."

"How much do you know about Reynolds?" *Does it count as betraying her secret if Mr. Darcy figures it out?*

"I know she is a loyal and talented servant, earning both the trust of my parents and myself. She is devoted to the good name of Pemberley."

Elizabeth picked up a book, pretending to read the back. "If she came to Pemberley when you were four, how did she know about the first person, the older man, to arrive on Stanton Moor?"

"I presume her proficiency and tact, and her position as housekeeper, made it imperative she be told in case another visitor out of time arrived. It happened in the year ninety-six with—with a child, and then with you. Had a servant in her position not been prepared, it would have been impossible to conceal them. I cannot always be at Pemberley."

Elizabeth was curious about the child, but stayed on the subject of Reynolds. "She cares about you and Pemberley very much. Did you ever wonder about her life before she came to Pemberley?"

"What is your purpose in such questions?"

"Nothing, idle curiosity." *I promised Reynolds that her story isn't mine to tell.*

July 1, 2011

"I wore white dresses and no underwear for three months! You can do this."

"*Shorts*"—Mr. Darcy's mouth twisted in disgust—"are not acceptable for a gentleman, no matter how hot it may be. Why can I not wear something in the manner of this?" He held out an advertisement from the newspaper she bought him.

"That is a suit." It was a lovely charcoal wool suit, complete with vest, tie, and complementing pocket square. She envisioned him wearing a well-cut modern suit; the July heat made her cheeks feel warm. The ensemble cost more than what she spent on his entire wardrobe yesterday.

"If this manner of fashion is available, that"—he emphasized his point with a stab of his finger against the paper—"is how I would choose to dress myself."

"They're for professionals to wear to work, or formal evening occasions. Or a date."

"A date? What manner of appointment constitutes an event worth wearing this suit? It may be worth it if I could be appropriately dressed."

The idea of Mr. Darcy taking anyone on a date made her stomach drop. "Never mind. The clothes I bought are neat, up-to-date, and they should fit. I thought you decided to try harder even if it was difficult. It was hard for me too, but I did it." *I had you to help me.*

Mr. Darcy cast a critical look at the clothes laid out on the bed, muttering something about damnable bare legs and his mother turning over in her grave. "Madam, I will wear the clothes, I will use a phone, and I will read novels that have not yet been written. I will try to learn the social and technological changes so I do not raise undue notice. But while you reverted to a time you found conservative but had a familiarity with through your knowledge of history and literature, *I* find myself in a time I cannot comprehend. How would you react if you were propelled forward two hundred years into the incredible?"

"You're being dramatic."

"I disagree. What if you found yourself in a world where instead of typing those text messages, you had only to think them? Or the vaccine for the disease most feared today, an incurable cancer, is given to all in childhood? If you woke up in the year 2211 and were told you had to wear a third of the clothing you were accustomed to, to the point of what was, in your own time, indecent, would you be eager to dress accordingly?"

I'd pitch a fit if I had to go out in only a bra and underwear to not face social ostracism. He was vulnerable, and it terrified him. She had hugged him on impulse once, after he showed her a kindness when he offered to help her learn to dance. If she didn't think he would pull away, she would hug him now and tell him everything would be all right.

"I guess this is a bad time to mention you should shave your side whiskers to blend in." Mr. Darcy's cold look was enough of an answer. "You're still a gentleman, you know," she kindly said as she left, "no matter what you're wearing."

DARCY DRESSED IN THE HORRID SHORTS AND A SHORT-SLEEVED SHIRT Miss Bennet called a polo. He was accustomed to his coats being formfitting, not his shirt, and hated the way the sleeves stretched over his biceps. He shivered, not used to his arms and legs being bare. He had been captivated for longer than he ought by the hooked teeth that folded together to hold the shorts in place. The sneakers were comfortable, but hideous to look upon. And it took him five minutes of staring in the washstand's mirror before he brought himself to shave his whiskers.

Miss Bennet's words had passed through his mind. Was he still a gentleman? Darcy scarcely recognized his own reflection. *I am without property, without breeches and stockings, without a guinea to my name. Am I still a gentleman for spending three months in the exclusive company of a single woman?*

He stopped at the doorway to the parlor, where Miss Bennet was using the mobile device. "I never realized," she called without looking up, "how wealthy you were. I mean, are. Ten thousand pounds is like the purchasing power of six hundred thousand pounds now. That doesn't even take into account the value of the land. There were only a few hundred families in England who were wealthier than you in 1811."

"I ought to be glad you befriended me before you appreciated my net worth. You might instead have paid me the same officious attention as Caroline Bingley does rather than share your opinions so honestly."

She started when she saw him, and he bowed. "You don't have to bow every time you see me."

"It is against my inclination not to show you the respect you deserve."

"Just stand when a lady enters the room or when she leaves the table." She rose wearing a satisfied smile. "It's strange to see you dressed as any other man on the street. I think I know why you couldn't recognize me when I first walked in on you and the colonel wearing that gown."

She stood close, and Darcy watched her look him up and down. She had never been shy about meeting his gaze, and he spent a moment looking at her bright, striking eyes. It took him longer than it should have to find his voice.

"It was because you were still wearing a bonnet. I could not at that moment see your face."

Miss Bennet gave a small laugh. "You couldn't recognize me because I wasn't yelling at you." She stretched her fingers toward his cheek. Darcy stood unmoving, closing his eyes at the moment he expected her fingers to make contact. The expected touch never came. He opened his eyes to see that Miss Bennet had pulled her hand away and was biting her lip.

"Sorry! I should show you the respect that you're used to. Touching your face isn't appropriate in the nineteenth century."

"I would by no means suspend any pleasure of yours." He dared not confess that he would not mind had she touched him.

"See, you're still a gentleman. You're just dressed like a modern one." She gave him another look before stepping away. "I'm used to you with sideburns, but you look good without them too."

To his fury, he felt himself blushing at her praise. He needed to take some action, do *something*, anything but stand here and have his appearance lauded by a woman he admired. "Miss Bennet, I want to go out."

She was taken aback. "You should be on bed rest for another week. There are possible complications if—"

"Your medicines have proven effective, and if I am not a danger to others, I should like to go out, if only for a walk."

"I understand. There's a pub called The Wheatsheaf off Bridge Street. Were restaurants a thing in 1811?" Darcy shook his head. "It's a place where people get together to eat. They choose the food they want from a list of possible choices, you stay and eat, and then pay the bill for the meal and service at the end."

"Unmarried men and women eat a meal in a public place, and this is done in perfect propriety?"

Miss Bennet took a deep breath. "This will be good practice." She seemed to be reassuring herself. "Shall we?"

Darcy nodded, but paused at the door, looking at his strange clothes again. Of course he *could* go out in these clothes. *It is still a damned well lot to reconcile.*

"Do you want to change into trousers?" Miss Bennet asked quietly.

"Yes!"

"I'll return the shorts to the store. Why don't you put on the chinos, the blue trousers?"

Before she finished speaking, he was already taking the stairs two at a time.

DARCY SAW LITTLE POINT IN LEAVING ONE'S HOME FOR A MEAL IF ONE WAS not traveling, but the experience was not a trial. It was simple enough to follow Miss Bennet's example and pick up the necessary cues by watching the other tables. He spent most of their time entreating Miss Bennet to explain the self-propelled vehicles he had seen on the street.

"You mean the power of these motorcars is greater than a hundred and fifty horses together pulling a carriage? How is that achieved? A steam engine that pumps water out of a mine could only do the work of ten horses."

"I can't explain how internal combustion engines work. Something about gas igniting and pushing down a piston that turns the axle that turns the wheels."

"These engine-driven machines have replaced horse-drawn carriages?"

She laughed. "Yeah, you won't see horses on the streets. Most people learn to drive when they're a teenager."

"You do not have one of these cars?"

"I did at home. I sold it since I didn't know how long I'd be in England with my father."

They went to the servant at the bar and asked for the bill. Miss Bennet was unusually friendly and grateful. "You seem disappointed," she said when the servant retreated. "Did you want to go for a ride in a car? You rode in one when that couple drove us from Stanton Moor on the solstice."

"I was in the midst of a fever that gave me delusions. I have no clear memories of that night or the preceding day."

"That's probably for the best."

The servant returned to settle the account. Miss Bennet was polite and familiar to such a point that Darcy wondered how blurred the lines of social class had become. When he asked about it on their short walk back to Bath Street, he was sorry he had.

"They're called waiters or servers; they are not your servants! Don't call anyone who performs a specialized task a servant. You don't want to be a walking anachronism."

"You forget I *am* an anachronism."

"Servants have disappeared in part due to the rise of the middle class and labor-saving machines."

"In my own time, it was not only the wealthiest of families who had servants. Even a man with a hundred pounds a year could afford one female servant. A family with five hundred could afford three servants, one of them a man."

Darcy watched a large red car speed past. Such incredible machines; it must have been traveling at thirty miles per hour. Miss Bennet continued walking and talking, and Darcy took a few quick steps to catch up with her.

"Women and men should be paid the same. Anyway, by World—by the early twentieth century, the number of servants fell, and so did the size of households. Who needs a servant to light a fire when you can flip a light switch? You need to struggle through the marching on of modernity and not cling so fast to the traditions of the past."

"It is only in the past for *you*."

"Then your best bet is to treat everyone equally, as though they're the same social class as you. Everyone is deserving of your respect, and they are all equal in the eyes of the law. Anyone can better themselves through education and determination."

"Is this time a pure meritocracy, and a world without prejudice?"

Miss Bennet sighed as she looked for her keys. "No, not at all. Discrimination against gender, race, religion, sexual orientation, wealth abounds all over the world. But from what I know about how you lived in your own time, I'd like to think if you had been born in 1984 instead of 1784, you would have been open-minded."

Before he replied, he heard an ear-splitting roar. Darcy stopped dead and looked up as the rumble grew louder. To his astonishment, a tremendous object crossed the sky between the clouds. It was large and terrifying. Darcy was about to shield Miss Bennet from the indescribable object, but its thunderous noise dulled to a low whine as it passed out of his sight. As quickly as it had come, it was gone.

"What was that?"

"What?" She finished unlocking the door and looked perplexed. Even if she had not seen it, she must have heard its terrible sound.

"That, that flying . . . thing!" He pointed to the sky.

Again, the pitying look he so hated, a mixture of sympathy and amusement. "It must have been an airplane. A machine using lift and driven by thrust from propellers or a jet engine to overcome gravity and drag so it can fly."

"How, how—" He could not form words. Darcy took a breath and tried again. "For what possible purpose was that machine created?"

"For transporting goods and people great distances. Different types of planes have military uses."

"You mean to tell me *people* are inside that engine-driven carriage, *thousands* of feet above the earth? Who would consent to such a thing?" The how was no longer a concern; it was the why that perplexed him.

"Most people have flown in a plane at least once. Some do it all the time for work or to visit family."

Miss Bennet opened the door and tilted her head toward it. Darcy looked to the sky, addressing his question to the clouds as much as to her. "For how long has this dream of Icarus been a reality?"

"The first sustained and controlled flight was by the Wright brothers around the turn of the *last* century, early 1900s."

Darcy felt ill at the thought of stepping into a machine like the car and being miles above the ground, hurtling through the sky at inconceivable speeds. He had thought the cars incredibly fast and powerful. "Flight is so commonplace you did not see fit to warn me I might see objects, carrying people, *soaring through the sky*?"

Miss Bennet came closer. When she grabbed his hand, he realized he was shaking. "I'm sorry. Mr. Darcy, it's okay. I mean, everything is well." They crossed the threshold, and instead of dropping his hand, she led him to the sofa and sat next to him. Her fingers were still threaded through his, and she squeezed tightly. "This will happen a lot. You'll discover something astonishing, and it will be something I'm so accustomed to that I don't think to mention it or question it."

The warmth of her fingers against his now held the entirety of his attention, rather than the airplane. His breathing slowed and the feeling of panic waned. He *would* survive in this world. *What could be more incredible than telephones, cars, and airplanes?* Miss Bennet laid her head on his shoulder for a moment before unlinking their hands and pulling out her phone. She typed a few words, then turned it on its side so they could both see the screen.

"While you're already shocked and amazed, there's another thing you ought to know that everyone takes for granted. I'm going to show you a video, and then I'll answer your questions."

Darcy translated "video" from Latin to "I see." "What am I about to see?"

Miss Bennet took his hand again. "Something that happened over forty years ago: the moon landing."

CHAPTER SIXTEEN

JULY 6, 2011

Hemingway was bare and abrupt. Darcy read a novel by a Frenchman named Verne, but he was confused as to what was impossible when it was written and what was now achievable. *Why is there a hot air balloon on the cover when he did not use a balloon in his race around the world?* He supposed the one with the consulting detective in Dartmoor was not terrible. And the short story by the American with the title from the Robert Burns poem was readable.

In two weeks of convalescence, Darcy slept more than he was willing to admit, had read four novels, and had learned how to operate a toaster and turn on the cooker to boil water for tea.

I am dull beyond all belief.

Miss Bennet listened to his observations on the novels and promised to bring him early Victorian literature after her jog. After finding a dictionary, he realized she ran for exercise and would bring books from the 1840s and 1850s.

He had not been out of Miss Bennet's home since the day he saw the airplane. Since then, he had learned people took vessels to the moon and to the bottom of the ocean, cities had subterranean rail-based transportation systems, artificial satellites orbited the earth and sent information around the world in an instant, and physicians administered drugs to make patients sleep through surgeries they expected to survive.

And in a world with such astonishing developments, one is reduced to opening a tin of soup with a crude device. Darcy struggled with the tin opener. He had mastered igniting the gas range on the cooker, but he would never enjoy preparing his own food.

Darcy forced all of the dishes into the overcrowded dishwashing machine to avoid washing them by hand when the front door opened. He went through to the parlor to greet Miss Bennet and stopped short at the sight of her.

"Good God!" Darcy turned his back.

"Are you all right?" she cried.

He knew what this phrase meant now. "I am well." He addressed his reply to the wall. "You left the house that way?"

"What is your problem? Your sister's gowns show off more cleavage than this."

He realized she meant nothing to do with geology, and blushed. "I am not referring to the shirt."

"I'm not talking to your back."

Deciding if she left the house dressed as she was, she could not be offended if *he* saw her thus, Darcy turned. Miss Bennet's hair was piled in a single tie atop her head, she wore the same yellow t-shirt he had seen her often wear, but she now wore tight black shorts that scarcely covered her thighs. Her arms were crossed and her lips pursed.

"There is *nothing* inappropriate about jogging in biker shorts. Women don't wear long skirts anymore. You need to move past this. I am not a slut for wearing shorts."

Miss Bennet had an annoying habit of presuming the worst of him. *In this case, that is better than admitting I find her bare legs enthralling.* "I did not presume you to be untidy for not wearing a gown. I am long past accepting that women wear trousers. You spent enough time in the nineteenth century to know I have never seen a woman dressed so sparingly."

"Untidy? That's not what, I'm sorry . . . A slut—I think the meaning of the word has changed. It means a woman who is thought to be shamefully, excessively . . . sexually active."

Darcy balked. "I dare not make such a presumption! You misunderstand me!"

"There is nothing wrong with women being as sexually active as men. Got it?"

Darcy tried to keep his eyes on her face, but they dropped to her slender legs. When he realized she had asked him something and he was still staring, he thought it best to agree. His gaze snapped to her face so quickly he felt the strain on his eye muscles. "Your servant, madam."

"Good." She then leaned over the dresser to pull at the cord that had fallen to the back. Darcy looked away, not willing to be tempted again. "I need to charge my phone. Jane is supposed to call soon. I'm going to take a quick shower. If she calls, will you answer it for me? I don't want to miss her."

"You wish me to receive a call for you?"

"It's not the same as *Mr. Darcy of Pemberley* answering his own door. Please? I don't want to miss this week's call. Between Jane's hours at the hospital and the time difference, it's hard to find time to talk."

What else could he do but agree?

"Thanks!" Miss Bennet gave this abrupt farewell and left. This time, he was not strong enough to resist the temptation of watching her leave. He stopped short of following her to watch her ascend the stairs, reminding himself that he was a gentleman even if he was currently wearing jeans and held no property.

He read the newspaper Miss Bennet had purchased for him. *I am resolved to fulfill the task of newspaper purchasing myself.* Darcy needed the dictionary often, but contentedly passed the next twenty minutes reading before a piercing chime rang through the room.

Darcy looked at the formidable box while it repeated its chime. *I cannot recall the Americanism Miss Bennet uses to answer the phone.* He disconnected the power cord. Miss Bennet asked him to do this and he had agreed; it must be done. He touched the green circle, closed his eyes, and held it along his jaw and said, "Miss Bennet's phone."

"Who is this?" an inquisitive female voice demanded.

"I may ask you the same question, madam."

"I'm Elizabeth's sister, Jane. Is she all right?" The tone was now a worried one.

"She is in good health; she asked me to answer should you call. Her phone was . . ." *Damn it, what was the word for when it is receiving electricity?* "Miss Bennet could not hear it ring from where she is."

"Well, can I speak with her? I need to begin rounds soon so if she's not there, I'll call her next weekend."

Darcy carried the phone upstairs, wishing this experience to be over. "That is not necessary. She wishes to speak with you now." The bathroom door was open and Miss Bennet's bedchamber door was closed, and he knocked.

"Yeah?"

Darcy rolled his eyes at this drawling colloquialism of "yes." "Your sister is . . ." *What was the phrase: at the phone, in the phone, on the phone?* "Your sister has called."

The door swung open to reveal Miss Bennet in a dressing gown. Her arms and torso were covered, but the dressing gown came not much lower than the jogging shorts she had on previously. He did not know if he needed to take proper leave of her sister, but right now he wished to leave the sight of Miss Bennet nearly unclothed.

"You answered the phone!" She had a grin as she whispered, "I'm proud of you. You'll be programming the DVR and ordering from Amazon soon."

He comprehended none of this; he was about to bow, but the motion would give him a longer glimpse of her pretty legs. "You know I have no idea of what you are speaking."

She laughed and caught his arm with her fingertips. "Thank you. I know it's not easy for you." He heard her say "Hi Jane" before closing the door.

Darcy descended the stairs, thinking this century allowed too much nakedness in women. He then recalled the monstrous shorts Miss Bennet had purchased for him and supposed the same applied to both sexes.

· · ·

"Who the hell was that?"

Elizabeth leaned against the closed door. "How about professional phone screener?"

"Did you have a one-night stand?"

"I did not."

"S'okay if you did." Her sister's voice raised an octave.

"You know me better than that."

"It's fine!"

"This coming from the woman who thinks looking twice at a man would make Mom hate you and derail your career."

"Is this man worth looking at twice?" Elizabeth's heart turned over. "Why is a guy answering your phone if he didn't spend the night?"

Elizabeth put the phone on speaker and tossed it on the bed to get dressed. "I told you, professional phone screener. Have you started your new rotation yet?"

"No, Queen of Deflection. Who is the guy?"

"A friend."

"Friend-with-benefits friend?"

"No! But even if he was . . . I know Mom thinks men are untrustworthy and a distraction from everything important in life, but I don't need to hear it from you."

"I love you no matter what. I was wrong to cut you off after you went to England. I didn't understand your reasons, but I should have supported you. So, what is the deal with Mr. Sexy Voice?"

"He's just a friend. He's living in the house too. He knows Professor Gardiner and . . . he needed a place to stay in Derbyshire."

"Your female academic advisor thought a strange man could squat in the house you're renting from her? How is that safe?"

"She vouched for him. I like h—the company, although he can't cook or clean worth a damn. He arrived a few weeks ago, and we've become good friends."

"He called you *Miss Bennet*. That's weird."

"Mr. Darcy is a little—"

"He calls you Miss Bennet, and you call him Mr. Darcy! You could have just said he's 75."

More like 227. "He's close to your age, he's just . . . formal. Hey, the house is on the market. It's a pain to take the bus, but two hours on a bus is better than me trying to learn how to drive on the wrong side of the road." Jane was book-smart, but easy to redirect.

"Now you can come back to where you belong."

"I'll wait until the house sells. I won't be home before the end of September." *Any time after Friday, September 23, at sunset.* She had spent four months already with Mr. Darcy. It was sad to think of what life would be like when he was gone.

"Since you're not finishing your MBA, have you looked for a job that will allow you to be independent and successful?"

Elizabeth smiled sadly. *Nothing about finding something that makes me happy.* "Soon. Jane, did you tell Mom we've been talking again?"

"I never told her you didn't respond to my texts, but she knows we're talking now. She doesn't ask about you, but she listens when I mention you. I think she misses you." Her sister paused. "Elizabeth, what were you doing?"

"I can't answer that in any way you could understand."

"Complicated grief is a term psychiatrists use when grieving has been particularly difficult, and the bereaved could benefit from professional help. Social withdrawal is a key—"

"That's enough, Dr. Bennet. I know you're trying to help, but I'm not isolated or depressed. I had a rough time"—*because I was in 1811*—"but I'm in a good place now." *With equal rights.* "Mr. Darcy is here, at least, and I'm getting together with Charlotte, and I'm selling the house. Just because I'm not ready to hop on a plane and become an accountant doesn't mean I need drugs or therapy. It means I don't want to do what Mom demanded of me like I always have."

"She wants the best for you."

"She wants me to find a job where I will be wealthy and never have to rely on a man for anything. The idea of us having a husband or staying home with children would put her in her grave."

"I think it will be easier for her when you're not in England. She's not heartless."

"I called her when our father died, and I tried to tell her about how I never had the chance to know why he left us. Mom said she expected me on the next plane, and when I told her I wasn't ready, she hung up on me." Elizabeth dashed away a few tears. "Tell me about your next thirty-six hours being the best resident your hospital has ever seen."

When she went downstairs, she found Mr. Darcy reading. He had stopped coughing, he had more energy, and he was getting bored. *A sure sign he's over his bout with "putrid sore throat."* To think how close she—they—had come to losing him. He rose when she entered and sat again after she did. At least he had cut back on bowing.

"Will you tell me why this book is still read nearly two hundred years after it was published? Why does one wish to read about the physical and spiritual abuse of a little girl?"

"It gets better after she grows up and becomes a governess. I brought you some poetry too. Lord Byron, Shelley, Keats. They'll be published not long after you go back, so be sure to buy a few first editions for Pemberley's shelves. Thanks again for answering the phone."

"It was no trouble."

"I suspect that it was, but you did it anyway." His quick glance away told her to not believe him while he politely disagreed. Mr. Darcy opened his book again.

"There's more," she dragged out the words, and Mr. Darcy raised an eyebrow and set aside the book. "My conversation with Jane made me realize a few things. One is we need an explanation as to why you're living in my house. When you answered the phone, Jane assumed . . . we need a story about why you're living here."

Mr. Darcy gave her a long stare. "Did we not once have this same conversation? You were incredulous when I told you all would assume you were my mistress if you lived alone with me at Pemberley. Matters are not as different now."

"Things *are* very different!"

"I recall you made some exclamation about 'what a world I live in' when I was afraid good society would make those same assumptions as did your sister."

"It's not the same!"

Mr. Darcy gave a self-satisfied smile.

His amusement was her undoing, and she found herself returning his smile. "Well, some things are the same, except now 'good society' *could* believe two people of the opposite gender can be friends and nothing more. I told Jane you know the woman I'm renting the house from, and since you needed a place to stay for a few months, it made sense that we be housemates."

"If your sister was satisfied, what further need have we of a complex history? I would rather focus on how to behave and how to operate these electricity-driven devices than remember my part in a drama."

"Even if you walk to the store to buy a paper, you have to be prepared to interact with people. Jane is on the other side of the world, but Charlotte and her friends will see you in person. It's not as rude now as it was two hundred years ago to want to know about the person you're chatting with."

"And Dr. Lucas will assume we are living together without the benefit of marriage?"

Elizabeth held in a laugh. *That's the cutest phrase ever for what Jane implied.* "That's one way to say it. I'm going to teach you a phrase to say whenever anyone implies we're . . . what you said. Say, 'we're just friends.' It means you're not my boyfriend."

"Despite the implication that I have not reached my majority, is that not what I am?"

"Talking to you can be so difficult," she mumbled. "Boyfriend. One word. If you are girlfriend and boyfriend and you live together, it means you are sharing a bed. That you are in an exclusive romantic relationship that could lead to marriage."

Mr. Darcy moved his hand to fiddle with the watch chain that was no longer there. He finally said, "When your acquaintances imply we are engaged, or married, or that I am your suitor, I am to say, 'we're just friends'?"

"Yes. You know Professor Gardiner because she is friends with your family and you needed a place to stay for the summer. I thought we could say you're a student on summer holiday."

"Am I not old to be at university?"

"You're earning a doctorate in Romantic literature and poetry of the early nineteenth century. You can pretend to be absorbed by books, so if you don't know what entertainments people are talking about, it won't seem too strange. You can be a trust-fund baby so you don't have to work."

He gave her a calculated stare. "What is that word you use to express your reluctant and dissatisfied agreement with an arrangement not to your liking?"

"Um, fine?"

"Yes. If anyone could believe I am seven-and-twenty and at university to read Wordsworth, that I live with a single woman with no damage to either of our reputations, and that I am disinclined to employment, then my response to your plan is 'fine'."

His tone told her it was not fine, but he would adjust just as he had to everything else. "Good job picking up the slang of a petulant teenage girl. Can you roll your eyes and say 'what-ever' slowly, as if it were two words?"

He did not respond to her playful taunt. "If there is nothing else, my—Miss Bennet, I should like to return my attention to the wretched existence of this orphaned girl." Mr. Darcy held up the book.

"Wait, you can't keep calling me Miss Bennet. I got so used to it that it didn't strike me odd until Jane commented on it."

That familiar wrinkle of confusion appeared between his eyebrows. "Unless your elder sister is coming to stay or you have married, I fail to see why you are no longer to be known as 'Miss Bennet.'"

"It's not the way friends and equals address one another. Colleagues might use titles and surnames, but if anyone hears you call me Miss Bennet, they're going to assume I'm your teacher or your employer."

"How am I to address you?"

She thought this would be obvious to a man who had previously demonstrated his astuteness. "Elizabeth."

"Such a thing is absolutely prohibited! To address an unrelated person by their Christian name suggests you are a child or an inferior." He stood and paced. "Or it demonstrates that the speaker is overly familiar and therefore terribly vulgar."

Elizabeth also stood, planting her hands on her hips. "It took weeks, but your sister was happy to let me call her Georgiana."

"Did you once hear me call Bingley 'Charles' or Miss Bingley 'Caroline'?" Elizabeth shook her head. "Gentlemen drop the title amongst men with whom they have a steady friendship, but I would never call a woman by her Christian name."

"Your options are Elizabeth or Bennet. I'll let you pick."

He gave an uneasy laugh. "Not a day goes by in this century when I am not taken aback by something."

She suspected the reason he was distressed. "You're not being disrespectful if you call me Elizabeth." He stopped pacing to look directly at her.

"It is unknown outside of one's family to address one another by their Christian name."

Elizabeth repressed the urge to stamp her foot. "Do you have any idea what could happen if someone finds you odd and asks questions we can't answer?" She felt her throat tightening. "You have no online presence, no birth certificate, no national insurance number, no passport. I have no idea what could happen to you if the police get involved. How can I get you to Nine Ladies if you're detained or put in a psychiatric ward? I didn't save your life to lose you to the authorities because you refuse to fit in. Will you *please* call me Elizabeth?"

She looked at him through watery eyes. The fight in his eyes died out, and he took a few steps closer, saying softly, "You forget—we both forget—that I have been in your place as you have been in mine. We have had the same fears and the same adjustments to make. Forgive me for being a trial to you."

"You're not a trial. I don't regret bringing you here."

"If I am to call you Elizabeth in public, I had better do so in private. I am liable to forget if I do not make it a habit."

"Thank you," she said softly. "Should I call you Fitzwilliam?"

"My sister was the only one left to call me that. I had suspected the next person would be my—" He stopped, biting his lip.

His wife. The only person Mr. Darcy imagined calling him Fitzwilliam *was his future wife.* An undercurrent tore through the room and her heart beat in a staccato rhythm as they looked at one another.

"Darcy!" she cried, and they both started. "I'll call you Darcy. We'll tell everyone you don't care for your first name, and when you shake hands, you ask them to call you Darcy."

He nodded once, and cleared his throat. "I am to be obliged to shake hands with a stranger? It is a frank, familiar custom reserved for much nearer connections."

"Then let's practice." She took a few steps back. "First you stand, look the other person in the eye, and extend your hand like this. It's not a funeral; smile when you introduce yourself."

His hand dropped along with his jaw. "I am to introduce *myself*?"

"I'll try to spare you the indignity if I can." He looked relieved, not realizing she was being sarcastic. "I would say, 'Charlotte, this is my friend Fitzwilliam Darcy. Darcy, this is my friend Charlotte Lucas.' Give a firm shake, not too limp because that implies weakness, but don't crush anyone's fingers. A few seconds, up and down twice. Ready to practice?"

Darcy held his hand at his side. "We have shaken hands. Not in introduction, but to seal our agreement that you would act in the manner of a nineteenth-century woman if I allowed you to remain in Pemberley House."

She had forgotten. Knowing him and his culture as she did now, she realized it must have shocked him. "Then you've already shaken hands with a stranger without gloves and lived to tell the tale." She held out her hand. "Hi, I'm Elizabeth Bennet."

She wondered if anyone else would have noticed the flash of unease cross his eyes before his determination fell into place. Slowly, he extended his right hand to grip hers. "Fitzwilliam Darcy. You may call me Darcy."

"It's nice to meet you, Darcy."

"The pleasure is mine . . . Elizabeth."

He gave her a firm, confident handshake. A hint of a smile reached the corners of his mouth as he said her name, and he still dipped his head as if he wanted to bow, but it was a good start. Darcy held her hand a little too long, but she didn't mind.

CHAPTER SEVENTEEN

JULY 15, 2011

Darcy rattled off the monarchs of the houses of Hanover and Saxe-Coburg and Gotha while Elizabeth scrolled a web page to confirm his answers. "His son, George the fifth, 1910 to 1936, changed the name in 1917 to the House of Windsor. You have yet to tell me why . . ."

Elizabeth was not about to approach the subject of not one, but two worldwide wars to a man who came from a time that did not have dynamite or automatic weapons. He would be traumatized and likely hate this time even more. "We'll get to that another day. Moving on."

When Darcy finished, he asked, "You were not teasing about the Queen's uncle who abdicated to marry a twice-divorced American?" She knew the abandonment of one's duty appalled him. *It's not a holdover from a bygone era; that's just who Darcy is.*

"It turned out better for England in the long run. That was impressive; your childhood tutors would be proud. Now, let's review—"

"I doubt that your friend is going to shake my hand and demand to be told who was the previous American president. What we have covered thus far is more than enough to be getting on with!"

His impatient tone stung, but the doorbell chimed. She gestured to Darcy, who pulled out the prepaid phone she bought for him yesterday after she sold another Georgian coin. He was to appear to be using it, but she knew it strained his eyes. He also typed excruciatingly slowly. She watched him use it, or at least pretend to. He felt her attention and sighed.

"Mi—Elizabeth, all will be well. Your friend, who you have been waiting and wanting to see, is at your door."

We can do this. He looked like any other guy lounging on the couch, one ankle resting on the other knee, checking his Twitter feed. *You wouldn't look at him and assume he was born before the United States had its first president.*

Charlotte came in smiling, and when she opened her arms to give her a hug, Elizabeth held back tears to see a familiar face.

"It's wonderful to see you again, Elizabeth. When I didn't hear from you, I thought you must have left England."

"I'm so sorry. I feel awful about the way I disappeared on you. I wouldn't have been surprised if you never wanted to see me again."

"Grief is a strange thing, and you don't have to explain." Elizabeth led her into the parlor, where Darcy set down his phone as though he was afraid it might break, and stood. Elizabeth had assumed that introducing himself might be too much for his outdated sensibilities, so she was surprised when he approached Charlotte and held out his hand.

"You must, of course, be Dr. Lucas. I am Elizabeth's friend, Fitzwilliam Darcy."

Charlotte shook hands. "Pleased to meet you, Fitzwilliam. I'm not wearing my clinical coat, so call me Charlotte."

"I prefer Darcy." His small smile softened his abruptness.

Charlotte gave Elizabeth an expressive look. "I see why Elizabeth has been out of touch. Have you been together long?"

"It's not—" Elizabeth began.

"We're just friends," Darcy said matter-of-factly. "Our mutual acquaintance owns this house, and since I am in Derbyshire for the summer, Elizabeth was generous enough to allow me to stay with her."

He's doing so well. She invited Charlotte to sit and expected Darcy to resume his place. Instead, he picked up his phone, slid it into his pocket, and announced he was going out. Charlotte nodded, but Elizabeth gave out a high-pitched squeak she hoped sounded like "what."

"I am sure you ladies have some secret affairs to discuss, and if I remain, I shall be in your way. Elizabeth, if you give me the shopping list, I shall make myself useful."

Elizabeth lost all power of speech, but walked into the kitchen to find the list; Darcy followed her. *He's never been to the store alone.*

"I need cash," he whispered. "I shall buy a newspaper and purchase what is on your list. I cannot remain idle, and I have no interest in interfering in your conversation with Dr. Lucas."

Darcy had introduced himself to a woman, shook hands, and offered to do the food shopping. "You *know* the word cash? Are you certain you can do this? What if you get lost?"

He gave her a superior look, and for the first time in recent memory, he looked like the haughty master of Pemberley. "You cannot doubt my ability to select an item and give the shopkeeper the required amount to purchase it. Do you recall showing me the Rutland Arms? I once stayed there the year it opened, 1804. King Street still meets Matlock Street, and it is as I remember it, save for the cars. So, yes, I am certain that I can walk down Market Street without grave injury."

"Fine, remember not to bow, and treat everyone equally regardless of gender or race or anything. Here's the list, and money. I ought to buy you a wallet."

"I can purchase my own necessities. Do not mistake inexperience with modern customs for stupidity."

"You're grumpy when you're bored."

"And you assume I cannot move about in this world. You had more freedom by this point when you lived amongst us at Pemberley." He bowed, giving her a cold look, and returned to the parlor, and Elizabeth followed in enough time to hear Darcy say goodbye to Charlotte.

"Darcy, wait! You're right." He turned back at the doorway, and she mouthed the words *I'm sorry* before giving him a smile. "Thanks for doing the shopping."

His posture changed, subtly. His shoulders relaxed, and he returned her smile. "A man who has nothing to do with his own time is an awful object, hence my willingness to buy whatever you put before me. Good afternoon, ladies."

After the door closed, Charlotte smirked and said, "Having a bit of a domestic? Looks like you're forgiven."

"No, we're just friends."

"Then I should have brought my doctor's bag because your face is flushed and you're breathing faster. Maybe you're ill from sleeping in separate beds."

Time to redirect. "How's Maria's library internship?"

THE HARSH LIGHTING AND THE BRIGHT COLORS OF EVERY LABEL WAS NOT the assault on his senses as it was when he first entered The Co-operative Food with Miss Bennet. *Elizabeth*, he corrected himself. If his mother could see him now: the nephew of an earl doing the work of a servant girl sent to a costermonger. Truth be told, he did not find the task demeaning since it was clear every manner of person, regardless of sex or circumstance, was obliged to also do their own shopping.

One item confounded him. *What is pasta?* Most people he observed were engrossed by their phones. Elizabeth said it could access information and had shown him the query tool. Were the other patrons confused as to what they needed to buy? Why were they more engaged with the screens than with the task at hand?

He felt ridiculous to be standing in an aisle of food shelves, his basket at his feet, staring at his phone. *At least I shall appear as everyone else does.*

It took him longer than he wished to type his question and learn that pasta was macaroni—the food made of dried wheaten paste, not the affected fop who ate the exotic cuisine. While he was at it, he learned that when Elizabeth said he needed a *wallet*, she meant a coin purse. Darcy stared at the bags and boxes of pasta, with their various shapes, and had no notion what to choose.

"You look like a visitor from outer space, mate. It's just pasta."

Darcy turned to see a short, slim man, older than himself, reach in front of him to select a box. The man gave him an amiable grin, and Darcy supposed his words had something to do with his own obvious confusion. Elizabeth had warned him that not speaking when spoken to would make him appear rude.

"I do not normally do the food shopping, and my housemate shall tease me if I cannot comprehend what she means by pasta."

The man laughed. "I hate food shopping too. My wife tells me to bring home De Ceccos, but I can't taste a difference between that and the supermarket brands. Cheers."

Darcy exhaled a sigh of relief at having survived his second brief social encounter. He grabbed the same long blue box as the other man. Food shopping was still preferable to listening to ladies lounge away the time with chitchat.

PURCHASING A WALLET WAS EASIER THAN BUYING FOOD. IT WAS NO different from any purchase he made in any London shop two hundred years in the past. He told the shopkeeper he needed a wallet, was shown four options, selected one of the four, paid for it, and left. This manner of shopping, he suspected, suited men of any time and place.

On his way back his attention was caught by raised voices near to where Elizabeth told him people waited for the public transport vehicle whose name he forgot. Darcy noticed the man who spoke to him in the market standing in a wide, defensive stance. Two modestly dressed women were seated, huddled together, and a man covered in tattoos abused them, while the man from the market intervened.

"I told you to take a walk!"

The younger man, who towered above him, spat at the feet of the women. "I'm putting Britons first. Fourteen words!"

Darcy immediately approached. When he was closer, he realized the man verbally abusing the women was more like a boy, whose largest tattoos appeared to be hooked crosses. Darcy set down his bags to join the man from the supermarket, who stayed between the angry youth and the frightened women.

"Go on, then!" The man from the market refused to yield.

"I'm saying what needs to be said!" He thrust a finger into the chest of the man before pointing at the ladies. "They are responsible for undermining the British race."

Darcy noticed the flinches of one woman and the tears of the other. He stood between them and the boy. "We have no interest in hearing anything you say. Take your leave and do it now." His voice was low and filled with fury.

The boy appeared ready to stand his ground, but Darcy and the man from the market were now joined by two others who came running at the commotion. The youth yelled a vicious oath before fleeing down the street.

The newly arrived pair asked the ladies if they were well, and both offered to remain until their bus arrived and to call the police. They were the most conservatively dressed women Darcy had seen since he arrived, with long skirts, their hair mostly covered, and longer sleeves.

"Goddamn neo-Nazi white supremacists!" The man drew Darcy's attention away from the women. "Never thought I'd see his sort in Bakewell."

"I am horrified beyond all belief." It was true, but he also did not understand. He had only seen two frightened women who needed help.

"My grandfather was in the 11th Armored Division during the war." He put emphasis on "the war." "He liberated Bergen-Belsen, and it haunted him for the rest of his life."

Darcy felt as though he were missing something substantial. He could only mimic the other man's mournful shake of his head. He began to bow before remembering such things were done verbally, and instead wished him a good day.

Elizabeth and Dr. Lucas were where he had left them. Elizabeth listened attentively, nodding and smiling, as he had seen her act with Georgiana. Something about her invited one's confidence. There was such goodness, such generosity in her.

"You weren't gone long," she greeted him as he entered.

"The only shop I can tolerate to spend any length of time in is a booksellers'," he answered before continuing into the kitchen to put away the food. Such a tiresome process: find the food, place it in a basket, unload the basket to pay, load the food into bags, carry the bags home, unload the bags, and put the items away. Darcy returned to the parlor and looked at his phone to indicate he did not need to be included in their conversation.

Could he use this to find a list of conflicts Great Britain had fought in to understand what the man had meant?

"It *was* a fun weekend. We'll do it again when I'm not on call. Willie Collins was asking about you last month."

Darcy did not care for the lilting tone in Charlotte's voice when she said that man's name.

"I thought I made my lack of interest clear."

Darcy smiled and resumed typing, slowly. *Why the hell are the letters arranged in such a strange order?*

"Oh, you were clear; and he knows it. But he still loves to show off his work and flatter girls. He asked if my 'pretty American friend' was still around."

"You promised me no ugly paintings if I came to Sheffield."

"I'm good to my word. Missy and Maria would love to see you again. Maria needs to get out more, and Missy never says no to an outing. It's not like her husband pays attention to her."

"Let me know when you're not on call, and I'll come. Until my father's house sells, I am a lady of leisure."

Charlotte looked at her watch and stood. "I have to run to get back in time for evening rounds." Darcy immediately rose. "Elizabeth," she drawled, "your roommate is invited too. I mean flatmate, sorry—you did say separate rooms. Darcy, would you like to join us?"

Darcy glanced at Elizabeth to have a hint as to her wishes, but Charlotte blocked his view and gave him an expectant look. He decided to be politic. "I thank you for the invitation, but I could not impose on your time with Elizabeth."

"You should come too, if you want."

"See, Elizabeth says you must come. We had fun in March; we toured Haddon Hall and spent the evening with pints and pool. Oh, and we saw the ruins at—"

"Don't let me keep you from your rounds!" Elizabeth leapt to her feet. "Those patients need their fabulous GP, and I won't have anyone's care neglected on my account."

Darcy thought Elizabeth parted from her friend hastily, considering the warm welcome she had given her. He had just discovered a list of conflicts involving the United Kingdom when Elizabeth returned from walking Charlotte to the door.

"You're getting a lot of use out of that phone."

"I observed an incident and had a conversation with a gentleman-like man. Something about the disturbance provoked him to speak of 'the war' as though I ought to know of it if I am to move about in 2011."

"What happened?" Elizabeth sat next to him.

"A boy no older than my sister harangued two women. They were not dressed as other women here; their hair was covered and their skirts were longer. They were distressed; one wept but the older woman tried to be stoic. The man intervened on their behalf, and I joined him, followed by two others. The boy fled, and the first man called him a name I did not know. He was ashamed of having witnessed such behavior in a fellow citizen, and described his grandfather's war service as though there were a connection."

Elizabeth bit her lip. "Do you remember anything else?"

He retrieved the grocery list and pen—a truly remarkable invention—and drew the symbol. "He had tattoos. The numbers 14 and 88 were clear, but the most prominent were these." She turned white. "What is the matter?"

"Are you telling me some kid, covered in swastikas, harassed two Jewish women at the bus stop? And you and another man chased him off?"

"What is this symbol?"

"A swastika." Her mouth twisted. "It's a symbol for Nazism, fascism, white supremacy, anti-Jewish hatred. It was the symbol of Nazi Germany in the 1930s and 1940s. It's still the core symbol for neo-Nazi groups."

"That is what the gentleman called him, a neo-Nazi. He then said his grandfather was haunted by what he saw when he liberated a town, Bergen-Belsen."

"Not a town," she whispered. "Bergen-Belsen was a Nazi concentration camp during World War Two, one of many. Most died of disease or starvation. I don't think there were gas chambers like at the extermination camps, but tens of thousands died there."

"I do not comprehend you." Darcy had a sickening feeling he did not want to.

After a deep inhalation, she began. "The Holocaust refers to the systematic, state-sponsored murder of more than six million Jews orchestrated by the German National Socialist Party, the Nazis, in the 1930s and 40s."

"Six *million* people?" London had only one million people when he had lived there. "Murdered by the government? That is beyond human comprehension."

"It was the Nazis's goal to eliminate their entire culture. The Jews were stripped of their citizenship and their property, deported, forced to work in appalling conditions, used in cruel medical experiments, and ultimately, or even as soon as they got off the train, poisoned to death with gas or shot or thrown right into crematoriums."

Darcy fought back the bile rising in his throat as she explained the most widespread, deadliest conflict in human history. Elizabeth occasioned this narrative with images from her phone. St. Paul's with raging fires in the foreground; a massive American ship engulfed in smoke, sinking into the Pacific Ocean; the leveled remains of a city in Japan. When she showed him an image from Bergen-Belsen of a ground-clearing machine pushing naked, emaciated bodies into a mass grave, he begged her to stop.

She wished to return to this world?

"I cannot bear to hear more. This was the *second* worldwide war? Naturally, there was a first? And has there been a third? Your world is a monstrous, evil place!"

"What about the defeat of these totalitarian ideologies and regimes? Their fall shows that freedom, peace, and democracy can triumph over evil."

"Is freedom and human dignity universal as a result of these wars? Is there now an end to violent conflicts between nations?"

She sighed. "I think people entered this century happier, freer, and more prosperous than the century before. There have been great achievements in public health, human rights—"

"Then tell me why this list of conflicts continues past your second world war? Why is a fifteen-year-old English boy pouring forth the hatred born of two generations ago in a different nation if this is a moral place?"

"But four strangers, one who couldn't have understood the depth of that evil, intervened. There *is* human decency in this time, like in yours."

"My time is *nothing* like this one. Why did you wish to return here?" He looked back at the list of wars. "And what is this about terrorism and bombing?"

"What's the general attitude of the English towards Jews, or any foreigners in 1811? Not to mention women. How have your soldiers behaved towards civilians while fighting Napoleon?"

Darcy grabbed her phone and enlarged the image from Bergen-Belsen, turning it back around to face her. "Neither we nor our enemies have done anything so monstrous as *this*."

"But they *will*. Your country will rain down a firestorm on Dresden. Your empire will crush civilian populations fighting for their independence in British colonies around the world. The German states as you know them will become the country that sponsors the Holocaust. The Americans will drop two atomic bombs. Your world *becomes* this one."

Darcy sat on the sofa and covered his face with his hands. How could Elizabeth have been eager to return to such a violent, wicked place? It turned his stomach to think of the depth of destruction and death the world now accepted as customary. The equinox could not come soon enough. "So it will. I cannot change it."

"And I thought *I* was bold in trying to save one good man from an early death. How could you stop World War Two?"

"I doubt so complicated an event could be forestalled. I could not set forth the intricate chain of events to preserve so many lives across the world so many decades after I am gone. What does that mean about my traveling through time? I was supposed to die, but you fell through time and saved my life. Was that always supposed to happen?"

"How could it? I knew that you died in 1811. If you were always going to be saved by being brought here, Pemberley—the books I read wouldn't have said you died."

"Then . . . whatever we did in 1811 would have *already* happened as those in 2011 knew it? I should have been known to have been alive after 1811 when you visited Pemberley."

"No, it can't work that way. I visited Pemberley in the twenty-first century and read that you died in 1811, and when I went there—then— I stopped you from dying. I changed that. I had assumed that I couldn't, but I did. Everyone who goes through Nine Ladies, one way or the other, changes the timeline."

"It defies all sense that events of the past can be altered."

"You're here, you're alive, and you're going to go back to live your life, and Pemberley's legacy will be preserved. Don't think about it any deeper than that. The world, then or now, isn't perfect, and it never was. Just enjoy what this time has while you can."

"How does one enjoy a world where the Jews of the European countries occupied by the German nation were murdered en masse?"

"Because we have principled people who stand up for what is right. And . . . you're allowed to go outside without gloves here."

"What?"

Elizabeth leaned against him and gave him a playful wink. He met her eye, smiled, and shook his head. They had no culture in common, no common experiences, barely even a common language, yet he understood that she wished to distract him and comfort him. This century was often incomprehensible, but it was not *all* wickedness. There were incredible achievements and decent people.

"I suppose there is goodness in this time and place."

"That's the spirit." Elizabeth rested her head on his shoulder. Darcy's breath hitched. "Is this all right?"

He knew this phrase meant did he approve. He ought not to touch her. They were not married or engaged. They were "just friends"; by any time's standards, he ought not to enjoy her being tucked against his side. Darcy brought his arm around her, moving her head on to his chest, pressing his cheek against her hair.

"Of course it is."

CHAPTER EIGHTEEN

JULY 22, 2011

They had begun taking short riverside walks when Darcy was first recuperating, but now that he was recovered, they were able to venture farther. Elizabeth redirected any walk that might take them nearer to where Pemberley's ruins lay a few miles away. Today's was a gentle walk on the Monsal trail.

It was while resting after these constitutionals that Elizabeth introduced her anachronistic friend to the television. He comprehended in concept how the satellite sent a signal to the television, and he realized the purpose of it and how to operate it. Darcy was just incapable of enjoying it.

Reruns of *Strictly Come Dancing* made Darcy demand she turn off "the damned thing." When she turned on the news, he said he preferred to read the newspaper rather than listen to "strangers talk at him." When she found something of interest on BBC America, he struggled to follow along and ultimately read instead, angling his body from the screen.

"I see you've set aside Byron and Shelley," Elizabeth said as she scrolled through the guide. "What volume of *History of the English*

Speaking Peoples are you on?"

"I completed the third two days ago. I now know how and when the war with Napoleon will end; I must feign ignorance after I return. Before I read Mr. Churchill's fourth volume, I have returned to the novels." He turned the book so she could read the title. "The scenes with the guillotine are written with terrible intensity—the Revolution was a true nightmare—but the rest of the story is slow by comparison."

Rather than debate a book she could not admit to finishing, she allowed something on the screen to catch her attention. "I binge-watched this on Netflix. Look, they have a marathon!"

"A what?"

"It means they're showing episodes of the same show one after another in the order they were made."

He set aside his book and cringed in anticipatory displeasure. Darcy immediately asked questions. She expected this; sometimes it was a machine, a phrase, a cultural reference, but there were always things to explain when they watched TV. Elizabeth had shown him costume dramas, thinking they'd be more relatable, but all he did was complain about the poor horsemanship of the actors.

He eventually cried, "This is an outrageous premise! How does the audience suspend disbelief to envision such strange occurrences happening in the real world?"

"Says the man who walked into a circle of rocks at sunset and went forward in time."

"And if she is the more rational of the pair, she would not solve crimes alongside a man who advocates such fantasies."

"That's what makes it so good, the bond between the believer and the skeptic."

Darcy stood. "Your program, indeed television in general, is a ridiculous pastime."

"So is your bullet pudding game, but I played it. Nothing beats combining humiliating yourself with live ammunition."

"I am amazed that people across the globe spend hours before this machine to the exclusion of intelligent conversation or any number of preferable activities."

"How many die annually from inhaling flour and choking to

death? Let alone accidentally swallowing the bullet. I may have saved you from diphtheria only to have you die in a parlor game."

Elizabeth did her best to keep her expression neutral. Darcy stood over her, his hands on his hips, trying to hold back a smile. Seeing the light in his eyes, she laughed first. Something about being the one to break his austere manner and make him laugh never got old. They both knew bullet pudding was a stupid game.

"I'll turn it off."

"No, I shall go to the Indian restaurant and pick up dinner."

He still hated dining in public. "I was shocked when you told me you had eaten it in the nineteenth century. Just don't say that you want the 'curried chicken in the India way' this time. I can call; they'll deliver it."

Darcy retrieved his phone and checked the bills in his wallet before putting both into his pockets.

"I do not mean to avoid the walk, and it will leave you more time to enjoy your *entertainment* without my astute observations on its deficiencies."

"At least I don't have flour all over my face!" He ignored her and was gone.

She had never seen the inner workings of a happy marriage, but her imagination couldn't come up with anything better than this. Her favorite times at Pemberley had been when she was with Darcy and could be herself. At some point, their time together had less to do with her being able to stop acting and more about enjoying his company.

And now I have his company 24/7. But on the equinox, he would go back and she would never see him again. His looming departure cast a long shadow over her heart and whatever feelings she held for him there.

DARCY PLACED THE ORDER AT RAJAS ON BRIDGE STREET AND WALKED around the corner to sit on a bench in front of the river to wait. It was better to sit here with a few ducks for company rather than watch Elizabeth's attention be engrossed by a box. Watching those sparkling eyes light up when she watched something intriguing, her pretty lips turn into an o-shape when something caught her by surprise, was maddening. He had to endure being near to Elizabeth only to have her looking *away* from him.

What manner of man is jealous of the attention a woman pays to moving images in a machine?

"Hey, it's the pasta man!"

The slight man from the market and the altercation came up the path holding hands with a woman his own age. Were they married, engaged, or dating—a concept he did not fully comprehend. The boundaries between relationships were blurred in 2011, and not just between men and women. If a near stranger hallooed at him two hundred years ago, it would be disgraceful. One conversation as a social nicety did not make them *acquainted*, but he would be wrong in 2011 to not rise and greet him.

"How do, Pasta Man?" The man held out his hand. *Why do strangers touch so often?*

He accepted the moniker with as much grace as he could. "How do you do?" Darcy shook his hand and lapsed into silence. *This is why it is preferable for a mutual party to assist with an introduction.* He was not inclined to society and was not certain how to speak to a stranger.

"This is the man who helped me with that Nazi last week, dear." She was his wife; Darcy saw a wedding band on her hand. Curiously, the man too wore a ring on his left hand.

"You can't go on calling him *Pasta Man* if he's a hero." The wife gave her husband a pointed look.

"I did nothing to claim the title of hero," Darcy replied. "I told him to be gone, as did your husband, and the boy used what little sense he had to flee."

"You being tall compared to me must have had something to do with it, because he sure as hell wasn't listening to me when I told him to clear off!" Darcy refrained from shrugging his shoulders. He must remember this man was not acting inappropriately for his own time. The man laughed and held out his hand again. "Francis Danconia, call me Frank. This is my wife Gwen."

Darcy's back muscles twitched; he repressed the bow his body wanted to give. He took the man's hand—again—and shook hands with his wife, mimicking his own introduction. "Fitzwilliam Darcy, call me Darcy."

"What brings you out on such a nice night?"

I am contemplating my jealousy towards an object the woman I admire but can never marry pays attention to. "I am waiting for a takeaway order."

"Did your girlfriend not like the pasta and send you out for something better?" Mr. Danconia's smile helped Darcy catch the good-humor of the inquiry. Girlfriend, not girl friend. A different relationship based on the space between two words. Sometimes the true meaning of simple words was more difficult to navigate than coffee makers and worldwide wars.

"We're just friends, and not at all. She approved of your recommendation, and I have you to thank for being relegated to the permanent position of food shopper."

The couple laughed politely, but *still* did not take their leave. Mrs. Danconia asked if he was new to Bakewell and where was he from. A brazen question for a stranger to ask, but in this world one exchange brought you to the level of acquaintance. "I was born in Derbyshire and have come down from university for the summer. My housemate came from America to care for her father in Sheffield, and our mutual friend is allowing us to rent her flat in Bath Street."

"Are you a doctoral candidate? What subject, and where do you attend?"

"Oxford," he naturally replied. "English literature, madam."

"*Madam?* Even the queen is content with Ma'am. Such a formal chap, isn't he, Frank? Clearly, I am on the wrong side of forty if he's calling me madam."

"I meant no insult, Mrs. Danconia." *Good God, it is impossible to talk to strangers in 1811, let alone now.*

"I'm not insulted, I'm amused. Do you call your housemate *madam* too, or is she under forty?"

The truth seemed appropriate. "I called her Miss Bennet, but she refused to answer to it, and I am forced to call her Elizabeth if I am to expect a reply."

Another polite laugh followed, then Mr. Danconia spoke. "She seems like a good sort of girl if she can get her man to do food shopping and she came abroad to take care of ill family."

The phrase "her man" did not feel correct. "We're just friends." What was once impertinence was now volubility, or amiability.

Mr. Danconia smiled as though he did not believe him. "Well, thanks again for your help with that Nazi kid. I doubt he'd have run off if not for you."

"It was nothing to do what was honorable. I thank you for your help in the market."

The exchange reached its natural conclusion, but Mrs. Danconia asked, "Since you're new to Bakewell, do you and your friend fancy meeting us tomorrow night? I work Saturdays, but Frank and I often have our tea at the Queen's Arms after I get home."

Strangers, to acquaintances, to friends dining together in public in the matter of minutes? Darcy suppressed his inclination to touch his hat and be gone. The Danconias were agreeable, too forward for his liking, but not too bold for their own time. Mr. Danconia was a well-judging man, and his wife had a humor that did not leave him with a bad impression of her. But were they being whimsical in their civilities and he ought not to take them at their word to dine together?

"Do you need to check with the missus?" Darcy knew he was taking too long to reply, and Mr. Danconia perhaps suspected a reason for his reluctance.

"I am *not* married. If it is agreeable to Elizabeth, then I accept your invitation."

"Right then, can I see your mobile?" Mr. Danconia's fingers moved rapidly, and his device was thrust back to him. "There's my number; ring me." Darcy selected Frank Danconia's entry, and the other man's phone rang. He answered it and hung up. "Now I've got your number." *Thank God he explained what he was doing.* "Text me if your friend says you can come out and play, yeah?"

"Of course." He was to ask if Elizabeth wished to dine with them, then contact Mr. Danconia to decline or accept the invitation. "I ought to see if the takeaway order is ready. I shall text you later this evening with an answer. Mrs. Danconia, it was a pleasure to meet you."

"I've moved from madam to missus. Hopefully, by the end of tea, you can call me Gwen."

Darcy bowed; in this instance, it seemed to be appropriate, and she smiled. Mr. Danconia held out a hand and said jovially, "Unless you want me to call you Pasta Man, it's Frank."

He took the outstretched hand, sick of the physical contact. "I agree to your terms, Frank. Good evening."

Elizabeth was still watching her program when he returned. She turned it off and took one bag from him, leading the way into the dining room.

"I thought you would insist on eating in front of the television, given how pleased you are with that bizarre program."

Elizabeth returned from the kitchen with utensils and plates. "I may not be bound by your outdated rules, but even I don't like screens at dinner. Too many years of Mom working late, and Jane and I eating peanut butter sandwiches on the couch watching *Wheel of Fortune*."

While they ate he said, "Something unexpected happened on my walk."

"Oh no! Not another neo-Nazi?"

"No, it was nothing untoward; at least, I do not believe it to be untoward in your time. I encountered the same man who I aided at the bus stop. He and his wife were walking past me while I waited for the food, and he stopped to speak with me." He described their manner and the invitation. When Darcy finished his account, Elizabeth smiled at him.

"You made small talk with people you don't know, who don't have an income based on the rent they charge on land they inherited over generations."

Darcy was indignant. "You cannot believe that I am incapable of engaging in pleasant conversation or that I cannot make myself agreeable to those who are not people of fashion."

"I never doubted your *ability*. I doubted your willingness to try."

"I did what I must to not draw unnecessary attention to myself. You know better than anyone how important that is."

"Then I guess we don't have to meet them if it was all an act." Elizabeth brought her food to her mouth, slowly dragging the fork out, and raised an eyebrow at him. She chewed, and stared at him with those dark, laughing eyes.

"It would be rude to decline if I cannot say you would prefer not to attend." He kept his eyes on his own plate.

"Darcy?" He looked up. "Did you like them?"

He set down his fork. "Yes. They were friendly, obliging, likely more fond of society than I am, but that is hardly a fault. I perceive there was nothing wanting in their manners in this time."

"That's enough for me. I find new people fascinating." After another bite, she shook her head.

"Fitzwilliam Darcy, born in 1784, with incomparable net worth, who was appalled by the notion of speaking to someone without an introduction, just made friends with a stranger on the street."

"Are you mocking me? After the trouble I have taken—"

"I'm proud of you. I'm impressed. You did what I couldn't do at Pemberley: you made a friend."

"You forget how my sister admired you." He did not mention the impossibility of a compassionate, intelligent woman like her befriending Bingley's sisters.

Her smile faded. "I liked Georgiana. She's shy, but so talented and kind. With encouragement and confidence, she'll blossom. When you go back, you have to make sure Mrs. Younge doesn't crush her spirit. Georgiana so much wants to be loved."

"If she believes I am convalescing, I expect she will be in Ramsgate when I return in September. I will keep your suspicions about Mrs. Younge in mind."

"I'll miss her. I left a letter for her, but she'll never hear from me again, and I'm afraid she'll feel I rejected her. Will you tell her the truth?"

He could not imagine any circumstance inducing him to confess passing through time to another human being. "I would not distress a girl already reluctant to speak. Keeping the secret might crush her and make her afraid to confide in people. She knows if I do not marry and have a child that Pemberley becomes her responsibility." For a moment, they both found their naan fascinating. "As she is now, shy and uncertain, I do not think she is up to the responsibility of knowing."

"She might be up to the task if you gave her the opportunity to prove herself. I can't believe she's only fifteen. She looks two years older."

Darcy knew full well his sister did not appear to be her stated age. "Georgiana will be sixteen this winter."

"You and Reynolds mentioned an infant who appeared after, after the old man appeared but before I did. That was in 1796. Georgiana must have been a baby; she couldn't have remembered. But what about *you*? How did they explain the appearance and disappearance of a baby to an attentive twelve-year-old?"

"I was being privately tutored and not at home to notice a child."

Her eyes narrowed. "An infant or a child?"

"The word 'infant' meant any young child, perhaps not breeched, not just a babe in arms. In a legal sense, it meant one under the age of twenty-one."

Elizabeth shook her head. "Sometimes I wonder how you and I can communicate at all. It must have been difficult to put a child in the middle of Nine Ladies after caring for it for three months, watch it disappear, and hope for the best. Why do you think it was even alone in Nine Ladies at sunset in the first place? It would have been freezing at the winter solstice."

"The only particulars I am acquainted with are related to *your* arrival. I could not even speak on my own travels, let alone another's that happened when I was twelve." Darcy was not in a mood to discuss anyone traveling out of their time. It made him think of his sister, and it distressed him to consider his upcoming departure. "I must text Mr. Danconia and tell him we will meet them. How do I compose an appropriate text?"

Elizabeth gestured for him to hand over his phone. "I'll do it. You take too long to find the letters, and you'd use too many four-syllable words." She gave him a saucy wink that from any other woman would not have been half so endearing.

July 23, 2011
Queen's Arms, Bakewell

"Not at all, Frank. To be retired at forty-eight after twenty-plus years of service is something to be proud of. You have to regale me with stories of your career, Squadron Leader."

"I'm retired, Elizabeth. Frank is fine." He leaned back in his chair, throwing an arm over his wife's shoulder. "I can't discuss my career in present company, now that I've learned Darcy here has never ridden in an airplane." Frank shook his head in mock disapproval.

"To be honest, war stories don't interest me as much as Gwen's restoration work at Haddon. I'd rather hear more about her windows."

"You hear that, Frank? She finds lead and resin and glass more scintillating than your illustrious career. I knew I liked you." Gwen tipped her glass in Elizabeth's direction.

"Oy, don't write me off! Since I'm retired, I work at Haddon too. I"—Frank paused for dramatic effect—"work three days a week as the ticket office cashier."

"And that's because he couldn't cut it as the car-park attendant!"

They all laughed, and Darcy was perfectly at ease. He began the evening fearful of saying or doing wrong. He was not given to shyness or self-doubt, but this situation was entirely unknown to him. Yet within minutes, he was assured of having a pleasant evening. Frank was good-humored and adored his wife. Both were sensible and amiable. Darcy even reconciled himself to dining in public.

The real reason he was able to survive an intimate party with strangers was because of the woman seated next to him. Elizabeth used her talents to prompt the others to speak, redirected topics that encroached too close to questions he could not answer, and led them in conversations both rational and playful.

"I'm surprised you're a student, Darcy." Frank gave him a long look. "You strike me more as someone more interested in leadership, someone strong-minded and comfortable with high-stakes decision-making. Why literature?"

"I wished to earn the title of doctor without having to attend divinity school."

The others laughed, especially Elizabeth. He did not have time to relish it because Mrs. Danconia asked Elizabeth about courses of study to earn an accounting degree. He followed attentively until Mr. Danconia gestured for his attention.

"Who's your team?"

"I beg your pardon?" *A team of horses?*

"Who do you support? You can't tell me university reading doesn't leave you time for football."

A schoolboy's game? "If we do not support the same, I fear it might start an argument between us."

"I've supported Man U since the creation of the Premier League in 1992. Are you a Derby County supporter since you're from here? There is always time to watch football, even for you studious types."

Darcy understood every other word. "It has been some time."

"You ought to join us to watch the FA Community Shield. Man U versus Manchester City, August seventh. You'll have to support United, though."

Darcy was alarmed by the seriousness in Frank's tone. "I should be delighted."

"Right then. I'll text you when we decide on a place. I love a Manchester derby! August seventh, remember."

Frank turned to his wife and spoke into her ear. Elizabeth glanced at him, silently asking him if he was well. Darcy nodded once, and she relaxed. He would have until the seventh to understand what it was he had agreed to.

August 2, 2011

"Frank Danconia texted me while you were jogging," Darcy said to Elizabeth when she came downstairs. "He and his wife asked us to join them on a walk this afternoon. He implies I ought to ask 'the missus,' then follows punctuation marks I cannot make sense of."

Elizabeth took his phone. "It's a winking face and a face sticking out its tongue. Turn your head." She held the phone out. "See?"

"No." He saw brackets and letters and colons. "What does he mean?"

Elizabeth turned a charming shade of pink. "He's teasing you about our being married. He knows I'm not Mrs. Darcy, and he hopes you know it's all in good fun."

Darcy did not feel their brief acquaintance warranted teasing on so important a topic, but had learned by now that such interactions were permissible. "I have repeated your 'we're just friends' phrase. Either he is far from clever, or he takes delight in trying my patience."

"I'm guessing it's the latter," she replied, distracted, and Darcy could tell she was scrolling through the previous messages. Her eyes went wide. "Frank mentioned the walks they're considering . . ."

"He mentioned ruins north of Rowsley, near Lambton, or a walk around Stanton Moor. I was about—"

"I'll type!" Darcy watched her thumbs fly across the tiny screen. "They'll pick us up and drive us to Stanton Moor."

Darcy felt a surge of annoyance. "I have no interest in going near to Nine Ladies until September. That place is formidable, eerie, and defies explanation. Why walk there rather than anywhere else?"

A strange silence stretched between them, becoming more perplexing to him every second. "I have zero interest in visiting the ruins of some house. And I just went for a jog so I don't want a long walk. There's nothing to be afraid of at Nine Ladies; it's not a solstice or equinox. Besides, there's plenty else to see on the moor. Let's get a move on so we'll be on time, okay?" This came out in a breathless rush, the phone was thrust into his hands, and she left the room.

He exhaled loudly and turned the device over in his hands. She was lying to him.

Elizabeth thought Darcy managed the car ride well enough. They were in the backseat, and their friends could not see his pale face, breathless manner, and that he kept his eyes closed from the moment Frank accelerated. The poor guy was nowhere ready to fly in an airplane. Darcy managed to unfold himself from the car with a fair amount of grace, and Frank and Gwen were too preoccupied with planning their route to notice how he braced himself against the roof for a long moment while he took deep breaths.

Frank called Darcy to his side, and they set out. Gwen and Elizabeth ambled behind them, more interested in chatting than setting a brisk pace.

Better Darcy looks at the time-traveling stone circle instead of seeing the crumbling façade of his ancestral home.

"That's the Cork Stone." Gwen called her attention to a mushroom-shaped outcropping with footfalls carved into its face along with metal handholds to allow people to climb it. Several boys at its top were teasing the boys remaining at its bottom.

Gwen laughed. "I pity their mothers. One of them is sure to get a call about a sprained ankle."

"You and Frank don't have children?"

"That's right. I committed myself to following Frank's career and my own interests. Children would have gotten in the way of our adventures. I don't think my mother ever forgave me!"

"Whereas my mother would be appalled if I marry and have children."

"Don't get me wrong; I enjoy children. But I'm not sad about my choices. Frank and I have been very happy."

"My mom was a struggling single mother. She hoped to save us from a similar fate by having my sister and me focus on careers rather than having families." On those nights when her mother worked late, Elizabeth had imagined her mother, father, and sister sitting around the table together as a family. That's what she wanted for herself.

They were silent for a while, but Elizabeth felt Gwen's eye on her. "I think, dear, every woman needs to choose the life she wants for herself and make it happen to the best of her ability."

Elizabeth looked to where Darcy walked with Frank. *What I want for myself has compelling dark eyes and a confident set to his shoulders. What I want is a clever, dry-humored man who loves his home and family with a fierce loyalty. But I'm not going back to 1811, and Darcy would never stay, so what's the point?*

Elizabeth kicked a stone down the path. The thought of children brought to mind the other time traveler: an infant or child left on the moor in the dark in 1996. And how did anyone with a heart in 1796 push a child into the circle at sunset and watch it disappear, hoping it would be safe?

What if it was kept in 1796 because whoever cared for him couldn't abandon him?

Young Henry said he had lived in Lambton before going to live with his grandfather after the death of his family. But he never mentioned his parents or his past before Pemberley. His grandfather, his devotion to the Darcys, and his desire to become gamekeeper were all the boy talked of.

Young Henry looked about fifteen. Roland was gruff, but could be the sort to have a heart of gold. Reynolds likely has a soft spot for children, given her history, and maybe Darcy's father wouldn't want to abandon an infant in the cold and hope it would be found in the future before it froze to death.

"This way. We want to head north."

"Gwen, you've lived here a few years, and you work at Haddon Hall. What can you tell me about Stanton Moor? Stone circles like Nine Ladies have been here thousands of years, right?"

"Since the Bronze Age. The moor is rather small for having so many circles. There are also remains of barrows and burial mounds."

"Has anyone excavated them?"

"Many were opened in the early 1780s by an amateur antiquarian named Major Rooke. He surveyed and recorded the main monuments and excavated a number of burial sites. There have been others, but he was the first to record his findings, if not the first ever to excavate them."

"Was there anything special about them?"

"Nine Ladies is unique in that it survived from the Bronze Age relatively intact. The druids think it has spiritual and mystical significance," Gwen said in a spooky voice and laughed.

I don't think they're wrong. Aloud, she asked how Gwen knew as much as she did about the moor.

"You can't work in a building with a history like Haddon without learning a bit about the moor nearby. There the chaps are. You join Darcy; I'm going to have Frank walk with me."

Darcy stood far from the circle with his arms folded. He listened to her tell him what Gwen had said while their friends were on the other side of the circle having a good-natured fight over who forgot the thermos.

"Do you think upsetting the burial sites caused the rift in time? That there's actual druid magic at work? The first time traveler didn't appear until after Major Rooke excavated around Nine Ladies. Druids believe the solstice and equinox are powerful, magical times. What if something happened in the 1780s—"

"Forgive me, but I cannot consider the why or the how."

"How come you're not curious about why the stones have their power?"

"I am more curious as to why you are lying to me about Pemberley."

Her stomach dropped, and she was sure the color drained from her face. "What? I haven't mentioned Pemberley at all!"

"The more I consider that, the stranger it seems. I can suppose you not wishing to distress me whilst I convalesced, but not once have you spoken of Pemberley or the family who would now live there. You have been eager to enlighten me on history, technology, society. Yet you have not once mentioned my home."

"That, that . . . silence is hardly lying!"

The Danconias looked back, and she gave a little wave, hoping they'd keep walking.

"Elizabeth, you do not speak of Pemberley, and Frank's text mentioned wishing to visit ruins near Lambton. One need not be clever to suppose it is Pemberley that is no longer standing." He stopped and stared at her. "You have been dear to—you have been my friend since nearly the moment you appeared on my doorstep. You saved my life, and I have not doubted your loyalty or"—he swallowed thickly—"or even your affection. Now I ask you to honor the friendship between us and tell me the truth: what happened to Pemberley?"

CHAPTER NINETEEN

August 3, 2011
Pemberley

Elizabeth watched Darcy pace Pemberley's perimeter, alternating his gaze between peering through the glassless windows, staring up at the chipped columns toward where the roof should have been, or gazing over the empty land where all he once owned was now lost. He then went inside, likely remembering when the interior walls were still covered in plaster, imagining the Adam fireplaces inlaid with Blue John where gaping brick cavities remained, and finding the exact place where the ornate mahogany staircase would be.

Pemberley wasn't just a house; she understood that after having lived there. While it was like a corporate entity that depended upon farming and whatever else the land produced, it also generated a loyalty among those who lived and worked there, had a history and a future there. It was a powerful combination of home and career, family and employment.

Watching Darcy walk its ruins was like watching a mourner approach a casket.

"You said I died in 1811 and my sister died without issue, and it is her husband who leads Pemberley on this path."

There was some force within him that was scarcely contained. Whether it was grief or fury she could not tell. "Yes. But when you go home, none of this will come to pass. Pemberley is in ruins *now* because you've disappeared at this point in 1811. That will change in September. When you go home, only three months will have passed. You don't die, your sister won't inherit Pemberley, and her husband won't drive it into the ground."

"What if she is married to the monstrous man who does *this*"—he threw out his arm and pointed at the ruins—"*before* I return, and I then have no children? Or how will I know if Georgiana's suitors, whoever they will be, is the man who does this?"

"If our timelines are somehow both parallel and linear, then you've only been gone six weeks. You'll go back after three months and—"

"When does Georgiana marry, and what is his name? I must know before I go through Nine Ladies. You knew the year I died; tell me about my sister." His eyes were as wild as they were when in the throes of fever.

She pointed at the placard. "All I know is from an entry in a guidebook and what's written there. It says what year *you* died, not Georgiana. No one has thought of the family at Pemberley for two hundred years, and the house has been in ruins for one hundred."

"Does not your phone have access to more information than all of Pemberley's library? Find it!"

She tried to keep her patience in the face of his frustration and fear. "We don't know her married name or when she died. The records may not even be online." There was more he ought to know, even though it would hurt. "Although it won't happen as soon since you didn't die of diphtheria, this may still happen to Pemberley."

"That"—he pointed without looking—"ravaged shell and barren land is not *Pemberley*."

Anyone who had seen it in its stately prosperity could not compare this roofless brick pile to all that was Pemberley in 1811. "These big estates aren't going to provide employment and housing and patronage after . . ." Elizabeth trailed off because Darcy walked away.

"Darcy, wait! Where are you going?"

"Lambton." He did not wait or even slow down.

"What's in Lambton? It was an estate village for Pemberley, so it might be abandoned."

"The church will still be there. St. Anne's has stood since Norman times." He did not look at her, did not slow his pace. After walking all the way here from Bakewell, she had a hard time keeping up with his long, determined stride.

Darcy was focused with a single-mindedness that bordered on frightening. When the honey-colored sandstone buildings were within sight, Darcy said, "The old road to Pemberley once passed through the heart of Lambton."

"It looks like it was bypassed a long time ago."

They soon came to the ancient church, and Darcy stopped. "The verge at the eastern churchyard gate was the village green. And where the car park is, there was an enclosed orchard." She wasn't certain he was really talking to her. "And that giant yew in the churchyard was no taller than I am now when I last saw it."

"Why are we here? It's nine o'clock on a Wednesday morning, and the vicarage is obviously abandoned. I doubt a hundred people live in Lambton."

"I have no interest in those now living." He strode toward the gate and threw it open. "We shall check the south side first."

"Check it for *what*?"

"Georgiana's grave."

The air was driven from her lungs.

"Will not you help me, Elizabeth?" His back was bent to carefully read each gravestone.

"Why are you doing this to yourself?"

"What did Georgiana suffer in the short life she lived after I was gone?" he cried desperately. "Did she know her husband destroyed Pemberley? That could *still* happen. I might not marry when I return, I might have no children, I might die young from something other than diphtheria, and Pemberley might fall despite your saving me. I need to know the name of the man she marries and make sure he never has the chance to ruin our home and livelihood. I do not know why I am saved when others died, but I will not forsake the gift you have given me by doing *nothing*! My sister deserves a better life, and the more I know, the more likely I can make that happen."

The pain in his eyes was unmistakable. Elizabeth was struck by a thought: did Georgiana's death have anything to do with who or when she married? Could he save his sister from her fate as she had saved Darcy?

"Are families kept together? Would she be buried near your parents if she inherited Pemberley?"

Finally, Elizabeth felt that when Darcy looked at her, he actually saw her. "Yes, that is astute; they sometimes are." He led them farther in and stopped before a still-impressive marble marker. After their names, and their ages and the dates of his parents' deaths, it read:

Christ calls us hence, we must attend
Death takes us from our bosom friends
Our children dear we leave behind
In heaven our souls shall be entwined

"It's a lovely tribute. Did you write that?"

He nodded once, and his throat bobbed with an audible swallow; he resumed his search. Stoic, nineteenth-century Mr. Darcy was the one with her today. The austere gentleman, the one whose loyalty to Pemberley and his family was above all else. The one who couldn't save his parents, but who would find a way to give his sister a better life than the one she was destined for.

Many gravestones had become victims of weather, erosion, or even vandalism. Elizabeth found Georgiana's stone first.

In loving memory of
Georgiana
daughter of George Darcy and Lady Anne Darcy
aged 21
who died December 29, 1817

"That's short compared to the elegies on the other stones. Why is her married name not there? The guidebooks and sign still say that she married and died without children, and her husband was the one who bankrupted Pemberley. That hasn't changed yet, so why doesn't it have her married name?"

Darcy ran his fingers on the simple slab. "It is not the convention of the time as it implies she was unmarried. Whoever buried her did not want to honor the connection."

"Would her grave focus on her connection to the Darcys and not on the husband if she inherited Pemberley?"

He shook his head. "What man would not insist upon inscribing the name he gave to his wife on her gravestone?" After a deep breath, he said, loudly into the quiet of the churchyard, "The parish register will have her married name in the marriage or death records."

St. Anne's large Norman door was locked. "We shall have to come back." He stared at the door as though the power of his will might be enough to open it.

"Darcy, even if you can get someone to open the church, they won't have registers from two hundred years ago available for you to read. If they were here, they crumbled to dust or were chewed by mice."

"I need the name and the date! I could not refuse her every suitor or disinherit my sister entirely. I cannot *help* her with what I have seen today."

"We'll find another way. A parish record office, or online records, or deeds, or . . . I don't know yet. We've seen enough for one day."

"Do not presume to tell me what I can and cannot tolerate." The words held all the power of righteous indignation, or pride, but the pain in his eyes softened their impact. "However, I see I can accomplish nothing more here today."

They walked around the church toward the gate they came in through. The morning sunlight hit a short stone near the chancel door. Elizabeth's heart leapt into her throat. "Fitzwilliam."

"Please—" Whatever words were on his lips died when he saw what she pointed at.

Sacred
to the Memory of

> *Fitzwilliam Darcy*
> *Lost 1811, aged 27 years*
> *His life a beautiful memory*
> *His absence a silent grief*

"That can't be your *grave*, right? You—you're not there." She pointed at the ground beneath their feet.

"A memorial, I suspect, given where it stands."

Darcy knelt in front of the low stone. Instead of a double-breasted cutaway coat and a waistcoat with a high collar covering every inch of him, Elizabeth saw how tan he was at his neck and arms where she had insisted he roll up the sleeves of his untucked Oxford striped shirt. At her gentle insistence, he had gotten his hair cut last week. On the outside, he looked like he'd stepped off the pages of a 2011 fashion magazine. *But he doesn't belong here.* Elizabeth blinked a few times.

"Many people loved or respected you. Colonel Fitzwilliam and Reynolds knew the truth and might have placed the stone. Maybe they thought the antibiotics didn't work and you died in 2011."

"You were right." Darcy's voice sounded raw, and he was still on the ground staring at the low marker with his own name. "I have seen more than I can bear for one morning, Elizabeth."

She placed her hand on his shoulder, repressing the desire to raise the other hand to his hair and run her fingers through it. Darcy brought up a hand and covered hers, still looking at his memorial stone. He gently lifted her hand and pressed a warm kiss into her palm. Elizabeth closed her eyes, and when she opened them, Darcy stood before her, looking lost.

"None of this *has* to happen. All we see here is the evidence of one possible outcome. You'll go back." Her voice caught. "They won't live lives without you, and it won't end like this."

Darcy reached out and held her hand in his, keeping a tight grasp on it all the way to Bakewell.

She couldn't see how Darcy belonged in the twenty-first century, but in this moment it seemed perfectly clear that he belonged with her.

August 19, 2011

Seeing the remains of one's ancestral home labeled as a Grade I-ruined Georgian building was not a suffering he would wish on his worst enemy. *Seeing my sister's grave and my own memorial stone was beyond all bounds of what one ought to endure.* It was a sadness that stayed with him longer than any of the other more harrowing discoveries he had made in this modern world.

Pemberley was now a destitute place of former significance, its partial verticality mocking all that it once was, all that it ought to have remained. The house had no weather protection, its dirty plaster chipping, its exposed bricks crumbling, and it was a matter of time, more time, before it came tumbling down.

Darcy could not account for how he passed the days after their Pemberley visit. He persisted in this pensive, sad state until Sunday when Elizabeth reminded him he was to join Frank Danconia to watch a football match. *"You need a distraction, and nothing I say or do is helping."*

Football was not enough to distract him from thoughts of Elizabeth. When she diverted him from his melancholy over Georgiana and Pemberley, when she engaged him in intelligent conversation, or when her spirits rose to playfulness, Darcy thought nothing else could complete such a perfect picture of domestic felicity. In other moments, when he remembered the few weeks left until Nine Ladies opened its gate, he wished he was not confined to such intimate quarters with her.

My affections are engaged, and if I understood her looks, her touches, her words, her smiles correctly, Elizabeth's are too.

"It's your turn."

Frank's voice shattered his reverie. Darcy blinked and looked at the backgammon board. "I'm sorry." He quickly scooped up the dice.

"Why are we playing this? Don't get me wrong, I like it well enough."

"We're playing because you invited yourself over when you learned Elizabeth was gone until tomorrow, and because there is nothing on television worth watching. We chose backgammon because you're terrible at chess." He gave a lopsided smile and finished his turn.

"Well, don't get snarky with me. Need I remind you about your unfortunate bowling performance?"

"Not if you call yourself my friend."

Frank *had* become an unlikely friend. He was amiable, far from foolish, a little too teasing. It was not in Darcy's nature to be in deep intimacy with so newly formed an acquaintance, but Frank was not the sort to demand more than camaraderie.

"Where did you say the missus was?"

Darcy rolled the dice. "I am not married."

"Y'know I meant Elizabeth."

"We're just friends."

"Right then, where is your pretty, smart, platonic housemate who you have no sexual feelings for?"

"If you mean Elizabeth, she went to Sheffield to spend the day with her friend and decided to remain until the morning rather than catch a late bus. She regrets not being able to meet Gwen as she had planned."

"No worries. She just invited some ladies over for a Friday night. Wine and girly movies and too much yakking." They played a few more rounds before Frank spoke again. "So you and the American have nothing going on? Gwen says she doesn't have a fella back home."

Darcy wondered if he could record his voice on his phone saying the phrase "we're just friends" and play it as necessary. "We're just friends; that's the truth. I don't understand why it's so hard to believe." *Using contracted words makes it sound as though I have no education.*

"Don't think I haven't noticed how you check her out. Make your move. Sounds like there's not much waiting for her in the States, with a family who hardly notices her. She might stay if she had a reason. You can't tell me you don't like her."

"There's quite a great leap from admiration to"—he was about to say "matrimony"—"to making my move. Besides, I am soon to return to . . . university." *I cannot bring Elizabeth back to 1811. She was unable to speak her mind, unhappy at being unequal to men, unable to truly be the person she is here.* Darcy's heart whispered perhaps one inducement *might* allow her to consider the prospect of life two hundred years in the past. He tossed his dice forcefully after rejecting this idea.

Frank placed them in the cup, but rolled the cup between his hands as he looked at Darcy. "University . . . and what does one do with a doctorate in English literature?"

"Frank, I can tell you with complete honesty that I have no idea."

AUGUST 20, 2011

"Lucy, I'm home!"

Elizabeth burst into the parlor. Darcy did not understand the greeting or the inflection in her voice, but stood to greet her. She gave him an affectionate embrace. It supplied the place of language to bid him good afternoon and express that she had missed him. The contact startled him, after a lifetime of such embraces reserved only for his mother and sister, but it was still longed-for; he wrapped both arms around her waist while she clung to him.

"This was the first time since the end of March we've gone more than twenty-four hours without seeing each other." She pressed her cheek into his chest. "What am I going to do when you leave in September?"

"I will miss you exceedingly." The words, the truth, came naturally to his lips.

She pulled back to look at him, her hands at his neck, the warmth of her fingertips burning the sensitive skin there. *How could I have once scarcely allowed her to be a woman because she wore jeans rather than a gown?* His hands were now on her hips, his fingers brushing back and forth. When her dark eyes stopped gazing into his own and looked to his mouth, his heart thundered in his chest so loudly he thought Elizabeth could hear it. He was drawn to the way her face tilted up toward him, her lips parted.

A sharp trilling sound came from the floor, and Darcy looked down to see Elizabeth's purse move to and fro. Both quickly removed their hands. She muttered a quiet "damn it" and struggled to find her phone.

"Yes?" He never heard her answer a call so abruptly. "No, now is fine." She whispered the words "estate agent" to him and left.

There was nearly a conquest of eagerness over judgment. *A gentleman does not kiss the woman he admires without making a declaration.* A gentleman would only kiss his betrothed or his wife in the way he wanted to kiss Elizabeth.

He could not fall sacrifice to what could become an irresistible passion. He had every intention of keeping command over himself as he would if he were in 1811. Walking hand in hand with Elizabeth felt natural. Leaning against one another on the sofa while they chatted away an evening made him smile. He could not regret the times she had hugged him. Clearly, he was adopting modern notions of behavior.

If Elizabeth had been born in 1787 rather than 1987, he would ask her to marry him.

But Elizabeth could not go to a time with no electricity, no antibiotics, no running water, no right to vote, no right to be a respected professional. She was accustomed to the independence reserved for gentlemen, doing as she pleased and speaking her mind. The notion of women's subordinate place insulted her deeply. Darcy doubted she would be happy enough with him in a time that would frustrate her.

What he did know was that he fervently wanted to kiss her, that he did not know how to leave her if he ever did, and that September twenty-third and their permanent separation threatened to break both of their hearts.

I should not be in love with Darcy.

When she came home and saw his eyes filled with adoration, hugging him felt *right*. Friendships could suffer a few hugs, especially considering the bizarre nature of their relationship. No one else would ever understand their shared time-travel experiences. It was bound to draw them closer.

But if my phone hadn't rung, I would have kissed him.

How many actions could be justified as friendship when they harbored so much love underneath? Would a friend cling to his hands in a darkened room and beg to tell him his future to try to save everything he loved? She couldn't pretend she saved him only for Pemberley, or for Georgiana.

Darcy had to return to protect his sister from an awful marriage and an early death. He had to ensure that Pemberley, and every soul tied to it, wasn't run into the ground before their time. She loved him for it. Besides, Darcy didn't have a birth certificate or a passport, and couldn't get a job or a credit card. He didn't legally, technically exist here.

It didn't matter how many moments like the one downstairs passed between them, one of those moments where they both tacitly acknowledged an undercurrent of attraction. She may as well go downstairs and tell Darcy what she had learned on her bus ride back from Sheffield.

And somehow she had to keep her heart from shattering into a million pieces because she couldn't have him.

"Charlotte invited us to stay for a weekend visit next time she's not on call," she said to him over the dinner table.

"Would you not prefer to spend the time with your friends?"

"Aren't you one of my friends?" Her question came out breathier than it should have. Their eyes met, and there was a blush to Darcy's cheeks.

"Yes, of course; you know that. A very dear one." Darcy stopped finding his own plate fascinating and looked at her. "My object is not to be in the way of anybody, particularly when you will return to America and may not see Dr. Lucas for some time."

"Couldn't I say the same about you? The equinox is a month away. I'd like to spend as much time with you as I can before—before it's too late." *Great job maintaining boundaries.* "I'd like you to come." She heard her blood pounding in her ears, louder with every passing second.

"I would not insult your friend and refuse her invitation. And—and I could refuse you nothing that it was in my power to give."

Elizabeth screamed, in her own mind, *Then let me ask you to stay here with me!* The one thing she wanted to ask for, but never would, was the one thing he couldn't give her.

"I've got news. I did a little research about where to find local records." Darcy narrowed his eyes, no doubt from the rapid change in topic. She hurried on. "I found Church of England parish registers by county online. Fifteen thirty-seven through 1918."

"That is incredible. Did you learn who my sister married?"

"I found Georgiana's christening record, but someone copied it wrong. It was from the fall of 1796, but you said she was born in winter of 1795, so I'm guessing it was transposed wrong." Darcy stayed silent. "I found your baptismal record; no mistakes there. But there's no record of a Georgiana Darcy getting *married* in Derbyshire."

Darcy's shoulders fell, and Elizabeth was quick to continue. "So, I searched burial records for Derbyshire with the date on her tombstone. You were right to look for her grave. I found *one* record with a woman named Georgiana who died in this parish December 29, 1817. I haven't found a marriage record. We still don't have the marriage date or his first name and, clearly, mistakes can be made, but I think this is it."

"What is her married name?"

"Wickham. She died as Georgiana Wickham."

CHAPTER TWENTY

Darcy felt as though he had taken a sharp blow to the chest, and a sickening feeling settled into the pit of his stomach. How did such a horrid event come to pass?

"The problem is we don't know his first name or where he was born, or—"

"George Wickham was born in the same parish, within the same park, as I. We are nearly of the same age. I was born in February 1784, and Mr. Wickham was born two years later."

Elizabeth looked up sharply. "You *know* him?"

"It is my misfortune, yes, to be acquainted with Mr. Wickham." Even he was surprised by the wrath in his own voice. The tightening in his chest worsened.

She narrowed her eyes. "You've mentioned Mr. Wickham before."

"Indeed I have not! I no longer admit to his society, and he is not welcomed at Pemberley."

Elizabeth shifted in her seat. "You were delirious with fever, raving about how he shouldn't come to Pemberley."

Darcy imagined several inappropriate things he might confess to and about Elizabeth while uninhibited by fever. "What did I say?"

"Something about paying him three thousand pounds and that he shouldn't be a clergyman."

Elizabeth would not be satisfied with his silence. Not because she was accustomed to a society that shared more personal information, but because their relationship was so intimate that both parties now expected such things be shared.

"His father was my father's steward. Old Mr. Wickham was a respectable man, and my father supported his son's education. If he took orders, a valuable family living might be his when it became vacant. He was also left one thousand pounds in my father's will. Mr. Wickham was careful to hide his true nature from his benefactor, but was not able to escape my observations, when I had opportunities of seeing him in unguarded moments, which my father could not have."

"When you were feverish, you called him a cruel man."

"A man of vicious conduct and a total want of principles! He has pleasing manners and he charmed my father, but Mr. Wickham's only true interest is himself."

"What does that mean? What was inappropriate then might not be what I would consider inappropriate now."

Darcy barked a mirthless laugh. "I think not paying your debts is still wrong! And is gambling with money you do not have and leaving debts of honor not always reprehensible? Is seducing girls who are unprotected not shameful? Is spreading lies to suit one's own ends not always inexcusable? Please, do not tell me that your century has lost all morality, and that not only is gracious living dead but so are your scruples."

Elizabeth looked abashed and silently took the plates into the kitchen. Darcy immediately followed. "Elizabeth," he began, and she put down the dishes and turned on the tap. "I do not mean to insult your—"

"It's okay. Just another cultural difference that divides us." She met his eye. "And you're not wrong; this Wickham would be as awful now as he is in your time. You obviously refused to give him the living, so what happened?"

"He expected some monetary advantage in lieu of the preferment. I *wished* rather than believed him sincere about preferring to study the law, but, at any rate, I was ready to accede to his wishes. After I paid him three thousand pounds, I dissolved all connection between us."

"Then why did he haunt your fevered nightmares?" Elizabeth handed him a wet pot and pointed to the cloth on the counter. He no longer rolled his eyes at humble tasks. The simple, repetitive motions helped to calm him.

"He wrote to me after he learned the incumbent of the living died. Mr. Wickham had run through his money—four thousand pounds within three years! He confessed his circumstances were bad, and he demanded the living my father intended for him."

"He did *not!* He must have been angry when you told him to . . . take himself off."

"He wrote me several letters this year and was violent in his abuse to me on the subject. I suspect he is equally reproachful and slanderous when speaking of me to others."

Elizabeth rinsed another pot and handed it to him. "But somehow Georgiana marries him? Why does a sweet, smart girl like her marry a lying gambler?"

Darcy set the dry pot down, turned his back to the counter and leaned against it. "I cannot comprehend how an attachment might be formed between them. At best, she might remember him as a boy on the estate who amused her when she was young."

"And we know he can't be reformed since he ruins an estate worth ten thousand a year."

"What will happen to the servants and tenants under my care, and their families, should Mr. Wickham ruin Pemberley? Twenty-five farms have been held by the same families since the 1770s and many have ten- or twenty-year leases. That is an incredible amount of stability." Darcy shook his head. "That such permanence could be ruined so quickly is astonishing."

"So aside from how he treats your sister, it's a mark of Wickham's degenerate behavior if he bankrupts Pemberley before he dies?"

"He has no goodness, no integrity, no benevolence. While I am not one to believe people cannot see the errors in their behavior and improve, Mr. Wickham, although given the best education, is not one of them."

"If you're presumed dead, or if you died without children, everything goes to Georgiana?"

"Yes. I stipulate a few bequests to friends and family, and annuities to servants, but my will leaves Pemberley's holdings to her and her direct descendants."

"But she's not stupid. Why would she allow Wickham to set any plans that are bad for Pemberley? She can make a will that says he can't sell any land she inherited, or break any leases, or whatever, right?"

He gave her a confused look. "Mr. Wickham would be her husband."

"So?"

What could explain Elizabeth's ignorance? "By marriage, the husband and wife are one person in law. The legal existence of Georgiana will be incorporated and consolidated into that of her husband."

"I don't understand."

"Coverture. A wife is under the authority and protection of her husband. A true gentleman considers it his most sacred vow, his greatest responsibility to well provide for his wife. Georgiana would not have the property rights of a single or widowed woman once she is married."

"A wife in Georgian England can't own property in her own name? She can't sign legal contracts?"

"You sound distressed." In fact, she breathed rapidly and her face was red.

"Coverture is obsolete now. And by obsolete, I mean discredited, archaic, and insulting to half the human race! What woman could be happy to marry under those conditions?" The words were like a knife to his heart. "He will have control over Pemberley's income, everything Georgiana has?"

"Once a woman is married, any wealth or property the woman brought to the marriage or later inherits comes under the control of her husband, unless some settlement contracted beforehand makes a different provision."

"Why would any self-respecting woman, especially one with any property, get married? I would never—" Elizabeth made an effort to compose herself before she spoke again. "They could never be happy together."

She turned off the tap and moved to stand in front of him. Darcy suppressed his desire to wrap his arms around her. "No, his cold-hearted selfishness would crush her gentle spirit."

"I don't get how it happens. If she's under twenty-one, she needs your permission. You go home, explain what a monster Wickham is, and they'll never marry. What I want to know is why a slick guy like this wants to marry a shy fifteen-year-old. Granted, she looks older, but she's so nervous and introverted."

"He must have one object in his view: to make his fortune. Georgiana has thirty thousand pounds."

Elizabeth paled. "If Wickham *hates* you, what would punish you more than his marrying your sister, making her miserable, and getting her money? If you died of diphtheria and she is Pemberley's heiress, that makes it all the sweeter for him."

"Revenge," he whispered. "His strongest inducement is revenge." He did not think he could lose any more respect for Wickham, but this was inexcusable.

Elizabeth made to reach for him, but then pulled back. "You can stop this. She needs your permission to get married. Just tell her to never speak to Wickham and explain why."

"Would that be enough? Am I to be like Oedipus and self-fulfill a terrible prophecy by trying to prevent it? Can I change her fate, or will my warning against him drive her willingly into his arms?"

"She's not that sort of girl. And Wickham isn't going to wait years for her to turn twenty-one, especially if you would sign one of these settlements to take care of her, as far as that could go." She rolled her eyes.

Darcy paced the small kitchen. "Something is wrong. Fitzwilliam is also Georgiana's guardian. If either my cousin or I are there her to advise and protect her, how could she marry Mr. Wickham before she dies in 1817?"

Comprehension flashed through Elizabeth's eyes. "How could they marry without permission?"

Darcy stopped pacing. "She elopes. It is the only way."

"She *is* lonely, desperate to be loved . . . and Mrs. Younge wants Georgiana married so she can move on herself. Even if you're right, that doesn't change much. Now that we know the who and the how, the why doesn't matter. You can still stop them from marrying."

"How can I without keeping her with me at all times? He is a silver-tongued serpent! Or do I accept it as an immoveable truth and disinherit her to save Pemberley from Mr. Wickham?" He *had* to preserve Pemberley and its people, but could he preemptively dispossess Georgiana? He could not imagine having children of his own, now that he knew Elizabeth; he admired her too much to marry anyone else, for all the good it would do him.

Elizabeth gestured for him to follow her out of the small kitchen and into the parlor. She was about to sit next to him on the sofa, then changed her mind and sat on the adjacent one. "You don't want to do that. Bloodlines are important in your time. Unless you have a thing against leaving property to women?"

"I am not one to say a woman should never be trusted with money. I would leave Pemberley to Georgiana without hesitation." It was not blood that mattered in this case. It was his sister's happiness and Pemberley's future. "We must determine when Mr. Wickham convinces my sister to elope. If they went off to Scotland between 1811 and 1817, can you not find a record of their marriage so I know the precise date?"

"I still say it's not going to happen while you're in 2011, and once you tell Georgiana the truth about him . . . Darcy, you know she'd never do anything to upset you."

"I wish to know all I can. I will be more able to protect her from a sad fate and possibly an early death if I know all."

She gave him an earnest gaze. "I know how you feel."

"How can you? Mr. Wickham will do worse than not love her as she deserves. He would stifle her spirit, bankrupt her home, restrict her movements, and limit her personal funds. It is preposterous to presume he would be faithful to her. And what if it is as a result of her marriage to Mr. Wickham that she dies so young? You cannot know how this preys upon me!"

Elizabeth rose. "I lived with your death hanging over me for three months. Do you know how hard it was to like you more and more, all the while knowing you would be dead by the end of the year?"

Darcy's heart leapt to his throat. "I do not doubt that your regard for me must have been a trial, knowing my fate as you did. And I regret that I did nothing to help you by refusing your every entreaty to tell me about what would come."

"When people started dying, and you got a sore throat . . ." Tears filled her eyes. "I hid in your dressing room while that doctor examined you because I thought the more I knew, the more likely I could keep you alive." He gasped in awe. "I told Reynolds to write to your cousin because he knew about Pemberley ending in ruins. I did it so we could convince you to do whatever was necessary to save you, but I was wrong." Her voice raised in pitch. "Nothing in 1811 would have saved you! So I *do* know what it feels like to know an awful truth about someone you love, and the fear there's nothing you can do to protect them."

The word struck *him* first, and he inhaled an unsteady breath. It was an unconscious confession, and Elizabeth closed her eyes, a few tears escaping from the corners and falling to her pinking cheeks. Darcy stood and raised a shaking hand to brush them away with his thumb, first one cheek and then the other.

Joy flooded his veins upon hearing the word "love," and then his heart sank with disappointment. He could not make his declarations in return. *A profession of love and admiration is tantamount to a marriage proposal, and she made her opinion on marriage in my time clear.* She could never be happier in the nineteenth century than she was here, and so his love could not be spoken or acted upon.

He curved his hand around the back of her neck to draw her closer, and pressed a gentle kiss across her forehead before resting his own against hers. Elizabeth's hand reached up to cling to his neck. Darcy closed his eyes, struggling with what, if anything, he could say.

"Elizabeth . . ."

"Don't."

Do not confess the depth of my own attachment? Do not ask you to return with me? Do not tell you that I cannot stay with you and forsake my sister and Pemberley? His balance was then thrown off, and he stumbled forward. Elizabeth had stepped away, and she dashed her hand across her eyes to wipe her remaining tears.

"You came for the penicillin, that's all. You need to save Pemberley and its people and, more importantly, Georgiana." Her voice was full of forced cheer. "I know about doing right for family. I left everything to take care of my estranged dad. At least Georgiana is deserving of you. Blood is thicker than water, right?"

She was trying to be flippant. If he could not admit the strength of his own affection, he could at least disabuse her of one idea, and confide in her a different truth.

"You assume that our"—Darcy swallowed the word "love"—"that a romantic devotion is beneath a fraternal one, and that bloodlines are more important to me than anything else. It is rather that responsibility to my family and the scores who depend upon the Darcys compels me to return."

"I know." He saw she did, as much as it wounded her.

"There is one thing you do not know. Georgiana and I were children in the same family, had the same first associations and habits, although separated by more than a decade. Despite our difference in sex, age, and manner, we are fond of one another. But we do not share the same blood."

He saw the deep interest, the absorbed attention in her eyes. "Georgiana isn't your sister?"

"By all accepted accounts, legal and filial, she is. But only three other people living know she was not born to my family, although she was raised and loved as a daughter."

Elizabeth fell into the sofa with an openmouthed expression of shock. "*Georgiana* was the infant found on Stanton Moor in 1796!" She gave a little smile. "My money was on Young Henry."

"He *was* orphaned, but from a typhus-like fever, not through rifts in time. Young Henry is Hank Roland's grandson and is fifteen years old. Georgiana, however, is not fifteen. Whenever you—indeed, anyone—commented on how much older she looks, I was reminded of what it was to lie, how I hated it, but had to for her sake. Her precise age is unknown, but since she toddled and babbled when Roland found her at Nine Ladies, she had likely had her first birthday."

"So Roland brought her to Pemberley, and your parents kept her like a stray dog?"

"No! They had to justify her presence in such a way that they could keep her near but three months later explain her absence. My parents . . ." Darcy looked away to gather his thoughts. "I was well loved, an only child, but my parents had the capacity to love more children than they were blessed with. They intended to keep the little girl well protected, and I suppose well loved, until the winter solstice. My mother was in town when my father wrote to her about the infant, so they announced Georgiana had been born in London the previous winter, that my mother suffered a long lying-in, and both she and the baby had been poorly for months."

"Wouldn't everyone have known if your mother was pregnant?"

"My mother was reserved and private. My parents claimed to be poor reckoners, having had no other children for twelve years. My mother came from town and pretended to arrive with the infant. With Reynolds's help, they announced Georgiana had been born in town months earlier, that mother and child had convalesced in the south in solitude, and now that both were well, it was time to bring her home to Pemberley. I know now it was their intention to send Georgiana back at the winter solstice and tell everyone she died."

"Babies died so often it wouldn't have been suspicious." Elizabeth threw up her hands. "I can't believe your parents got away with it. They told everyone Georgiana was born in the winter of 1795 after she came through Nine Ladies at the autumnal equinox in 1796?" She frowned. "How did they pass a one-and-a-half-year-old as a ten-month-old baby?"

"My fair-haired mother came home with a fair-haired infant, who grew into a tall little girl that my tall father claimed to be his. Reynolds was my mother's lady's maid at the time and said she had known her mistress to be with child. To be blunt, my family is wealthy and influential, and as they already had a son to inherit, nothing could be lost if Georgiana was not born to my mother, which between her loyal servants and her respectability, no one questioned since my father accepted Georgiana."

"What about you?"

"My feelings could not have changed years later when I learned the truth of her origins."

"No, I mean when you were a kid. You weren't suspicious as to where this baby suddenly came from?"

"I was sent to the home of a gentleman scholar to be tutored. I saw her but once before the solstice when I came home for Christmas holidays." Darcy shook his head with a bemused smile.

"I was a boy more interested in finishing my lessons and playing games than wondering about the appearance of a sister. That she was my family was enough for me. Over time I grew fonder of her, rather doting for an older boy unused to children at all; and when I learned the truth, it changed nothing. Georgiana is my sister."

Elizabeth crossed her arms. "Let me guess the rest. Your mother, who by Reynolds's accounts loved you and Georgiana to pieces, couldn't put *her* kid in the stone circle, in the dark, in winter, hoping she would be safe when she got back to 1996."

Darcy considered sitting next to Elizabeth, but decided to remain standing at a distance. "All I know for certain is that when she appeared in autumn, they did not intend to keep her forever. In the winter, they dared not leave Georgiana to die of exposure if no one found her in the future, and by the time the chance to return her came again the following summer, Georgiana would not stay in the circle. She kept running out, screaming for Mamma. What parent, even an adoptive one, could turn their back?"

"My father turned his back, threw out his wife and two daughters—never mind." Darcy took two steps toward her, but she held up her hand. "This isn't about me." She gathered her composure "That explains why the christening record I found says Georgiana was baptized in the fall of one year when she was allegedly born in the winter of the previous one."

"We did not—we *do* not have the personal authentication demands as you do. My father said she was born in town and had yet to be christened. It was easy, all matters considered, to pass her off as their own."

Elizabeth leaned back in the sofa, drumming her fingers against the armrest. "Georgiana thinks she's nearly sixteen . . ."

"But she is, in truth, already over seventeen."

"I'm the last person to judge about meddling with when and where people belong, but did your parents wonder about Georgiana's birth parents?"

Darcy finally sat, not next to her, but adjacent on the other sofa. He leaned against the arm, toward her, selfishly enjoying how she leaned closer in return. "I know my parents loved her completely, and when the time came to send her away from the only home she knew, to perhaps end up abandoned or dead, it seemed crueler to Georgiana than the cruelty of keeping her away from the mother who had born her."

Their hands were inches apart on their respective sofa arms. Darcy watched her fingers stretch, then close into a fist. He wanted to grasp her hand too. Her attention was still on the gap of space between their fingers when she spoke. "You'll go back to keep Georgiana from a miserable fate because she's your sister. That you see her that way even after learning the truth is one of the things I—I admire about you."

"I cannot undo what was done to bring her to us. She *is* Georgiana Darcy of Pemberley. She hardly remembers our mother, and our father died when she was a schoolgirl. She needs her *brother*, and for more than to keep her from marrying Mr. Wickham."

"In your time, she's an adult, ready to land a husband if Mrs. Younge has anything to say about it. If she lived in this century, she would be trying to convince you to let her stay out later with her friends, getting ready to attend university. If she did get married, she would have rights distinct from her husband."

"I do not doubt the near limitless opportunities here for young ladies. But Georgiana is *loved* there, and it is the only home she knows."

Elizabeth stood, and he rose out of habit. "Then you'd better find a new companion, because Mrs. Younge will push her into the arms of anyone who will take her, even this awful Wickham. She does need you. Your sister—whatever I think of her being kept there, Georgiana *is* your sister—needs to spend more time at Pemberley, with you. You have to show her it is her home and that she *is* loved and needed. She's as much a Darcy of Pemberley as you are. Give her responsibility at Pemberley, something real for her to be proud of herself about."

"It would be appropriate for a gentleman to keep a sister more than ten years his junior in his home if he was—" Darcy stopped. The wife he wanted, but could not have, stood in front of him.

She understood what he had not said. Her eyes dimmed, and her insincere smile returned. "Isn't that what you're supposed to do when you're a single wealthy man? Find a wife to be the lady of the house and have children. Given your devotion to Pemberley, you don't strike me as unwilling to commit."

"I am not unwilling to commit myself; I am unwilling to commit my affections unequally. My mother's family, my aunt in particular, expect me to marry my cousin to unite our fortunes."

"Marrying cousins is going to fall out of fashion, let me tell you. Still, there's the solution: marry her, have children, keep your sister at home until she finds a wonderful husband, and Pemberley is saved." Bitterness crept into her voice, no matter how she tried to be lighthearted.

He strove to answer playfully. "I *could* marry Anne, but I value my ability to do as I please without reference to anyone else. She is not worth the sacrifice."

"You tried to convince me, months ago, that you weren't a selfish man."

"My aunt would take my marrying her dreary, uneducated daughter as an invitation to manage all of my concerns. She is an arrogant woman and would always be at Pemberley with us. It is not selfishness to not marry my cousin, it is self-preservation."

Elizabeth laughed, although tears hovered in her eyes. "I always found you surprisingly funny, Darcy. I doubt many people get to see that wry, humorous side of you. Still, it could be a quick fix to most of your problems."

Darcy could no longer maintain this pretense. "I do not marry Anne because I do not admire her. I could not *love* her as a husband ought."

Her normally bright eyes now showed a tortured dullness. "I don't need to hear about how much you ought to love your wife. It's been a long day." She turned, but he caught her hand in his own.

"Tell me, Elizabeth, do you think I will not regret leaving you?"

Pain was carved in merciless lines around her eyes and mouth. He suspected his own face reflected the same grief. "Does it matter? Even if you've thought of a life at Pemberley, preserving your legacy and your sister's happiness, but with the loneliness of being without—" She pressed her lips together.

"Without you?"

A few of the tears fell. "Right. You might have a few sleepless nights struggling between duty and desire, and comparing saving Pemberley and being alone against the temptation of what is essentially a life in exile in the twenty-first century. But there's too much at stake for you to stay."

"And I dare not consider how you would fare in 1811 without the rights and choices you are accustomed to. But you forget a life here, in what you call exile, would be with *you*, a life with companionship as such I will never know again. I dare not ask a question of you when I know I would not receive a favorable reply. I would not ask you a question that would pain you to refuse. But as to how I think of remaining or leaving, you must know both are unbearable."

CHAPTER TWENTY-ONE

SEPTEMBER 7, 2011
ALVASTON, DERBYSHIRE

"You didn't have to do this, Frank."

"Don't be ridiculous." Gwen answered, twisting around from the front seat to look at Elizabeth. "You are not taking the bus to your father's house. Besides, Darcy insisted. We've decided to walk along the riverside park after we drop you off. Have Darcy text Frank when you've finished."

He had insisted Frank drive her to pack up her father's house before its contents and the house itself were sold, but Darcy didn't talk to her much lately. He acted like a modern twenty-seven-year-old in public, but when alone with her now, he was reserved. The affection and casualness he had displayed with her was now hidden behind the hauteur she had first seen from him at Pemberley all those months ago, and it made her angry.

Did they love each other? *Is it even love if it can't be acknowledged?* She could ask him to stay in 2011, but he would never sacrifice Pemberley and Georgiana. And they could never justify his existence here without documents to prove who he was, let alone find him a career in a world that he could scarcely comprehend. Darcy might have asked her to go back with him, but they both knew that she would be miserable there without any of the rights she once took for granted here.

"Which house am I looking for?" Frank called.

She blinked and snapped her head to the side. "There, number 32."

Darcy unbuckled the seatbelt and flung himself from the car. Elizabeth suspected Darcy was using all the power of his formidable will to not throw up.

"Give us a text when you're done, yeah?" Frank called to Darcy.

Darcy gave a careless wave over his shoulder. His head was bent, and he put both hands on his waist, and was breathing slowly.

Gwen and Frank shared a confused look; Elizabeth mentioned something about motion sickness, thanked them as she got out, and unlocked the front door. The lounge's walls were covered floor to ceiling with bookshelves. It made the room appear small and dark. One wall was filled with books about advanced physics and math. On the other wall, across from the oversized chair, where most people might have placed their television, were more shelves. These were filled with novels, biographies, and, of course, poetry.

What an interesting juxtaposition. What sort of conversations would we have had over the dining table if my father had stuck around?

"Should you like to keep your father's books, Miss Bennet? I am willing to pack your selections for you."

Elizabeth had not heard Darcy come in. "No, I just need to look inside each one and make sure there's nothing there."

She began at the top left of the first bookcase, pulled out a book on general relativity, held it open by its covers and shook it, flipped through it, and when nothing fell out, she put it back and began on the next. To her annoyance, Darcy stared at the physics titles over her shoulder.

"I'll be here all day if I have to explain physics since Isaac Newton," she snapped. Out of the corner of her eye she saw Darcy flinch. They were in an untenable position, and she didn't have to make it worse. "Jane was the one who inherited the science aptitude; I'm just good at math. I can hardly explain to you what makes up an atom."

Every so often he pulled out a book, furrowed his brow, returned it to its place, and looked up something on his phone. Elizabeth examined every book before searching the dining room, but there were no family dishes, no embroidered napkins in the drawers.

She went upstairs to search through an office. Not a single picture frame graced the room. She had gone through his pertinent papers after her father had his stroke; she now searched what little remained. It was more cluttered than any room she looked through, but the search yielded nothing personal.

There has to be something.

"Physics seeks to explain the rules of the world, and of what substance, what matter, these atoms make up the world." Darcy startled her as he appeared in the doorway. "Those who study it wish to comprehend the structure of the universe."

"In your time, the church is so prevalent, and scientists are only hobbyists. Is it hard for you to reconcile faith and science?"

"Not at all." He held an Einstein book on the general theory of relativity. "Embedded in these calculations and theories are the workings of the universe, hidden forces, and relationships so complex only God could have created them."

He never ceased to surprise her. "That is a remarkable observation."

They looked at each other longingly. Darcy recovered first, his expression gaining in austerity. "I think time travel has little support in theoretical physics."

"And yet here you are," she said drily.

"All gentlemen—forgive me, all *people* have a profession now; what was your father's? I suspect he was a natural philosopher, but how does this have an application in the marketplace?"

"Something about fabricating nuclear reactors for the Royal Navy submarine fleet." She stood quickly, her legs tingling after kneeling for so long. She stumbled, and Darcy reached toward her. Elizabeth recoiled, and he clasped his hands behind his back.

"How does a vessel—"

"Google submarines while I check the bedrooms." She moved past him without another word.

There were no photographs. The journal on the bedside table had scrawled calculations and not personal reflections. She pulled open the drawers in the chest, being sure to check underneath every item and under the bed. The last room was a small bedroom at the end of the hall that had been turned into a cozy television room. It could have belonged to any man in any country in almost any time.

The loft!

It was dim, dusty, and she learned the hard way that she couldn't stand upright. But there was a single trunk in the corner.

"Hey Darcy, I need your help."

He appeared at the foot of the ladder. "Your servant, Miss Bennet."

"Can you help me with this trunk?"

Elizabeth shoved the trunk to the top of the ladder, and before she could climb down with her end of it, Darcy took it from her and left the room with it. *Show off.* Her mother always did say the best thing about men was that they could more easily do heavy lifting.

She eagerly raised its lid. Diplomas, his dissertation, yearbooks, newspaper articles with her father's name dated no later than 1982. No pictures of her or Jane, no clippings of their birth announcements. No scribbled drawings. Not even a crinkled, forgotten wedding picture.

My mother wouldn't have taken every single photograph with her. Did he throw them away?

There was no indication in the entire house that he had ever been married or had two daughters.

"Damn it!" She slammed the lid, bracing her hands on the trunk as she hung her head.

"Good God! What is the matter?"

"Nothing."

"Forgive me, but you are very ill."

She drummed her fingers on the lid. "What does ill mean? I'm sick, I look badly, I'm acting immorally?"

"I mean that you are troubled, and seeing your distress brings me sorrow."

She looked at him emptily. "What does a nineteenth-century gentleman do when a lady is distressed, *Mr.* Darcy? You wouldn't ask me what's wrong. That was an impolite, emotional mistake. Your self-control is slipping, *sir*."

"I wish . . . a gentleman would ring for your maid or sister to comfort you. If you were alone, I would offer you a glass of wine."

She snorted. "You did that for me once, when Colonel Fitzwilliam was going on about how women were beneath men in every way and I didn't think I would survive one day in 1811."

"I am concerned for you." He said the words as though he was saying it looked like rain.

"And there might have been a time when you would ask me what was the matter as if you cared about the answer!" She stood, kicking aside the trunk with a forceful shove. "I'm done; I'll hire the firm the realtor recommended to clear out the house."

"Please, look at me." She did, with a sigh. "What were you searching for?"

"Something to tell me about who my father was or what he thought of missing out on his daughters' lives. His will says his estate should be liquidated and the proceeds split between Jane and me. That's the only proof in his entire life that he had two children."

Darcy watched her in silence as tears welled up in her eyes. The rise and fall of his chest was the only indication that he was a living, breathing man and not a marble statue.

"I used to imagine my father had a pile of unsent birthday cards for me and Jane that he couldn't bring himself to mail because he felt guilty. Or I'd find years of letters marked 'return to sender' because my mother wanted to keep him from us. I was so stupid!"

Darcy shook his head.

"There's no collection of the letters I wrote to him as a child. Did he even read them? The photos I gave him the two times he saw us when we were teenagers aren't here either. I thought I'd find a hint we meant something to him. But there's nothing, Darcy. Because his daughters were nothing to him. The proof is right here in this house."

Darcy looked pained, but was still silent. It fueled her already burning anger. "All you can do is stand there like a gentleman who would as soon put his hand into a fire than overstep the bounds of propriety."

"Miss Bennet, a man who feels—"

"Are you going to call me *Miss Bennet* until the equinox?"

"I mean you no disrespect, madam."

"Madam? No, you mean to treat me like we're strangers to make it easier for you to leave." Elizabeth breezed past him toward the front door, seething with annoyance.

"Miss Bennet." She didn't stop. "Elizabeth, please!" She stopped, and he came around to face her.

"You are so quick to think the worst of me. Do you believe that reestablishing the boundaries I ought to have maintained whilst I was here is what I *prefer*? That it is easy for me to watch your suffering and not act as I wish?"

Her voice was shaky as she admitted, "I can't bear to be stuck with you until the end of the month and have you act coldly towards me."

"Neither can I bear to do it. It was badly done. I want to comfort you but I have no right, and that is painful to me. I was preparing myself for my inevitable departure."

"Will it make it easier if you treat me the same way you'd treat Miss Bingley? Because it's making it worse for me."

"No, particularly when I recall all of the times you have been a comfort to me in this strange place. I could not have seen Pemberley's ruins and the graveyard if I had not you with me." His gaze turned intense. "Mr. Bennet does not deserve your tears. You were a poorly fathered daughter, and in spite of this, you have become an admirable and accomplished woman, full of humor, love, and intelligence." She then found herself pressed to his heart with the words, "My dear Elizabeth."

She was stunned *he* pulled her in to hug her. This was what she needed, even if they both knew it couldn't last.

"There is nothing to justify his abandonment because what Mr. Bennet did was unjustifiable. He was an indolent man more content with his books than doing what was right by his children."

She refused to cry. Darcy was right; her father did not deserve her tears. "Why didn't he want to know his own daughters?"

"I can think of no decent excuse, only plausible explanations. Perhaps the distance or a dislike of your mother kept him absent. It appears he was not a man inclined to strong attachments or exertion."

"You must think me naïve, expecting to find hidden photographs and unsent letters when every piece of evidence over the past twenty years showed he didn't care."

"I have thought many things about you from the moment you appeared from Nine Ladies, but naïve was never one of them. In spite of Mr. Bennet's abandonment, you have become clever, confident, and self-reliant, capable of love and laughter."

"I want to leave. Can you text Frank?" She went outside and sat on the steps to wait. When Darcy joined her she said, "Thank you. I mean it—thank you for coming with me."

"My parents made mistakes, as all parents do, but how any father—how could he desert you? I cannot comprehend it."

"Because you have this ingrained sense of duty I've never seen in anyone else. And you're capable of more love." She looked away. "And that's why on the equinox you're going to save Georgiana from marrying Wickham, you're going to make sure she's happy and confident, you're going to take care of Pemberley and the people who depend on it. And someday you're going to be a good father. You're a better man than my dad ever was."

She sat close enough to Darcy to feel the brief tension course through him. "I dare not think of my future as a father, but I thank you for the praise. Was it—was it painless for you as the solstice approached? Did the eagerness of returning home make it easier to think about leaving"—his lips pressed together—"to leave Pemberley?"

She cast him a dark look. "I thought you were on your deathbed! I knew I'd miss you, and Georgiana too, and it was a thousand times worse when I realized no doctor in 1811 would keep you alive after I left. Electricity and equality weren't in the front of my mind anymore. As soon as I had the idea to bring you with me, I would have begged, borrowed, and stolen to get you into that stone circle."

"Too good, too excellent creature!" She supposed that was a compliment. "Your disappearance went unnoticed given your temporary estrangement from your family. I wonder how mine shall be explained."

"Colonel Fitzwilliam and Reynolds are doing all they can to keep your disappearance a secret. You don't remember signing them, but they drafted letters to your family, to Mr. Willers, to Georgiana, to be delivered at various times during your alleged convalescence. I think you'll be okay."

Elizabeth did not even notice the airplane passing overhead until she saw Darcy look up and flinch.

"How can one commit oneself to flying at such height and such speeds? I can scarcely tolerate to ride in your cars. What, if anything, should I say to the few who know the truth? How could I explain one can fly thirty thousand feet above the earth and travel from London to New York in seven hours? I shall have none to confide in about all I have seen and done."

"Talk to Reynolds."

"You sound confident that she would be both willing to hear me and be able to comprehend me."

Darcy didn't sound suspicious, but Elizabeth cringed at her mistake. She had promised Sandra Reynolds that she would keep her secret. "She loves you like a son, although she'd never admit it. She's known about Nine Ladies since the beginning, and she's calm under pressure. If you want to talk to anyone about this century, she could handle it."

Elizabeth felt her cell phone buzz, and read the text. "Charlotte asks if we want to come to Sheffield next weekend."

"I have said I would join you should she invite us, and you wish to go."

"Are you going to call me Miss Bennet and not stand within three feet of me?"

"I will act as I had done before I—before we . . ." He sighed. "I do not want for my last days in 2011 to be filled with animosity. Leaving will be . . . difficult, however necessary—it will be difficult regardless of how I act with you."

Elizabeth knew he was embarrassed, and looked back at her phone. What she read made her groan aloud. "Charlotte wants to go to a club on Saturday. Her friend booked a VIP table at a new place called the Viper Rooms. I get the impression Missy goes out a lot." How was she going to explain an upscale nightclub, the alcohol and sexual innuendo, with a DJ playing house music, and laser lights on a dance floor?

"Is a club like Brooks's or White's but for both sexes?"

Elizabeth giggled. It soon became a full-blown belly laugh. Darcy gave her a look of pure confusion.

"You thought public assemblies were bad. This will be hysterical. Or go horribly wrong. I promise we can leave after an hour, but I *have* to take you clubbing!" She was still gasping for air and laughing.

"I comprehend that now female laughter no longer has the negative connotations it once did, but forgive me, what the hell is wrong with you?" Darcy pulled her to her feet, looking at her askance.

"Nothing. I just needed a good laugh after today, after the last few days. Remember that suit you saw in the newspaper advertisement? It's lucky I sold the rest of those Georgian coins because you're going to need it. In order to go to an exclusive nightclub and sit at a VIP table, you'll need to dress to impress."

September 15, 2011
8 days until autumnal equinox

Darcy stood before the mirror, his phone propped on the bathroom sink, practicing tying the neckcloth to his newly purchased evening dress by watching videos on YouTube. He had managed a four-in-hand knot and was now determined to master a Windsor knot.

In another week, I will have my valet to do this for me.

He had done well without servants. His modern clothing required less care to maintain. There were no fires to light, and the vacuum and hot water heater were astonishing feats of engineering. Food shopping was tiresome, but he managed to prepare a toasted cheese sandwich without doing irreparable harm to either the pan or the cooker. Or his fingers.

I refuse to leave this mirror before I can tie this knot. He tugged it off and tried again. Not knowing how to tie the damned thing caused him embarrassment at the tailor, and he was not going out without knowing how to tie it impressively. He considered asking Frank, but he did not want to admit that, as someone supposedly born in 1984, he was a twenty-seven-year-old man who did not know how to tie a tie.

With only the instructions from Elizabeth that he "not look like a banker or an undertaker," he placed himself in the hands of the shop attendants. He thought it a wasteful expenditure no matter how pleased he was with the result. However, Elizabeth insisted he would not be allowed into some establishments were he not attired in the gray suit with deep blue silk lining now packed in a garment bag along with what Elizabeth referred to as her "swanky new cocktail dress."

Given how ladies' evening necklines plunged in 1811 and how hemlines are scarcely decent now, I dare not to imagine how Elizabeth will appear.

His poorly considered and poorly executed plan to distance himself had failed spectacularly. They meant too much to one another to sustain the aloofness while they lived in isolation with one another.

If I chose her, if I stayed, I would have an extraordinary source of happiness. I would never be alone again, but I would have the everlasting guilt of having chosen desire over duty. To confess he wanted to marry her was impossible. He could not ask her to sacrifice every modern convenience and privilege for his sake. Even if she was willing now, she would ultimately resent living two hundred years in the past, and that would lead to her resenting *him*.

Darcy ripped the tie off again, cursing his lack of focus. He must go back, and go back alone. That did not mean he was right to treat Elizabeth coldly. He could not forget the tenets of being a gentleman: honor, courtesy, generosity. He would act honorably toward Elizabeth and not give in to temptation, he would treat all he encountered with the good manners of this time, and treat his dearest friend with the kindness she deserved.

There was a knock. "Darcy? I left a bag in your room to pack your stuff for tomorrow."

He opened the door. The purple and gray silk necktie hung around his neck. Elizabeth took one look at him and raised an eyebrow. "How's it going?"

"Perfectly well, I thank you."

"I can remember my grandmother tying my grandfather's ties when he was alive. Do you want me to give it a try?"

"No! Any respectable adult member of my sex is able to tie his own necktie. I am determined to master this on my own."

Elizabeth picked the phone up and held it at eye level so he could more easily watch the video. He thanked her with a look, and her gentle smile showed she was happy to do it. These non-verbal understandings would be one of the many things about her he would miss when he left.

CHAPTER TWENTY-TWO

Sᴇᴘᴛᴇᴍʙᴇʀ 16, 2011
7 ᴅᴀʏs ᴜɴᴛɪʟ ᴀᴜᴛᴜᴍɴᴀʟ ᴇǫᴜɪɴᴏx

"Why can I not tell your friends I prefer the music of my own time?"

"A millennial Englishman doesn't love Beethoven and Haydn."

"I told Frank to select whatever music he preferred whenever I ride with him, dreadful experience that it is. I speak of the car, not of the music. I fail to see why I cannot speak of historiography or literature. *You* speak of books."

"Nobody can talk about books at a nightclub."

"We will not always be at this nightclub."

"Can you accept I know what I'm talking about? I didn't put up a fight about learning how to play whist."

"Fine. What would you have me do?"

"Pick a decade between 1950 and 2000. I'll find songs for you to listen to and articles to read. Memorize the bands and their hits. That means commit their popular songs to memory."

Elizabeth and Darcy caught the bus to Sheffield. It was lucky there were frequent stops and the bus never had the opportunity to travel at high speeds for long because Darcy felt sick whenever he put his fate into the hands of a machine that traveled more than thirty miles per hour.

"The 1990s or 2000s will do."

"What made you pick then?"

Darcy shrugged and threw up his hands. He was more open with his gestures and expressions than he had been in 1811; she liked it. "If I was born in 1984, my musical preferences would have been established before I reached my majority. The end of the 1990s and early 2000s would be appropriate to that time in my life."

Elizabeth wondered if she could convince Darcy to argue the artistic merits of "Oops . . . I Did it Again" or profess how much he admired the Backstreet Boys. No, she couldn't be that mean. Taking him clubbing would be bad enough.

"Let's say that Fitzwilliam Darcy, master of Pemberley, is a Britpop fan. You like Oasis and Blur. You should listen to the Smiths and the Kinks, and the Beatles too. Let's find you an earworm. Close your eyes so you don't get carsick." She plugged in the headphones, placed one earbud in her right ear, and handed the other to Darcy.

Darcy took it and placed it in his ear. "I understood less than half of the words that came out of your mouth."

"And I don't understand the difference between full-dress and half-dress. But we make do, don't we?"

THEY WERE WAITING AT THE BUS STATION WHEN DARCY SAID, "Will not Dr. Lucas soon arrive?"

"You mean, 'won't Charlotte be here soon?'" Elizabeth looked at her watch. "Yes, she worked until seven but was coming straight here."

"Is there anything I need know about those whom I will meet? Specifically, is there anything I need know of them, their lives, or professions that I may not readily comprehend?"

Elizabeth turned on the bench to get a better view of Darcy's face. Had she not spent three months in absolute privacy with him, she might not have been able to read the alarm in his eyes. All of Darcy's lately acquired knowledge of what was practiced now was on the point of being called into action in the company of strangers.

"You're doing well here. I don't tell you that enough."

He sighed. "I do not think I told you the same while we were at Pemberley. I ought to have done."

"For all the differences between us, who else could understand what you and I have been through?"

"There are always experiences we can only share imperfectly; however, you are right that none but you could empathize with what I must do to pass in a strange land out of my proper time."

Elizabeth resisted both the urge to peck him on the lips and to tell him to speak with Reynolds.

"You know Charlotte is a physician. She's sensible and attentive, and doctors are respected professionals because they're trained and save lives. Her friend, Missy King, is married and is a mental health nurse. Mental health problems aren't something to be ashamed of. I gather she works to make things better for other people because she gets no attention from her husband who married her for her money."

"I thought those of this century make marriages based on mutual affection."

"People still take into account how responsible someone is with money and their financial future together. Missy will be the first to tell you her husband married her for her money, but I don't know why *she* married *him*. I think you'll find her a little brash. Don't be surprised if she calls me Liz, even though I hate it and asked her not to."

"How charming. Dr. Lucas has a sister?"

"Yes, Maria is years younger than Charlotte and their brothers. She makes Georgiana look talkative. She has an internship at a library, something about newspapers. Last is Charlotte's childhood friend Willie Collins. He calls himself an artist and is desperate for praise. He will be . . . what's the phrase? He will be a 'tax on your forbearance.'"

"I am used to parading and vulgarity from those forced upon my notice, and from those who feel they have a claim upon my interest. I can tolerate Dr. Lucas's friends with admirable calmness and decent composure."

"For my sake?"

"No, because it is right to be done."

Rather than tell him how proud of him she was, Elizabeth teased. "I doubt you can take the trouble to be civil to strangers beneath you in consequence, Mr. Darcy."

"You take great pleasure in professing opinions that are not your own."

"You know me too well. And I know *you*; you can roll your eyes when they're not looking and I'll still consider you a gentleman."

"Miss Bennet, you insult me." Darcy's tone was low and even, but his eyes were bright and a smile tugged at his lips. "You dare to presume I will not behave in a gentlemanlike manner?"

"Well, you *are* a proud, unpleasant sort of man."

Darcy smiled. He rested his arm along the back of the bench and bent his head toward her. "This is your opinion of me? It cannot be, because I am a man without defect."

"That might be true now. You've learned to laugh at yourself since I first met you." Elizabeth tilted her head up and leaned closer.

"I have at least learned to allow *you* to laugh at me." Darcy's gaze lowered along with his voice.

"There you are!" They jumped apart as Charlotte strode toward them. Elizabeth stood to give her a hug. "I'm so pleased you're both here!" Charlotte turned to Darcy, who swiftly held out his hand.

"I'm guessing after seeing Haddon and the Pemberley ruins, you don't want to tour any stately houses?" Charlotte asked after they were on their way.

Did Darcy flinch at hearing Pemberley and ruins in the same sentence? "Not this time."

Darcy spoke from the backseat. "Isn't it interesting how some country homes have remained intact for centuries and others were lost forever?"

"I think Haddon being mothballed for hundreds of years had a big part in its being preserved."

"Whereas with Pemberley House, for example, one irresponsible owner destroyed the work of generations."

Elizabeth looked at Charlotte, but her eyes were on the road, her expression bland. *How could she not hear the fear in Darcy's voice?*

"It's more likely heirs couldn't afford the upkeep." Charlotte paused as she merged into traffic. "Parkland gets sold off, or the buildings requisitioned during war got damaged but never repaired, death duties..."

Charlotte focused more on the road than her conversation, but Elizabeth knew Darcy was worrying about the people who depended on Pemberley. "It must be expensive to maintain a place like Haddon now."

Charlotte slowed at a roundabout. "Guess most of the money comes from visitor admissions."

"Yet Haddon is not a museum." Darcy's reply was forceful. "It is a home that has somehow remained in the same family for centuries."

"Not many of those left." They exited the traffic circle, and Charlotte's full attention returned to the conversation. "Why so curious?"

The last thing Darcy needed was to show too much interest in a timeworn brick pile. Besides, now that they drove faster, Darcy would throw up if he tried to talk.

"A friend of ours is a project manager at Haddon," she answered for him. "What is your sister up to? Is Maria happy at her internship?"

"As happy as I can tell. She's at the Sheffield Local Studies Library. Something about preparing newspapers for microfilming. Maria will join us for sightseeing, and tomorrow night Willie and Missy will meet us to go to dinner along with some other girls, and then we'll go to the club. Let's go out for a curry tonight." Elizabeth nodded, but the back of the car remained silent. "You all right back there?"

Charlotte accelerated. Elizabeth turned to look at Darcy, who leaned against the window with his eyes closed. "He's fine. He loves Indian."

SEPTEMBER 17, 2011
6 DAYS UNTIL AUTUMNAL EQUINOX

They passed the morning at the Weston Park Museum so the ladies could enjoy an archeological exhibit. Darcy suspected Elizabeth wanted to see if anything regarding the digging in Saxon and Celtic grave hills might explain the events at Nine Ladies. However, another reason appeared to be to give Elizabeth and Dr. Lucas ample opportunity to walk and talk at length.

Darcy was absorbed by the Social History collection. It was not that the range of items was vast—from small personal objects to entire shop interiors, relics from wars to children's toys—it was that every item required him to read the description, consider both its construction and purpose, and use his phone to seek out more information.

Living in this time held an exciting prospect of perpetual discovery. This century was at times incomprehensible and yet so extraordinary he still wished to learn all he could. But in six days, it would not matter at all. Georgiana and Pemberley needed him.

A true gentleman always does what is his duty, with vigor and with unfailing resolution.

Darcy was considering the perfect cuts and vivid picture of a jigsaw puzzle when he realized Miss Lucas was in the same exhibit hall, peering into a case with the now-understandable typewriter. Darcy forced himself to speak, remembering not to bow.

"Hello, Maria. How are you enjoying the museum?"

She whispered, "I've been before." Even under his expectant gaze, she stayed silent.

He dared not express to anyone, save Elizabeth, his genuine wonder at the Life and Times Gallery. "Perhaps we should find the others?" They crossed the gallery toward the entrance, and she still did not speak. "If you've already seen Sheffield's museums, what do you recommend we do this afternoon?"

A desperate look that begged him to not ask her to express an opinion was her answer. Perhaps direct questions would draw her out.

"Charlotte says we are dining at a restaurant named Rafters with other friends before going to the nightclub. Have you eaten there?"

She shook her head. This made his first conversation, with Frank Danconia and his wife, seem effortless. Sometimes the blame for his trouble conversing with strangers could not be laid at his feet. One last attempt, and then he would accept his failure, though not for lack of trying.

"Charlotte said you're assisting in a project to maintain newspapers. Forgive me, but how is this relevant?" It was easier to accept that women now had professions than believe anyone could be employed for the purpose of saving newspapers.

"Preserving newspapers is incredibly important! They chronicle defining historical events and provide insight into daily life that's invaluable to researchers."

Miss Lucas would speak at length of newspaper preservation, of all the things in this incredible world? "What do you do?"

"I cut the binding of the volumes to remove the pages, then I use a humidifier and an iron to de-wrinkle the paper, and I repair damaged sections so the pages can be microfilmed. That's the most economical way to preserve the intellectual content. Right now, I'm working on volumes of the *Sheffield Daily Telegraph* from the 1920s."

He nodded, deciding to look up "microfilm" later.

To Darcy's amazement, she continued. "They're inherently acidic. Crumbling," Miss Lucas added when she saw his confusion. "And they take up substantial space. I help preserve the content of Sheffield's papers, but there are newspapers being digitized or microfilmed across England spanning hundreds of years. They're invaluable historical resources."

"How pleasant that you found employment that—" Darcy was struck by a thought. "Maria, are you saying that newspapers, from across the country, from hundreds of years ago, can be read today?"

She nodded. "In a few months, the British Newspaper Archive will officially launch. Some of the librarians I work with are helping to facilitate online access and test—"

"Maria, do I ask too much—it might be of the utmost importance." Darcy's thoughts ran faster than his words could keep up with. "I'm attempting to learn my family history, and a newspaper article may hold the answer."

Since the topic was no longer paper, she had trouble finding her voice. "I don't—maybe a birth and death register—"

"No!" What happened to his equanimity in this century? "I suspect my . . . relation eloped to Scotland, and this distressing event came to the notice of the newspapers. If you knew the names and a range of dates the event was likely to happen could you find an article about the elopement?"

Elizabeth was unable to find a Scotland irregular border marriage record for his sister. He had come to hope, as Elizabeth did, that Georgiana was unlikely to run away with Wickham once he told her the truth about him. Still, to learn the exact circumstances of Georgiana's meeting with Wickham, to be able to prevent it ever happening, would be a comfort.

"I'm just supposed to work on my papers."

"Didn't you say these newspapers are preserved for the sake of research?" He forced her to meet his eye.

"I could ask the librarians helping with the Archive's launch to look it up as practice to see how the search functions work."

"I am indebted to you." She gave him an odd look as she pulled out a notepad and a pen. He wrote *Georgiana Darcy of Pemberley, Derbyshire and George Wickham, married, eloped between July 1811 and December 1817.* "I shall leave on Friday. I cannot express my gratitude if you could share anything you learn before I depart."

She nodded without looking at him.

"Don't you need my number so you can share with me any information you find?"

She fidgeted with the pen and shrugged. Darcy wondered if he made a social blunder. *Does one not give out one's number to unmarried ladies, or is she very shy?* "Would you prefer to tell your sister what you learn, and she can tell Elizabeth?"

She finally looked at him and nodded.

ELIZABETH AND CHARLOTTE WERE AMBLING THROUGH THE SPORTS LAB exhibition when a horde of children rushed past them to take over the interactive exhibits. They shared an amused look as the children pushed their way on the bicycles, played tug-of-war with the headphones, and pounded on every button. The noise level in the room drove them to the relative quiet of the hall.

"They're a lively group!" Elizabeth laughed.

"They're not so bad." Charlotte looked over her shoulder at them, still smiling. "Do you think about having kids?"

A flash of what it must be like to be a mother in 1811 with high infant mortality, no epidurals, limited hygiene, and a preference for boys crossed her mind. *Even for Darcy, how could I do that?* "Someday. I guess."

"That's ambivalent."

Would being with Darcy in 1811, having children with him, make up for everything else I would lose? "I want children, but my life and career are too much in limbo right now. My mother would loathe the idea of my getting married and giving up working to be at home with kids."

"Who says you have to stop working?" Charlotte sounded wounded.

"No one has to; *I'd* want to. My mother was a resentful single mother. When we were older, she took a job an hour away at a job she hates because it was at a university and employees' children received discounted tuition. She was never home for dinner, never had time for a piano recital or to plan a birthday party. It's not that I don't appreciate her sacrifices, but she was so obsessed with paying for our college education that she never spent time with us." She noticed Charlotte's sympathetic stare. "Yeah, I know, not very modern of me, is it?"

"Do what makes you happy, that's what I say."

"I'm missing the other half of the equation anyway, so it's irrelevant."

"It doesn't have to be," Charlotte drawled. "I've been contemplating intrauterine insemination."

Elizabeth pulled Charlotte to a bench. "Are you telling me you're trying to get pregnant?"

"Not at this very moment. And thanks for announcing it to the whole museum. You're surprised, I see. But I've always wanted children."

"You might find someone you want to have children *with*."

"I'm not a romantic; I never was. I want children more than I want or need a husband. If the right guy for me came along, he'd accept me and any kids I had. And I don't have a lot of time."

"What's the hurry?"

Charlotte laughed. "How old do you think I am?"

"There's no good way for me to answer that."

"I'm thirty-seven. And before you say I have time, my mother had a surprise baby at forty-five and, as happy as she was, I know she was exhausted, physically and emotionally."

"It sounds like you've already made your decision."

"I'm ready to be a solo mum."

"I wish you every happiness!" Elizabeth hugged her. "What's the first step?"

"I've done the patency health tests. I just need to find a donor I know or go through a donor bank." They caught notice of Darcy and Maria walking down the corridor. "*There's* someone who would pass genetic muster."

I cannot imagine explaining this to Darcy. "Charlotte, when baby Lucas arrives, I will be first on a plane to spoil it and help out . . . but please, please, do not ask Darcy even in jest."

Her friend bumped her shoulder with her own. "Why not? He's good-looking and a PhD candidate. And our kids could be half-siblings."

"We're just friends." She was sick of spitting out that both true and false phrase. "I am *not* having kids with Darcy, he is *not* my boyfriend, and he's leaving on Friday."

Charlotte's smile fell. "Even after you go back to the States, what's a little distance when you two are head over heels about each other?"

A little distance? Try two hundred years, my contentment with day-to-day living, the life of his sister, and a sense of duty unparalleled in time. "It doesn't matter how much we like each other. After Friday, I won't see him again."

CHAPTER TWENTY-THREE

Darcy sat in Dr. Lucas's parlor wishing he'd brought a book. He had changed his clothes and attended to what grooming needed doing exactly as he would have done before he left for a ball. Despite his lack of a valet, and taking two tries to master the Windsor knot, Darcy followed the same methodical preparation routine and was finished with time to spare to await the ladies.

That was forty-five minutes ago.

The ladies left for their toilette thirty minutes before he dressed and still they were not ready. *For every matter that is improved now, other things are irritatingly unchanged.* Women ought to begin their preparations earlier or not waste half so much time before the glass. The frivolous distinction of one gown over another was a waste of time.

While settling this point in his mind, Darcy was roused by the sound of the doorbell. The other members of their party for the evening had arrived.

"Hey Darcy!" called Dr. Lucas. "Can you please get the door?"

A woman wearing some . . . *thing* was on the other side of the door. Only her abdomen and the top of her thighs were covered with ornamental spangled fabric; to say her breasts were covered would be an overstatement. Her heeled shoes brought her nearly to his own height.

Behind her was a tall man wearing an ill-fitting black suit without a tie; he did not look up from his phone.

"Holy crap!" The woman in the glittering construction that was allegedly a purple gown appraised him openly.

Darcy kept his eyes on her heavily made-up face. He had never before seen so lavish a use of powder, rouge, and lip paint.

"I'm Missy King, and this is Willie Collins. We're Charlotte's friends."

Darcy stepped aside, repressing the natural compulsion to bow. "I'm Darcy. Do come in."

"Char said Liz's man was hot, but she's so whatever about men in general I didn't believe her," Mrs. King said as she breezed past him. Mr. Collins tilted his head at him in an awkward gesture.

Darcy inferred some of her meaning. "We're just friends." He followed them into the parlor, gaping at her indecent attire. The typical fashion he had seen other women wear was not half so revealing as what this woman wore.

Mrs. King perched on a chair arm and crossed her legs, and Darcy kept his eyes from the indecency of it. "Anyone who says 'just friends' is never just anything, but whatever."

"I have heard it said"—Mr. Collins wagged his finger at him—"that the best relationships are those based in friendship. You do yourself a disservice by accepting no as an answer the first time you ask a woman with whom you have a friendship for something more."

"Willie, you sound like a sexual predator." Mrs. King managed to roll her eyes despite the weight of makeup adorning her eyelids and lashes.

"I don't mean a man ought to force himself on anyone. However, by paying a female friend compliments on her attractive qualities, one has a greater chance of moving that relationship toward a romantic one. I, for one, practice complimenting females on how their likeness ought to be captured, by me, on canvas. Don't you agree?"

It took Darcy a moment to realize the vulgar man addressed him. "I think a woman would rather be paid the compliment of being believed when she declines to accept a man's proposal for something more than friendship."

"You need practice, and I'm the man to help you. Allow me to demonstrate. Missy, may I say how—"

"I'm married, remember."

Mr. Collins shrugged and promised to demonstrate, for Darcy's benefit, on the other ladies. Darcy found him downright stupid.

Mrs. King leaned forward to capture his attention; Darcy prayed her gown would stay where it was. "Are Char and Lizzy getting dressed? What about Maria?"

"Maria did not wish to go to the club, and Charlotte and Elizabeth are still dressing."

"Then I have time for a smoke. I know, I should know better." Mrs. King rummaged through her purse and pulled out what he had learned was a cigarette, a means by which one burned their throat with acrid paper and vile tobacco. "I'm a social smoker. Damn, I forgot my lighter. Char! You got some matches?"

After Mrs. King shuffled up the stairs, Mr. Collins asked, "Are you a patron of the arts? I ask because I am an artist, one of local renown, if you will permit me to admit."

The foolish man prattled on, and Darcy wished for a time when to be addressed by such a man, in such a manner, would be an impertinent freedom. Now he could only eye this man in unrestrained wonder and silently beg for the ladies to come downstairs. When he heard a door open, he turned hopefully, but it was Mrs. King descending with a strong grip on the handrail and defying the laws of the natural world by walking in such high-heeled shoes without injuring herself.

"I'm going out for a fag. Want to join me, Darcy?" Mrs. King spoke through the end of the cigarette. He weighed the ridiculousness of both parties and joined her.

"How do you know Lizzy?" Mrs. King pulled out a wooden stick from a box. Darcy stared as she scraped it against the box, and a flame appeared at its end. She lit the cigarette, shook her hand to snuff the flame, and dropped the stick to the ground. She asked him to hold the box while she smoked. He took it lightly, fearful of tightening his grip lest it combust in his hand.

"What is that?" He could not tear his eyes from it.

"I said, how did you meet Lizzy? Char knows her because she has rounds at the hospital where her dad was being rehabilitated. And we crossed paths because she's a GP and I'm a mental health day nurse, and I know Willie because they've been friends since they were kids. So, how did you find your way into Liz's life?"

Darcy pulled out one of the tiny cords. No striking flint and steel, no tinder and spark, no using a spill from a vase next to the fire. *A cord and friction, and one has fire at their fingertips!*

"Earth to Darcy. Are you high?"

He dropped the thing into its box and slid its cover on. He ought not to show how amazed he was by the fire-starting tool. "I am on holiday from university and needed a place to live. My family knows the professor from whom Elizabeth is renting her flat, and she was gracious enough to allow me to stay for the summer."

"Char said something about you being a PhD candidate. When do you go back?"

He recognized the impressed tone; it usually occurred when a lady realized his income or learned he was single that he became more fascinating than he was a moment earlier. Darcy stepped to the side so her cigarette smoke blew away from him. Mrs. King turned to face him. "I leave Friday."

"Smart *and* sexy; win-win. Is Darcy a first name or a last name?"

"That's my family name."

"What's your first name?"

He did not care for her familiar tone and bold stare. "It isn't your concern since you shall not be addressing me by it."

"A secret! Maybe I'll get it out of you by the end of the night." He raised a disapproving eyebrow, yet she took a step closer. "Does Liz know your first name?"

"Of course."

"But she doesn't call you by it?"

He had no wish to explain how having Elizabeth address him by his name was an intimacy in which his heart could not afford to indulge. "I prefer Darcy."

"You and Liz are just friends?"

"She prefers Elizabeth, and yes, we're friends."

"And you and Liz are *really* just friends? I'm not a poacher. You're not sleeping together?" He did not feel this question merited a reply. Mrs. King rounded her lips and blew out more smoke.

"You and she are staying with Char tonight?"

Darcy nodded. Incredibly, he now preferred the company of Mr. Collins.

"Want to come home with me instead?"

"I beg your pardon?" Darcy felt uncomfortably breathless.

"You heard me." She sucked on her cigarette and exhaled. "Wanna fuck?"

A married woman, to whom I have just been introduced, and to use such language! "No!"

"Why not? You said you and Lizzy were just friends."

"Regardless of my relationship with Elizabeth, your husband would not be pleased to find me with you when he comes home."

Mrs. King shrugged; Darcy was surprised her dress did not fall off. "He and his friends flew to Dublin to drink all weekend, if that's your hang-up. Besides, he's fucking some slag right now, and there'll be a different one tomorrow." She looked as though she now expected a different answer and gave him a sultry smile.

"I am perfectly serious in my refusal!" It would not be the first proposition he received in which it was suggested that his, as well as some woman's, integrity be compromised, but it was the most unexpected of them all. The threat to his morality aside, he was not hypocritical enough to feign affection for such a lonely woman to succeed in her unhappy design.

She tossed her cigarette to the ground, crushing it underfoot. "Had to ask; nothing worse than going home alone. Not that someone with your noble principles would understand. No hard feelings! I'll find someone to fuck at the club. Let's see if Char and Lizzy are ready, and Harriet and Pen should be here any minute."

Darcy followed her inside. To indicate he had no wish to engage with Mrs. King and Mr. Collins, he pulled out his phone. Worldwide wars, a breakdown of both communication skills and social bonds, and now he could add blatant indecent propositions to the wickedness of the modern world. *Such fantastic achievements exist amid such an appalling loss of gentle manners.*

"*Char*-lotte *Lu*-cas, you are not wearing that green dress!" Mrs. King cried. "You look hot, but you wore that last time."

"No one's going to know it's my only 'club outfit.'"

"My dear Charlotte, you will be the brightest ornament to adorn the Viper Rooms this evening."

Dr. Lucas thanked Mr. Collins; Mrs. King shrieked, "Lizzy! You look so cute! Hey, you're wearing purple too. We match!"

Darcy put his phone away and looked up as Elizabeth came down. His throat closed, and his heart skipped a beat. While Mrs. King underwent an examination into the value and make of Elizabeth's gown, the color of her shoes, and the arrangement of her hair, Darcy openly admired her. Both ladies did wear purple, but that was where the similarities ended. One elegant in every respect—quite beautiful—the other vulgar.

"You'll get your pick of men tonight, Liz!"

The idea that Elizabeth might be looking for the same temporary, scandalous company Mrs. King offered to him made Darcy feel a surge of jealousy. He exhaled sharply. Elizabeth looked at him and blushed. "Not looking, Missy, but thanks."

The doorbell rang, and everyone's attention, save for his, turned. He did not realize he was still staring until Elizabeth came to his side.

"You look as though you've never seen me so well-dressed. Or maybe my dress is too short for someone who's not used to seeing ladies' calves, let alone their knees."

He tried to find words to describe how lovely she looked, no matter the century. "You are an excessively handsome woman." She drew her fingers up and down his tie. Her hair was curled more than he had previously seen it; he touched a strand before tucking it behind her ear. They stared at one another until high-pitched shrieks and greetings from the doorway forced them both to blink.

"I'm glad you're not horrified that you can see my knees. You've come a long way in accepting what's appropriate for this time."

"There is nothing wanting in your appearance, and shorter hemlines and women wearing trousers are nothing compared to other, more significant changes." He lowered his voice. "Besides, have you seen what Mrs. King is wearing—or, rather, not wearing?"

She laughed, leaned closer, and lowered her voice, as well. "I think you'll hate everything about this evening: the music, the noise, the dancing. Missy's dress won't be the worst of it. We can leave early."

"I may have already experienced the worst that this evening will hold."

"What happened?"

"I do not wish to speak of it. Suffice it to say, the twenty-first century ought to incorporate a tenet of my own time: never do anything that is unpleasant to others."

They could say no more because everyone was ready to leave. The newcomers were both dressed in bodice-squeezing shirts, which were spangled in the same style as Mrs. King's dress, and tight trousers called skinny jeans. Dr. Lucas introduced them as Harriet and Penelope Harrington, but he was not certain which girl was which. After five minutes in their insipid company in the cab, Darcy realized it did not matter.

After dinner, they traveled to a brick building that had the look of a warehouse rather than assembly rooms. Darcy could hear a low-pitched thudding. There was a long line of young people outside, most of them women dressed as Mrs. King and the Harrington sisters. A large man was before the door, holding back the throng.

"We need to show ID?" Elizabeth cried. Her fear all along was that he had no identifying papers. "Charlotte, wait. Darcy and I have to leave!"

"Why, did you leave your passport at home?"

Mrs. King strode to the front of their group and led them past the noisy line of would-be patrons toward another entrance. "I told you guys I booked a VIP table! Sharlene and I are like this," she said, crossing her first two fingers. "Like someone with as much money as my family has stands in a queue, pays a cover, and shows ID? Please!"

Mrs. King spoke with a man guarding a different door, and their party was ushered inside. Darcy was at once assaulted by a darkness punctuated by bursts of unnaturally colored lights, a pulsation of sound that came from no instrument he could imagine, and the calling of scores of people.

They were led through a barroom toward a space defined by glass walls and clusters of sofas and chairs around tiny tables. "VIP corner booth, as much champagne as you can drink, and our own waitress. First round is on me! Our table seats fifteen, so if you find someone on the dance floor, bring them; there's plenty of room!" Mrs. King's boasting served to partially explain where they were going and what would happen.

The Harrington sisters pulled Charlotte and Elizabeth to their feet after they were seated and demanded they had to dance, right now, this song was the best, the DJ was amazing, and they would come back for drinks. Mrs. King ordered something called shots for the group, and Mr. Collins pulled out his phone. The darkness, the noise, and the confusion as to the purpose of such a place made it impossible to think.

"You don't mind if I dance, do you?" Elizabeth gave him an apologetic look.

She was herded toward a dance floor on the other side of the glass wall. The music was a racket with a fast beat. Elizabeth and her friends were pulled into a small group of women around the same age who appeared to be either very happy or very drunk; he could not tell at so great a distance. It appeared all one need do was move any part of one's body in any manner, so long as it was in time with the noise. Group dancing, if it could be called dancing, seemed typical among the ladies, most of whose clothing did an inadequate job of covering their breasts.

The dancing between couples was . . . terribly horrifying. Conversation between couples was rendered impossible by the volume of the music. The swaying and thrusting defied description.

Mrs. King had been speaking with the waitress who brought a tray of drinks while Mr. Collins looked at his phone. She slid along the bench to sit nearer to him.

"I always spring for a VIP table wherever I go. The DJ is great, and I love the glamorous atmosphere. Not to mention the bartender is hot!" Darcy took in the crush of drunken humanity pressing against the bar, the discordant noise that was allegedly music, and the glasses with a green liquid. *Have the words glamorous or atmosphere changed their meaning in the last two hundred years?*

"I'm going to get the girls so we can do shots!" Mrs. King threw back the champagne in her glass and disappeared after casting it down.

Darcy decided to attend whatever nineteenth-century ball he was next invited to without complaint as the waitress returned, bringing Mr. Collins a pink-colored drink with a paper parasol in it. Women at the other tables had similarly shaped glasses with brightly colored liquids.

"What can I get you?"

Darcy was not one to drink any more than to elevate his spirits and never enough to confuse his intellect. He did not wish to become overset, but to tolerate the evening, he would need assistance. Before he could answer, Mr. Collins spilled most of his frothy drink into his lap. "Perhaps you can suggest something that won't damage my self-respect."

The waitress looked at Mr. Collins and held back a laugh. "A man after my own heart. How about a Lagavulin?"

"Fine, thank you." *Fine*? What would happen next week if he used such language or mannerisms in 1811? He did not have the chance to ruminate; the ladies had returned. Elizabeth moved across the bench seats to sit close to him. Her eyes were bright and her cheeks were flushed from dancing.

"Who's ready for shots?" Dr. Lucas cried.

A chorus of enthusiastic screeching answered her. Everyone reached for one of the tiny glasses; Darcy reluctantly followed.

"Neon cocktails are popular now. These are Green Lizard shots." Mrs. King mistook his distasteful expression for a confused one.

"What's in them?" Elizabeth asked.

"Does it matter? Midori and something." Mrs. King threw back the contents, and so did everyone else. Darcy wondered what he had done to deserve this punishment, and swallowed the whole of the sickeningly sweet and vile liquid.

There was more chatter, which Darcy followed as best he could amid the modern vocabulary and din. The waitress brought him a drink that was not an unnatural color, and it appeared like what he observed men at the bar to be drinking. The men came in dressed as he was, but after consuming several drinks, their jackets were removed, as so often were their ties. Their state of undress was appalling, but given the state of undress the women *entered* the nightclub wearing, he supposed a man removing his jacket was unobjectionable.

"You gotta admit, this place is pretty swish," one of the Miss Harringtons, who was dead drunk, said to him later while Elizabeth danced with Dr. Lucas. Mrs. King had found a man more amenable to her intentions for the end of the evening and was seated in his lap.

Darcy nodded in ignorant agreement to either Harriet or Penelope, and was pleased to see the waitress had replaced his empty glass with another. The whisky drink was gaining in his estimation.

"Downstairs is for the real party people. Best house music around. Wanna dance?" the other Harrington sister asked him, also reeling drunk, and who leaned toward him in a manner that, regardless of the century, failed at its attempt to be alluring.

"I thank you, no." He remembered to smile and look apologetic. Disguise was a social nicety in this instance.

The sisters pouted, shrugged, and announced their intention to go downstairs for some real fun. They wobbled on unsteady feet toward the stairs. Elizabeth passed them on her way back to their table. The hum of sounds from male shouting, female shrieking, and uproarious laughter was oppressive.

"I don't suppose you'd dance with me?" Elizabeth asked him, taking a sip from her second glass. The hem of her flared skirt rode up above her knees as she crossed her legs and shifted her weight; he gallantly kept his eyes on her face.

"In another *time* and place, I would solicit your hand." They had to speak into one another's ears to be heard.

"Haven't you learned anything about women in this brave new world? *I'm* asking *you*."

"I should like to dance with you, but I dare not attempt what now passes for dancing."

"What are you afraid of?"

"Whether I have more apprehension due to the infringements on morality or the anticipation that this dancing will bring an attack of peritonitis is uncertain."

He was rewarded with a trill of laughter. Elizabeth was explaining the rituals and purpose of this place when they were distracted by the sight of Mrs. King thoroughly kissing whomever it was she was seated upon. Even Elizabeth's cheeks turned pink, and she angled herself away from the exhibition.

He thought of his own time when his sitting so near to Elizabeth and engaging in gentle conversation would be scrupulously avoided. The sight of such a tête-à-tête would be shameful to their reputations, and they would be supposed to be engaged.

"You have that look on your face, Darcy."

"How do you mean?" He had nearly to yell for her to hear him.

"That you're holding back some scathing reprimand on these wicked times."

He shook his head. "You mistake me. I cannot but think of the difficulty which secret lovers must have in finding a proper spot for stolen interviews in my own time. It is easy now for lovers, clandestine or open, to be alone with one another."

"Are you jealous?"

Darcy coughed on his whisky. She could not mean that he was jealous of whoever it was Mrs. King was embracing. *Does Elizabeth wish to kiss me in the same manner?*

There could be no private conversation between them since Charlotte Lucas and Willie Collins returned and sat next to them. Darcy was forced to listen to Dr. Lucas and Elizabeth discuss the former's intentions of sowing seeds and having children that he could not comprehend. All he understood was Dr. Lucas's excitement and Elizabeth's gentle encouragement.

"Hey, Lizzy! I'm going to the smoking room. Keep me company?"

Elizabeth took her drink and followed Mrs. King. Mrs. King's stranger gave him a superior, drunken, self-satisfied smile. Darcy pulled out his phone. He would miss having a convenient means by which to ignore fools when he returned home. He sighed and looked up what time the sun set on Friday.

. . .

The crowded, enclosed smoking space smelled like musty tobacco, sweat, and spilled beer. "Missy, I can't stand here any longer." The smoke burned her eyes and clung to her clothes. "Why did you ask me and not your guy?"

Missy crushed the rest of her cigarette into an ashtray. "I don't like smoking alone, and I'm not hooking up with what's-his-name for his conversation skills."

"I'm going back. I hate to leave Darcy by himself."

"Hold a tick, I wanted to have a chat and didn't feel like dragging you to the ladies'. I asked Darcy to go home with me tonight."

She felt ill, and it had nothing to do with the smoke or the alcohol. "What did he say?"

"He said no."

"Did he understand what you meant?"

"Lizzy, he talked intelligently at dinner, and he's at uni for a PhD in *English*. I told him to *fuck* me. I was clear."

"Oh my God!" That must have been the worst experience Darcy mentioned before they left Charlotte's.

"I asked him if you were just friends, and he said you weren't sleeping together. I don't go after my friends' boyfriends."

Missy misunderstood her exclamation. "Darcy's not my boyfriend. You're free to do whomever you want, I guess." *As long as your husband doesn't care.*

Missy crossed her arms over her chest. "You think I'm a slut for fucking guys I meet at nightclubs? What am I supposed to do when the husband I'm stuck with forever doesn't look at me twice unless he's asking for a bigger spending allowance from my trust fund?"

Elizabeth didn't think Missy wanted suggestions such as marriage counseling or divorce. "Even if I wouldn't make the same choices, slut-shaming isn't my thing, so live your life how you want." *What shocked Darcy more: Missy's lack of fidelity, or her use of the f-word?*

"Whatever, I wanted you to know I asked him to fuck me—since I thought you were just friends—and he said no."

"I'm not mad. You know, you didn't *have* to tell me."

Missy laughed and linked an arm through hers as they left. "Yeah I did, because you two need help. Darcy might've turned me down because I'm married, or because he's not a one-night-stand type, but I don't think that's it. I don't know what the hell your problem is."

"*My* problem? What do—"

"Why aren't *you* fucking him?"

Was there any use in pretending? "It's not that simple."

"That guy latches on to your every word. He looked like he wanted to take you up against the wall when you came down in that dress. And you? Your longing gazes and little smiles are disgusting."

"At the end of the week, he's leaving, and I'm going back to the States. After Friday, we'll never see each other again."

Elizabeth, to her shame, felt herself tearing up.

"If that's the case, you may as well give him a good send-off, yeah?"

When they returned, Missy's latest conquest jumped when she resumed her seat in his lap, as though he had forgotten he had been waiting for her. Darcy had been watching Elizabeth approach and set his phone aside. He stood and bowed when she reached him, and Elizabeth saw in his eyes the moment he realized his mistake. He winced, and Elizabeth felt the attention of the surrounding tables.

She gave an exaggerated curtsey and held out her hand. Darcy's expression clouded in confusion, but habit and custom won over three months of retraining. He took it and kissed it gallantly.

"Mr. Darcy, what a courteous greeting. Did you regret my short absence?"

"My dear Miss Bennet, I have great pleasure in meeting you no matter the length of your absence."

He gave her a grateful smile and led her toward her seat, gesturing to the bench as though he had been standing to allow her to move farther in. No one paid them attention now, but she could see Darcy was upset by his mistake.

She often had a sense he was holding back some powerful force that was scarcely being contained—not physically, but mentally, emotionally. Darcy couldn't be who he was meant to be here; he was always cautious, but in this time it was the vigilance of one always on alert for fear of doing wrong rather than the restrained self-possession of one who held himself to a high standard of behavior.

He wouldn't be happy here, even if he didn't need to save Georgiana and Pemberley.

"No one thought anything of it," she whispered, but with the noise of the music and conversation he did not hear. She had caught his attention, though, and he leaned closer. She read the wariness, the tension, and the barely concealed impatience in his face. She felt a surge of affection for him. He tolerated so much for her sake.

"Do you want to leave?"

He looked surprised. "You appeared to be having a pleasant time dancing and talking with your friends. You need not cry off early on my account."

"The girls could be out for hours, although I think Missy will head to bed soon." They looked at Missy, who again had her tongue down the throat of this evening's conquest. "I know you hate everything about this place with an abhorrence unparalleled in time."

"I do not hate it."

"You're a good man, Fitzwilliam Darcy, but you are a bad liar. What do you honestly think of this?"

He leaned closer to speak into her ear. "I read an epic poem translated from Italian, written five, seven hundred years ago," he said. "This evening reminds me of one of its early lines: 'Oh! Ye who enter here, Ye heirs of sin, leave every hope behind.'"

He was entirely serious. "I don't recognize it, but that's dismal. Shall we leave?"

"Yes. Forgive my irreverence, but by God, I want to leave and never return."

She handed him her phone after bringing up the number for the cab company. "Think you can go out front and call a cab while I get the key and say goodbye?"

He nodded and was gone. Elizabeth slid down the bench to tell Charlotte they were leaving, and Charlotte gave her an extra key.

"I'll be home in a few hours, don't wait up," Charlotte murmured as she kissed Elizabeth on the cheek.

Missy pulled her lips from her companion with an audible smack. "Lizzy! Leaving already? It's not even one! Where's Darcy?"

"He's calling a cab. He asked me to say goodnight to all of you." Elizabeth gave a little wave and stood.

"You gonna give Darcy a send-off like we talked about?" Missy reached into her purse and handed her a square, foil packet. "I'll bet he'd give you a different answer than he gave me!"

Elizabeth, feeling the effects of the second cosmopolitan, along with a strong regard for the man in question, took it. "I might do that."

CHAPTER TWENTY-FOUR

SEPTEMBER 18, 2011
5 DAYS TO AUTUMNAL EQUINOX

There may as well have been an inscription over the nightclub door that read "Thro' me pass mortals to the realms of woe, Thro' me they pass to everlasting pain, Thro' me to meet the race forever lost." The twenty-first century itself was not Dante's hell, but the Viper Rooms were close. Darcy could be certain about one thing: *he* had not lost the good of intellect. He was not a neutral soul who could not choose between right and wrong.

Although he admired the suit above the other clothes he had worn, Darcy was pleased to remove the last vestiges of this taxing evening and go to sleep. If only the ringing in his ears and the lights he still saw when he closed his eyes would disappear.

Any public assembly would be preferable to three hours spent in the Viper Rooms.

There was a knock at his door. Darcy turned on the bedside lamp—such things were second nature now—and rose to answer.

"Can I come in?" Elizabeth entered without waiting and shut the door behind her. She had taken off the becoming purple gown in favor of her sleeping clothes, and her face was no longer made-up. After enquiring after her health, he had nothing else to say as she persisted in silent anxiety.

"I thought I could sleep here with you."

A quickening of his heart rate was the only reaction he could give. He would assume nothing, no matter how intently she stared. When he made no reply, she crawled onto his bed and leaned against the headboard to face him. The depth of feeling in her eyes rendered him immoveable.

"I know this is the second time you've been propositioned, but I thought we could say goodbye properly. You're leaving on Friday, and we'll never see each other again. I don't want your last memory of me to be a handshake or a curtsey."

He was overwhelmed and shocked. "You know I need no such . . . memento to remember you."

"Maybe I need one."

He gave her a long look. "Need?"

She sighed. "Let's not get hung up on needs versus wants. I want you to stay in this century, but I know you can't and shouldn't so I won't ask you. You might want me to go with you, but you won't ask me either."

"I cannot ask you a question when I know the answer will not be in my favor."

"We have to let something precious slip through our fingers, so we might as well make the most of the days we have left." She patted the other side of the bed. "Come here."

He shook his head, wounded and thrilled all at once. "Do you believe I will be able to walk into that stone circle on Friday if I join you now?"

Elizabeth pursed her lips and crossed her arms. "Of course you will. You're *Mr. Darcy of Pemberley*, paragon of loyalty and duty. I know nothing I offer you tonight is going to entice you to stay. I'm starting to think you're not as interested in me as you led me to believe."

He tried to keep his frustration at bay. "You think I am unaffected by your attractions, and *that* is why I am standing here when you are sitting on my bed?"

"Maybe you can't reconcile me with your outdated sensibilities on how you think women are supposed to act. I guess you'll be happy to go back to a time when sexual desire is limited to men only."

Her words were a bitter aggravation. He was never the sort to agree with a gentleman who prevailed on a woman's virtue and then despised her for it afterward. Elizabeth's straight, unabashed look was a feminine defiance against what was expected from women of his own time.

"Of course desire exists in both sexes. This energy requires restraint and should be confined to the matrimonial bed. I will not dishonor myself, or you, with wandering lust."

"Is that why you said no to Missy?"

"Need I actually state my reasons for refusing that sad woman? Shall you like me to write the list down for you? I can arrange them alphabetically or by any rule of your choosing!"

"I'd rather know why you would refuse *me*!"

"It would not do to raise expectations I cannot fulfill! You *know* what I feel for you. Do not make this harder for me."

Elizabeth threw up her hands. "Do I know what you feel? I know you don't want to go to bed with me. What I know is that you have to leave and you won't ask me to go with you."

"And you have not offered to come. You would sacrifice your independent status to go back to a time with only my integrity to protect you? Is that the world you want your daughters to live in?"

Elizabeth exhaled angrily and looked away.

"And if I did ask, or you did offer, how could I bear it if you became ill and left me because this century has medicines to keep you alive?"

"You think I would leave you so easily?"

"Then what about your children?" Her mouth dropped open. "We both know that if your *child* had cancer that you would stride into Nine Ladies and never look back. What if, even if you promised to return to me, the stones lost their power and I never saw you again? I cannot live with that sword of Damocles hanging over my head, Elizabeth! So, yes, I feel too much to ask a question when I know I will not receive a favorable reply, or you would ultimately be miserable if you gave me one."

"How do I know what you feel for me when you don't say? I thought *this* would make it easier." She gestured to the empty space next to her on the bed. "I thought you would enjoy it."

He gave her a long look, taking full notice of her figure stretched out on the bed. "Oh, I have no doubt that we would enjoy our evening thoroughly."

At her hopeful smile and widened pupils, he looked away. He wanted her, wanted to love and comfort her. But if he did that, he would never be able to leave. "I would not have you, who mean more to me than I dare put a name to, after both of us drank more than usual . . . You are a respectable woman and would not wish to go farther than decency would prevent you from mentioning to anyone in the morning."

"Women aren't immoral because they have sex outside of marriage." She dropped her feet to the floor and stood. "We have nothing whatsoever in common! I'm amazed we could have fallen—" She narrowed her eyes and tilted her head. "Are you a virgin?"

To his ever-increasing fury, Darcy blushed. "That is not a term applied to men." Elizabeth's expression darkened; being evasive would not suit either of them. "All the familiarities of man and wife are known to me," he muttered to the floor.

"Me too."

Darcy's eyes snapped back to her face. He was naïve to presume unmarried ladies were as chaste now as they were expected to be in 1811. His rational mind knew he ought not to judge her. However, the thought that other men had experienced what he, in good conscience, could not, drove Darcy toward an unreasonable fit of anger and jealousy.

In a voice of forced calmness, he asked, "It may be of small importance to you, but how many lovers have you had?"

"No, the people who get to know about my sex life are the people currently involved in my sex life. And since you made it clear you don't want to go to bed with me . . ." She stood and walked past him, her elbow unnecessarily bumping into his chest. He reached out and gripped it, spinning her around to face him. She glared, and Darcy bent lower to look right into her eyes.

"I did not say I do not want to go to bed with you! I want very much to throw you on the bed, and myself with you, kissing you violently and yielding to everything we could possibly—" He stopped and let her go. "I need say no more," he finished quietly. They both breathed heavily, and their lips were too close together. "Even if I forsook my sister and stayed, or you renounced all the independence and advancements here and returned with me and were actually *happy* there, my ring is not on your finger."

"That wouldn't stop two people who cared about each other in 2011, and it didn't stop you in the past if you're not a virgin."

"You cannot compare the actions of a responsible landowner who is close to thirty to the foolish indulgences of a younger man. Young blood is hot, and passion and curiosity are potent forces. A brief infatuation with a courtesan and a diversion with a merry widow do not mean I am willing to disregard what it means to be a gentleman, as well as disregard what *you* mean to me!"

She shook her head as though he were the one being unreasonable. "That is *exactly* what you're doing by rejecting me!"

"Your offer has more implication than one night's passion. You are demanding of me what I cannot give!"

"And you're refusing me for reasons I can't understand!" She now looked at the floor, her hands on her hips.

"Look at me and tell me that sharing my bed makes it simpler for us to say goodbye. For me, it will break my heart more to know precisely what I must turn my back on. For me, the memory would serve as an ever-present, vivid reminder of what I left behind. Tell me truthfully: if you were my lover for one night, would it not make you mourn my absence more, or make you hate me for choosing Pemberley over you, or ruin your potential happiness with anyone else, as I know it would for me?"

She raised her head. "Would it torture you that much?"

"Would it not torment *you*?" He would not believe her if she said it would not.

"I hate this." Her voice dropped to a harsh whisper as her eyes filled with tears.

Darcy barely resisted the desire to take her in his arms. Instead, his palms clasped her cheeks gently as his thumbs brushed away her tears. "I do not want to be the cause of your tears, but I know it is not that simple."

She roughly removed his hands and jerked her head away. "I am afraid you have long been desiring my absence, Mr. Darcy." With a curtsey and a glare, she quit the room.

SEPTEMBER 22, 2011
ONE DAY UNTIL AUTUMNAL EQUINOX

```
Pasta Man! Coming over 2 say bye tomorrow?

            Yes, I will be there at half past three.

Elizabeth coming?

                                                  No.

But she likes us :) What did u do?

            I did nothing. She is well.

Then why isn't the missus coming?
Darcy? What happened?
Did u make your move like I told u 2?

            No, but Elizabeth did; I declined.
Now she does not speak to me more than necessary.

You said NO? Why?
She must've been gutted.

            She is returning home.
```

> *They have these things called airplanes!*

>> *We will not see one another again.*
>> *It would not have been appropriate.*

> *But u FANCY her!*
> *Don't u?*

>> *Yes, I admire her.*

> *So what's the problem?!*

>> *It would have been wrong when we both know it could never happen again.*

> *She offered a one-night stand but u said no?*
> *And now she's cheesed off and won't talk to u?*
> *Nice one, mate*

Darcy tossed the phone aside with a clatter. Darcy hated that Frank would think he had dropped his acquaintance after he left. He might have asked Elizabeth to reply to Frank's texts as though she were him, to allow the friendship between them to sink gradually, but he was no longer in a position to ask Elizabeth for anything.

He suffered from disappointment and regret and wishing for what could never be. Elizabeth felt humiliated and was angry, and no words of his would change that. And so four days had passed with cold politeness, avoidance, and sharp words, and he suspected his final day would be the same.

I did what was right to be done. He held too much respect for Elizabeth and what she meant to him to throw it away for one night. He had pushed back the boundaries of proper behavior farther and farther, and finally came to a line he could not cross because they could not be together.

She would not be happy in the past, and I would always fear she would leave me to return to a time that can offer her more than I can.

September 23, 2011
Autumnal equinox
Nine Ladies

Earlier that afternoon, Darcy had found an empty box for all of his clothes and accoutrements, finally placing the phone on top before setting the lid. He parted from Frank and Gwen, deceiving them when he said he would stay in touch, but not when he said he valued their friendship and would miss them.

Darcy could have said a great deal to Elizabeth before he left her, but it was safer to leave untouched her importance to him, lest it should betray her into thinking he could stay or betray him into saying what could not be said. Elizabeth only nodded when he thanked her for saving his life, and she gave no inclination of having wished for more than to keep him alive. It was a reserved leave-taking, complete with nineteenth-century courtesies and not even a handshake.

The sun would set at 6:57; his watch showed it was now past six.

Instead of his worse-for-wear 1811 clothes he wore when he was dragged from his deathbed three months ago, he was dressed in a twenty-first-century raincoat, jeans, and sneakers. They would have to be burned. Today was Friday, September 23, 2011. He would return on the autumnal equinox in the year eleven on Monday, September 23.

There will be servants to do for me what I have lately done for myself. There will be hours of meetings with Willers, Roland, and Reynolds, to say nothing of the personal correspondence to reestablish and a believable explanation for my absence to create.

He must write to his sister before he did anything else. The sooner he told her about Wickham, the safer she and all of Pemberley's servants and tenants would be.

How shall I explain if I enter a dark room and turn to the wall to flip a light switch that is not there?

Elizabeth said Mrs. Reynolds would listen to his descriptions of this place, but he saw no indication his housekeeper had any interest in the future. He was not sure if, or when, he would be ready to speak of what he had seen and learned in 2011. Besides, after six months of knowing her, with three months in her near-exclusive company, the only person he wanted to converse at length with was Elizabeth.

Elizabeth had gone on a long run, cleaned the flat, and packed her things. The last things to do now that Darcy was gone were to text Charlotte and Gwen goodbye and to board her plane tomorrow.

She placed the linens on a shelf in the spare room and was leaving a note for the Gardiners to say she washed them when she saw a box on the shelf. She opened its lid and gasped. Elizabeth stared at Darcy's modern clothes and his phone, and scribbled "Darcy" on the box lid before shoving it aside and stomping out of the room.

She couldn't bring herself to even touch his clothes. *Out of sight, out of mind.* She'd leave another note for the Gardiners to donate them when they reclaimed their flat.

Her phone chimed. She went downstairs to retrieve it, hearing it chime, three, four, five more times before she got to it. Charlotte had sent her a bevy of texts, and, fearing the worst, Elizabeth dialed her friend.

"Hi, are you okay?" Charlotte asked about Darcy, and Elizabeth refrained from giving in to her anger. "No, he already left. He asked Maria for what? What did she find? Yeah, thanks. I'll miss you too. Bye."

Maria found newspaper articles that mentioned Georgiana and Wickham. *What made Darcy think to ask her?* Maria had sent the first few lines of each article:

- September 29, 1811 *Kentish Gazette*: "Miss Darcy, a Derbyshire lady of 15, who is ward of her brother, a bachelor, eloped on morning last with a young man of about 25 years of age. Miss Darcy's faux pas with the young man took place at an inn near Ramsgate..."
- October 2, 1811 *The Derby Mercury*: "From the effect of the late elopement of Mr. Wickham with Miss Darcy, an orphan under the care of her brother, it may justly be said to have been, on the gentleman's part, a pact with the lady's

companion. This respected family in Derbyshire are plunged
into . . ."
- October 3, 1811 *The Morning Post:* "Miss Georgiana Darcy, a
lady of a respectable family with handsome fortune, eloped
from Ramsgate with Mr. George Wickham, who had
previous connection with that family, with the purpose of
being married in Scotland. The brother of the damsel is
convalescing and his whereabouts are unknown . . ."
- October 13, 1811 *The Morning Post*: "Married—Lately, Mr.
George Wickham to Miss Darcy, only daughter of the late
Mr. George Darcy of Pemberley."

It was the dates that gave her a plummeting feeling in her stomach and forced Elizabeth to grab her keys and coat with trembling fingers, and scramble to find a flashlight. Her love for Georgiana overrode her reluctance to pass another moment with Darcy. It was already six o'clock, and she had to catch a bus and then cross the moor to Nine Ladies.

IF ANY WALKERS WERE TO COME ACROSS HIM IN THE CENTER OF THE CIRCLE, they might imagine him to be engaging in druid spiritualism. It was growing dark, and Darcy brought his pocket watch near to his eyes: 6:50. His watch was less accurate compared to the precise timekeeping now practiced, but it could not be much longer.

He heard the pounding of feet and looked over his shoulder. Someone gasping for breath and carrying a light was fast approaching. It was only when the person charged up to the circle that he recognized her.

"Elizabeth!" He took several quick steps toward her, scarcely daring to hope what her presence meant. Her hair was plastered to her forehead and sweat dripped down the side of her face.

She waved him off, still panting. "No, stay inside; it's almost time."

"Why–"

"Shut up and listen! Maria found out when Georgiana marries

Wickham. You asked her to find their marriage announcement in the newspaper?"

"Yes, what did she learn?" His hopeful feelings vanished as he realized Elizabeth's coming held little good news.

"The announcement is dated October 13, 1811. *The Morning Post* says they were lately married."

"Good God! They marry this year?"

"It's worse." Elizabeth gave him a fretful glance before looking at her phone. "There are articles mentioning their elopement as early as September twenty-ninth. They left the morning before from Ramsgate and ran off to Scotland. And Mrs. Younge was in on the whole thing!"

Tonight was Monday the twenty-third. "They are in Ramsgate *now*, and are seen leaving together on the morning of Saturday the twenty-eighth?"

"Yes! That's why I came. You won't have much time to stop them."

"I shall have no time!"

"You have five days."

"There are no trains or cars, Elizabeth!" He lost his patience. "It is two hundred and fifty miles to Ramsgate! It could take five days to get there."

"What if you intercept them after they leave Ramsgate? I know it's bad if she's seen leaving with him, but you might recover her on the way to Scotland. Better her reputation is ruined than she marries this guy. We both love her—and Pemberley—too much for that to happen."

Darcy bit back the question, "Is that the only reason you came?" because he knew the answer. For a long moment, neither said anything.

Elizabeth spoke in a rush. "If you tell Georgiana the truth about Nine Ladies, about me, tell her I wish we could have been friends."

"*She* would be fortunate to have been your beloved friend, and Georgiana would be comforted to know that although you must remain apart, *she* is remembered fondly by you." He could not keep from his tone the bitter implication that Elizabeth would never understand his sacrifice was for both their benefit.

"I don't hate you."

"No, but you are angry and embarrassed, and will soon become indifferent to me."

"You're the one who—" She stepped toward the circle.

"Stay where you are!" Darcy took a few steps backward toward the center. "We both know you would never be happy there." Elizabeth looked at her phone to check the time; its light illuminated her face. He could not take his eyes from her, drawing in every detail of her. He was angry that she would not forgive him for refusing her. And still, he wished to hold her and never let her go, not tonight, not tomorrow, not ever.

Before the phone's light disappeared, he caught the reflection of shimmering tears in her eyes. She may overcome her disappointment, and remember him with some of the affection she previously held for him. Maybe his refusal and departure would not make her hate him, but it did not matter. Soon they would part forever.

"Goodbye, Elizabeth. Please accept my best wishes for your health and—"

ELIZABETH STARED INTO THE DARK, EMPTY CENTER OF NINE LADIES. HE had been right there, and then without a sound, Darcy was . . . gone.

CHAPTER TWENTY-FIVE

SEPTEMBER 23, 1811
AUTUMNAL EQUINOX
NINE LADIES

It was as though a bolt of lightning had struck him back apace, scorching his body and compressing the air from his lungs; and in an instant, he was wrenched forward to the same place. Darcy was thrown off balance by this instantaneous and violent pushing and pulling; and when he opened his eyes, he was on the ground. He blinked twice before sitting upright, wondering if he had fainted from that brief lack of air. Before he was on his feet, he knew by the height of the trees he was back.

He heard an exclamation of surprise and saw Mr. Roland holding a lantern aloft, its light illuminating the gamekeeper's features enough to see that he wore a triumphant smile. Standing next to him was his cousin, who brought a hand to his mouth. Darcy was too dazed to exit the stone circle. When Fitzwilliam approached, he stared at Darcy, shaking his head before pulling him into a fierce embrace.

"You are alive! I dared to hope but . . ." Colonel Fitzwilliam released him, but kept his hands on Darcy's shoulders. Darcy felt a hot, prickling feeling behind his eyes at the sight of this dear and familiar face. "Are you well? You are cured of the putrid sore throat?"

It had been weeks since he had thought of his bout with diphtheria. "I am, and have been healthy these two months."

"Miss Bennet's medicines cured you! To what do we not owe her?"

Darcy's stomach dropped. "Yes, and I owe her more than my life, because through her, I learned about Georgiana and Pemberley's fate. I must be off, and without the loss of another minute!" He strode from the stone circle. "Roland, have any of my horses been kept at the inn in Matlock? No matter, my own can rest there overnight; I shall leave from there at dawn. I need horses ready for me at Nottingham before midday. I leave for Ramsgate within the hour."

Roland gave Fitzwilliam a look of concern. "Yes, sir. Glad you are back, sir."

The gamekeeper ran ahead to his cart. Fitzwilliam stared at Darcy as though he had taken leave of his senses.

"Darcy, it will be pitch-dark before we return to Pemberley. It will take you two hours to go ten miles, not even accounting for the darkness."

Darcy went to where two horses were next to the birch trees. "What did Miss Bennet tell you about the future?"

"That more than your life would be saved if she kept you alive. I dare not confess more."

His closest friend looked pained at whatever he was recalling. "Did she show you pictures inlaid in a box that she held in the palm of her hand? I know it all. I saw Pemberley's ruins myself."

"Then you know why Reynolds and I agreed to let you go. We hoped you would forgive our interference if it was for the good of Pemberley."

"It is for that greater good that I go to Ramsgate. Miss Bennet told you Georgiana's widower bankrupts Pemberley, everything is sold, and my tenants dispersed?" His cousin nodded as they reached the horses. Darcy mounted, not without briefly losing his balance. To think he had not ridden a horse in three months. "She elopes with George Wickham from Ramsgate before Michaelmas."

"Why would she—But how did you—"

"There is no time!"

"It is *dark*!" Fitzwilliam stood in front of Darcy's horse. "And you cannot go anywhere but to your dressing room. I bribed your valet to remain in your employ in idleness—you are welcome, by the by—and you ought to make use of him. You have neither hat nor gloves, to say nothing of that thing. Is that a coat?"

"Fine! I'll change, but I need to get to Matlock tonight to be at Nottingham by midday tomorrow."

"*Fine*? What does that mean?"

"I will answer your questions, but I must leave now if I have a hope of being in Ramsgate in time!"

Fitzwilliam swiftly mounted. "No, *we* must leave now. You cannot think I will allow you to make this journey alone!"

SEPTEMBER 24, 2011
O'HARE INTERNATIONAL AIRPORT, CHICAGO

Elizabeth was bleary-eyed and ragged after she made her way through customs and the baggage claim. After she found a spot away from the crowd and turned her phone on, she learned Jane had to work and was not coming after all.

Damn it. Elizabeth had given up her car and her apartment to go to England for her father's sake. She had planned on staying with Jane, but now she didn't have a place to sleep for the night. Elizabeth fought against the urge to cry in frustration.

Her phone chimed. Elizabeth was shocked to see "Mom" with a message saying, "In the cell phone lot. The board says your flight landed. On my way."

Will wonders never cease? My mother actually came.

She put her luggage into the trunk before getting in the passenger seat. She leaned over to hug her mother, but Mrs. Bennet only tilted her cheek toward her and Elizabeth gave her a peck instead. She pulled away before Elizabeth buckled her seatbelt.

"Mom, why are you here?"

"You're welcome for the ride, Lizzy. It's nice to see you after nine months. I'm well, thank you for asking."

Passive-aggressive or aggressive-aggressive: her mother's two favorite attitudes. "Sorry. It's not that I'm not grateful. I expected Jane."

"I only came because it isn't a school day."

After Jane began high school, their mother had taken a job as an administrative assistant in the athletics department of a college an hour away. The reason: the college had a tuition grant program for children of its full-time staff who worked for three years. By the time Jane was a senior, most of her daughters' college educations were paid for.

"Now that we're done with undergrad, you don't have to work a job you hate anymore. You're only forty-six; you could find something you enjoy."

"I'm not looking for a new job now. Do I have a husband to share the financial burden with? No. You and Janie had no undergrad loans because of that job. Now she's off to be a *doctor*! I knew she couldn't have been that smart for nothing. But how will *you* support yourself with *just* an accounting degree? You could've earned an MBA or become a CPA and doubled your income!"

Elizabeth did not like where this conversation was headed. "What did Jane have going on?"

"The University of Chicago Medical Center doesn't let their residents come and go because you need a ride. This is Janie's last year as a resident, and she's about to start her Emergency Medicine senior rotation."

"Right." Elizabeth gazed out the window. She realized they were headed the wrong way. "Where are we going?"

"Janie has two other med student roommates. You lounging on their couch would be depressing for those hard workers. You'll stay with me while you job-hunt."

"Mom! I had it all set with Jane!"

"I know. But I told her you'll be more motivated to move out of your teenage bedroom than you will be hanging around Hyde Park. You need a job, Lizzy. No one else in this world is ever going to take care of you."

"Let me guess: Jane was happy to agree. She *loves* to make you happy." Her head throbbed.

"Don't take that tone with me. Be grateful I've forgiven you for gallivanting around England."

"Gallivanting? I went to take care of my father, who had a *stroke*. And then I was settling his estate."

"And did he deserve your sacrifice? No! Men never do. So what *did* you get from your time in England?"

Saw some grand houses; made a few friends. I learned for certain my father didn't give a damn about me. Spent three months in 1811. I fell in love with a guy I couldn't have, who left thinking I hate him.

OCTOBER 31, 1811
PEMBERLEY

Darcy intended to walk to Mr. Willers's house before breakfast, but learned he was in his office at so prompt an hour. His steward had come into his service not long after the death of Darcy's father and with the recommendation of their former steward, old Mr. Wickham. Mr. Willers had been an attorney and had shown such promise for a young man that old Mr. Wickham, who knew he was ailing, insisted he was the best man to manage Pemberley's concerns.

As Darcy entered, he was caught by the organization, the precision of everything in sight: shelves perfectly neat; ledger books ordered by date; sheets of paper stacked tightly.

There was also no avoiding the black ribbons Mr. Willers wore for his wife.

"Mr. Darcy!" Mr. Willers looked up and rose. "Have you been standing there long? Come in, please."

"Forgive me for interrupting your early hours."

"I cannot pretend to not be more disposed for employment than usual." A shadow passed over Mr. Willers's countenance; his face held more lines than Darcy remembered. "I find steady employment better for the spirit."

"I do not doubt that employment may aid in dispelling melancholy." Darcy could well imagine that remaining alone in the house he shared with his wife would be painful. "That is part of the reason why I am here. Given my lengthy absence and time spent in reestablishing myself at home, I have not told you how exceedingly sorry I was to learn of the death of your wife."

"Thank you, sir."

"Mrs. Willers was a lovely, amiable woman, and a credit to you."

The steward cleared his throat and straightened a sheaf of papers that did not need straightening. "We lost many good people. It is a comfort to all of us at Pemberley that you were spared."

Darcy was struck, quite struck, by guilt. He rationalized that Elizabeth could not have saved everyone, and her affection for him, the certainty that he was to die and what that meant for Pemberley, and his already knowing the truth of Nine Ladies made him a logical choice for her to save. Nonetheless, it was still a blow. He had been saved, but twenty other people connected to Pemberley had died.

"Sir? Mr. Darcy?"

"Forgive me. I was contemplating the incomprehensibility of Providence. I also came to say that I have relied upon you heavily these three months. You are a tremendous asset to Pemberley."

"I did no more than you would expect from your steward. Many landowners, if you will give me leave to say, are not half so committed to their properties as you."

"You do yourself too little credit. You were my secretary, you saw that rents were collected, you oversaw the renewal of two leases on agreeable terms, you set forth the contract to begin lead mining next year, you dealt with a tenant dispute as I would have done, and, furthermore, you kept a meticulous record of every activity."

"It was a pleasure to do my duty."

"We have run a profit this year because of you."

"You were gone but three months, sir. Pemberley's success cannot be measured by what happened from summer to autumn." Mr. Willers turned an unmanly shade of pink, but Darcy was not finished.

"You, with Reynolds's assistance, took over my charitable concerns. There is not a tenant who suffered from the effects of bad harvest or weather or sickness because of your care. You made certain a haymaking party followed the mowing of the fields. You sent apples and a joint of meat to every widow associated with Pemberley. I understand you even met with my solicitor in person."

"I had to travel but once to London, but it was no trouble. I spent most of my time in my office or walking the estate, and contentedly, I may add."

"Your current salary is two hundred and fifty pounds per annum, is it not?"

Mr. Willers blinked at the change in topic. "It is, sir."

"I will double it."

"I beg your pardon?"

"I am fortunate, indeed blessed, to be dependent on so well-educated, so attentive, and so honest a man. You do not broker unscrupulous deals with tradesmen for your own benefit, you do not overcharge on bills to line your own pockets, and you do not fail to renew a lease of an industrious family to move in an acquaintance of yours. You have proven your worth a thousand times over."

"I do not know how to express my gratitude."

"It is I who must express mine, Mr. Willers."

"I ORDERED YOUR CARRIAGE FOR NINE O'CLOCK, DARCY. YOUR GOING TO the first assembly will dispose other people to attend the second. Besides, everyone will want to congratulate you on your good health. Consider it your civic responsibility as a principal landowner to start the Season off well."

"Why bother? I come late, I do not dance, and I go early. Everything about me speaks to me being out of my element in a ballroom."

Darcy was sitting with Fitzwilliam and Georgiana in the breakfast parlor. The spirits of the former were playful; the spirits of the latter were subdued, but no longer as disheartened as they had been after Ramsgate. Darcy's own temper, today and over the past month, he dared not vouch for.

"A public assembly is five miles away. Young ladies wishing to dance are in desperate need of my attention. Besides, Georgiana might like to attend."

The siblings looked up quickly. Fitzwilliam went on, "You need not look at me that way, Georgiana. I am not suggesting we look for your future husband tonight. But Darcy, I think she ought to be seen with her brother, even if she does not dance. It is not as though we have reason to be ashamed of our girl."

Darcy cringed at the oblique reference to the near-disaster at Ramsgate. He and his cousin had arrived at the inn—exhausted, anxious, and having nearly killed one horse in the attempt—precisely in time. Before his cousin descended after him, Darcy saw his own sister through the side-glass of a carriage pulling away ten yards from him. He had run toward it, calling to its postilion while Fitzwilliam wrenched open its door before it came to a stop.

They were gone from Ramsgate after Darcy verbally eviscerated Wickham and severed Mrs. Younge's employment. Fitzwilliam added his own, more physical, dispatching to Darcy's sharp words. Once inside Darcy's coach, Georgiana's confused tears gave way to guilty weeping, and then to ashamed sobs while Darcy unfolded the black heart of George Wickham.

The one potential threat to his sister's reputation was an article in the *Morning Post*. It implied an elopement had been prevented, but no names were given. It was thought the lady might be from Derbyshire, but none could say for certain whom she was.

Georgiana—indeed, we all—are more fortunate than I had reason to hope for.

Had Elizabeth not run to Nine Ladies with what she had learned, he would never have stopped his sister from eloping. Thanks to Elizabeth, Georgiana's happiness was preserved, and Pemberley's future along with it.

"What say you? Darcy?" A linen napkin struck him on the head and landed in his lap. His sister eyed Fitzwilliam nervously, his cousin glared at him, and his servant struggled to hide a half smile.

Darcy balled up the offending napkin before remembering that he was twenty-seven, not seven, and could not throw it back. *At least not while my servant is in the room.* "She should not attend public balls before she has paid morning visits or invited close friends to supper. We shall proceed by degrees after her new companion joins us; perhaps we might invite Dr. Ferris and his sister to tea."

Georgiana's sigh of relief caught everyone's attention. "When does Mrs. Annesley arrive?"

"Reynolds tells me to expect her by the end of the week. She was governess to a family of girls for ten years and preferred to be a companion to a young lady rather than begin anew teaching another brood. Do you look forward to knowing her?"

"I am not comfortable with strangers, but she shall soon cease to be one. My former companion was not . . . compassionate. Elizabeth once said—did you tear that napkin, Fitzwilliam? She said, and I agreed with her . . . though I dared not then confess to you, that . . . Mrs. Younge was not fond of me."

Darcy told the servant he could go. He set aside the frayed napkin. "I am exceedingly sorry for not seeing the deficiencies in Mrs. Younge's character."

"Elizabeth said she was cruel to me and eager to see me married to anyone so she could move on to a new situation. I did not see Mrs. Younge's actions for what they were. I thought it was *I* who was lacking."

Darcy reached across the table to press her hand. "You are not deficient in any way. Miss Bennet was correct, and if I had taken action based on her observations, Mrs. Younge could not have facilitated your intended elopement."

"I must take my share of the blame. No, do not shake your head. I fancied myself in love. Mr. Wickham tended to my concern for you with believable affection and sympathy. I felt worthy of another's attentions for the first time." Georgiana's lips quivered, but the tears Darcy thought were certain to fall never did. "I hope my new companion will not dislike me."

"My dear Elizabeth did not fail to see your worth, and neither will Mrs. Annesley." Darcy saw his cousin's eyebrows rise. Darcy took a long sip from his teacup, thinking about where he had paused. "*My dear, Elizabeth*" *sounds like* "*my dear Elizabeth.*"

"I miss Elizabeth." Darcy's teacup slipped from his fingers. "I received a letter from her after she arrived home."

"How was your friend's voyage?"

"She arrived in York, but did not describe the voyage or the ship.

She reminded me to not sacrifice my self-respect, that I am a capable woman despite my shyness, and not to be in a hurry to marry and leave my home. It was as if she thinks I might do some good at Pemberley. I know nothing more of the Canadas or her home than I did before."

Fitzwilliam and Darcy shared a look. The colonel smiled at his young cousin. "She is an excellent friend. I am glad she is in good health."

Georgiana twisted her fingers in her lap before squaring her shoulders. "Elizabeth passed her love on to Reynolds and me, and you as well, Fitzwilliam."

Darcy then left with the excuse that he had correspondence to attend to. During his alleged convalescence, he was sometimes thought to be in Bath, at other times at the estates of friends. Between his cousin, his housekeeper, and letters he had signed in the midst of fever, he was thought to have recovered in relative solitude.

After Ramsgate, Darcy had reinstated himself in the wonted concerns of his Pemberley life. Just as Mr. Willers said, there was nothing like active, indispensable employment for relieving sorrow.

The aloneness, after having had her intimate company for six months, is at times unbearable.

"You *are* attending that assembly." Fitzwilliam eyed him as he leaned against the doorframe. "You must do something other than meet with Mr. Willers and ruminate."

"How do you mean?"

He entered, throwing up his hands. "You dwell moodily in this room. I am here for one more day, and then there will be no one to draw you out. Did not your friend Bingley invite you to Hertfordshire?"

"I do not wish to leave until Georgiana is settled with Mrs. Annesley, and I cannot spend too little time at Pemberley after three months away. I shall escort my sister to London after Christmas and will see Bingley there on occasion."

"I hope you go into society more than 'on occasion.' That is unsociable, even for you. I fail to see why you are dispirited. Your sister is saved from a miserable marriage, and her reputation is secure; your absence was explained; Pemberley's wretched fate has been avoided. And let us not forget that you are not dead!"

"What possesses you to say I am unhappy when I am undeniably blessed?"

Fitzwilliam held his gaze, and for a few moments, he said nothing. Darcy was deep in thought likewise, trying to harden himself against further questioning.

"I am determined to make this last day one of thorough enjoyment. Tonight you are dancing—yes, *you are*—and now I want to go out shooting." Darcy agreed, and both men moved toward the door. "Oh, and Darcy, if you begin another sentence with, 'when I was in the future,' I will box your ears."

DARCY COULD NOT READ THE CLOCK WITH ONLY A CANDELABRA BEFORE the mirror and the light of a dying fire to illuminate his library; he suspected it was closer to four than to three in the morning. He had gone to the assembly and danced with ladies who were in want of a partner, as he had promised himself after having attended that nightclub.

He still could not help thinking of Elizabeth. When would the longing for her stop? He doubted her anger would linger, but did it mean that anger could ever be replaced with a more tender emotion? *Not that it matters.*

The door opened without a preemptive knock, and the intruder gave a sharp gasp of surprise. Reynolds was dressed for the day, holding a candle aloft.

"Sir! I did not see you in the chair. I thought one of the maids left the candles burning."

"No, I am just not rational enough to go to bed when I ought."

Darcy kept his gaze averted, and his housekeeper said nothing. He could still sense her displeasure.

"Shall I have the fire built up? It is near enough time for a maid to clean the grate and lay and set the fire in any event."

"No. I could do it myself, if I wanted it done."

"Yourself, sir? Is this perhaps a symptom of your time spent away from proper servants?"

He rose and ran his hand along the cornice and corbel, remembering the gaping hole and exposed brick of Pemberley in 2011. "There were no servants, and I did not need them." He tapped on the mantle a few times. "Can you comprehend setting a fire without needing a tinder box? Or lighting a candle without using a spill from the vase on the mantle? Can you imagine how much easier these tasks would be with a small, self-igniting piece of wood?"

The silence stretched for so long that Darcy turned to look at his housekeeper. She was inscrutable. "I daresay, if such a thing exists, setting your own fires and lighting your own candles in 2011 must have not been laborious."

Darcy laughed; he dared not attempt to explain electricity. "I did well without servants, I will say only that."

"You are a gentleman, and you need not perform any task that ought be done by those you employ for that purpose. We have no matches, and I have maids who would be appalled to know the master suggested he would light his own fire. If you intend to sit up and think over your fair dance partners, you ought to build up this fire."

"I assure you, I am not in love with any lady in the neighborhood. I danced three dances with ladies who were obliged to sit down for want of a partner."

"It is just as well, as I do not know who is good enough for you, if you will give me leave to say."

Darcy's mind went straight to Elizabeth. "Not in this neighborhood." He felt his housekeeper's attention and said he needed nothing else. She was at the door before he changed his mind.

"I should like you to show Georgiana your system of domestic economy and household accounts."

"Sir?"

"Your experience in every department of housekeeping is invaluable. Georgiana should see your servants' register, to know when they entered our service and what their wages on quarter days are. She ought to know what is paid for in ready money and what is in the cashbook for weekly sundries, as well as the bills paid weekly, quarterly, or monthly, and what is consumed and how much."

"Yes, sir."

Darcy knew this was a reluctant accord. "Would instructing her take much time away from your responsibilities?"

"Not at all, but I suspect Mrs. Annesley will take the matter of your sister's education in hand."

"I want her to learn about Pemberley's management. I need for her to feel the same connection to its well-being, its history and future, as I do."

"Miss Darcy is handsome, has excellent connections, has been given a good education, and shall be introduced into the world when she is ready. Her fortune aside, a girl like Miss Darcy will marry and leave us to manage her own household."

"Elizabeth"—Reynolds's eyes widened—"Miss Bennet suggested Georgiana needs to know that *this* is her home as much as it is mine, and that she is needed here. That she is as much a Darcy of Pemberley as I am."

Reynolds, along with Mr. Roland, Fitzwilliam, and Elizabeth, were the only ones who comprehended the full impact of those words. "I shall also show Miss Darcy our expenditures on food, menu planning, what a dinner for fourteen costs and its menu. I will see she has charge of those matters before Christmas."

"It will help her confidence, thank you."

"Sir? Miss Darcy is an intelligent, though sensitive, girl. When you marry and your wife supersedes her, will not Miss Darcy feel displaced after she has learned how to manage this house?"

"That is not likely to happen anytime soon."

Reynolds curtsied and left Darcy to resume his investigation of the empty grate.

Not likely ever.

DECEMBER 10, 2011
ROCK RIVER TOWER APARTMENTS
ROCKFORD, ILLINOIS

Happy Holidays!

I've returned to the States after nine months in England. The first three months were spent caring for my estranged father who suffered a stroke, then he died of a heart attack. In the spring, I was in a place that defies common sense. In the summer, I met and lost a great guy. In essentials, he's dead. It's complicated.

I spent the fall in my mother's house. She lives, sleeps, and breathes getting her daughters in lucrative paying jobs. After two months of job searching and depression while I nursed my broken heart and dealt with my mother's passive-aggressive hints that I was a freeloader, I settled for a job with the Winnebago County Health Department as a staff accountant.

I scraped together enough cash, as I wait for accountants and lawyers on two continents to disperse the funds from my father's estate, to buy a '95 Civic. It's silver and the duct tape blends in perfectly. I'm in an 800-square-foot apartment that costs $900 a month. I can walk to work, which is important given the state of the aforementioned Civic.

Christmas newsletters are nauseating to write when your life sucks. Elizabeth deleted the document.

Facebook didn't improve her mood. The humble bragging of every friend planning a wedding, finishing their master's, expecting a baby, hosting Christmas dinner for in-laws, or working in Chicago or New York made her want to scream. As she did every evening since she first saw the article on the BBC News website, she opened the link to read again:

British Newspaper Archive launched online

An ambitious project to digitise every newspaper, periodical, and journal ever printed in Britain has launched, making more than a million pages of pre-1900 newspapers available to readers online.

The British Newspaper Archive will allow readers to search by date, title, and keyword, and will include material previously only available at the British Library.

The project aims to build to four million digitised pages over the next two years, and to 40 million pages over the next decade.

29 Nov 2011

She went to the British Newspaper Archive's site. Since the equinox, she had wanted to know if Darcy had saved Georgiana. She searched by keyword "elope" and "Ramsgate" between September through October of 1811. Only one article was returned, from September 29, 1811, and Elizabeth paid to subscribe so she could read it in its entirety:

> *A hustle took place yesterday in Ramsgate in a post chaise, in which a young lady and gentleman, from the conversation and warmth of both parties, appeared to be intending to elope. They were, however, intercepted by the lady's friends in the stable yard. One man dragged the gentleman from the chaise and struck him. The other man escorted the tearful lady into his own coach and drew up the blinds. There are suspicions that the lady was from a respected family in Derbyshire; but as the man in question fled immediately, and exhibited bruises around his nose and eyes that, along with the blood, left him unrecognizable, and the lady was immediately removed, their identities cannot be confirmed.*

He did it! Darcy, and probably Colonel Fitzwilliam, made it to Ramsgate in time. Georgiana was safe, would never marry Wickham, and Pemberley might still be standing. But Elizabeth felt she couldn't find out about Darcy's or Pemberley's fate if she wanted to move on.

Darcy lived the rest of his life thinking I hated him. She had been disappointed and angered by his rejection. But now she was angry at herself for not sympathizing with his reasons. Darcy was right when he said that she couldn't imagine living in the past, and could never have lived with himself if he had put his own desires ahead of the life of his sister and the fate of Pemberley.

She had saved her friend from diphtheria and had helped him to save his sister from misery. That they were so much more than friends couldn't matter now when two hundred years separated them.

CHAPTER TWENTY-SIX

DECEMBER 22, 1811
PEMBERLEY

"I know a Sunday evening with nothing to do turns you into a fearsome object, but could we not have found something to do *inside*? Beating my brother at billiards or entertaining my nieces with a seesaw in the drawing room could not have lost their appeal already."

"Admit it, you are just cold!" Darcy called as his cousin drew his horse nearer.

"I would never admit to something so unmanly." Fitzwilliam bent and flexed his fingers, and looked around. "Are we nearly at Bakewell?"

"So we are. Shall we find somewhere to rest indoors, even though you are not cold?"

"No, I would prefer to return to Pemberley before the sun sets."

"Since we are here, I wish to show you a place."

Darcy felt Fitzwilliam's steady gaze as he led them into the village. He had not been here since he left in September, two hundred years in the future.

"There it is," Darcy pointed to a gray stone building.

"How dreary. It appears to be a girls' boarding school. Why are we here on this frigid day?"

"It was—it *will* be divided into three private residences, and I lived in the second with Elizabeth. We shared one parlor, a dining room, a kitchen, a bathroom, and two bedchambers. We needed no servants because of the harnessed power of electricity, this elemental force, like gravity or magnetism, which provided light and heat and movement to labor-saving machines. I do not mean electric as in friction, but a charged energy that made remarkable things possible."

"What is a bathroom?"

In two hundred years, Elizabeth would lease this place. "How might one preserve a sheet of paper? I know it can be done, but I do not know how. Do you think if it were sealed in a vial and kept out of the light, that it could be read in two hundred years?"

"What a thought-provoking subject. I would love to discuss *paper* with you . . . in front of a fire with a glass of your aged claret."

"Do you suppose the ink would fade?" Darcy felt his cousin's incredulous gaze and turned his horse to face him. "It is not a philosophical discussion."

Fitzwilliam shook his head. "What will you do? Ask the mistress of the school to put a letter in a wall and plaster over it with the expectation that in two hundred years it will find its way into the hands of the right woman at the right time? That is impossible."

Darcy sighed. "It was a fool's hope."

"What would you write to Miss Bennet that you did not say while you were together? And if she did find your letter, what if she found it while you were in the future with her? Would it not be odd to find your own letter that you did not remember writing? What if she read it before she ever went through time and met you? I cannot rationalize such a thing! The logic of time travel is beyond my comprehension."

He would write to Elizabeth that he loved her but could not marry her and bring her here, thereby making her miserable. He ought to have been brave enough to ask her to come and suffered her refusal to assure her of his affection. If she read his letter, she would know for certain what he felt. *Would that comfort her or wound her further?*

"Darcy, why are we here on this bitter afternoon when it is nearly dark and your relations are all over your house to celebrate Christmas?"

Darcy tightened his grip on the reins. "You are keeping me from temptation. It is nearly sunset; we can return now."

"I comprehend you have not recovered from a tender affection for her, but what is this about temptation?"

"Today is the winter solstice." Darcy kept his eyes ahead. Fitzwilliam's confusion lasted but a few seconds.

"You damned stupid man! You would never be so selfish, so—"

"Likely not," he sharply interrupted. "But a brief fancy of seeing her again crossed my mind when I awoke." The specific thought, and one more lasting than he implied, was, *If I walk into Nine Ladies at sunset, if Elizabeth is still in Bakewell, I can hold her in my arms before the day is out.* "I appointed you my keeper until the sun set, although we both know my abandonment would be a near-criminal neglect of everything I value. Let us return to Pemberley."

"Your peculiar attachment to the American from the future becomes clearer. To think that Fitzwilliam Darcy lived with a woman without the benefit of marriage. Oh, how wicked you became in those future times!"

Darcy cast him a cold look, but Fitzwilliam just laughed. "It was not as you imagine it to be. We're just friends." Darcy shook his head. "We were friends, not lovers."

"If you did not succumb to the allurements of your pretty traveler, why are you indulging in a flight of fancy of returning to her?"

Darcy would not speak his answer aloud. *Because while we were not lovers, I do love her.*

JANUARY 3, 1812
PEMBERLEY

Darcy left Mr. Willers on his way to the housekeeper's room. Mr. Willers had begun to wear white with black, although he still did not wear gilt buttons. His steward had been more involved in helping him, Reynolds, and Georgiana distribute gifts of money, food, and clothes to the tenants than a man in his position needed to be, but Darcy could not fault him. He wished to remain active, and his steward's sense of responsibility to Pemberley was almost as absolute as his own.

Reynolds no longer asked him what he needed when he came to her rooms. If he required his housekeeper, he rang the bell or sent a message with a footman. When he required a confidant who understood he spent three months not in this century, he went in person.

"If you have something to say, I am willing to hear it. However, with your permission, I have not the time to waste while you struggle with what to say about some twenty-first-century curiosity or a mistake you made since you returned."

From who else but a servant who had known him since he was four, and who demonstrated her loyalty every day, could he allow impertinence? "You are perfectly right. Forgive me for often taking up so much of your time." She bowed. "I had a conversation with Mr. Willers this morning about a housemaid, Millie."

"She became maid last July when Polly did not return after her brother died."

When would he stop feeling guilty for surviving when others had not? *Perhaps never.* "Mr. Willers said Millie mentioned she wished to earn a hundred pounds for a dowry to marry a laborer at Hill Close Farm. She does not love him, but she knew being a maid was the work of a young woman and did not wish to become a burden to her family."

Reynolds's eyebrows drew closer together. "Many female servants work only until they save enough to set up their own home, and will find other employment after they marry. Miss Darcy has been learning alongside me not even three months, and she understands this."

"Mr. Willers's comments about Millie's intentions did not catch me by surprise. However, *my* reply took him aback." Reynolds gestured toward the chairs around her table, and he sat.

"You said something appropriate to two hundred years in the future, but not credible in this day?"

"I said that why did we not educate and apprentice the village girls the same way the boys are so that, as young women, they are in a position to support themselves without a husband."

Reynolds winced. "What did Mr. Willers say to your singular notion?"

"He said Millie's family would not cast out a spinster, and he added that if she worked at Pemberley for as long as she was able, he suspected the Darcys would provide for her in her dotage. I would have said more, had I not remembered myself."

"It is not as damaging as when Sir Wesley and his son Mr. Clarke were here and you sought a light switch when the room darkened after the sky grew cloudy."

"You may be right, but I have a greater problem. After living in Miss Bennet's century, I would now have women enjoy the best educational opportunities their abilities afforded, and have them enter into the arts and professions they choose, and vote, the same as any man. I would be labeled as a radical if I espoused such views to the wrong person."

"I would not worry about Mr. Willers's indictment of your notions on female education. He thinks too well of you to speak against you, even if he strongly disagreed."

He hoped his trusted steward did not believe female education, particularly of poorer girls, was pointless. Darcy planned to have the parish school admit both boys and girls. He changed the subject. "My sister said Mr. Willers aided you both in delivering her gifts this season."

"Mr. Willers was happy to be of use in identifying those with the greatest need. Miss Darcy spent a great deal of time making baby clothes, blankets, and shawls. I do not think there is a villager or tenant wanting within five miles of Pemberley."

"I ought to have given Georgiana more responsibility sooner. I must make up for the time I lost, and I would rather be here than anywhere else."

"If I may say, sir, you were very much missed."

"You mean as a nuisance is missed when it is gone: merely that an improvement is noted?" Teasing Reynolds would have been incomprehensible three months ago. Her willingness to advise and listen to him, to be a confidant, had lessened his natural reserve around her.

"You were never a nuisance, not even as a little boy with your occasional scrapes."

"You are blinded by a maternal-like devotion, I fear."

To his astonishment, his housekeeper's cheeks pinked, and she stood. He rose as well, and she turned away.

"I did not mean to embarrass you, Reynolds. However, you must know how much—"

"I am not offended. I am affected by your words more than I ought to be." He should have realized sooner how much Reynolds loved the Darcy children. "Master Fitzwilliam, think no more on equal rights for women or light switches. These progresses will happen in their own time."

"Progresses," he said softly as he walked to the door. "The advancement of science, the incredible technology, the engineering feats of the future, its social improvements . . . it is remarkable. Although I do feel those in 2011 ought to remember that there is a right way to do everything, and that is the way that pleases the greatest number of people whilst offending the least. Consideration for rights and feelings of others is scarcely a rule for public behavior in the future, and it is no longer the foundation upon which their social lives are built."

"It sounds as if you resented the twenty-first century, sir."

"Not as much as you might suspect. I only realize with some bitterness that if these progresses do reach England, it will be too late for me to enjoy them. Good night."

Reynolds recalled the name for every new noun he mentioned, like the match and the light switch, as well as what each did. She was an unexcitable woman; she did not balk at educating women and men on equal terms, or airplanes traveling across the world in mere hours. Elizabeth had been correct: Reynolds was the best person for him to speak of his time in the future.

January 14, 2012
Rockford, Illinois

It was past time to take down her Christmas decorations, but now Elizabeth's small home looked bare without the green boughs and the twinkling lights. As she fought with a tangled string of lights, her phone rang.

"Hey, Jane!"

"Happy New Year! I'm sorry I haven't been able to call. I finally have a stretch of time to myself, and I wanted to catch up before I go to sleep."

"I know how hard you're working. And even if I didn't, Mom is eager to inform me about your dedication."

"She does like to boast about her own children."

"One of them."

"That's not fair; she talks about you. Last week, she said your starting salary was over fifty thousand."

"Did she then say how my pay won't increase much with experience, and in order to be a credit to her, I should earn a CPA or MBA? Because that's what she told me at Christmas."

The extended silence on the other end of the phone spoke volumes. "Well, I am proud of you. Don't let Mom's thoughtlessness bring you down."

"In her mind, my whole life hinges on earning those three letters."

"Tell me what you've been up to, because you do *not* want to hear about what I've seen in the emergency room. Consumer fireworks are illegal for a reason. Did you go out on New Year's Eve?"

Elizabeth poured the contents of a hot chocolate packet into a mug. "I went out with some girls from work."

"Didn't you go out when you were in England too? You said something about buying a dress to go to a club."

Elizabeth remembered how Darcy looked, in his impeccably fitting and modern gray suit, gazing at her as she came down the stairs. "What's that? Sorry, the water was boiling. Did I tell you I've been doing trivia night with a group from work? I got a question right about the number of bones humans are born with because of you."

They chatted until Jane went to sleep, and Elizabeth tried the British Newspaper Archive again to find Georgiana's missing person's information from when she disappeared as a child. Internet and newspaper searches about missing or abducted children in England in 1995 yielded nothing.

Even if she found the family of the girl who became Miss Darcy of Pemberley, what could she say? *Don't worry, your daughter is safe and has a loving older brother and is living in 1812?* She couldn't tell them that, if Darcy took her advice, their daughter learned how to manage one of the wealthiest estates in England and had a respected family with as much security as a woman in that time could have.

Being the mistress of a house was like being the CEO of a major corporation, and Georgiana would build up her confidence if she oversaw Pemberley's operations. With Reynolds to help her and Darcy to trust in her, Elizabeth liked to think that Georgiana would not have settled for marrying someone who wasn't worthy of her.

Elizabeth stared at her laptop. A few keystrokes, and she might know what happened to the Darcys. Elizabeth hoped Georgiana had found her confidence at Pemberley. *Maybe she ended up with Mr. Bingley.* She tried not to think about who Darcy had married.

That's the real reason I don't want to look into Pemberley's fate.

Her phone rang again, and Elizabeth was grateful for the distraction. She smiled when she saw the FaceTime caller, and combed her fingers through her hair before holding the phone out in front of her. "Hi, Charlotte! Did you have a nice Christmas?"

Charlotte shrugged and gave a little laugh. "It was interesting."

"What happened?"

"I've been to the clinic and, even though I have no fertility issues, given my age, I have about a ten percent chance of success. So, after Christmas dinner I told my family I'm going to start my first IUI cycle as soon as I pick a donor."

"You said, 'Merry Christmas; I'm off to get sperm'?"

"They all think I'm nuts. My father said, 'No sane single woman gets pregnant on purpose!'" Elizabeth watched her blink twice and take a breath. "Once there's a new grandchild to spoil, they'll come around, though. They're old-fashioned."

"You look upset." Elizabeth had reservations herself. If it didn't work, her friend would end up heartbroken.

Charlotte's eyes filled with tears. "I wish they were supportive! I know the traditional happy-ever-after isn't for me. They keep going on about how hard it will be. Even Maria, who is on my side, is afraid I won't get pregnant and I'm going to end up broke and disappointed."

I need to be less judgmental. Elizabeth resolved to be the most encouraging friend Charlotte would ever have. "Then you get to tell them a big fat 'I told you so' when baby Lucas arrives. You're going to be a great mother! What happens next?"

Charlotte's face lit up. "Thanks, Elizabeth. I needed to hear that." She sniffed and dried her eyes. "Well, I flip through pages of donor information and make my choice."

"Are there pictures of the guys when they were little so you can rule out the ones with buck teeth and lazy eyes?"

Charlotte snorted. "They only cover ethnicity, height, weight, education, job, hobbies, and basic medical history. How do I pick?"

"This will be fun! Like online dating, but without the pictures."

They laughed for an hour while Charlotte read through the descriptions.

"I think I've narrowed it down between these two."

"You won't tell me which one? Is it the dentist who likes rock climbing? Or that guy who's six-three with the doctorate?"

"No telling, it'll be a surprise!" Charlotte looked up from her tablet, chewing her bottom lip. "What if it doesn't work?"

"It will."

"I could adopt, but I had my heart set on having a child of my own. I don't know how many failures or misc—"

"We're not talking about failures today, we're talking about possibilities! And I'm sure your donor is tall, handsome, smart, and athletic, with an unremarkable medical history. You can move on to the next step because you're ready."

"Thanks. I *am* ready." Charlotte gave her a brave smile that then turned more sly. "We've been talking about me forever. Speaking of tall, handsome, and smart, have you heard from Darcy?"

The mere mention of his name robbed her heart of the last of her pain at his rejection and stole her lungs of air. It felt good that someone knew Darcy had been here and that he meant something to her. "I know nothing about what he's been up to, and I care less."

"You look pretty annoyed to not care at all." Charlotte raised an eyebrow.

"I'm not annoyed, but, yeah, I *do* care. I miss him more than I should."

"Why did you break up?"

"We were never together in the first place." Charlotte rolled her eyes. "It's true! I never even kissed him."

"What! Are you having a laugh?"

"We were just friends. And we had a fight, and he went back and I came home. End of story."

"If you and Darcy were just friends, do you think you'll start dating?"

"Says the woman having a child on her own because she doesn't want to wait for Mr. Right."

"You and I aren't in the same place, and we don't want the same things."

Elizabeth forced false cheer into her voice. "Sure, I would date." They had been apart for months, and that was more than enough time for a person to get over their romantic disappointment. She should start acting like a rational creature and move on. Darcy was a sensible man; *he* would have.

Charlotte looked at her with such a sympathetic gaze that Elizabeth was afraid she might cry, and she had promised herself not to shed more tears over Fitzwilliam Darcy. "I need to charge my phone. I'm so proud of you for moving forward! I want you to text me as soon as you have your first IUI."

A long run on the treadmill would clear her mind. She was ashamed of herself for having been so angry with Darcy for refusing her and for not saying that he loved her.

I do want to be with him—but not in 1811. Darcy wasn't wrong when he said she would leave the nineteenth century if she thought twenty-first-century medicine would save someone she loved. And while she knew Darcy would treat her well, she wouldn't want her daughters to be second-class citizens. Besides, she could never have been herself in his time.

Darcy was long dead, but through Nine Ladies, he was still alive. As she tugged her laces, she longed to know what was passing through his mind at this moment. Specifically, she wondered whether, in defiance of how she had treated him before he left, she was still as dear to him as she once was, and as he still was to her.

CHAPTER TWENTY-SEVEN

MARCH 24, 1812
ROSINGS PARK, KENT

It was duty rather than affection that brought the two cousins to their aunt's home at Easter. Fitzwilliam came because Darcy implored him to save him from being the sole object of Lady Catherine's attentions. Darcy knew his aunt spoke of him to others in the terms of highest admiration, but privately, her satisfaction in his visit came not out of love but because, in her mind, Darcy was destined to marry her daughter.

Anne rarely spoke to him, or anyone, if it could be helped. *Such a miserable creature; silent, petulant, and dull.* Darcy resigned himself to no conversation at the breakfast table and took up his letters. He sorted through them until he stopped at one from Mr. Willers. He tore it open, but after scanning its brief contents, he tossed it aside with a frown.

"What is that, Darcy? You appear exceedingly troubled. Did you read something that disturbed you? Who is that letter from? I must know."

"My steward," he said when he could no longer avoid giving his aunt an answer. "Nothing is amiss; he passed along information from my gamekeeper."

"A gamekeeper should have nothing worth concerning you with at this time of year. Some estate matters ought to be beneath your notice. It shows a lack of perception as to what is and is not important to Pemberley if your steward thinks you should be troubled—"

Darcy was on his feet instantly. Little infuriated him more than the suggestion he should not be concerned with any matter about Pemberley. Still, he took a calming breath and remembered whose house he was in. "Forgive me, madam, but I have business to attend to."

He was a mile from the house before he reopened the letter. When he left Pemberley in February, he had instructed Roland to inform him, through the steward, if there were any events from March 20 that would be of interest to him. Mr. Willers had not understood, but passed on the reply: "Young Henry saw to the matter himself and had nothing to report."

You are a fool, Fitzwilliam Darcy! You cannot go on in this manner. He had no expectation that Elizabeth would come through Nine Ladies, and yet here he was, mourning a loss no rational man should feel. He had not confessed the depth of his attachment to her; she had no reason to return. He was a man of action; but if he could not forget Elizabeth, and she was not returning to him, what was he to do?

"Darcy!"

Fitzwilliam came up behind him. Darcy attempted to be more animated than he felt. "You are not one for a walk unless you are escorting a lady."

"Of course I prefer the company of a pretty lady, but anything is a relief to the company at Rosings, even a walk with you. Why did you abandon me?"

"If it is not my aunt's allusions to nuptials that will never happen, then what drives me away is her presumption that she knows more about the proper management of my ancestral home than I do."

Fitzwilliam adopted a mock-earnest expression. "If you are so ashamed of her ladyship's ill-breeding, why not tell her so?"

They both laughed. "You know I will not insult my mother's sister. Besides, Lady Catherine would not heed me even were I to take out an advertisement announcing that Mr. Darcy of Pemberley will never marry Anne de Bourgh and that I find Lady Catherine to be an arrogant, meddlesome fool."

"No, you would never set her down in public. What you *would* do is write Lady Catherine a long, persuasive, stern letter!" Fitzwilliam barked a laugh. "No one has been put in their place until your unyielding temper has been put to paper with four-syllable words!"

Darcy smiled at this picture of himself. "Shall you remain as I walk this grove for a few hours, or return to the house?"

"I shall keep you company. Lady Catherine will be displeased at your staying away. She is not as attached to me as she is to you, even though *I* humor her."

"That is why you are here: to give me a reprieve." They shared a long laugh.

"You should marry Anne and save us this aggravation."

Darcy heard his cousin's teasing tone and took no offense. "I want an excellent woman, sensible, intelligent, amiable, of good judgment. Anne has no elegance of mind or sweetness of character, not to mention she is superlatively stupid."

"Well, well, are not you a fastidious man?"

"Since *you* are not, why do you not marry Anne?" His cousin huffed; Darcy smirked. "In fact, since you are not as fastidious as me, if *you* marry Anne, I shall grant you a legacy of five thousand pounds for the simple pleasure of having the matter of my marrying her dropped forever."

"All of Anne's property is not enough to make me sacrifice my every happiness and comfort to have Lady Catherine always with me."

They continued in this style for the rest of their walk, but the idea that he must take definitive action regarding Elizabeth had taken a firm hold in Darcy's mind.

May 5, 2012
Rockford, Illinois

Elizabeth was getting ready for bed when she went to charge her phone and saw Charlotte had called three times while she was out, each voicemail message asking her in stronger language to call back no matter the time. She cast a longing look at her turned-back sheets and inviting pillow, then dialed Charlotte's number.

"Hi, I didn't wake you, did I?"

"No, I'm so excited I woke up early. What time is it where you are?"

"Just past one. I went on a date, and before you ask, no, he's not here, and he will *never* be here."

"Not a lot of luck on the dating front?"

"My heart isn't in it." *You can't go on dates if you keep comparing them to a guy who's been dead for two hundred years.* Eager to redirect discussion away from her life, she asked, "Why did you call so many times?"

"It worked. I'm still shocked, but it worked."

Elizabeth yawned and crawled into bed. "What worked?"

"The IUI! The second cycle worked! I'm pregnant."

Elizabeth let out an exultant shriek. "That's wonderful!" Charlotte had suffered one unsuccessful cycle, and it had been a dark time for her. "When are you due?"

"The transfer was on April twentieth and I found out on the fourth. I'm due January eleventh!"

"Congratulations! How do you feel?"

"Physically, I feel fine. Emotionally, though, I feel like I've been on a rollercoaster."

"That's understandable, but nothing worth having is ever easy. What did your family say when you shared the news?"

"Mum and Maria are already fussing over me about cutting out caffeine. I know my brothers and dad will be excited when the baby is actually here." She was silent for a moment. "I won't let their lack of enthusiasm disappoint me. They'll come around."

"That's very practical." *If she ever got married or chose to be a single mother, her own mother might disown her.* "You have a great attitude."

"I'm a practical sort. But it's not practical for me to spend three hours on Babycity's website researching buggies!"

She laughed. "Baby Lucas will ride in the safest and highest-rated stroller available. See, you're a good mom already." Elizabeth tried to stifle a yawn, but Charlotte heard her.

"You don't have to stay up. I just couldn't wait to tell you!"

"I'm so happy for you!"

"Elizabeth? Did you mean it when you said that you'd come to England after the baby was born?" Elizabeth's sleepiness vanished as she heard the hopefulness in Charlotte's voice.

"I said I'd be on a plane as soon as baby Lucas arrived."

"Would you really visit me next spring? The baby will be born in January, and after things settle in, I'd love for you to come."

"I will! I wish I was closer. I'd go to appointments with you and pick out maternity clothes and paint a nursery. But you don't need me there, because you're going to do great."

She heard Charlotte sniff on the other end of the line. "Thank you. Most of my friends . . . they're worse than my dad and brothers. Missy can't look at me without rolling her eyes. I want this baby, more than anything else."

"Give them time to get used to the idea, but if they're not giving you the support you deserve, kick them to the curb. You have to take care of you and baby right now, and if they don't realize how lucky and happy you are, they're not what you need."

"I know it's expensive to fly here, and you'd need to take time off—"

"I'd love to come!" Elizabeth meant it. "I get three weeks' vacation, and my father's estate is settled. After taxes and paying the lawyers, I inherited eighty thousand dollars. This time next year, I *will* be landing in Manchester airport, ready to spoil baby Lucas."

MAY 31, 1812
PEMBERLEY

"If I understand you, Mr. Willers, by improvements, you mean not only agricultural improvements, but also the exploitation of mineral resources on Pemberley's land?"

"Yes, Miss Darcy."

"Such as the lead mining lease you put into place?"

"Mr. Darcy and I discussed the terms last spring. I would not have taken the liberty—"

"Forgive me for interrupting, but Miss Darcy was not chastising you," Darcy said. "She is curious, and knows the matter was done with my full support."

The three were on horseback overlooking a well-drained field. Since Easter, Darcy had invited Georgiana to observe how he dealt with his most pressing matters as an estate owner: consulting with his steward frequently, advising his tenants, taking an interest in the lives of his workers, and offering assistance to his neighbors. She had already spent the last six months alongside Reynolds overseeing the household accounts, the stores, the management of the servants, and the estate's charitable concerns.

"What do you think, my dear?" Darcy thought his sister looked troubled.

"Fitzwilliam, I had no notion you were deeply involved in so many matters." She stared toward Hill Close Farm and then turned her horse to look to where a flock of sheep grazed.

"If I may, Miss Darcy, it is like you not omitting the smallest article in keeping household accounts," Mr. Willers said. "Mrs. Reynolds would not have you ignore weighing the sugar or meat when they come in to compare them against the charge?" Georgiana nodded. "Although the housekeeper may do the work, it is up to the mistress to oversee it. It is the same as with Mr. Darcy's duties."

"Pemberley is my responsibility, and any respectable landowner is not above concerning himself with livestock and hay," Darcy added.

"How does one balance such responsibility and know what to delegate and what to manage yourself?"

"It is not always a simple case. One must place great faith in those in his—or her—employ. I cannot always be at Pemberley." He gave his sister a long look. "Mr. Willers's role is particularly necessary when I must attend to business elsewhere. The steward sees to every aspect of Pemberley's management. He communicates with lawyers, suppliers, and tenants when I cannot, and not a week goes by when he does not write to me if I am away."

Darcy thought his steward looked embarrassed to be praised, but he did not know why his sister looked discomfited. He came alongside her horse, asking her softly what the matter was.

"I am ashamed to admit I thought Mr. Willers a mere rent collector," Georgiana whispered. Mr. Willers prodded his horse forward to give them more privacy. "How am I to learn about Pemberley's concerns if I did not even know Mr. Willers is such an active manager on your behalf?"

Darcy smiled. "On *our* behalf. Now you know we have a steward who has made it his business to improve the Darcys' property to the utmost." He gave his sister's hand a light squeeze. "You are a Darcy, and I have been remiss in not giving you responsibilities at Pemberley. Should you like to know as much about the land as you do about the house?"

Georgiana nodded eagerly. "Although Mrs. Annesley expects me now since I have not sat down at an instrument in a week. I have been so pleasantly occupied with Reynolds, and now with you and Mr. Willers, that I had not noticed. I prefer to spend my time with more important matters than music."

Darcy called back his steward's attention. "My sister is returning to the house, but she thanks you and hopes to meet with us again tomorrow." Mr. Willers touched his hat, and Georgiana and her groom left. "It may not be conventional, but my sister must be acquainted with *all* of Pemberley's concerns."

"Miss Darcy is intelligent, and I suppose to know the small scale and the large scale, the house and the land, is beneficial. It is . . . original, but it will make her a better mistress."

"Then you will aid me in instructing her on our ongoing concerns?"

"Miss Darcy is capable and, more importantly, you wish it to be done. I am not so backward that I cannot instruct a lady." Mr. Willers's self-conscious expression faded, and a more thoughtful one replaced it. "It is as though, sir, you are treating Miss Darcy as your heir."

After Darcy knocked on his housekeeper's door and was bid to enter, she surprised him by inviting him to sit and poured him a cup of tea. He raised an eyebrow at this uncharacteristically welcoming gesture.

"I was about to sit with my ledger book, sir. I cannot help it if I must discuss the twenty-first century rather than review what is paid and unpaid from the twenty-fifth to the thirty-first, but I can be certain my tea is not interrupted. Miss Darcy will do this tomorrow, but I prefer to review it so I can answer her questions. Although she asks fewer now."

"Shall I return when it is more convenient?"

"No, there must be a matter on your mind."

"That is partly why I come here; you keep me from doing anything that will demonstrate I might be living out of my time."

"You are precisely where you belong." Her voice rang out like a bell. "Has Miss Darcy been a credit to your intention to have her understand your concerns as landowner and master?"

"Yes." He smiled. "Mr. Willers is not opposed, and I take pride in seeing her so interested in land, tenantry, rents, and livestock." He once held the same interests himself. However, what had been tranquility and comfort before was tediousness and vexation now. His longing for Elizabeth was not improving with the passage of time. Instructing Georgiana was the first part in rectifying that.

"I thought your campaign for equal rights for women in estate management would send Mr. Willers looking for a new situation. I am pleased to be wrong; he is too valuable to lose." The light was fading, and Reynolds brought candles to the mantle where she struggled a few times with the flint and steel to light the first one. "One of your matches would not go amiss," she muttered.

Something about Reynolds's phrase "equal rights for women" struck Darcy. It sounded like something Elizabeth would say. Darcy watched Reynolds light the candles. He had described the thin combustible cords, but had he known their name? He must have; how else might his housekeeper make a comment about wishing for one of his matches?

Unless Elizabeth told her more about the future than I realized.

"Reynolds, what did Miss Bennet tell you about the twenty-first century?"

His housekeeper stirred her tea, eyes downcast. When she raised them, her expression was impassive. "Nothing of consequence. I had no wish to know, and I had too much to teach her about this time to be interested in what Miss Bennet left behind."

"She did not speak to you about matches, men and women having equal rights and privileges, how they travel, how they communicate?"

"She described medical advancements when she explained what she might do to save you. Miss Bennet also mentioned Pemberley's sad fate." Her teacup was put down with authority. "I do not wish to dwell on either."

"Did she show you images of Pemberley from 2011? I know Colonel Fitzwilliam saw her pictures of the ruins." There were currently over five thousand acres of land at Pemberley, thirty farms, hundreds of people. How many of those established families could still be attached to Pemberley in two hundred years?

"It was heartless of her to trouble you with photographs of Pemberley's ruins."

"I surmised the truth on my own and insisted to see the remnants of the land and house myself." Darcy cleared his throat. "It was terrible."

"I fail to see why you are melancholy, if you will give me leave to say." Her tone was just short of scolding. "Was not the purpose of sending you to the twenty-first century to be cured, in part, to prevent that from happening? We knew you would not go for your own sake, but you would if it meant your sister and your home were preserved. You are alive, Miss Darcy does not marry a dishonorable man, and Pemberley will remain a prosperous estate to be passed on to your heir."

The silence stretched out, and Darcy drummed his fingers against the table. "Pemberley is on a better path now."

"Then why, may I ask, are you here this evening?"

"A prosperous estate, like Pemberley, is centered on the house, with its parkland, gardens, and stables, and from this center is the home farm and the tenanted farms and cottages. I would have Georgiana comprehend how these agricultural enterprises and rents are the mainstay of a landowner's well-being."

"You mean a *gentleman's* well-being."

He met her gaze for a silent moment. "I have given the matter thought for months, and Georgiana will be Pemberley's heiress. I shall see what might be done so she can enjoy the income from her land but not sell it, and thus dissipate the inheritance for her son, or her daughter. I shall do what can be done to ensure that *she*, and not her husband, if she marries, remains in control of Pemberley."

His housekeeper's mouth gaped, and then closed with an audible snap. "Yes, sir."

"You may as well have overturned the table in your shock."

"I do not know why you presume you will not have children!" Reynolds inhaled, and was once again composed. "I suspect when the new Mrs. Darcy, whoever she may be, gives you children, you will undo what you are about to set into place in favor of Miss Darcy. What remains to be seen is why you have come to tell me of it."

"I am responsible for passing Pemberley intact to my heir, who *will* be my sister. Miss Bennet suggested Georgiana needed to feel proud of herself beyond the typical ladies' accomplishments, to feel a sense of pride in being a Darcy of Pemberley. Instructing her in Pemberley's management is one part of ensuring that my sister feels the same connection to her home as I do. Although she is shy, her fear of doing wrong when it comes to managing this house is gone." He prepared himself to say the next words aloud. "Part of that also involves passing on the traditions that go with Pemberley, and that includes telling Georgiana the entire truth about Nine Ladies."

JUNE 23, 2012
ROCKFORD, ILLINOIS

Elizabeth tugged on a storage bin to yank it out from under her bed. Sweaters, boots, gloves, and winter coats were piled around her. When the summer clothes were in the drawers and the bulky winter clothes were crammed into the bin, the last to be done was to hang the skirts and dresses in the closet. She reached into the back to pull out a hanger, and Elizabeth's hand brushed against muslin.

It had been one of Georgiana's gowns, reworked for her benefit last spring, the one Elizabeth had been wearing when she dragged a feverish Darcy into Nine Ladies. It was trimmed at the bottom with two rows of violet stitching, and decorated around the bodice with bows and ends of violet-colored ribbon. The green kid slippers were still in the back of the closet, but she had forgotten the bonnet and gloves in her rush to get Darcy to Nine Ladies in time.

That was nearly a year ago to the day.

Was he as lonely as she often was? Whenever she had no one to talk to, when she read a book that reminded her of life in the past, when she saw a happy couple, if someone asked her if she was seeing anyone, Elizabeth thought of Darcy. She still didn't dare look up anything about Pemberley, but it didn't mean he wasn't in her thoughts.

Even though he had to leave, he was still tempted to stay.

Elizabeth found the rumpled petticoat, chemise, and short stays. The stockings were long gone, but she peeled off her own clothes and struggled into the two-hundred-year-old ones that looked as though they were only just made.

She looked at herself in her bedroom mirror and put her hair up. The effect of the hairstyle and gown was astounding. She could walk through 1812 Lambton and up to Pemberley's front door.

Sandra Reynolds lived a lifetime there and had been content. *Would being with Darcy make me happy enough to not miss every privilege I would leave behind?*

She went to the closet to put on the slippers and noticed the time on her alarm clock. If she hoped to talk to Charlotte before she went to sleep for the night, they would have to FaceTime now. Charlotte picked up after five rings, bleary-eyed, her face creased with red lines.

"Charlotte, did I wake you?"

"Time's it?" Charlotte rubbed her eyes and sat up.

"It's four o'clock here. Sorry, I thought you'd be awake."

"'S'all right." Charlotte gave a wide, loud yawn. "I put my head down to take a nap, and I think I've been asleep for hours."

"Go back to sleep. I'll call you tomorrow."

"No, I'm up."

"How are you feeling?"

"Tired," she said flatly. "And morning sickness is a misnomer. It should be called 'every moment my stomach is empty and whenever I smell anything' sickness."

Elizabeth smiled. Charlotte still looked happy for a low-grade narcoleptic who couldn't keep down dry toast. "Growing a baby is hard work. How big is baby now?"

"Like a cocktail olive. At my next appointment, I should be able to hear baby's heartbeat."

Elizabeth's heart clenched as she realized she would never share that with Darcy. "That's exciting!"

"My mum is going with me, since Maria started her job at the libr— what are you wearing?"

"Nothing."

"Go to the mirror and hold up the phone." Charlotte was alert now. Elizabeth trudged to the mirror and hoped the light was poor enough to hide her crimson cheeks. "You look like the cover of a Georgette Heyer novel."

"Is that a compliment?"

"Look at that detail! Go in closer and show me those ribbons. It looks so authentic, like it belongs in a museum. It must have cost a fortune. What's it for?"

Elizabeth turned the camera around. "Just a costume party."

"And you felt like trying it on on a Saturday afternoon? You need to get out more." Charlotte laughed, but Elizabeth felt the truth of it.

"I really do." It was time to deflect the focus from herself. "How have you been managing at work feeling so tired? Is it hard to do rounds when you need to visit the smallest room all the time to throw up?"

Elizabeth let Charlotte talk, content to listen and not discuss her own life. After they hung up, Elizabeth was left staring at her reflection. The nineteenth-century clothes she could accept, and the general attitudes toward women she might tolerate since Darcy wouldn't allow anyone to treat her poorly. *But would my own daughter be that lucky?*

She could learn the distinctions of class, and if Georgiana knew the truth, she would help her adjust. Even if business pursuits were abhorrent in women, she could be mistress of Pemberley and use her talents there. Darcy deserved, and wanted, everything she was prepared to give: companionship, loyalty, honesty, and affection.

The truth was she had let Darcy go without considering returning with him. Stupid, selfish mistake! It might be the greatest, all-consuming regret of her life. So what was she going to do about it?

If I walked into Nine Ladies in September, what would happen? What would I have to do?

Leave her job: easy. Leave her friends: difficult but doable. Leave her sister: harder, but only from remorse in causing her worry.

Could he forgive me for how I treated him before he left? What if he's moved on, like any sensible person would? If his feelings for her weren't what they were last autumn, she would once again be thrown on to his charity for three months. Only this time she would be trapped with a man who didn't love her back.

What if he's married? Elizabeth had been looking at the mirror, and saw the color drain from her face at this dreaded thought. She had never found a marriage record for Georgiana when they knew she had married Wickham; not finding a record about Darcy's marriage wouldn't mean he was still single.

What quality of life would my daughters have? Women were thought too feeble for real exercise. I would be thought intellectually inferior to every man.

And Darcy had never said that he loved her. *Even if he did, what if he doesn't love me anymore?*

"I'm not brave enough," she said aloud before bursting into tears.

CHAPTER TWENTY-EIGHT

JULY 1, 1812
PEMBERLEY

Darcy sat alone in the summer house after he had distressed Georgiana by his confession about Nine Ladies' power. Once his guilt at upsetting her lessened, his mind passed over dancing here with Elizabeth. He no longer struggled to define the source of his longing to be touched, his yearning for physical contact. It was an extension of his longing for Elizabeth, for love, friendship, for home, for fulfillment that he had not entirely figured out how he could have.

I will speak to Mr. Willers; he might be able to advise me.

Georgiana sought him out an hour later, saying nothing as she sat beside him, slowly untying the ribbon on her bonnet. Once it was off her head, he might have had a clearer view of her face, but both Darcy siblings stared straight ahead at the garden, sitting in silence for a long time.

"I am sorry I ran from the room."

"You need not apologize. You were overcome by great surprise."

Their conversation—if a situation where one person confesses and the other doubts, cries, and then flees could even be called a conversation—had gone about as well as Darcy had expected. When he had first learned about Nine Ladies, *he* accused his dying father of being addled by laudanum. It was only after Roland's and Reynolds's testimonies of the first traveler that he gave his father's confession credence. His acceptance followed after seeing the proof of his sister's origins and was further strengthened when Elizabeth appeared.

"Whether or not you ever believe—"

"I believe you."

Darcy's neck cracked as he turned sharply to look at her. "Why? Traveling through time is an astonishing notion!" *The proof of her own origins has yet to be laid before her.* He had not even approached the subject of his own journey to the future or Elizabeth's true history. "I did not accept the truth easily, and I had evidence laid before me that you have yet to hear."

"Since I was too young to read joined letters without help, I saved every letter you wrote to me." She looked away before she spoke again. "In town this winter, Lady Catherine showed me the letter you wrote her whilst you recovered from putrid sore throat. Her ladyship wished to show how attentive you were, even though you were ill. It was exactly the same as the one you sent after I left Pemberley to escape the infection."

His sister handed him a letter.

Dear Georgiana,

Thinking you must feel surprised at my prolonged absence, I write these lines to acquaint you that I am convalescing in solitude. It is useless to seek me, but rest assured I improve daily. I have very little more to say, except to remember me to our family. I should have written sooner to ease your mind, but until recently I did not feel well enough nor did I have anything of interest to report. I dictate this to save my strength so I might return to you sooner.

I am your fond brother,
Fitzwilliam Darcy

"Save for the greeting and closing, it was the same, word for word. The one to me was dated in July and the one to Lady Catherine was from early September."

"What has this to do with Nine Ladies?" Darcy asked the question, but feared he knew the answer.

"Both were signed by you but written by Colonel Fitzwilliam; I know his hand. He and Reynolds informed me of your condition while you were ill. You said they and Roland are the ones who know about Nine Ladies." She turned to look him in the eye. "You were gone from June to September, solstice to equinox. You signed these letters before you left through the stone circle to hide your departure."

The summer warmth did nothing to stop the cold dread creeping up his spine. "It was not my intent to deceive you. I wished to begin by telling you what was possible at Nine Ladies before burdening you with the rest."

Georgiana teared up. "That such a thing is possible is a struggle to comprehend. But that you left for three months, alone, while deathly ill? If our foremost responsibility is to conceal and return any who arrive from the future, what possessed you to go?"

Darcy handed her a handkerchief and gave a dry laugh. "You guessed so much; I am surprised you cannot realize what else remains. I did not leave by choice or alone, although I chose to return." *Alone.*

His sister exhaled a shuddering breath and frowned. "What?"

"You remember Reynolds's cousin, who remained with us last spring?"

"Elizabeth Bennet, of course. I was fond of her, and I believe she was so of me, although she never replied—oh!" Georgiana shook her head while Darcy nodded. "She was from the future, not Upper Canada, and you hid her. She feared you might die of the fever and wished to heal you in the future?"

"She *knew* I would die before she ever came here. She told Fitzwilliam and Reynolds that medicine from the twenty-first century would likely save me. I was delirious with fever and did not realize what happened until it was done."

"How was Elizabeth certain one man was to die two hundred years in what was for her the past?"

"Suffice it to say, she knew I would die if I stayed in 1811, she knew you would marry poorly after I died, that you would die young and without children, and that Mr. Wickham's control of your fortune would be the beginning of the end of Pemberley. It was her hope—*our* hope—that by using her medicines to save me, I could return and prevent you from marrying Mr. Wickham and keep Pemberley from ruin."

Darcy put an arm around her to draw her near as she dried her tears. "The rest we shall save for another time. It is a shocking thing to know that such an incomprehensible power exists within a few stones."

"I am not so distressed. You must tell me what you learned in the year 2011. What medicines saved you? And how did dear Elizabeth—"

"It is too much for my sensibilities to recollect it!" He spoke more harshly than he ought, and he gave Georgiana's shoulder a squeeze before whispering an apology. Of what remained to be confessed to his sister, Darcy resolved it would be soon, just not in this moment.

"Were you not afraid to be trapped there?"

"Reynolds knew that the other visitor, the old man, had returned in 1783 to his proper time."

"How did she know you could go to Elizabeth's time and return? All Reynolds or our parents could have known for certain was that one entered Nine Ladies and disappeared."

"Miss Bennet had the same fears. I daresay we had to take it on faith."

"It is not like you or even Reynolds to accept anything of great importance without evidence. Although, I suppose wandering in and out two hundred years ahead of one's time is not something that can be verified."

Reynolds, who only heard of the old man's return, had approved of the decision to send the master of Pemberley into the future, certain that he could return. *On what was that certainty based?*

Mrs. Reynolds, who Elizabeth had suggested would listen to him speak about the twenty-first century, who remembered what a light switch was, who used the word "match," who was not shocked into silence at the notion of women voting. Reynolds, who had no doubt Nine Ladies would send him and Elizabeth to her century, and that he could come back when he was cured. How was it that his housekeeper knew every detail about the old man who appeared in the early 1780s, but had not worked at Pemberley herself until 1788?

Did Reynolds arrive from the future, return to it, and then come back to Pemberley? Darcy kept his eyes straight ahead, his fingertips lightly pressing on his sister's shoulder, and kept his breathing under control, while he felt the summer house spin.

"Fitzwilliam, are you well?"

Georgiana's voice anchored him. He forced himself to put Reynolds out of his mind for now. "For Miss Bennet's sake, I am pleased she could return. She would not be content here. From what I know of the advantages she has in the future, my dear El—I feared for her happiness had she been forced to remain here."

"And, of course, you are glad to be home for your own sake, and mine, and Pemberley's. You would not have been happy there either, I suspect."

"Of course," Darcy said flatly, hating the deceit.

"You spent a great deal of time with my friend Elizabeth." It was a statement, not a question.

"Yes." Darcy paused to find the breath to speak. "Her nearly last words to me were about you. She wished you to know the truth so you would not think she heartlessly dropped your acquaintance. Elizabeth had great faith in you and in your abilities."

"Her actions towards me now appear in a different light, but that is not to say I think less of her. She befriended me and wished for my happiness, and she took a great risk to save you. For that alone, I am grateful to her. Although we will never meet again, I will always think of Elizabeth as my friend."

Darcy swallowed thickly. "As will I."

"When you marry, will you tell your wife about Nine Ladies?"

"I am not the sort of man to keep such a thing from a wife, but I do not intend to marry."

Georgiana turned quickly, and Darcy's arm fell from her shoulder. "You are unwilling to marry? Why?"

"I value my privacy, my ability to do as I please without reference to another. Besides, you will be an even better mistress of Pemberley than our mother was. What need have I to marry?" He gave her an approving smile, but it fell when his sister, who had no blood tie to him, gave him the same appraising look that had belonged to their father.

"Are you lonely without Elizabeth?"

His sister was clever. "Every day." Darcy could not look at her. "Elizabeth is the only woman in the world, then or now, whom I can think of as my wife. If I did not believe she had some regard for me, I should not say this to you."

Georgiana rested her head against his shoulder. "I am sorry, Fitzwilliam."

It was quite late when Darcy entered his housekeeper's room. He looked at her, trying to see some evidence in her face that she was born in another century, but she appeared no different to him.

"I suppose it is done, sir?" Reynolds spoke into the stillness he was not ready to break. "You did not tell Miss Darcy the whole of it yet?" Darcy, having decided to come here, had not decided what to say. Uncharacteristically, she filled the silence. "Time, sir, time will help her to grasp the strangeness of it."

"Georgiana is a resilient young lady. I dare anyone to mistake her youth and shyness for weakness and foolishness. All that remains is to tell her that *she* is from the future. I did not come to speak of her."

His grave tone caught her notice, but other than a brief widening of the eyes, she did not react.

"What can I do for you, sir?"

Darcy paced, hands clasped behind his back. "I require mending, and my valet is not capable of seeing to it."

Reynolds bowed. "You need not have come to me this way with such a thing. A message with the footman would do. How can I help you?"

He stopped pacing and pierced her with a stare. "The zip on my jeans needs to be repaired."

She diminished in stature before his eyes. "She told you?" his housekeeper whispered harshly. "Miss Bennet promised me she would not—"

"No, Elizabeth did not betray you." He shook his head. "Only one who was from that century or had spent much time in the future could suspect you. I am ashamed it took me this long to reckon what she must have realized long before the solstice."

Reynolds trembled, although from shock or rage he could not tell. *Or fear. Did she think I would force her to go back?* Darcy's anger at having been deceived was replaced by admiration for someone who had sacrificed so much for the sake of his family. He was ashamed she did not know what she meant to him.

"I must say this: I am wounded that since I have been master, you did not confide in me. After I went to the future myself, why could not you trust me? Pemberley is your home, Reynolds, and we are your family."

His enigmatic housekeeper burst into relieved tears.

July 17, 1812
Pemberley

If Mr. Willers was surprised to see his employer in his parlor, he did not show it. If his interest was further piqued when Darcy would only speak after he was assured they were alone in the house, Mr. Willers barely allowed a wrinkle of confusion on his forehead to make an appearance.

"I am certain you wish to ask why I came."

His steward bowed. "You must have your reasons for coming to speak with me in absolute privacy. What may I do for you, sir?"

"Your experience as an attorney as well as my steward shall now be called upon in a unique way. What can you tell me about Pemberley and strict settlements?"

"A strict settlement is formed on the concept of a limited life tenancy of an estate. A father leaves the estate, for life only, to his first male heir, and thereby entailing possession of the estate on the life tenant's son. If Pemberley had such a settlement, as heir of the entail, you would have when you inherited made another strict settlement that would in turn keep Pemberley intact for two more generations."

"I was not willing to entail Pemberley away from my sister. It was not my father's wish, either."

"If you wish to do this now, I—"

"I have no wish to make a strict settlement; an entail that cannot pass *to* a woman also cannot pass *through* one."

"Am I correct in assuming you wish to leave Pemberley to your daughter if you have no sons?"

Darcy looked at Mr. Willers for a long moment. "I wish for Pemberley to go to my sister and her children."

He saw the word "why" form on his steward's lips and then fall away. "Sir, I advise you against creating a will that will disinherit the children you are likely to have."

"You may advise me on what I asked." Darcy was forced to use a tone he did not want to use on so trusted and gentlemanlike a man, but it served its purpose. Mr. Willers nodded, and for a moment was lost in thought.

"In Pemberley's case, the eldest son was the person selected to hold the estate. A daughter could serve the same purpose, not unlike how your cousin Miss de Bourgh is an heiress. But you already inherited, and only on your death could Miss Darcy inherit Pemberley from you."

Darcy suspected this would be the case and, in his frustration, rose to pace. "That shall not suit my purposes. I cannot be dead."

"What could be your purpose?"

"My purpose is for her to manage Pemberley as though it were her own, with full access to its income, without it falling into the hands of her husband, and without my being dead."

Mr. Willers looked as though he wished he were anywhere else, having any other conversation, with any other man. Darcy took a breath, walked to a chair, and settled himself calmly. "Forgive me; I know this sounds peculiar. May we continue? I wish for Georgiana to control the Pemberley properties and leave them to her oldest child, son or daughter."

Darcy was not in the twenty-first century, and so he was not to be pressed to explain himself to one in his employ. He still lived in a time and place where deference to one's superiors, a knowledge of proper social niceties, and a position of influence would allow him to get away with behaving strangely, without having to answer for it.

"Yes, sir. Even when a woman inherits property, her husband would have given directions for its disposal in his will. Your sister may not be able to leave Pemberley to a daughter. Whatever Miss Darcy owns becomes her husband's when she marries. This still cannot take place until your death, however, so it is irrelevant."

Darcy tapped his fingers on the chair arm. "I cannot risk that the Pemberley properties be necessitated away from Georgiana's children, especially if she has only daughters, or dispersed in any way that might make them not exist in the future."

"In the future, sir?" Darcy did not reply. "What about a trust for Miss Darcy's sole use?"

Darcy stood eagerly to pace again. "Yes, but not merely a separate fortune that a husband could not access. *Pemberley* must be held in trust for her benefit, and with the obligation that the use of the Pemberley properties and income would be for Georgiana's sole benefit and within her control, and not her husband's."

"For her lifetime?"

"No, it would pass to her direct descendant, male or female, for their lifetime."

"You cannot mean to disinherit yourself and your future children!" Darcy saw the look of incomprehension cross his face as Mr. Willers slumped into his chair. Mr. Willers was typically of a cool and calm temperament, but Darcy did not mind his steward's more open, modern manner.

"I wish to leave Pemberley, its assets, the property, to my sister and her direct descendants, male or female, for . . . for a time." Darcy hesitated. "I then want to return the Pemberley properties to my own line at a later date. If after several generations, there is no longer a direct descendant of hers, I wish for Pemberley to be held in trust until it can return to my own direct descendant. Could this be accomplished?"

Mr. Willers also rose, and brought a hand to his mouth, shaking his head and pacing. Darcy noticed he had stopped wearing black crepe and had completed grieving for his wife. For a man normally capable and composed, his steward looked befuddled and bursting with questions.

He turned back to Darcy, his eyes alight. "What know you of your lease in town?"

"The house in Mayfair is leased from Lord Grosvenor." Darcy did not know what this signified.

"The original lease on the house expired in 1796 and was renewed for ninety-nine years." Mr. Willers held up his finger again, looking as though he was a professor before his pupils. "The renewal was made to the owner of the original lease, your father, from the present Lord Grosvenor's ancestor. That your father is not the current occupier is obvious, but you have proven to be a beneficial tenant to Lord Grosvenor, and there is no reason to suppose you and your descendants would not be treated for renewal."

Darcy stared for a long moment. "How can you recall these details?"

His steward gave him an equally disbelieving look. "It is my responsibility. You can lease Pemberley in a similar manner. If funds are set aside in a trust to pay for taxes and other duties, and a separate trust for her sole use is established for Miss Darcy, you can lease Pemberley to your sister, and you or your descendants can renew the lease to her and her descendants indefinitely."

Darcy shook his head, although the idea had merit. "I cannot renegotiate terms with every successive generation of leaser and lessee. The term of the lease must be set and must pass through her direct line without needing to be renewed."

"A year-to-year lease to your sister will serve your purpose, and you and she, or your children and hers, can regularly renegotiate—"

"The lease term *must* be set, without any renegotiation between me and Georgiana, or her descendants and mine. If she has no children, Pemberley shall not go to her husband or to anyone else. If her line ends, then the property can be held in trust for my heirs until the term of the lease is over." His steward stared at him as though he were mad, but Darcy liked the idea more and more. "Can you do this?"

Mr. Willers threw up his hands. He had given up all deference and reserve, and Darcy did not mind his genuine reactions. It reminded him of the twenty-first century.

"If we set aside the problem that Miss Darcy is not yet one-and-twenty and cannot enter into a contract? If you lease Pemberley to your sister, *and* stipulate all the rights and privileges of landowner go to her and her eldest child and their eldest child, then when the lease term is complete, you, your own children or descendants, may have nothing. You can stipulate a separate contract that says what Miss Darcy may or may not sell or lease or mortgage, but that still does not mean she and her children will leave you anything when those rights return to your line."

"But the house could be standing." Darcy gave a wry smile.

Mr. Willers only blinked.

Darcy cleared his throat. "Pemberley, indeed any grand estate, is dependent upon the survival of the family, the household servants, the tenant farmers, and their families and workers. A successful estate owner needs a good head for business and a sense of duty and responsibility, and my sister and her sons or daughters will be as dutiful as I would be."

Darcy waited to counter Mr. Willers's argument against women as proper estate managers, but his steward bowed in agreement. *That is promising.*

"Not for the first time, your background as an attorney has proved useful, but your aptitude with business is considerable. My sister will need your guidance, but her commitment to Pemberley is equal to mine. You shall not forsake her if I leave Pemberley to her? Would you be the same able, loyal steward to her as you have been to me?"

"I would be as dedicated to any Darcy, male or female, who showed the same care and commitment to the Pemberley properties as you have done."

"Thank you."

Mr. Willers gave him a shrewd look. "How long will the lease term be?"

Darcy shook his head, and retrieved his hat and gloves. "Another question for another day. Perhaps you might first investigate how this best can be done so that none shall question its legality. Time is of the essence. Good day."

Was he mad, risking everything for something that might never work?

July 30, 1812
Pemberley

Darcy's confession about Georgiana's true origins, with Reynolds's and Roland's testimony as to how she was found on Stanton Moor as an infant, were not as easily accepted as the rest of his account about Nine Ladies. *It is one thing to know your brother visited the future for medical care; it is another to learn that you were born in the twentieth century, you were adopted, and are a year older than you were led to believe.*

When Darcy entered his sister's sitting room, she was with Reynolds. Georgiana pulled him to sit next to her. "Reynolds was showing me a sketch my mother drew of me with the clothes I wore when I appeared in Nine Ladies."

"I did not know my mother drew you wearing clothes from the future."

"Do you think she wished to have some proof of my origins in the event it was needed?" Darcy shrugged. "Do the clothes look familiar? Reynolds did not think them strange for the time and place she once knew."

The child had Georgiana's nose and eyes, although her hair had darkened as she grew. Bow-shaped clips held back wispy hair, and Darcy knew they were made of plastic. The little girl wore a pink dress in a style Elizabeth had called overalls. Underneath was a short-sleeved white shirt with ruffled trim and pink hearts across it. Her bare, chubby legs stuck out from beneath the knee-length skirt and ended in tiny sneakers.

Darcy could not take his eyes from the sketch. "The shoes, the material, the length of the dress . . . I imagine a child born even in 2011 could wear something similar. Reynolds, what happened to these clothes?"

"The clothes were burned after it was decided Miss Darcy would remain with us. As were my own when I returned here after my husband died." For his sister's sake, Reynolds was more open than Darcy might have supposed possible a fortnight ago. The secret and their shared origins had forged a bond between the ladies. "I suspect your brother has burned his clothing as well."

His clothes from 2011 were, in fact, in a closet, hidden in a battered trunk his valet would never use. He had not been able to bring himself to burn them.

"Fitzwilliam, why do you suppose my parents went to such lengths to deceive everyone that I was their own child even before they could not bear to send me back?"

"Adoption is not legally recognized, and I imagine they did not want you to be treated as anything less than their proper daughter." There was a distinction between the position of a birth child with all the rights that come with that versus assuming the care and custody of a child in an informal way.

Georgiana shook her head. "I know why it was done, of course, but my age, my parentage, Nine Ladies' power—it was an unprecedented deception."

"You were deceived, but you must not doubt that you were loved."

Georgiana smiled and nodded. Darcy looked at both ladies, ready to ask the question he needed to ask. "Now that the entire truth is known to everyone involved with Nine Ladies, do either of you feel any desire to return from whence you came?"

They doubted and stared, and while his sister's mouth hung open, his normally inscrutable housekeeper made the most vehement speech he had ever heard her make.

"I would rather deny myself the necessaries of life than return! I came here because I could find contentment, fulfillment even, such as I would not have known in the world I left behind after my husband's death. It is harder in this time in many ways, but I would never leave my life here. Your parents were generous to me, and I shall not scruple to say that I am invaluable to this family. Pemberley is my *home* and will be until I draw my last breath."

Reynolds's refusal did not surprise him. Darcy was tempted to embrace the dear woman, but supposed she would be made embarrassed by such a display. He turned to Georgiana. "Please, say something. You cannot imagine what is possible for you there. If you wish just to see it once for yourself, you need only speak."

"Speak? In a word, no! Pemberley will always be my home!" His sister stood and backed away, as though he was about to drag her to Stanton Moor this moment.

Darcy held up his hands. "I am relieved, although not surprised. I needed to be certain before I proceed."

His sister returned to her seat, looking as though she had avoided her own execution, but Reynolds narrowed her eyes. "Proceed with what?"

CHAPTER TWENTY-NINE

August 24, 1812
Pemberley

"Must we meet out of doors, Fitzwilliam?" Georgiana asked.
"We are such a disparate group; I cannot think in what room we might appear together without attracting undue attention." A more incongruous gathering Darcy could not imagine: his gamekeeper and that man's grandson, his indomitable housekeeper, his young sister, and his cousin, the son of an earl.

"That is true." The siblings walked farther across the lawn. "I suspect Reynolds will not be pleased by your summons. I intended her to review the candles and soap stores, and you are interrupting her work."

Darcy smiled at his sister. "I am not surprised that *you* are giving the orders. Nothing has fallen below your notice at Pemberley."

"If I am to be Pemberley's custodian, is it not right that there is nothing below my notice?"

Elizabeth was correct to suggest he give his sister responsibilities. By showing he had confidence in her, Georgiana had developed more assurance in herself. Had he known better, he would have done more for her years ago. Darcy shook his head; he could only look forward now. "Yes, you are quite right."

"I am glad, because I invited Mr. Willers to join this unorthodox committee meeting."

He stopped short and tugged his sister's elbow to stop her progress. "You have not!"

"Indeed, I have."

"We cannot discuss Pemberley's future, and your place in it, without reference to Nine Ladies. He knows nothing about time travel!"

"I think, given of how much importance his aid in writing this bizarre lease agreement will be, and Mr. Willers's value in guiding me on certain matters of business, he ought to know what your *true* objective is. I thought you trusted in him."

"It is not a matter of my trust in his abilities. As someone I employ, indeed, as a gentlemanlike man, I respect Mr. Willers. I readily admit that I like him. That does not mean I am willing to disclose being able to travel through time! Cannot you see the danger in this?"

Georgiana clutched the handle of her parasol and twisted it. "There is danger in all of this, Fitzwilliam. That is all the more reason to have a capable and loyal man in his position know the truth."

"He could ruin our reputation or our safety—I mean by accident, rather than design. What might happen to every tenant, every servant, our family, if he unintentionally makes the truth known? We shall either be thought mad if we are disbelieved or accused of being selfish deceivers if we are believed. To say nothing of how my fragile plan would fall apart. Your children, if you have them, must know, but I cannot accept that anyone outside the family be told."

"Is it your place to say?" The words burst forth from her. "You are entrusting me with *Pemberley*. If this plan has any hope of success, we need Mr. Willers's help. I judge a man in his position must know. Do not you think me capable of judging what is best for Pemberley after all?"

The consequence of giving up the right to make every choice for Pemberley was before him. It was temporary, but it was more painful than he had thought it would be. Georgiana was less fearful of doing wrong since she became involved in Pemberley's management. If she was shy in the drawing room, she had poise when it came to making a decision for Pemberley. He could not crush her budding confidence, not now when it mattered the most.

"I do. Let me tell you something our father told me: learn all that you can and ask questions of those who know more than you, but do not allow anyone to challenge your position as mistress of Pemberley. It is difficult for me because I must now include myself in that number."

Georgiana set her shoulders. "It is a step I take from my own judgment, after considering the judgment of those whose counsel and opinions I am bound to consider. And I do consider your opinion and your fears, Fitzwilliam. However, we must tell Mr. Willers what Nine Ladies can do, and what you are *truly* hoping to accomplish."

"*Where no counsel is, the people fall: but in the multitude of counselors there is safety.*" Darcy only nodded as they continued toward the summer house.

"Reynolds grudgingly supports you, and you ought not to assume that Mr. Willers will be as outspoken an opponent as our cousin." Georgiana sighed sadly. "I hope he is less violent in expressing his opinions today than he was last night."

"There is no lack of people who will find fault with the path I choose. But I am confident in my decision; those people cannot feel for me."

"Yes, I cannot imagine you being so in love that it robbed you of your judgment of right and wrong. This can work—for your sake, I want it to—and Mr. Willers's full participation will make that more likely."

"It is *your* participation that will make this work, Georgiana. Your willingness and your commitment, along with your natural abilities, are more important than anything else. I am proud of you."

The summer house was now in sight. Roland and Young Henry stood together discussing how best to preserve a section of his woodland. Reynolds gave no indication whether or not she approved of what Fitzwilliam was articulating to her. They quieted when the siblings approached, but before Darcy could speak, his cousin swiftly stepped forward.

"You still intend to do this!" It spoke to the strength of his feelings that Fitzwilliam confronted him in front of the servants. "Did nothing I say last night convince you to forget this madness?"

Darcy's temper blazed. "It is not madness—"

"It *is*! It is complete folly, and I will not let you do this."

"You are in no position to stop me!"

The colonel's mouth snapped shut, and he ground his jaw. They glowered at one another for a long moment. "Are you saying you are beyond the reach of reason?"

"I have done nothing for months but reason how this is best to be done! My judgment is sound."

"Well, you cannot do this without Georgiana, and as one of her guardians, I will prohibit her from aiding in your scheme. She is a woman, and she is sixteen. You said it yourself: you need me until she is one-and-twenty; if I cannot dissuade you, then I will stop *her* from helping you!"

Darcy felt the blood draw from his face, and his hands shook. This agitated response lasted only a few seconds before a righteous indignation took its place. "How dare you! You need not help me if your conscience will not allow it. But how dare you presume that you have the right to disrupt my—"

His sister urged them apart with gentle hands on their chests. In a voice that was perfectly calm, Georgiana said, "Stop." She turned to Fitzwilliam. "My brother is a complete enthusiast on the subject, and we shall not move him. Moreover, I *want* to help him! You know how unhappy he has been."

The colonel's reply was a deepening color on his cheeks. Georgiana dropped her hands and turned to Darcy. "You must know the real reason he opposes your plan."

The cousins' eyes met, and his anger fell away. "Forgive me?" Darcy's voice was a whisper. "I will not ask you to help me, but you must know I do not aim to hurt you."

When Fitzwilliam spoke, his voice faltered, although his manner showed the wish of self-command. "If this is what you deem best, I can do nothing but help you."

"Mr. Darcy, what is all of this?"

Everyone turned and saw Mr. Willers. Darcy supposed that to an onlooker, it was a strange scene to stumble upon. The master and his noble cousin looking as though they might come to blows, a girl half their size between them as though she had any chance of stopping them, and three servants giving every impression of not being the least bit interested whilst watching with bated breath.

Darcy and Georgiana shared a look, and then he turned to Mr. Willers. "Thank you for joining us. Perhaps we might move out of the sun? We have matters to discuss."

January 6, 2013
Rockford, Illinois

It felt as though year-end closing would never end. Elizabeth found something bordering on comfort in precision and methodology and the necessity of every number being in balance. Managing business details came easily to her. However, living the drudgery of annual reports and audits for a bureaucracy was another thing altogether.

I'm good at it, but I hate this. She had been at her job with the Winnebago County Health Department a little more than a year, and it was going nowhere.

What is Darcy doing in January of 1813? Gathering with family and friends for Christmas festivities? Or would he have gone to London by now?

He would have settled into life as master and landlord, enjoying the company of his friends and neighbors. Would enough time have passed for him to meet and marry someone worthy of him? Darcy wasn't the sort to brood; he would act rather than dwell. If he had any sense, he had forgotten about her, and she should do the same.

Sometimes it feels like I never will.

Elizabeth jumped when her cell phone vibrated. She saw the close-up picture of an infant's face, screwed up mid-wail. Then followed the words, "7lb 4oz Mary Olivia Lucas. Everyone doing well."

Elizabeth felt a rush of unadulterated joy. With her vision clouded by tears, she typed her congratulations with an excess of exclamation points and emojis. After promising to call Charlotte after she went home from the hospital, Elizabeth looked back at the spreadsheet on her screen.

All of the delight and gladness drifted away. It was time to make some changes in her life.

February 4, 2013
Harvard, Illinois

Her mother's home, purchased following years of living in a cheap apartment, was in a town of fewer than 8,000 people. It was near to a hospital, the library, and the pool, and was in walking distance to the high school. That had been useful, since neither Elizabeth nor Jane were allowed to buy a car when they were sixteen, as it would have taken money away from their college funds.

Elizabeth laughed when she realized her hometown would fit inside Pemberley's 1811 park.

"What's so funny?"

"Nothing, Jane. What were you saying, Mom?"

Since Jane's schedule didn't allow for much time off, and Elizabeth's job didn't allow for time off at the end of the month or the end of the year, the Bennet ladies were only now able to celebrate Christmas together.

"I said Janie is almost finished with her residency. She'll be making over two hundred and fifty thousand a year. I knew you couldn't be my smart girl for nothing." Mrs. Bennet kissed her cheek.

Jane cast an embarrassed look at her sister. Elizabeth rolled her eyes. Some things never changed. "It's a good thing you didn't want to be a neurosurgeon, otherwise you'd have another five years to go."

"Then she'd make twice that. But her salary will continue to go up. Extra shifts are always available. I'm so proud, Janie!"

Her mother's strategy to program them to be independent had been primarily repetition. The prompts to study, go to college, be a lawyer or doctor, and make six figures so you don't need a man had been sewn into every conversation like lead weights since they were children.

"Elizabeth has an accounting degree and makes nearly sixty thousand, Mom. You should be proud of her."

"I never said I wasn't proud of Lizzy."

You never said that you are. "I quit after month-end closing. My last day was Friday."

Her mother narrowed her eyes "You're . . . *unemployed*?"

"I'm on my three weeks of paid vacation, so the end of February is when I'll technically be unemployed."

Mrs. Bennet opened and closed her mouth but was unable to speak. Jane stepped into her familiar role as peacekeeper.

"Stay calm, Mom. I'm sure Elizabeth had a good reason. Maybe she will end up making more at her new job."

"I haven't looked for a new job yet. But I haven't felt so liberated in my life."

"You should have found another job before you quit!" Her mother was now an unbecoming shade of purple. "I know you're not as smart as Janie, but come on!"

"I was miserably unhappy. I had to make a change."

"Who cares if it wasn't what you *liked*! Your sister will never have to worry about how she'll pay her bills, and she won't have to rely on anyone, ever. What the hell are you going to do?"

"I have a plan, just not *your* plan. I won't waste any more time doing what I hate and being unhappy. As for money, I have eighty grand in the bank from my father's estate."

Her mother looked as though she proposed selling her body on the streets. Jane tried again to mediate. "You must have some idea about what you'll do."

"I always liked history, and . . . I have a thing for historic homes. I could use my business skills working for a historical society. I want to do work that matters, like historical preservation. I want to see the results of the work I do."

"Have you applied for a job?" Her mother gripped the edge of the kitchen table, her knuckles white.

"No, I have a trip coming up, but that's the sort of job I'll look for after I get back." Her mother raised an eyebrow. "I'm going to England to see Charlotte."

"That friend who's having a baby alone, on purpose? And she's a doctor! What a waste."

"You make it sound like she's a drug dealer, not a single mom by choice. Charlotte was brave enough to go after what she wanted. I missed my chance with Darcy, and now it's too late." She had never known for certain if Darcy loved her, and even if he had, too much time had passed for her to go back to him. "It's time for me to make changes in my life."

"Who's Darcy?"

"Never mind. *I* have to be the one to make my life better. I sublet my apartment, and I'm going to the UK. I've booked a ten-day tour and I'm going to see all the monuments and museums and houses I missed the last time."

Her mother and sister looked appalled and nervous, respectively. Her family would never understand her.

"After that, I'm spending the rest of March with Charlotte and baby Mary. She's asked me to be her godmother."

Still they stared in silence.

"I need to do something for me before I reset my life. I have plenty of savings. And when I come back, I'm going to find a job doing something I love that puts a roof over my head."

Jane bit her lip and looked as though she wasn't a woman who managed the controlled chaos of a hospital emergency room. "I hope you know what you're doing. I guess you can stay with me when you come back until you find a job."

"Good, because Lizzy's not stepping through my door until she has a j-o-b!"

There was her sister and her mother in a nutshell.

MARCH 17, 2013
SHEFFIELD, ENGLAND

"And *this* little piggy went 'wee wee wee' all the way home!"

Elizabeth accompanied this with tickles and was rewarded by a smile. Mary Lucas, aged two months, gave a happy shriek.

"This week is the equinox, Mary. On the twentieth, the length of the day and the night are equal." Elizabeth punctuated this explanation with enthusiasm and smiles. "And do you know what Elizabeth can't do, Mary? She can't go to Nine Ladies, no she can't!"

Mary stared at her sagely and shoved her entire fist in her mouth.

"I've thought about going back since my plane landed, because I still love Darcy. But Elizabeth is too afraid Darcy doesn't love her."

The toothless gnawing on her tiny fist continued. Elizabeth held out a rattle and encouraged Mary to reach for it when Charlotte entered after finishing her shower.

"You two having fun?"

Mary looked in the direction of her mother's voice and began to gurgle and coo.

"Mary is an excellent conversationalist."

Charlotte filled the kettle and set it on the stove. "Did you give any more thought to visiting your friend Gwen? Your trip is coming to an end."

"Trying to get rid of me?"

"We love having you here, and that's not because you make it so I can shower by myself. It seems like a waste not to visit Gwen."

"We haven't talked in a long time, and I feel badly about that."

"That's more of a reason to meet up. We'll drive you to Bakewell if you need us to."

Elizabeth texted Gwen and expected a polite demurral, but was surprised when Gwen asked if she was free on Wednesday to join her and Frank on a walk. She even suggested that Charlotte and the baby come. The plan was satisfactory, but reading Gwen's location of their meet-up drove the air from Elizabeth's lungs.

"Did you just groan in dismay?" Charlotte asked as she picked up Mary.

"They want to walk at . . . at the Pemberley ruins." She managed to say *Pemberley* out loud without her voice shaking. Pemberley might be a derelict place of former significance. She wanted to remember

Pemberley as imposing and alive, like its master, rather than a neglected shell without weather protection.

"What ruins?"

"Pemberley. Remember, we went there when I came over the first time?"

"We walked around the building and saw the grounds, but I wouldn't call a shut-up house *ruins*."

Elizabeth's skin felt cold and clammy. *How much did we change things?* "What do you remember about our visit to Pemberley?"

Charlotte gave her a wary stare as she shifted Mary in her arms. "We went there after Haddon with Missy, Willie, and Maria. No one has lived there since the 1970s or '80s, and I think it's held in a private trust. I don't remember the details Willie threw at us. Parts of the grounds are open to the public. Don't you remember?"

Elizabeth blindly nodded, but wasn't ready to speak. Since she couldn't bring herself to go back in time to Darcy without hearing him say he loved her, she had no business at Pemberley and pretended a disinclination for going.

"Don't be stupid!" Charlotte cried as she set the baby on her activity mat. "Don't you want to see Gwen?"

The house would be empty, after all. She wouldn't run in to some great-great-great-grandchild of Darcy's. Besides, she'd be spending the time chatting with Gwen and Frank.

So, they would go to Pemberley.

MARCH 20, 2013
VERNAL EQUINOX
PEMBERLEY

Trapped in a car with a screaming infant is a form of torture. Elizabeth freed herself from the baby's bone-rattling wails. Then, as though Mary had been protesting the car itself, she cooed and kicked her legs happily when Charlotte put her in the stroller.

"Does it seem busier than the last time?" Charlotte asked, looking around the car park.

"I can't remember," Elizabeth hedged, knowing full well their memories of that visit were vastly different. "I want to take a closer look at the house."

It was breathtaking. The porticoed entrance was still there, all the columns whole. The Darcy coat of arms was on the pediment. Every window had glass. It was as much an architectural splendor now as it was two hundred years ago. Instead of abandoned fields surrounding the house, there was still a courtyard and a maintained lawn.

Elizabeth found herself tearing up with joy at seeing how Pemberley had survived. She knew Georgiana hadn't eloped with Wickham, but life after that must have gone well for the Darcys.

"Elizabeth!" Charlotte pushed the stroller back and forth while she stood still. "Mary's on the verge of a meltdown. Can we start walking?"

Some of Pemberley's parkland was left, albeit less than two hundred years ago. Elizabeth was silent while they walked to keep herself from commenting aloud on the changes she noticed.

When it grew closer to the time to meet Gwen, Elizabeth and Charlotte made their way toward the house. They passed a few joggers, people carrying binoculars or cameras, and others enjoying a quiet walk. Even though no one lived at Pemberley, it was nice to see that, in some sense, the estate was still alive.

"I wonder who takes care of the parkland and maintains the house?" Elizabeth asked.

"I read on the placard that it's held in a private trust with funds available for its basic maintenance. If no one from the family is left, I wonder why the house was never sold."

They were now out of the park and along a hedge, well in sight of the house, and Elizabeth knew that on the other side of the tall shrubs was what had been Mr. Willers's cottage. It made her smile to think that if Darcy saw Pemberley now, much would still be familiar to him.

Elizabeth heard a conversation from the other side of the hedge growing louder as their paths began to converge.

"Did you want me to have your solicitor call you?"

"If you know nothing of me by now, you should know how much I dislike talking on the phone. If you can't deal with it, she can wait until we meet in person on Monday."

"Right, sir. Be back later with the car."

She heard pounding footsteps as someone jogged away. Elizabeth stopped, and felt a tingling in her fingertips and lips. She breathed faster, but had a hard time filling her lungs with air.

"You look a little pale," Charlotte said.

The owner of the other voice came into sight. Darcy absolutely started. Then astonishment on his face gave way to delight.

"Elizabeth!"

"Darcy?"

Someone might have been speaking, but she heard not a word over the thundering of her own pulse in her ears. Elizabeth stared, doubting what she saw before her, as a wave of dizziness overtook her. She saw spots in front of her eyes before her vision blurred, and after she felt her knees buckle, she saw and heard nothing at all.

CHAPTER THIRTY

SEPTEMBER 23, 1812

"Sir, what would you have me say?" Mr. Willers asked him. "You must know that this will be much talked of."

"You may say that out of love and affection I did what I could to legally transfer Pemberley to my sister."

"While you sail to the Canadas to marry your housekeeper's cousin, whom you met when she visited England in the year eleven?"

Darcy nodded. "Colonel Fitzwilliam will be the lessee for the present, but once my sister is of age, the truth of her and her future family's extended custodianship will be open to gossip. You might do what you can to limit the peculiar length of the term of the lease from becoming common knowledge."

Mr. Willers held up his hands in surrender. "I will not announce the two-hundred-year lease between you and your sister. However, it *will* be a legal contract, and your new will shall also reflect the terms. It cannot remain a secret, but you can be certain I will discuss the details only when necessary."

"You have been exceedingly calm in regards to everything." Darcy and his steward were in his office at Pemberley, speaking softly with the door shut. "I did not expect you to believe us. My sister was right to confide in you."

Mr. Willers leaned back from his desk. "I do not believe you are going forward two hundred years because of the position of the sun while you stand in a stone circle. Nonetheless, *you* believe it, and so does Miss Darcy. For the present, I shall act as though you are going to Upper Canada indefinitely, and until you or your son or daughter returns, you intend for Miss Darcy to manage Pemberley in your absence."

Darcy gave a tight smile. "I suggest you accompany Georgiana and Fitzwilliam to Nine Ladies on the solstice."

Mr. Willers inclined his head. "You are more a man of business than is usual with gentlemen of large property. Wherever you are going, your loss will be deeply felt."

"It has been my greatest interest to attend to my properties; I could do so again."

His steward dropped his voice. "You are convinced that you will find a Pemberley you recognize? Miss Darcy will not borrow or mortgage, but misfortunes could befall Pemberley that are outside of the family's control. And no one can know for certain if this is structured in a way as to prevent you from being taxed beyond your means in the twenty-first century." Mr. Willers cleared his throat. "Not that I *believe* you are going into the future to reunite with Miss Bennet."

"You had a concern about something I might have control over..."

Mr. Willers's curious attitude disappeared and a serious one replaced it. "Yes, it is the phrasing of this line: 'Unto the first and nearest of his kindred, being male and of his blood and name, that should be alive at that time.'"

"If I present myself in 2013 as though I am my own descendant, this could refer only to me. There would be no other Darcys save for any of my sister's family, and they would always have known that the lease would conclude at the close of 2012, and Pemberley would revert to my line."

Mr. Willers shook his head. "If you wish to reclaim Pemberley from Miss Darcy's descendants or reclaim it from the trust, your claim must be beyond doubt. My fear is that you shall have every distant cousin taking the surname Darcy to be a claimant, or for his son to be a claimant."

Darcy leaned forward to stare at the pertinent line. *Can it be as bad as that?* "I trust your judgment; what must be done?"

"I am not certain," he said, as though this was a personal failure, "short of a record of your baptism in a contemporary register. Miss Darcy's falsely recording your line in the Darcy family Bible may not be sufficient for the law. I realize that repossessing Pemberley is not your primary objective, but you might have no way to substantiate your claim against another claimant." He paused. "Not that I believe you are going to the future."

Reynolds ought to have known I would need to prove my identity to navigate the twenty-first century. Why had she not mentioned the importance of such a document any of the times the group met to plan? *I might need proof of identity to obtain a passport to travel to America to find Elizabeth.* Darcy drummed his fingers on the arm of his chair.

"Sir, if you are thought to be in the Canadas, and are composing letters to your friends and family that they will receive over the next several years that will appear as though you have found Miss Bennet, have wed her and had children by her, and are remaining abroad, when you arrive in 2012, how shall you prove that *you* were born in England in the 1980s and that you—and *only* you—are the rightful heir of Pemberley?"

MARCH 20, 2013
VERNAL EQUINOX

Darcy had been so struck by the sight of Elizabeth that he could only cry out her name. She had more reason to be surprised by his appearance, understandably, and he saw it in her face. The disbelief flooded her countenance like an incoming wave that knocks one off their feet and pulls them under. The sight of him was such a shock that Elizabeth fainted right away. He had not noticed Charlotte until she rushed toward her friend.

"Hand me the bag under the buggy. Darcy?"

It took Darcy a long moment to realize he was being addressed, and to realize a buggy was a wheeled chair with an infant atop it. By the time Darcy brought it, Charlotte had rolled Elizabeth to her back and unfastened her jacket. She shoved the bag under Elizabeth's feet to elevate them.

"Elizabeth, Elizabeth." Charlotte shook her shoulders while Darcy hovered uselessly. "Darcy, give us some room." A displeased wail came from nearby. "Help me out: push the buggy into the shade and give the baby a toy."

He did not wish to let Elizabeth out of his sight, but the tone in Charlotte's voice told him not to argue. He pushed the buggy away and turned it so the sun did not shine in the infant's eyes.

Whose child is this?

He had not been attentive enough to see if either woman wore a wedding ring, but Darcy knew he could assume nothing about relationships and families in this time. A baby did not mean Elizabeth was married, but it meant she had a lover at least a year ago.

As long as she is not married, I will do whatever I can to convince her of my affection. He was not about to squander the opportunity when she had fortuitously appeared on his doorstep. He had expected it would take months longer to find her in America.

The baby began to wriggle unhappily. Darcy picked up a rattle, inadvertently touching something that made lights flash and music play. The fussing stopped, and Darcy handed the child the rattle. A delighted shriek followed, as did a wide smile that he naturally returned.

"And who is your mamma, little one?"

ELIZABETH'S SENSE OF SOUND CAME BACK BEFORE SHE WAS READY TO OPEN her eyes, and she heard Charlotte telling her to wake up.

"I'm all right." She swatted Charlotte's hand to stop her from shaking her again. Her eyes fluttered open and she tried to sit up.

"No, not yet. How's your shoulder and arm? You landed on your side, but that saved your face from getting hit."

Elizabeth took a deep breath and stretched her left arm. "It's fine." She swallowed thickly. "Did . . . did I see Darcy?"

"Yeah. And then you crumpled to the ground. It might've been romantic if he caught you, but you passed out like some gothic heroine cow while he stood there like a tosser."

Charlotte looked at her like she had lost her mind. "I thought . . . I heard a rumor Darcy was dead." *That sort of explains it.*

They heard a dissatisfied cry. "I'm going to check on Mary. You ready to sit up?"

Charlotte gently pulled her upright and, when she was certain Elizabeth wasn't about to tip over, walked to the stroller. It was only after she struggled to her feet that Darcy came near.

"Elizabeth." He looked steadily at her. "I am so happy to see you again."

His words struck her, and made his presence more real. *Fitzwilliam Darcy is standing right in front of me.* She felt his body heat down the front of her, though they were not touching. "When did, what, why are you . . .?" Her throat was dry and she could not string the words together.

He took her hand, and when she squeezed it back, his eyes glistened. Some of her confusion must have shown through in her slackened jaw and inability to speak. "I *will* answer every question you have, I promise."

Darcy enveloped her in a tight hug. She twined both of her arms around his waist and pressed her cheek into his chest. His hand rested on her head, holding her against him.

"I thought I would wonder about you for the rest of my life," she whispered. "I thought I would always wonder if you had been happy." She could not choke out the rest of her thought: that she expected to wonder until the day she died if Darcy had ever loved her.

Darcy searched her eyes, but before either of them moved or spoke, a throat cleared. Charlotte was looking at them, one hand on her hip and the other on the stroller handle, rolling it forward and back.

"Charlotte, it's nice to see you again as well." If either of them was capable of acting politely and pretending their reunion was perfectly normal, it would be Darcy. Nineteenth-century civility wasn't dead and gone as far as he was concerned. "Congratulations on your happy news," he added, giving a smile in Mary's direction.

For the next few minutes, Darcy praised the intelligence and beauty of the infant who was attempting to shove an entire rattle into her mouth while Elizabeth was acutely aware of her own quick pulse and rapid breathing. She thought she might be sweating even though she felt cold and clammy.

"Tell me, Darcy, how does it feel to be back amongst the living?" Charlotte asked.

He gave her a strange look, perhaps fearing some idiom no one born in 1784 would know. "I'm sorry?"

Charlotte pushed the stroller as she and Darcy fell into step next to her. "Elizabeth said she fainted because she thought you were dead."

Elizabeth bit her lip and shrugged; Darcy nodded once in recognition. "What a terrible misunderstanding. I've been . . . preoccupied, and only came to . . . the area in December."

She gasped. *Of course, he came on a solstice. He's been here three months already.* He gave her a remorseful look. She felt her breath coming even faster. "Elizabeth, you cannot think that I—" His eyes darted to Charlotte, and Elizabeth heard his soft sigh of frustration. Darcy started again in a conversational tone that was for Charlotte's benefit. "I assumed you were in America, but I had *always* wanted to see you again. What brings you both to Pemberley?"

She stared dumbly at his polite conversation, and Charlotte answered for her. "Elizabeth's been touring England before she starts a new job, and now she's here to visit us." Charlotte threw her a meaningful look.

Words, put words together in your brain and speak them. "We came to Pemberley to meet Gwen and Frank. They'll be happy to see you again."

Darcy cleared his throat. "I have seen them, nearly since the moment I . . . arrived. They're here because I wished to show Gwen parts of the house and ask for her advice. She has managed conservators at Haddon Hall for years, and I suspect I'll need much help with Pemberley."

He saw his friends immediately, but when it came to me, he just "always wanted" to see me again? She was confused, light-headed, and her throat was dry.

They met Frank and Gwen near the house. The following minutes were consumed by hugs, handshakes, introductions, and more baby-admiring, during which Elizabeth wished they would all go away so she could interrogate Darcy.

"I thought I wasn't going to see *you* until this afternoon," Gwen said, turning to Darcy. "I thought I'd have time to chat with Elizabeth before we pored over restoration plans."

She saw the slightest shift in his shoulders and knew he stifled an inclination of his head, or even a bow. "I encountered Elizabeth and Charlotte by accident along the path near Mister—near the steward's cottage. It was a welcomed surprise." He gave her a warm look and a smile. "However, I have no intention of interrupting your visit."

No, be rude, interrupt the visit, send them away, explain everything to me now! She had a hard time following the conversation, and her vision went blurry again.

"You don't look up to walking the park, dear." Gwen's soft voice crashed into her thoughts.

"She's right, you look peaky." Frank peered into her face.

"She fainted ten minutes ago." Charlotte took her pulse and asked how she felt, but Elizabeth could only stare at Darcy. "Elizabeth, I think you're suffering from shock. I'm taking you home."

"No!" she shrieked as Frank and Gwen nodded and murmured their assent.

Darcy's face hardened at the suggestion, but then he looked at her closely. "You do look pale." He sighed sadly. "You ought to go with Charlotte."

She widened her eyes, tilted her head, and looked several feet away before leaving the group. Darcy followed, and when they had some relative privacy, she whispered, "Stop being agreeable to everybody. And don't you tell me to leave without us having a real conversation!"

"I do not *want* for you to leave!"

"You've been here since *December!*" Her voice shook, and so did her hands. She forcibly blinked again to clear her vision.

"I will tell you everything, but I cannot in front of the others, and what I have to say will take a long time to explain to your satisfaction." He gave her an appraising look. "Besides, you look ill. For how long shall you remain in England?"

"Another week."

Darcy looked stunned. "That is hardly any time at all. Would you consider coming—"

"It's the equinox!" If she had missed Darcy before, what sort of pang of loneliness would she feel long after he was gone this time? "Are you leaving tonight?" Before she could confess a desire to go with him, he shook his head.

"No. I was going to ask you to leave Charlotte's house to stay with me *now* at Pemberley so I can speak with you, so I can convince you that I came back with the best of intentions."

"At Pemberley? But I thought the house was . . ." She shook her head, feeling dizzy again. *What best intentions?* Darcy put an arm around her shoulders and guided her to their friends, who were doing their best to look both concerned and disinterested. "Elizabeth has decided to go back to Sheffield; I think it best if we reschedule our visit."

Frank and Gwen said their goodbyes, and while Charlotte put the baby in the car and folded the stroller, Darcy asked, "What can I say to you to convince you to come back to Pemberley?"

Did he think she would drive away and never see him again? "Try 'please.'"

He gave a relieved laugh, and then his eyes darkened. "Please, will you come back as soon as you are able? Frank said he would bring you from Sheffield whenever you like."

Right, because Darcy can't drive a car. She gave a nervous giggle at the thought of Darcy driving some A road in a curricle. Maybe she did need to lie down. "Tonight he can—"

"You are not going anywhere tonight or tomorrow." Charlotte was using her "Dr. Lucas" voice. "You are suffering from the effects of delayed shock."

"Then *I* will come to Sheffield this evening to talk—"

"No, you're not," Charlotte interrupted. "She is absolutely gobsmacked. Look at her!"

Maybe Charlotte was right; Elizabeth wasn't certain whether she was closer to throwing up or passing out. "Frank can come get me the day after tomorrow." Elizabeth looked to Charlotte, who nodded and then got into the car after waving to Darcy.

"And you will stay at Pemberley for a while?"

"I'll stay," she said, raising her eyes to his. "For a while."

Darcy opened the door for her, and Elizabeth was grateful because her fingers still tingled; she even struggled to buckle her seatbelt. When the car pulled away, she looked out the window and saw him watching the car for a long moment before walking toward Frank and Gwen. The silence in the car lasted as long as it took Elizabeth to exhale a shuddering breath.

"He's a *Pemberley* Darcy? I never knew that."

"What do you mean?"

"Remember what Willie Collins told us? That house you're so fond of used to belong to the Darcy family until the '80s. It's in a trust now, but if Darcy is talking about restoring the building, I'm guessing Pemberley has his name on it. Plus, he asked you to stay with him *at* Pemberley, like it was his house."

Elizabeth grabbed her watered-down iced coffee from that morning, hoping its generous heaping of sugar would help her focus. "I have no idea, but he sure as hell better tell me *everything* on Friday."

"I forgot Darcy was his last name and not his first. What's his first name?"

"Fitzwilliam." Charlotte blew out a whistle. "I know; it's a family name. It doesn't roll off the tongue."

Charlotte shrugged. "It suits him."

Clearly, she needed more sugar. After a long swallow, she held the cup against her forehead, but it wasn't cold enough to calm her. "I don't follow."

"He's a tall, handsome, serious, intelligent guy who doesn't stand in a room so much as take a position in it. He has a lot of confidence and authority for someone who doesn't look thirty. If anyone could walk up to a stranger and introduce himself as 'Fitzwilliam' and be taken seriously, he could."

If anyone other than Georgiana gets to call him 'Fitzwilliam," it's going to be me.

"You *really* didn't know he was alive?"

"Nope."

"And he wasn't your boyfriend?"

"Nope."

"You *never* slept with him?"

"Nope. I never even kissed him."

"Really? What the hell is wrong with you?"

October 10, 1812
Kympton, Derbyshire

The Kympton parsonage was a charming prospect. Georgiana called often to speak with Dr. Ferris's sister to discuss the charitable concerns of the surrounding villages, but Darcy had not been inside the parsonage above three times. He did not wish to come at all today, but Georgiana's council of advisors decided this was a chance for him to possibly have a birth certificate, and therefore a passport, in two hundred years.

Disguise of every sort is my abhorrence. It was one thing to tell people he was going to British North America rather than he was traveling through a druidical stone circle to the twenty-first century. What he was about to do now could be gilded with words like "inducement" or "enticement," but it felt corrupt. *Have I lost my integrity?*

Darcy's horse was led off, he was ordered to come in out of the wind, divested of his outer clothes, and pressed into the chair closest to the fire, and a glass of sherry was set down beside him. Dr. Ferris was a hale, hearty, well-looking man of about forty. He was a good scholar, and his house was kept by his sister who was over ten years his junior.

"Forgive me for intruding on a Saturday. I do not like to interrupt your sermon writing."

"Not at all, Mr. Darcy!" Dr. Ferris gave a wide smile and settled into his own chair after pouring himself a sherry. "You are always welcome. However, I suspect you have a specific reason for coming to see me on such a blustery day."

There was nothing for it now.

"Among other reasons, I came to tell you that at the end of the year I am going away for some years. You may not recall, but last year my housekeeper had a cousin from the Canadas stay at Pemberley. You met her at an evening party at the home of Sir Wesley Clarke."

Dr. Ferris folded his hand over his ample stomach. "Yes, young girl, pretty dark eyes, unique voice, barely tolerable at the instrument."

"Elizabeth Bennet." Darcy gathered his courage. "I am sailing to the Canadas at the end of the year to marry Miss Bennet."

The sherry glass that had been halfway to his lips came down. To his credit, Dr. Ferris did not verbally express his incredulity. "I wish you joy."

Darcy bowed. He tried to find the words to continue this production when Flora Ferris entered.

"How many blankets did Miss Darcy say—" She stopped short at the sight of their guest, who stood to greet her. "Forgive me; I did not hear the doorbell." Darcy asked her to join them. The Ferris siblings looked a little surprised, but Miss Ferris sat.

Georgiana had suspected Miss Ferris's mutual *tendre* for Sir Wesley's son, Robert, had not abated. Darcy never noticed their attachment, but Elizabeth had seen it after observing them once. He was not pleased to bring a second person into this system of deceit and corruption, but the others had determined it necessary.

"Flora, Mr. Darcy tells me he is sailing to British North America to marry Miss Bennet, whom we met last year at Stadler Hall."

"Miss Darcy's houseguest, your housekeeper's relation? Yes, we were together one evening at Stadler, and we met when I called on Miss Darcy. What a remarkable, romantic choice. I congratulate you!"

What she meant was that she was surprised Mr. Darcy of Pemberley would marry someone beneath him in wealth and consequence. Still, her enthusiasm appeared genuine; that was a good sign.

"Thank you. Dr. Ferris, I would prefer to be married in England; however, that shall not be the case. The future Mrs. Darcy and I will be in Upper Canada a long time, and I want you to record our marriage in the parish register."

"I beg your pardon! You are asking me to forge the signature of you and your wife, as well as the signatures of two witnesses? To *pretend* you were wed in my parish? To what end?"

"I want any who might inquire, many years from now, to know I was married and that my child is legitimate."

"And the marriage record from the Canadas is insufficient?" Dr. Ferris gave a little disbelieving laugh.

I am not going to be in Upper Canada. Darcy only nodded. He gave every appearance of being an influential gentleman expecting to get what he had asked for. Inwardly, the scenario made him cringe.

The clergyman looked torn between obliging a wealthy and powerful man, and being dutiful to his office. "I suppose . . . only for the sake of my patron . . . I could record your marriage in the parish register."

"As well as the birth of a son, named for me, one year after the marriage is recorded."

Dr. Ferris slammed down his glass and stood; Darcy refrained from wincing. Miss Ferris's mouth gaped. Before the clergyman could harangue him, Darcy asked, "Miss Ferris, may I ask, what is your fortune?"

This change in topic caused further confusion, but Miss Ferris raised her chin. "One thousand pounds, sir."

"And you are how old?" He hated to be impertinent.

"About as old as you."

"How unfortunate that a capable, intelligent woman with a thousand pounds, in this neighborhood, is not yet married." Miss Ferris flushed. Before Dr. Ferris threw him out, Darcy went on. "I suspect the only son of a baronet would offer for a worthy woman who immediately, and anonymously, had another five thousand pounds settled on her."

She brought a hand to her mouth. Miss Ferris understood him, but her brother sputtered, "I do not comprehend you!"

"He will settle five thousand pounds on me so I can marry Robert if you forge the registers and record his marriage and the birth of his son."

"It is not Robert, it is Mr. Clarke." To Darcy, this sounded like an old argument.

"Come now, he has been 'Robert' to me for a long time. Sir Wesley and Lady Clarke's greatest opposition to our marriage will be swept away if I brought six thousand pounds!"

Darcy watched the siblings stare at one another, one with pleading eyes and the other with stubborn fury. Dr. Ferris ultimately nodded, and his sister cried happily. "I cannot understand your purpose, but for the sake of my sister's happiness, I will do as you ask. If there is nothing else . . ."

Dr. Ferris wished him gone, but they had only begun. Darcy leaned back in his chair and crossed his ankle over his knee. The clergyman sighed and returned to his own chair, taking a long draught of sherry.

"I should like this to be done several more times."

"Several more times?"

"In 1813 and 1814, I need you to record my marriage and my son's birth, and in twenty-five to thirty-five years, I want you to record my death, my son's marriage, and, the year after that, the birth of his son. You can choose any name you like for the lady, but the son's name shall be mine."

Dr. Ferris shook his head. "Have you run mad? I shall record your marriage and your son's birth in return for my sister's happiness, but no more. To record the entries here could perhaps be viewed as a repetition of what will properly be done in Upper Canada, but anything beyond that is an outright falsehood."

"I realize it might be impossible for you to add those entries in thirty years, although I hope you are still the incumbent. You would be about seventy. I shall depend upon you to recommend to Miss Darcy, who will at that time have the right to grant the Kympton living, who among your family should replace you."

"Good heavens!" Miss Ferris cried, and she and Darcy shared a knowing look while Dr. Ferris looked as though he had never been more puzzled in his life.

"Flora, what is he saying?"

"Mr. Darcy says that if you do this, he will give you the right to name the future incumbent of Kympton. If you marry, you could grant your son the living! If your son agrees, then he can appoint whomever *he* likes when the time comes, so long as he registers the marriage and birth of a son of that generation of Mr. Darcy's family." For all of Dr. Ferris's scholarly learning, he was perplexed. "He is promising you the right to pass the living on to your son!"

Dr. Ferris gave Darcy a long look. "I am not insensible to the opportunity you are granting me in return for what, to some, is merely ink on a page. However, you cannot motivate me in this way, as I am quite happy as a bachelor." Dr. Ferris gave a self-satisfied smile.

Darcy's jaw popped, and the pain of it made him realize he had been clenching his teeth hard enough to break a molar. "Perhaps the new Mrs. Clarke, the wife of the future Sir Robert, may suggest who might be worthy of the living. Her second son might prefer the church. I would leave the decision to choose a respectable man, who is also amenable to doing my family an invaluable service, to you and your sister. I am confident you would select someone willing to oblige the family who improved your families' prospects."

Miss Ferris, nearly on the shelf and unable to marry the man she loved, had gone from confirmed spinster, to potential bride, to securing the future of her unborn second son in a matter of minutes. "Mr. Darcy, I would be pleased to help my brother remember to add your son's marriage to the register. I am certain we could find a worthy incumbent who will be amenable to your wishes. Without a doubt, I know future generations of my family will be happy to be of service to yours."

Dr. Ferris may be the scholar, but it was his sister who was quick-witted.

Darcy stood. "I thank you for your assistance in a matter that is dear to my heart. Should either of your families need anything in the years to come, you need only apply to the Darcys. For the present, if you would both call at Pemberley on Tuesday so we might commit to the details, my sister and I would be pleased to have you to dinner."

"Mr. Darcy, I have not agreed!"

Darcy exchanged another look at a determined Flora Ferris. *Miss Ferris will see that you do.* "I am certain you will decide what is right to be done. Good day."

Darcy could not persevere in the self-deception that bribery was *right* to be done. Had he lost his honor on a scheme that was unlikely to succeed? *None are injured by my ruse, and I used some of my fortune to unite two respectable young people.* Nonetheless, he had done something deceitful to have the chance to more easily find Elizabeth. He was struggling with his guilt while in the hall retrieving his great coat and hat when Miss Ferris joined him.

"Are you truly going to the Canadas to marry Miss Bennet? I do not know why you ask this of us, and I suspect I do not wish to know; however, you must tell me if *that* part is true."

Darcy smiled for the first time since entering the house. "If anything in this is beyond all doubt, it is my devotion to Elizabeth Bennet."

CHAPTER THIRTY-ONE

MARCH 22, 2013

"I don't suppose you can shed any light on the mysterious reappearance of our mutual friend," Frank asked after she waved goodbye to Charlotte and they were on their way to Pemberley.

"I haven't heard from Darcy since I left England in 2011."

Frank made an indistinct sound. "He asked for your address the second after he crossed my doorstep."

Her heart turned over in her chest at the same time as she felt a surge of jealousy for not being the first person Darcy sought out. "When did you first see him again?"

"The whole thing is strange. Darcy refuses to discuss what happened between the time he left in 2011 and the time he appeared at my house in the middle of the night. Doesn't say what happened with Oxford, doesn't explain why he never mentioned Pemberley, doesn't explain anything."

"What happened?"

"It's a few days before Christmas, well past dark, and he knocks and asks for a room for a few nights. He's all apologetic for intruding and for not replying to a single text or email—very polite and dignified, you know how he is. But Darcy is carrying a box of clothes like he's been thrown out of the house! He won't say where he's been; he just begs us to forgive him and asks for a place to stay until he can meet with his solicitors about Pemberley. Gwen falls for his puppy-dog eyes and says he can stay as long as he likes. Mind, I wasn't going to refuse him, either"—Frank looked at Elizabeth for emphasis—"but it's *bizarre*. Who shows up in Bakewell with his clothes in a box, eighty quid in his wallet, no interest in charging his phone, and claims to have nothing else in the world until after he meets with his lawyers?"

Box of clothes? Realization struck her. She had left Darcy's things in Professor Gardiner's house, choosing to ignore anything that reminded her of him. Had she forgotten to tell them to donate the box? Darcy must have gotten it from the Gardiners. *He went there looking for me.*

"You said he asked about me?"

"I'm putting the kettle on while Gwen tidies up the guest room. I come in with the tray, and Darcy is staring at the cards on the mantle like he's never seen a Christmas card in his life! He's got yours clutched in his hand, and he asks what your address is like his life depends on it. Gwen gives him your address, and that was the end of it. I thought he'd have written to you."

Yeah, me too.

NOVEMBER 19, 1812

Darcy considered the two important things now at hand that were to fix his fate for life: the solstice and Elizabeth. Half of his plan was thus determined, but the other half might not prove straightforward. His responsibilities at Pemberley, however he found it, could eventually be established, but the person to share with, to animate, to reward those responsibilities might not be attained. Who knew how long it would take him to even find Elizabeth?

To say nothing about how long it takes one to get a passport, and that is assuming there is an inarguable birth record awaiting me. To say nothing if she loves me as she once did.

"Does your hand hurt?"

Darcy looked up to see his cousin enter. He still held the pen, but had ceased writing as his thoughts wandered. "Yes, but I am near done."

"You must regret your style of writing now, after all of the letters you wrote these past months."

"I shall not regret their length so long as you do not regret posting them." A question hung on his words.

Fitzwilliam gave him a long look before sinking into a chair. "Of all the things you could doubt with this scheme, you need never doubt me." He gestured to the stack of folded letters. "Whose years'-worth of letters are you finishing now? Everything else to stage this drama was finished weeks ago."

"Bingley." He looked at the salutation. "I saved his for the last because I struggled with what to write. He is my closest friend, but he is so removed from Nine Ladies and Pemberley's well-being that I cannot justify his knowing the truth. My other friends' letters, even writing to your father, to my aunt, those were easier."

"Easy?" Fitzwilliam breathed the word. "Nothing about this shall be easy. I worry for you. How many times will you be afraid of the unknown? How many times will you be caught by surprise by your own ignorance of what everyone else seems to know?"

"Perhaps every day."

"How can a man such as you stand it?"

"I did it once, you forget."

"I think anyone can endure trials when there is an end date for their suffering. This is indefinite at best."

"You ask how I can stand to live in unfamiliarity. A better question is how can I happily live without her? I must do something before it is absolutely too late to hope. It is over a year already since I last saw her."

"What if Pemberley does not survive as you intend it to? That might guarantee your plan will fail."

"Having to sell an estate indicates financial mismanagement, or the holder living beyond his or her means. Georgiana would not allow that any more than I."

"And what of her children? Her grandchildren? Miss Bennet aside, you have set yourself on a fool's errand. For this to work as you wish, this must progress near faultlessly over generations."

"That is why Mr. Willers's lease agreement says the inheritor must be named Darcy and the custodian must also take the name Darcy; what can be sold is limited to certain sections of timber or land, and it dictates the amount of funds be set aside annually to pay future death duties, as well as the formation of a trust for the remainder of the lease term in the event there are no direct descendants of my sister then living. Between Flora Ferris and my sister, at least two generations will be recorded." Darcy shrugged. "It is incredibly complicated, and that is why the matter is under the direction of Mr. Willers."

"While I lease Pemberley and play lord of the manor until Georgiana is twenty-one."

"Try not to kill every bird in your first season."

Fitzwilliam was silent for a few minutes. "Can you even remember what Miss Bennet looks like?"

"Do you?" he quipped, not looking up from his letter.

"I am not the one throwing—I am not the one in love, so I do not have to remember if her eyes were blue or brown."

Darcy laid aside his pen and blotted his paper. "She is not quite tall, a spare person since she is in the habit of running, but with a pleasing figure. A sweet face, a small but well-shaped nose. Her eyes are brown; they are joyous and intelligent and show a keen sense of humor."

"Well, at least you are leaving your friends for a woman you would recognize should you find her." Fitzwilliam looked down when he spoke again. "And if you do not find her, or she is married or dead, or cannot love you—"

"Is this how you want to spend our final weeks together?"

The colonel shook his head, and waited in silence while Darcy finished his letter. Darcy knew his cousin would miss him terribly, as he would miss him. Sometimes words intruded into understandings that were better left in silence.

MARCH 22, 2013

Darcy wished for his cousin's advice now. Fitzwilliam's manners were admired by the opposite sex, and he might suggest something to make his conversation with Elizabeth easier. *Or he would tease me for my stupidity.*

When the car appeared, Darcy had been standing outside Mr. Willers's cottage, waiting in agitation, for half an hour. Frank gave him a mock salute and a wink while Elizabeth pulled her bag from the car, and they were finally alone.

It took him a long moment to speak, as his hands and feet had gone numb, and he had forgotten how to breathe.

"I'm pleased to see you again. You look lovely."

She flushed, looking down and smoothing a hand over her hair. It was shorter than it had been when Darcy first knew her, and he liked it. "Thank you." Her eyes finally met his; he wished to do something to see a spark of approval in those dark eyes. "What are we doing at the steward's house?"

"Pemberley is not habitable at the moment, and Mr. Willers's house, as well as Mr. Roland's, were two of the estate properties that survived in good repair. Now that Pemberley is mine again, I can make the house fit to be lived in, but until then, I am living in the steward's house."

"Pemberley still looks better than it did the last time I saw it."

"Quite."

They stood in awkwardness until Darcy remembered his manners and gestured that they ought to go inside. Mr. Willers's house had been maintained through the nineteenth century, updated with electric light and indoor plumbing in the early twentieth century, and renovated again in the 1970s. There was a fitness and beauty that the two stone homes that remained on his grounds had belonged to two men who had been invaluable to his family.

He offered to show her the house and her room, but she shook her head, abandoning her bag and walking to the looking glass over the mantle. She ran her finger across its gilded frame. "This mirror was in your study." Elizabeth turned to the center of the room. "And that chair was in Georgiana's sitting room."

"Yes, I understand a great deal of Pemberley's furniture was moved when a girls' school occupied the house during World—"

"Georgiana!" Elizabeth interrupted him. "You found her in Ramsgate in time, didn't you?"

"Yes." He smiled. "If not for you, and Maria Lucas's newspapers, I would never have recovered her. You would be proud of the woman Georgiana became; in fact, given her confidence compared to when you first knew her, she is quite altered. Still shy, but more assured. She is—she *was*—a remarkable mistress of Pemberley."

"I'm so glad." They stared at one another for a long moment before Elizabeth gave a nervous laugh. "If only Regency English high society knew that Mr. Darcy of Pemberley lives in his steward's house."

"I am not now to learn that such things are not as significant as they once were. More importantly, I know for certain that wealth and connections are nothing to you."

Elizabeth ran a hand through her hair, not knowing where to look. Darcy had never before seen her so lacking in confidence, not even when she was two hundred years out of her time. "You must have been surprised to meet me that way on Wednesday."

Her expression hardened. "You've been here since the winter solstice! I would have left England next week and never known you were here! I left two days ago with Charlotte, and you didn't bat an eye."

He stepped quickly toward her. "Have you *any* idea that it took all of my self-control to let you drive away from me?"

"You've been here for months! Why did you come if it wasn't to see me?"

At the note of pain in her voice, he reached out to take her hand in his. His thumb rubbed soothingly over her knuckles, and he felt some of his own pain lessen as she squeezed his hand in return. "What other reason could I have had for coming back?"

"Why don't you tell me why?"

Darcy let go of her hand and lifted his own to frame her face and, without a word, kissed her firmly on her mouth. A powerful relief filled him to feel her lips against his. It was a slow kiss that contained but a hint of the accumulated passion from months of desire. For a few precious moments, he relished in the sweet feel of her lips against his before he spoke.

"I love you. I have always loved you."

She breathed faster, and her skin flushed, but she did not seem capable of making any speeches. Still, Elizabeth had not pulled away or struck him, so Darcy took that as leave to continue. "I would never forgive myself if I said nothing again and I lost you because of that, if you thought I have not loved you all this time."

His hands still cupped her cheeks, and she reached up to clutch his wrists with her fingers. "I never wanted you to choose me over Georgiana's happiness and Pemberley. But why didn't you say that you loved me before you left?"

"To me, true courtship consists of gentlemanly attentions that are not so pointed as to alarm while not so vague as to be misunderstood. I had done that without even meaning to; my interactions with you felt perfectly natural. But to explicitly say that I love you . . . for one from my time and place, it would have been tantamount to a marriage proposal. And I could not confess that I loved you and wished to marry you when we both knew you would never return with me."

Elizabeth blinked her eyes, and a few tears spilled out. "I'm so sorry that I wasn't ready to go then. You don't know how many times I've thought about going to Nine Ladies. But I was too afraid that you had moved on or never loved me in the first place. Why don't you hate me for being unwilling to go back with you?"

Darcy shook his head. "Hate you? Never. I wanted to tell you that I loved you, but I could not ask you to marry me and thereby bring you back and make you unhappy. I could not do that to you, so instead I said nothing. Can you forgive me for leaving you in doubt of my feelings and wishes?"

"There isn't anything to forgive." She gave him a trembling smile. "I suppose I could forgive you for not calling me the second you appeared on Stanton Moor, but why didn't you?" She let go of his wrists and he dropped his hands, but he was unwilling to step away from her, not when he wanted to pull her into his arms and never let go.

"I cannot pretend to know the etiquette of how to communicate an undying affection in this century, but certain things deserve to be done in person. I could not have you learn that I ardently admire and love you from a text rather than from my own lips. I have only been waiting for a passport . . . and the courage to use it."

Her eyes widened. "You were brave enough to travel forward in time two hundred years to find me, but you're not brave enough to board an airplane?"

"I am not used to traveling above ten miles an hour! I suffer from travel sickness in a car that goes above thirty. You cannot imagine how frightening the thought of traveling hundreds of miles per hour, tens of thousands of feet above the earth, is for me."

She shook her head, smiling. He so badly wanted to touch her, but she still had said nothing of her own feelings.

"Elizabeth, please, end my apprehension and anxiety. I love you and wish to marry you and have long felt this way with an unwavering devotion. I will make it the study of my life to contribute to the happiness of yours."

Her breath hitched, and she pressed her lips against his in a gentle and deliberate kiss. Her touch sent a tremor through his entire body. Darcy wound his arms around her waist to hold her closer. Her hum of approval vibrated against his lips; he lightly touched his tongue against her lips, and finally tasted her mouth. She teased him with her lips and tongue and pushed her fingertips through his hair. It took a tremendous effort to pull away from her.

"As delightful as that was, I dare not assume what your feelings are."

"I love you too, and of course I'll marry you!" Her hands on his shoulders gripped him tighter. "We'll go back together, like we should have the last time. What held me back was not knowing for certain that you loved me. I'm sorry I didn't find you before the equinox, though. Now we'll have to wait until September."

She was still in his arms, and Darcy nearly dropped them from her in surprise. "That is not why I came."

Her mouth hung open. "Didn't you come back to find me?"

"Certainly I did."

"Then why wouldn't we go back to Pemberley in September?"

"We *are* at Pemberley. I never intended to bring you to the nineteenth century. Everything I have done for the past year was done so I could leave and stay here with you."

December 10, 1812

Since his intention of going through Nine Ladies was known to her, Reynolds had drawn back her subtle warmth. She was as capable and dutiful as she had been these twenty-five years, but Darcy noticed the withdrawal even from so staid a woman. He had to mend their relationship before they parted.

His housekeeper stood before his desk, awaiting orders, and Darcy wished for the Reynolds he once knew. She had never been affectionate, but her comparative severity was a harsh change from the woman he had known since he was four years old.

"We have little time left, my dear Reynolds. Do not spare me your feelings."

She started. "I am sure I do not know what you mean, sir."

"You do. You and I value forthright conversation. I have made my peace with my cousin. I do not wish for us to part this way."

"You will think me selfish if you allow me to speak freely." There was no inflection in her voice.

Darcy shook his head. "You have been nothing but generous and selfless in all the years I have been fortunate to know you."

"When you decide something, it is as good as done, and what I think matters little."

"It does matter to me. You may not wish to acknowledge it, but I will say it: you have in many ways been like a second mother to me. Please, say what you must so we might part as friends."

Reynolds released some of the tension that had been around her eyes and in her shoulders for months. "I thought your first concern was always for Pemberley, even above your own interests, sir. To cast it all away for any woman is selfish."

"I have taken great care to preserve Pemberley and protect it for the next two hundred years. I have faith in Georgiana to keep us on this path."

"Pemberley is your responsibility, not your sister's."

"Pemberley is the responsibility of the *Darcys*. You cannot tell me Georgiana is incapable, or that she does not have the wisdom of sensible counselors. You cannot say that she does not want this. Nor can you, born in the twentieth century, tell me that a woman is naturally less capable than a man."

"Be that as it may, I cannot understand your choice, Master Fitzwilliam. Everything you love will be lost to death and time."

"Not everything. Not every*one*."

Tears welled in his housekeeper's eyes. "I cannot believe you love Miss Bennet to such an end."

"I am more worried with whether or not she could love me."

Reynolds's eyes narrowed. "You are not risking Pemberley without having reason to hope."

"My conviction of her regard for me is strong, but I left her. If she is single, I first have to find her and determine if she cares for me enough to forgive me for not declaring myself when I ought to have done."

His housekeeper made a dismissive sound. "You did not see her determination to save your life when you were ill. She cared for you. But she did not love you enough to forgo the advantages and freedoms of her modern life to come back with you."

"I would never ask her to." Darcy rose and came around his desk. "Simply because you found contentment here, it does not mean Miss Bennet would be happy with this life. And, as Fitzwilliam told the group when we last met, there is a possibility I may not be gone forever."

"If they believe that, they are fools! You have no intention of returning." Darcy had the good grace to look away. "If you learn that your sister managed Pemberley well in your stead and was happy, you would not take that bright future away from Miss Darcy any more than you could ask Miss Bennet to sacrifice what she has to return here."

"You comprehend me better than I can understand you. You did not tell me I need a birth record to prove my identity and to obtain a passport. You must know something about what large estates faced in the twentieth century, but you refuse to aid Mr. Willers. You are not angry because you fear for Pemberley's well-being, and you are not angry because you think I will be disappointed in love. I wonder if you wish me to remain unhappy."

Darcy had meant this as a way of inciting her to speak, but she suddenly rested her head against his chest and put her arms around him. "I want you to find happiness, and if you find it in 2013 with Miss Bennet, so be it. But Master Fitzwilliam, you are the closest thing I have to a son. My own little boy! And I will never see you again!"

March 22, 2013

"You can't mean to stay here forever?" Elizabeth cried.

"I wish to be with *you* forever, and this is where you are." Darcy brushed his lips against hers again.

It was so unexpected. But Darcy's staying here made no sense. "I wasn't ready before, and I didn't know that you loved me. I needed to hear the words. You left behind too much! Whereas I barely get along with my family, I only have a few friends worth knowing, I've quit my job—"

"You would be made miserable in 1813!" The gravity in his tone struck her. "You would have been thought bold when you would now be thought honest. Your laughter would have been thought of as a hint of reprehensible sexual freedom when now you would be called lively. You would have been thought too weak to control your passions and unsuitable for business or politics. Your presumed proper place would be a lower one than mine, with fewer legal rights, no power, and less respect, only because you are a woman."

"You're forgetting I would be with *you*. I'm not saying it would be easy, but you can't assume I couldn't have a meaningful life in the past."

"Your talents would be wasted then, and that injustice would hurt you in a way different from what women of my own time know. You would have led a life deprived of the opportunities that only as a man might you have had in that time."

"But what will you do here? How can you be as happy here as you were being Pemberley's master?"

"Pemberley needs a proper function in this time, and there are still three tenants who rent and work their land. And I shall relish every moment I am with you."

"How is that fair? I should have to sacrifice something too."

"You will have to sacrifice your peace of mind to be with me. Think of it: How many times in a day will you need to explain something to me? How many conversations must you carefully manage to hide that I am bewildered by the topic? Any curiosity about my life before 2013 will have to be deflected; any confusion as to why I cannot reply sensibly will have to be explained. Think of the extent to which you had to prepare me when I was last here, and that was amid a small social circle for three months. You might resent your role, and thereby me."

Elizabeth shook her head as she smoothed his hair and laid a palm on his cheek. "Never," she whispered, and silenced his next question with an affectionate kiss. Instead of pressing against him to kiss him harder, she pulled away with a thought.

"We can't go back and forth, can we? We might change something in the past and have nothing to come back to."

"It would be foolish to interfere in time any more than we already have, and I, for one, would not risk our being trapped in the past should Nine Ladies lose its power."

"I feel guilty that you gave up so much."

Darcy shook his head, his bright-eyed face smiling at her as he led them to the sofa. *Who knew that Darcy was so expressive in his joy?* "All of my reservations I told you that night at Charlotte Lucas's house still hold true. You would be made unhappy in the past and ultimately resent me or leave me, and I could not bear either."

"I love you. Not a day went by that I didn't think of you, that I didn't wonder if you were happy or if you were as lonely without me as I was without you. Whatever we do from here on out, we do it together. I wasn't ready to commit to a life in the past before, but I know now that I would never, ever leave you."

"You could still be miserable in every other aspect of your life in the nineteenth century. I love you too much to wish that upon you, especially when I know that, challenging as it may sometimes be, I can be happier in this time than you could be in mine."

Her throat felt tight and her chest ached right beneath the breastbone. "What about the people who loved you?"

Darcy's expression clouded slightly. "My absence was a severe stroke to my family. My friends never understood my choice, as little as they comprehended what I had done. A few—Georgiana, Bingley—were truly happy for me."

"What did you tell them? Who knows the truth?"

"The account was that I sailed to Canada to seek the hand of my housekeeper's cousin and remained there with you. I have learned I was branded an eccentric romantic. I leased Pemberley to my cousin for four years, and then to my sister and her issues through 2012. By the duplicitous means of clergy and my sister's descendants who forged parish and civil records, I was able to present myself as my own descendant and the rightful heir of Pemberley. Georgiana, Fitzwilliam, and Mrs. Reynolds knew the truth, along with Mr. Roland and Young Henry." He gave a small smile. "And Mr. Willers was lately brought into our confidence, with interesting results."

"That sounds like quite a story," she whispered. Darcy must have spent the last year planning something this elaborate. He left behind a wealthy estate with hundreds of people and a family who dearly loved him to be with *her*. She was awed that someone adored her this much, and a little guilty; but to look at him now, smiling and bashfully touching her fingertips, no one would say he looked unhappy.

As she gazed at him, Darcy leaned forward to kiss her, gently and confidently. Her arms slipped around him, and when her hands were in his hair, a low moan escaped him. Warm fingers slid along her neck, curling around the nape, holding her close. As she considered how shocked someone born in 1784 might be if she climbed into his lap, another thought crossed Elizabeth's mind.

"Wait! How did they believe you're Pemberley's heir? And you said you were waiting for a passport? How is that possible?"

Darcy went to the desk. "I had to first find the solicitors who managed Pemberley's trust, once I learned there were no Darcys now living at Pemberley. Any information those who knew the truth thought I might need to know was to be left in Mr. Roland's house. Robotham & Co are solicitors that had been undertaking wills, trusts, and property law since 1837, and Mr. Willers had moved Pemberley's concerns into their care years before he died, and so they there remained." He came back with a large envelope and dumped papers between them on the sofa. Some were filled in by hand on yellowing paper, but most were crisp and white with typewritten words in the blanks.

"It is a long story that involves me meeting many times with the solicitors who succeeded to the trusteeship of Pemberley after Georgiana's last descendant died thirty years ago, justifying why I have little recorded presence, spending a great deal of time applying for records from the Government Record Office, and my encouraging their suspicions that my grandfather's and father's death certificates must be lost as a result of that office's move from Somerset House, and convincing them that I was the rightful heir now that the lease was concluded."

"I know you wanted to declare yourself to me in person, and I can appreciate that. But if you planned to stay in the twenty-first century, I would have helped you. You didn't have to establish your life here on your own."

"I absolutely did." Darcy's voice grew serious. "I am wholly committed to living here, and to make that possible . . . Elizabeth, I needed more than to hope to manage here tolerably well. I had to *know* for certain I could take care of myself, and you. While I awaited a passport, I had to prove I could be the same capable man in this century as I was in the one that I left behind."

As she nodded her understanding, Darcy handed her a document that said "Certified Copy of An Entry" and "Birth" in large letters. Every box was filled in, everything stamped and sealed and signed. "You have a birth certificate," she said flatly. "This is you?" She waved the paper. "They think you, Fitzwilliam Darcy, were born in 1984?"

"I ought to be satisfied the year is correct; that is more than I expected. I have had a hard time remembering I am now thought to be born in the summer rather than in February."

Elizabeth picked up a blue and red number-card, then a form with purple ink announcing an NHS card, and shook her head while Darcy held out a yellow and green tinted ID with his picture.

"You got a provisional driving license? How do you even drive without getting sick? And how did you get these other numbers?"

"Apparently, six weeks after my birth was recorded, a National Health card was sent to my 'parents" address, which was Roland's house. A National Insurance Card followed before my sixteenth birthday, as it once did for everyone. It was not difficult, relatively speaking, to find them in his house. The license, for which Frank agreed to be my referee, was another necessary step to get a passport to find you in America. I cannot drive a car." He took the card from her, frowned at it, and put it in his wallet. "I do not care for the picture, although Frank tells me that is to be expected."

Elizabeth swore under her breath and leaned into him. He loved her and had given up everyone and everything to build a new life here with her. "You have to tell me how this was done."

"I will. I wish I had begun the scheme as soon as Georgiana was recovered from Mr. Wickham." Darcy pushed tendrils of her hair aside and kissed her behind her ear. "We have lost so much time."

"You must have told Georgiana about Nine Ladies and where she came from?" Darcy exhaled loudly and nodded as he pulled away from her neck. "She was such a sensitive girl. How did she take it? I know she could do anything she set her mind to, but was she ready to manage Pemberley without you?"

Darcy gave her an enigmatic smile. "Should you like to know what I learned about Georgiana's life?"

He pulled her to her feet and told her they were walking to Pemberley. Along the way, he talked of bribing Dr. Ferris, and how his sister, Lady Clarke, and her children saw to it that the parish registers reflected three generations of births, deaths, and marriages of his make-believe line.

"Civil registration of births began in 1837, but I have learned that reporting was not compulsory until years later. And even then, they were not always reported. The living at Kympton was held by my sister's family until 1924, with the secret knowledge that the incumbent could name his own successor so long as they entered false birth and marriage records of a missing Darcy family member. At some point, death notices required a doctor, so the parish burial records ceased.

"The final Darcy birth and marriage entries were recorded in the Kympton register before a measure passed in 1924 to abolish the sale or inheriting of livings after two vacancies. English Sees began to acquire them for parish churches, and after that members of the Darcy family needed to report to civil registers."

"You can't tell me Georgiana's descendants bribed county clerks for the rest of the twentieth century."

"I know not who was recruited to feign to be my grandparents to register my father's birth, but it appears pretending births were at home rather than in hospital helped. I suspect my sister's last remaining descendant found a woman with an infant to claim to be the mother, and a man hired for the purpose brought 'proof' of the 1924 baptism and claimed to be the father, although they could not falsify a marriage between them. That was done in 1956 to create a record for my father, and in 1984 the same was done the final time for me."

"Even though the birth was registered by both 'parents,' you and your father are considered illegitimate now."

They held hands as they walked. "Inheritance laws have changed, and illegitimate children thankfully have rights to their father's property. As far as the solicitors are concerned, my father's name on my 1984 birth certificate and the parents' claim to residing at the same address—Roland's cottage—is sufficient. Since there was no activity of his life beyond my father's name on my birth certificate, asserting his death was simple. They would rather not be trustees of a neglected estate whose small income from rent on three farms they can only draw from to keep the grounds and house in minimal good repair. In the absence of other claimants, and my official birth certificate and other documents, as well as those going back generations, I was able to assert my claim."

"You were lucky."

"I do not dispute that, but my sister and her descendants were also determined. Registering a fictitious birth is a crime, and although none were injured, I am not insensitive of the wrongdoing done on my behalf."

They walked around to Pemberley's front façade, and at the door, Darcy brought a key from his pocket. "I thought the house uninhabitable. Is it safe?"

Darcy scoffed as he turned the key in a modern lock set in a hundreds-year-old door. "Pemberley is a listed building, and I cannot alter it without permission from a local planning authority. It is safe, but until its roof, electrical wires, and plumbing and heating are seen to, I am not supposed to live in my own house."

After he shut the door, the space returned to darkness before Darcy pushed aside the window coverings and turned on a few light switches. "That does not mean, however, that its contents are not mine and I cannot enter Pemberley House whenever I choose."

The entrance hall had its bright, spectacular plasterwork. Darcy was going on about how he hated the electric lights and how they lit areas of the ceilings that were never meant to be seen, but she didn't care; it looked splendid.

"Come, what I wish to show you about Georgiana is in the library."

When they entered, she saw some of the furniture was uncovered and the curtains were already pulled back. From the footprints in the dust on the wood floors, she knew Darcy had spent time in this room. The bookcases were full, and the Adam marble fireplace was as grand as she remembered.

"During the Second World War, Pemberley was occupied by a girls' school, and this was the only room they were not allowed to use."

Darcy talked about how fortunate it was that the house was occupied by students rather than soldiers, and the improvements done to accommodate them, but Elizabeth was scarcely listening. A book lay on a table, and in gilt letters on the cover were the words, "Pemberley House Library Catalogue." She opened it to the last used page where someone had written 'rmvd to the drawg room Oct. 1984.' She remembered standing in this spot, with a single candle, holding Darcy's hand and pleading with him to let her tell him about his future.

"Should I be alarmed that I lost your attention so soon?"

She shut the catalogue. "This was a home until the early eighties. It's amazing so much is still here at Pemberley. It's as delightful as I remember."

"If I did not know better, I would suspect you of trying to earn my favor by flattery like Miss Bingley did."

"Never. You were going to tell me about Georgiana. Did she marry Mr. Bingley?"

Darcy shook his head and gave an enigmatic smile. "No, not Bingley."

December 15, 1812

"It is exquisite, and the style is *au courant*."

"Perhaps it is too sentimental?" Darcy asked as they looked at what was in the jewelry box.

"Elizabeth would appreciate so considerate a gift." Georgiana's expression grew thoughtful. "She was the first person who said that they thought me a capable woman. She is dear to me too. We spoke about my apprehensions about being in company, and she told me she had no doubt that I would do anything I set my mind to do."

"I should have encouraged you long before I did. I am exceedingly sorry—"

"You need not be sorry. I only wish I had the chance to thank her, to know her better." Georgiana brushed the back of her hand across her eyes. "Fitzwilliam, you must bring so lovely a lady more!" Georgiana pulled out other jewelry boxes, and Darcy wondered how much he could fit in his pockets. He was not about to carry trunks into Nine Ladies.

"Women do not wear jewels like this in the twenty-first century. Perhaps they save them for formal occasions, but I cannot imagine Elizabeth wearing these."

"You would know better than I, but you said my mother wished for something of hers to go to your wife so, for her sake, select something."

Darcy stared at the gold and gemstones and, remembering the purple gown Elizabeth had worn to the nightclub, selected a small amethyst parure to go along with his own carefully selected choice. He doubted she would wear them, but if it respected his mother's memory and pleased his sister, so be it.

"What about a tiara?" Georgiana selected a diamond one that had belonged to his mother.

"I don't think so."

"I will hide it in the house for you to find someday. Miss Ferris wore a pretty one last evening that belongs to her future mother-in-law." Georgiana sat. "I fear I spoke too freely in front of the ladies at Mr. Clarke and Miss Ferris's engagement dinner."

"I do not remember you speaking after the gentlemen returned to the drawing room."

"It is not in my nature to converse spontaneously with those with whom I am not much acquainted. Mrs. Annesley suggested I speak of my interests, and I put myself forward to speak of my charitable concerns with Miss Ferris."

Georgiana plucked at the embroidery of her skirt. Darcy set aside the jewelry and joined her on the sofa. "There can be no fault in that."

His sister set her shoulders and splayed her hands when she clearly wished to slump into her seat and fidget with her fingers. "I mentioned how I relished reviewing the tenants' contracts and doing rent collection alongside Mr. Willers. I said that I wanted to improve Pemberley's profits without having to increase rent more than five percent. Mr. Willers and I agree we need to do something after lead mining is exhausted."

"Am I correct in assuming none of the ladies shared your enthusiasm?"

"Lady Clarke asked that I not mention profits in her presence, and another woman insisted I leave land management to men. Miss Ferris tried to draw me out again, but I could not speak a word after that."

Darcy knew his sister was intelligent and capable, but her shyness was still a hindrance. And at a time when the pursuit of business by men was at best a dubious virtue, polite society deemed it distasteful in a respectable woman of good family. "You must not question your talents and doubt yourself. In those affairs which may be called business, I would not be ashamed to have you known to be an expert."

"Lady Clarke said a man wished to marry an agreeable woman to keep his home, not one who knew more than him and who might put him to shame."

Darcy shook his head. "You have none of the usual inducements to marry, and you can wait until you find someone who admires you as you are."

"I must marry and have children for your plan—"

"Stop, I can hear no more! You need not marry if you do not wish it. My hopes of living again at Pemberley are second to being with Elizabeth, and if there is no identifying record awaiting me, I shall manage without it. Live your own life, and find your own happiness irrespective of me."

"Do you think it possible a gentleman would concede to live on an estate he cannot pass on to his descendants in perpetuity? I shall never leave Pemberley, nor allow anyone to make decisions for it. Could any man marry a woman on such terms?"

"I would not have a girl of intelligence and feeling marry a man who may be a tyrant or a fool or both. No sister of mine would be under the necessity of marrying for her support. If you marry, be it to someone to whom you will be as beloved and important as you are to me."

Georgiana started quietly weeping.

"My dear, you cannot assume no respectable man would marry you because you alone are entitled to make Pemberley's decisions. And a man who cannot respect your abilities and your position is not the man to spend your life with."

His sister looked at him in despair. "I am not crying over not finding a husband! Even after you learned where I came from, I was always your sister. You are the person who loves me best, and you are leaving!"

Georgiana threw her arms around him, and Darcy felt tears in his eyes. "I shall miss you more than anything in the entire world," he told her. "Promise me something: Do not lose your peace of mind for any male creature breathing. Do not marry for Pemberley's sake."

March 22, 2013

"My sister was a shy woman, but she kept the Pemberley properties well. Georgiana became a conservative, but wise, investor. She had a reputation for compassion as well as for being a formidable woman of business, and she lived until 1877."

"But who did she marry?" Elizabeth cried. "I am not looking for her gravestone again to find her married name."

Darcy was tempted to see how long he could tease her, for he enjoyed the curiosity in her eyes. "If you did go to St. Anne's, the name on her stone would read 'Georgiana Willers.'"

When her jaw closed, Elizabeth smiled. "Mr. Willers was never the sort to gamble away an estate or live the high life in London, but you probably had someone from a different social class in mind. Does that bother you?"

"No," he replied with complete honesty. "Philip Willers was scrupulously polite, a man content with his responsibilities and never shied from them. A dutiful man. He mourned his first wife, but that does not mean I think him incapable of loving a second time. Likely he was a devoted husband and a doting father."

"When did they marry?"

"Many years after I was gone. Georgiana was thirty; Mr. Willers must have been in his early forties."

"I think if he was your brother-in-law, you could call him Philip now."

He acknowledged her teasing by saying, "*Mr. Willers* and my sister worked alongside one another for years, but I do not yet know how their relationship changed from a business partnership to one that was more amorous."

"What do you mean 'not yet'?"

He held out the family Bible and gently opened it to the family record pages. "The births, marriages, and deaths were diligently recorded, including my own fictitious line. Georgiana also kept diaries for the rest of her life. Letters to me, in truth," he corrected himself. "After her death, they were placed in a box in the library with my name on it, and her will stated they were not to be moved until her brother's descendant claimed Pemberley in December 2012."

"She must have missed you so much," Elizabeth said softly.

"Yes. I skimmed them, but decided to read them in order. I have not read ahead of 1813."

Elizabeth took the Bible, carefully turning the pages. "They had one son, Philip Willers-Darcy, in 1829, but he died in April 1855."

"Their son wished for a profession, and I suspect Mr. Willers encouraged some employment. Georgiana's letters said he begged for an army commission, and he was a captain in the 77th regiment. He was stationed in the United Kingdom until 1854. He died of disease in the Siege of Sevastopol."

"Poor Georgiana. This says he was married in 1853 and had a son before he left for the Crimea."

"I know not what happened to their son's wife, only that she remarried and left her son to the care of his grandparents at Pemberley. Mr. Willers died not long after his son—I gather his heart never recovered from his loss—and Georgiana raised her grandson at Pemberley."

"Your sister lived a long time, but her grandson didn't marry until 1893. I wonder why he waited until he was nearly forty."

"I found few papers of his. Perhaps he married to entrust Pemberley to his own children rather than commit the properties to a trust. Or perhaps he had not yet found the right woman." He gave Elizabeth a warm look, and she blushed. "He and his children forged birth records. That is likely due to Georgiana's influence from raising her grandson."

Elizabeth looked at the names in the Bible. "Georgiana's grandson had three children: Philip, born 1894, James, born 1896, and Catherine, born 1900." She turned the pages to the 'deaths' record, and her face fell. "Both boys died in France."

"Their mother died of the influenza, their father died in 1924 at the age of 70, and Pemberley was left to young Catherine Willers-Darcy, who never married."

"There were few men left after the Great War." Elizabeth sighed sadly.

"Catherine was a woman for whom nothing about Pemberley was beneath her vigilant attention. The girls she met while Pemberley housed a school during the Second World War might have helped her in forging birth records for my benefit." He took in the room in a sweeping glance before returning his attention to Elizabeth. "So much might have gone amiss during those years; I could not truly appreciate it until today. Finding a Pemberley I recognized was never my object, only a means through which I might more easily find you. I know how fortunate I am, but never more so than now that I finally have you, dearest Elizabeth."

He ought not to dwell on the time they had lost, not now that they were together. "Let me show you the portrait of my sister's family. I have not even told you what Reynolds arranged to be left behind. You shall have to tell me what is best to be done."

"No." She set the Bible down gently.

Darcy's smile slipped. "No?"

"It can wait a little longer." The longing flicker in her eyes was alluring.

"You would rather stay in the library?"

She nodded, and Darcy drew in a slow, deep breath. "Have you something else you would rather do?"

Her voice lowered to a throaty whisper. "I can think of a few things."

"And what might we do in the library other than read?" Darcy looked at her with false innocence.

He had expected Elizabeth to roll her eyes, but instead they burned with a passion he had until now only imagined. Darcy caught her by the waist, drew her against him, and kissed her deeply. Excitement raced through him as she pressed her body close to his and trailed her hands over him, her touch reassuring him that what he had hoped for for so long was now a reality.

Her hands were on either side of his face, her fingers pushing into his hair when she pulled away to say, "I love you."

Elizabeth's eyes were luminous and steady on his. Darcy gave a breathless reply, but before he could express himself sensibly as to why he loved her too, and how much, she returned her lips to his with a fierce intensity. To think he once lived in a world where the woman he loved ought not to have flirted with him and not explicitly invited his kiss.

CHAPTER THIRTY-TWO

MARCH 22, 2013
PEMBERLEY, STEWARD'S HOUSE

"There is no way you cooked this."

"If nothing in all I have done to get here indicates my cleverness, you should know me well enough to not doubt my ability to read and follow step-by-step instructions."

Darcy's tone was severe, but he smiled, not that Elizabeth could see with her eyes closed as she euphorically pulled her fork from her mouth and chewed.

"You hated to cook when we were in Bakewell. The best you managed was boiling water for pasta or making a grilled cheese sandwich."

"I had to learn self-reliance since I came back." *And I shall run mad if I must live on toasted bread and cheese for the remainder of my life.* "I hired someone to drive me when necessary and someone to do laundry, but the chores of grocery shopping and cooking have fallen to me if I wish to eat."

"Nice shirt, by the way, even if you didn't iron it yourself. You look handsome."

Darcy blushed; he suspected that was her purpose. "One ought to make some alteration in one's dress before dinner, although one does not always do so when at home."

"That's what we are now, aren't we? At home, together?"

The dining table separating them was what kept Darcy from kissing Elizabeth again upon hearing those words and seeing that affectionate gleam in her eye. Some kisses had been tender and fleeting; others had been passionate and lasted a long time. "Sadly, you are a visitor, and we ought to speak to your mother so we can marry."

Elizabeth coughed, and set down her fork. "No. You have my permission to marry me."

"I did not expect to ask for her consent, not in this time, but I do not mind showing her the courtesy."

"I realize the absurdity in someone like you being a disappointment to the mother of the woman you want to marry, but she won't care that marrying you will make me happy. I will *tell* her what we are doing. Besides, you'd want to ask in person, and you don't have a passport yet. Who wants to wait that long?"

Darcy knew her mother was a subject Elizabeth did not wish to discuss. "Perhaps you might name the day when you will make me the happiest being in the world."

"Are you eager to make an honest woman of me?"

He blinked. "That implies seduction has already taken place."

"Here's hoping. I can remember you telling me on one of our walks that you couldn't imagine sharing your life with anyone." Darcy felt her foot slide along his leg underneath the table.

"I assumed that if I married, it would be a match of unequal affection, if there was any affection at all. I had not expected to find a woman to speak the truth to me and not always defer to me, who was not swayed by wealth and connections. I had not expected *you*. So I ask again: when will you marry me?"

"As soon as possible. I'm a British national who lives abroad, but I'm also a US citizen who traveled into the UK on my US passport. I have to leave and then come in with permission to marry and live here. While I'm waiting in the States, I can close my accounts and pack what little of my stuff I want to ship here."

"I had not considered all you would leave behind as well, your family, your country."

"Emigrating is nowhere near equal to what you gave up."

Before Darcy could mention not needing to settle a score of sacrifices between them, Elizabeth went on. "Visas and emigration are nothing compared to a wedding spectacle. Some people spend thirty thousand dollars and are engaged for a year and a half."

Darcy could not understand how entering into a marriage became an expensive and prolonged event. "What man who is able and willing to marry is also agreeable to waiting over a year for his bride?"

"I bet you the first word out of my mother's mouth is 'pre-nup.'" She pulled out her phone. "Look, you can give notice at a registrar's office and be married twenty-eight days later." She came around to his chair, resting her hands on his shoulders, and gave him a pleading look. "How horrified would you be to just get married at a registrar's office?"

She appeared to be asking for some sacrifice on his part. All Darcy understood was that some weddings took place a year after the engagement, they were expensive, and Elizabeth preferred to be married privately as soon as she was allowed to do so.

"Dearest, I would rather marry a month from the day you have permission to remain in England than wait any longer."

Darcy saw the relieved expression on her face before she hugged him. She might have done more if the insistent chimes of his phone had not interrupted them. He would have ignored them, but she stepped out of his arms to clear the dishes and told him to answer.

When she returned, he was nearly finished typing his reply. "There's a sight: Fitzwilliam Darcy, texting at the dinner table. Who were you texting?"

"The young man who is renting Roland's house. He has been in my employ since I returned. He was employed by the solicitors in charge of Pemberley's trust to maintain the grounds, and he rents the house now that I hired him to do that as well as other tasks. He is a man who prefers to play video games since he has neglected his education, but he is willing to work because it means he can afford not to live with his mother in Lambton."

"He sounds like a terrible employee."

"He is no Young Henry. However, he is nineteen and has skills that I lack, and he has little curiosity in me. He drives a car, does not mind speaking on the phone, and can type faster than I can. He has yet to fail to do anything I ask or answer any question, although there is a fair amount of eye rolling. Despite that, I see his aptitude if only it were fostered."

Elizabeth walked into the parlor, and Darcy followed, still struck that there was nothing wrong in his sitting near to her, nothing wrong in his enjoying her affectionate glances and touches, nothing wrong in his being alone with her.

"Who else lives on Pemberley's land?"

"Three other tenants. One is the Taskers at Hill Close Farm. They have been here for eight generations as Pemberley passed through my sister's family. They have a three-generation long-term tenancy for three hundred acres for grazing sheep and haymaking. Another family has a dairy cattle farm also of respectable size, and a third a smaller holding with pasture land."

"Are you disappointed only three tenants are left?"

"No, the plan was to sell property steadily and invest elsewhere. Mr. Willers knew land needed to be sold to pay taxes and death duties, and that scheme was continued by Georgiana's grandson and great-granddaughter. Roland was instrumental in mapping out a small park near the house to remain whilst land, timber, and holdings were progressively sold. Young Henry devoted himself to Pemberley's land for his entire life. His name featured in Georgiana's letters, and his son was land manager after him. His descendants live in Lambton."

"This kid you've hired is Young Henry's great-whatever grandson?"

"Yes, but he does not know about Nine Ladies. He texted me to be certain I need him to drive me to meet with the District Council about Pemberley's improvements." Darcy set his jaw. "Since Pemberley is now a listed building, I must seek the approval of strangers on a committee."

Darcy's eyes fluttered closed when Elizabeth ran her fingers through his hair. "What's the problem?"

"To transfer the Pemberley properties out of the trust into private ownership again, an exit tax was due. Inheritance taxes due when Catherine Willers-Darcy died were paid by the estate, and the ten-year anniversary charges have also been paid by growth on the income from tenants, but I had to pay an exit charge on the money in the bank, the land, and the buildings now that the trust has ended." Darcy tilted back his head and rubbed his eyes.

"Are you telling me you're broke? I mean, insolvent?"

He gave her a long look. "I know what 'broke' means! Why do you think so many words developed their meanings only recently? And no, I am well enough considering I have, literally, appeared out of nowhere."

Elizabeth kissed his cheek. "I'd marry you if you were broke. Don't worry, I'll provide for you in the style to which you are accustomed."

Darcy knew he was being laughed at, but let it go. "I must find a way to afford to keep Pemberley, so until then, I dare not spend the remaining money. As for Monday's meeting, there is a procedure for obtaining consent to restore listed buildings. The house must be improved before it can be lived in, but I ought to delay the work required until Pemberley has means of earning a sustainable income."

Elizabeth scrutinized him. "You're worried, aren't you?"

"I have a duty of care to occupants and visitors that the house will not catch fire and that pipes will carry water, but it shall be some time before I can do what I must, and do so in accordance with the rules set forth by council members who presume to know Pemberley better than I do."

"You're frustrated you can't live in your own house, but you don't want to spend what money you have until you know how you'll afford to keep Pemberley?"

"Mr. Willers did well by me to bring us to this point." He felt grateful, even while he also felt overwhelmed. "I could use his advice."

"I can do it."

He looked at her in confusion. "Do what, my dear?"

The endearment transformed her considering eyes glossy. "I can pay for improvements to be done to move things along. I inherited eighty thousand dollars from my father."

Darcy shook his head, but Elizabeth went on excitedly. "That's enough to make Pemberley livable while we figure out how to keep it."

"Eventually, tenants' rents shall pay for what must be improved without my incurring debt." He was not certain as to Pemberley's future beyond that.

"Everything I have will be yours, and everything you have will be mine. Isn't that how this is supposed to work?"

He struggled with the idea that she would endow him with all of her worldly goods, not the other way around. "I am not quite thrown back to the starting point. I would not have you think I need your fortune or that we cannot marry before Pemberley is seen to. I was awaiting a passport before finding you, not Pemberley's restoration; that might never happen."

"I want to do this for us. Think of it like my dowry. The man gets my property, and in return, you save my family from having to maintain me." She laughed. "Seriously, *we* will figure out a way to keep Pemberley. In the meantime, I can afford to fix some lights and pipes. I love Pemberley too, you know."

It was time to accept help along with love, and be appreciative, no matter the cost to his pride. When he agreed, she kissed him again before chuckling. "By the way, brides don't promise to obey anymore, just so you know what you're getting in to."

"I am a sojourner in a strange land, dearest Elizabeth."

"This time isn't strange to you still, is it?"

"I possess a tool capable of accessing nearly all of human knowledge that connects people in a way unparalleled in history. However, your contemporaries use it to look at videos of cats and engage in quarrels with strangers. It is, indeed, a strange land."

With a laugh, she shifted and stretched her legs across his lap. Darcy's eyes widened, but he rested a hand on her knee. "And yet you came back, despite everything you hate about it."

"I would never use the word 'hate'; I even missed things about this time. But I came because *you* are here, and you are dear to me."

"I never dreamed you would come back. I imagined going back, even if I wasn't brave enough to do it, but I couldn't begin to imagine you coming here." Darcy's pulse was arrested by her tone and the look in her eye.

"I knew since last spring that I must come back, and as an avowed lover this time."

Elizabeth pressed closer and kissed him in so fervent a way as to warm the blood. Darcy gathered her tightly into his arms. He loved the feel of her quickening heartbeat against his chest, and was encouraged enough to give a slow caress over her hip. He held her crosswise on his lap with one hand on her back for support that left his other free to briefly caress what he had until now only imagined. Hot desire shot through him. He stroked his hand across her abdomen, along her hip, coming to rest again on her knee. She made a sound in her throat that told him he had best bring his hand back up and responded to him with a moan and swift, open-mouthed carnality.

They were breathless when she drew back. "Let's find a proper bed."

"But we have not even named the day when we will marry." Darcy knew his voice trembled.

Elizabeth's forehead creased. "You don't want to make love to me?"

He narrowed his eyes at the phrase in this context, but he understood the idiom. "I do, exceedingly. However freely engaged persons might act now, I cannot help but feel that you deserve better from me. It has been for many years that I felt the only woman I would take to bed would be my *wife*." Elizabeth gave him an appraising look. "Are you angry with me?"

"No. I love you, and I want to show you how much right now. You love me, and you want to show me how much by waiting." There was a mischievous look in her eye that he did not dislike. Elizabeth moved away and stood. "We should compromise if we're going to be happy in the meantime." Darcy blinked. "I'm going to go upstairs, take off my clothes, and think about you. You're welcome to watch. Or help."

Darcy was still nonplussed, with his heart pounding in his chest as though it were looking for a way out, when the shirt Elizabeth had been wearing was tossed down the stairs.

He went to the first step to pick up the still-warm shirt, and when he climbed the stairs, he saw Elizabeth had entered his room. He was still a gentleman, but he was nevertheless a sensible man who thought it practical to find the middle ground between the values of his former time and the one in which he would spend the rest of his days.

Elizabeth was standing next to the bed, stepping out of her trousers, when Darcy strode into the room and shut the door behind him.

March 25, 2013

When Elizabeth woke up, her nose was pressed against a chest that rose and fell to the steady rhythm of its owner's breathing. Today was only the third morning she had woken up this way, but she was happily becoming used to it.

She hadn't been surprised when Darcy followed her up the stairs that first evening, but she was startled by how unrestrained he'd been once the door closed. She had severely underestimated what Darcy was willing to do before they were married. After, when she confessed her amazement at how unguarded he was, Darcy chuckled softly. *"You thought I would be reserved? In bed, with you?"* She had never been so happy to be wrong.

Darcy looked tousled this morning; it was very attractive, and she was tempted to wake him. Instead, she gently untangled herself to get dressed. After she prepared coffee, she saw Charlotte had sent several texts over the last two days. She hadn't looked at her phone since Friday, and Charlotte's latest message implied she feared she was dead.

"If Darcy was going to kill me, he would've done it when we lived together," Elizabeth said after Charlotte answered.

"After the way Darcy looked at you, I figured you died by accident from a sex injury."

Elizabeth laughed into her coffee cup. "No, Darcy doesn't believe in premarital sex."

"Seriously? Your loss."

"He admits that he's not above temptation. Still, as eager as I am, we'll get married first. I'm okay with that."

"Sounds like you two found something to satis—wait, what?"

"Oh, did I forget to mention Darcy asked me to marry him?"

"Elizabeth! You said you weren't together. That you hadn't even kissed him!"

"That is true."

"Darcy *proposed* after you got out of the car, when you hadn't spoken for a year, having not ever dated, and you said yes?" Before Elizabeth could answer, Charlotte said, "I'm sorry. Congratulations, that's brilliant news."

"You went from 'you're crazy' to 'congratulations' in three seconds. Which one is it?"

"You supported me when I wanted to be a solo mum. My other friends, my coworkers, even my family, all took a long time to come around. Some never did. But you were with me every step of the way because you wanted me to be happy. So, best wishes on your happy news."

"Thank you. I don't blame you for being surprised."

"I can't say I'm surprised Darcy was in love with you. I only wonder why he waited until now to say anything."

"The timing wasn't right, but he loved me and wanted to marry me all along. How is Mary?"

"No deflecting! We're talking about *you*. Were you stunned Darcy asked you to marry him instead of dating first? How exactly are you trying to seduce this morally upright man? What *is* he willing to do?"

Elizabeth, who felt too much sensitivity to Darcy's sense of privacy to answer, was glad when she heard Darcy's tread on the stairs. "I can't give you those details right now."

"Is he there?"

Darcy crossed the room to the couch, and with a contented sigh, he pulled her into his arms until she lay across him. "Yes." He pressed a kiss against her temple, and Elizabeth reached for his hand to lace their fingers together.

"I won't keep you, but before you go, text me a pic of your engagement ring."

"Oh, I don't have a ring."

"He's letting you pick out your own? How progressive for someone who says no sex before marriage. You're not leaving next week now, are you?"

"I'll have to, but I'll come back as soon as possible."

"Brilliant news, congratulations! Text me later with details, and I want a ring pic!"

Elizabeth hung up and settled further into Darcy's arms. "The engagement news is out, Mr. Darcy. No reneging now."

"Do you think you might call me something else?"

She knew what a familiarity it was for him, to call someone by their first name. "I can call you 'Fitzwilliam.' Should I not call you that in front of anyone else?"

"I wouldn't mind if you did." Elizabeth suspected he might. Darcy combed his fingers in her hair. "What ring was Charlotte speaking of? I could not help but overhear."

"Nothing." She felt him looking at her. "Most men present a ring when they propose, but some women choose their own after. A diamond ring on your left hand is a symbol of the agreement that you're about to get married, but most women wear it with their wedding band after they're married."

The fingers running through her hair stopped. "And the world would expect you to have one, if not now, then soon?"

"It's just a custom." She sat up to look at him; he looked pensive. "A diamond engagement ring is an advertising campaign invention. I don't need one."

Darcy shifted her off of him and climbed the stairs without a word; Elizabeth's stomach dropped. The rest of his life would be filled with moments where he realized how out of place he was. There were so many conventions that would catch him by surprise, to say nothing of the larger matters of politics, science, history, and even entertainment that would constantly show him how uninformed he was.

How can someone used to being one of the smartest and most respected men in the room stand it?

Elizabeth hurried upstairs to console Darcy and nearly ran into him as he came out from their room. "Don't worry about it, please? There will always be experiences we're only going to be able to partially share."

"Do you suppose I feel embarrassed or discouraged because I did not know a woman in 2013 expects an engagement ring?"

"I did . . . until you said that." Darcy's expression was neutral. "The last thing you can stand is to be ridiculed. What happens when everyone knows something you don't, and the things we can't completely share become too hard—"

"You fear I might leave you? You judge me harshly." His eyes darkened, and his lips formed an angry line. Before she could speak, he sighed. "I cannot fault you, because the fear that you would resent my time and leave me is the greatest reason for not bringing you to the past."

"I love you too much for you to be unhappy here."

"I have my home, and will eventually have a profession worth doing. I have the hope of a family. I *want* to be here, I want to live here and *now*, with you. Petty differences in our conventions will never supersede what I want. What I want, with a fierce and consuming passion, is *you*, my dearest, loveliest Elizabeth."

His voice was rough, and there was longing in it. It brought the soreness of unshed tears to her throat. "There's nothing I want more than you." He drew her close enough to press a soft, lingering kiss on her mouth. "Darcy, why did—"

"Darcy?" he asked in a low voice.

"Fitzwilliam," she tested the name. His brown eyes darkened even more. He leaned in close and pressed his cheek against hers.

"Thank you." His warm breath against her ear thrilled her, and her question escaped her while he placed slow kisses along her neck. Her hands skimmed under his shirt, but when she tugged it higher, Darcy stopped and rested his chin on the top of her head.

"You shall have plenty of time to captivate me, but I need your opinion now. Let me get dressed and we can walk to the house. Since you cannot stay on your current visa, we have a short time left. I must show you something."

An hour later found them at Pemberley, and Darcy led her up a back staircase she had never used to the third floor.

"Every space of this floor now has boxes and trunks stored in them, and they are filled like this one." Darcy lifted a box off of a pile and placed it before her, raising the lid as he spoke. "I cannot understand why these were left, but perhaps you can."

Inside was a gown with wide sleeves and a high neckline. Even without taking it out of its box, Elizabeth noticed it had a fuller skirt than she had worn in 1811, and there were hideous ruffles all over it. "It's an ugly Victorian gown that looks like it walked off the set of *Gone with the Wind*." Darcy frowned. "An American movie set in the 1860s."

"The floor is filled with my sister's gowns, and each is numbered to correspond with a notebook entry that says the year it was made and the materials used. There is one morning gown and one full-dress gown from 1813 until 1877. For some reason, two gowns from each year of my sister's life were preserved and their facts recorded." Darcy shut the lid. "And Catherine Willers-Darcy must have known of it, because from the time she first managed Pemberley on her own, until she died in 1984, she saved clothes in the same manner."

"Pemberley's entire third floor is filled with clothes Georgiana and her great-granddaughter wore in the nineteenth and twentieth centuries?"

"I cannot understand it. Clothing was torn apart to make other items; they were dyed and reused, sold, passed on to a lady's maid, used for rags. I read of austere conditions during wartime, and still Catherine Willers-Darcy preserved clothing. She may have been inspired by what she discovered of Georgiana's, but why did Reynolds tell Georgiana to do this?"

"You're certain it was Reynolds's doing?"

"Reynolds did not, at first, approve of my plan, and refused to help despite all she knew of England in the twentieth century."

"You weren't just her employer; you and Georgiana were the children she never had. Of course she didn't want the closest thing she had to a son to leave."

Darcy swallowed thickly. "I realized that far too late. I always valued her, but I did not understand what we meant to her. Reynolds was so private, but I am ashamed I never knew how much she loved us."

He was lost in silent self-reproach for so long that Elizabeth wrapped her arms around him. After a moment, he grasped a notebook atop another pile. "One of Georgiana's early letters mentioned Reynolds's recommendation and directed me to this floor."

Elizabeth took the notebook and, after flipping through pages of box numbers, dates, and descriptions, opened to the brief letter on the first page.

> *My dear Master Fitzwilliam,*
>
> *Although I do not wholly approve of your plan, I desire for your happiness above all things, and suggested that Miss Darcy leave this selection for Pemberley's benefit. What has negligible value now will be of wider interest in the years to come and, therefore, will be of use to you in establishing Pemberley's purpose in the future.*
>
> *May you find who you are looking for, and may she bring you joy.*
>
> *I remain your devoted servant,*
>
> *S. Reynolds*

Pithy but heartfelt, and a little inscrutable, not unlike the woman herself. "She wanted to help you find your place here after all. It's brilliant."

"What benefit could gowns have for Pemberley? Why did Reynolds encourage my sister to keep her clothes?"

"Fitzwilliam, this is a treasure trove! You need to hire a conservator to decide how to preserve them. You probably need a costume historian too, to appraise them."

"Reynolds wanted me to have a collection to sell, like the coins she gave you to pay for my antibiotics? Who would want hundreds-of-years-old gowns?"

He had no idea of their potential value. "The Victoria and Albert or the Met would buy these in a heartbeat. A collection of dresses from two women from the same family, spanning their lifetimes, nearly one hundred years apart? The exhibit practically makes itself."

"Who?"

"Museums! People would pay to see them, not to mention costumers would love to get their hands on them to learn how they were constructed." Elizabeth sneezed. "Can we talk downstairs?"

Even in its disused state, Elizabeth thought the library was the coziest room in Pemberley. She pulled a dustcover off of a chair near a window and sat to watch Darcy pace. He was not pacing with anxious energy, but slowly, with arms folded and his head bowed.

"Reynolds knew agricultural or mining rents would not sustain Pemberley in this century. You think she wished me to sell those gowns and invest that money to keep Pemberley?"

"Of course. You could sell the lot for hundreds of thousands of pounds. Maybe there's a rare couture find in their collection? Or maybe auction the ones in the best condition if that brings a better price?"

"Even if what you say is accurate, how does that help Pemberley in the long run?"

"Reynolds knew they'd have value to collectors and that we could use the funds from their sale at Pemberley."

"How is a one-time investment going to help us keep Pemberley a home for the long term?" Darcy stopped pacing and stood before her. "Reynolds wrote that they would be for Pemberley's benefit. If the clothes have value, not only monetary but educational or cultural value, they ought to remain here. Why sell them if I could display them here? If you, and Reynolds, believe anyone would want to see this collection of old gowns, then they belong at Pemberley."

Elizabeth squinted. "You want to turn Pemberley into a museum? You really want tourists traipsing through your house?"

"People regularly applied to see Pemberley. Reynolds collected gratuities and conducted them through the house. When Fitzwilliam first saw you, we thought you were a lost tourist. People in my time traveled to the seaside, went on trips in the Lake District, and visited stately homes like Pemberley. They were open to visitors who only needed to ask to see the principal rooms."

"They paid a tip to the housekeeper, and they got to walk through someone's house?"

"Why is that strange? You toured Haddon Hall. It is privately owned, yet people view the house although the family lives there."

"Reynolds thought you could keep Pemberley if people came to see the clothes! The clothes would draw people, and even the architecture and whatever furniture we can salvage and the portraits in the gallery are still here too. But instead of leaving the housekeeper a tip, you could charge a twenty-pound-per-person ticket fee."

Darcy frowned and looked around the library. "But could Pemberley survive as a museum and pleasure grounds for the use of the people? We had fewer than fifty visitors a year."

Elizabeth laughed. "I think thousands will visit! Pemberley's been dormant since the 1980s, and even with the updates, it still looks like a Regency-era home, and it will be even better when it's restored." Elizabeth pursed her lips. "There have to be hundreds of gowns. Do we have space to display them *and* live here?"

Now Darcy grinned. "The ground floor has two drawing rooms, a dining room, a billiard room, the library, the oak parlor, and my study. Not to mention the servants' hall and offices. There are five principal bedrooms on the first floor, three dressing rooms, and four secondary bedrooms, six smaller rooms, and now four bathrooms and four water closets." He pulled her to her feet, gripping her hands tightly. "What need have we of a twenty-six-by-forty-foot ballroom in 2013? I think we shall have enough space, my dear!"

Her mind raced over the idea of mannequins displayed in different rooms. "You could showcase two centuries of the fashion of Pemberley's women caretakers. The exhibit can compare the two women, or show how styles changed over a lifetime, or compare daywear versus evening wear. The possibilities are endless."

"Scholars would study clothes that have been packed away for more than a century?"

"Absolutely! People will want to learn how they were constructed, what fabrics and dyes were used. You could have events catered for people who make period clothing with presentations and lectures. This is how we keep Pemberley. Reynolds knew Pemberley couldn't operate based on agricultural rents, so she made sure there was a reason for people to want to visit it."

"She showed astonishing forethought, and it demonstrates how much she loved my sister and me without expecting anything in return. To say nothing of how grateful I must be to my sister and her family's stewardship that allowed me to come back the way that I did."

Elizabeth wrapped her arms around him and rested her head against his chest. "I think a good way we can thank them is to make sure that Pemberley is still here in another two hundred years."

He kissed the top of her head. "I have a gift for you, although I had not planned to give it to you until we married. Had we become engaged in 1813, I would have bought you a new carriage, but I see now that this is closer to the current etiquette."

He brought out a gold ring with a split shank, with a round diamond surrounded by a rainbow of six smaller round stones. It was unlike anything she had ever seen, and she softly asked where he found something so pretty.

"Acrostic jewelry had become fashionable among both open and secret lovers before I left. I wanted something made for you that was distinctive of the time I was leaving." Elizabeth held out her hand, and Darcy slipped it on.

"This is why you left the room after my call with Charlotte." She felt foolish, but had to ask. "What is acrostic jewelry?"

To her surprise, Darcy blushed and lowered his eyes. "It's a bit . . . sentimental, I suppose. The first letter of each gem spells out a message or term of endearment."

The diamond in the center of the cluster was obviously the beginning, but it took her a full ten seconds to figure out the order and what diamond, emerald, amethyst, ruby, another emerald, sapphire, and topaz spelled. "It spells 'dearest.' You had a ring made for me that announces to everyone that I am dear to you? You romantic soul." *Who else in the world, living or dead, knew that Fitzwilliam Darcy was a passionate man?*

"It can stand the place for a modern engagement ring for the present."

"I'm not taking it off until a wedding band is about to go on next to it!" This came out louder than she intended but, thankfully, Darcy interpreted her determination and ardent gaze properly.

He came full-length against her and, with one hand on her hip and the other hand in her hair, drove her backward to press her against the wall. She set her mouth on his and opened to the pressure of his tongue, making a low noise of contentment when his hand moved underneath her shirt. She slipped her arms behind her back and unclasped her bra. Her moans grew louder when his warm hand swept over her breast, and she strained in anticipation. Darcy slowly traced a finger around the curve, then cupped it roughly as he rocked his hips against hers.

When he drew back to kiss along her neck, Elizabeth thought of all they had done so far and what she had to look forward to, and made a faint, longing sound. Darcy's teeth grazed the sensitive skin behind her ear, but even though she panted the words "don't stop," that was what he did, with a shuddering sigh of frustration.

"You deserve better from your future husband, and I cannot imagine you would prefer our first time to be a flyer against a wall in the library."

She didn't know what a flyer was, but the latter part sounded perfectly fine. "I think I do."

Darcy had his hands on her hips, gripping them firmly while keeping a few inches between them. He ran a finger along the waistband of her jeans with a curious expression on his face.

"You're trying to figure out how to take trousers off a woman to even make that work, aren't you? This would be easier in a skirt. Say the word, and the jeans are gone."

"This is why courting couples are never left alone."

"Are there any made-up beds left in Pemberley's bedrooms? Are you tempted to go look for one?" She was still panting heavily as she refastened her bra.

"You know very well that nothing in all the world and time tempts me more than you."

She watched him force stillness on himself, limb by limb, muscle by muscle, until he was in a fit state to be in public. "You might be the most determined person I've ever known, but I wonder if we're going to make it until we're married."

"That is becoming less likely with every passing hour."

"Would that be so bad?"

"It bothers me less with every passing hour."

CHAPTER THIRTY-THREE

March 30, 2013

Frank was going on, with the enthusiasm of a proud parent, to anyone who would listen about how United had now set a record by winning twenty-five out of their opening thirty games. Darcy gestured to the bartender to bring him another pint, when his friend clapped him on the shoulder.

"I said every round was on me, Romeo. You said you were just friends when I called her the missus, but who was right?"

Darcy smiled. "You were wrong at the time, and you're still wrong, for another two months." Silently, he cursed passport processing times, notice of marriage wait times, and residency requirements that prevented him from marrying Elizabeth immediately.

"I'm glad you got yourselves sorted. Did you get your leg over?"

Although he had not heard this particular idiom, Frank had not stopped asking some variant of this impertinent teasing question since Darcy told him Elizabeth had agreed to marry him. "Did Gwen give you the names of her museum and conservator colleagues?"

Frank huffed and texted him with a dexterity that Darcy envied.

"Done. Godspeed in turning your new mansion into the premier stately home and fashion museum in England."

"'Tis not new," Darcy muttered over the rim of his glass.

"What was that?"

"Nothing. Have you reconsidered my offer? It'd be only fair."

"I told you, no. I'll teach you to drive, but there's no way you're getting me on a horse. So, where's the missus—I mean, fiancée—today?"

He had learned this French word replaced *betrothed*. "She's speaking to an immigration advisor since, although she was born here, she isn't a permanent resident and she traveled to England on her American passport. Although she applied for a British passport already, her tourist visa will expire before it will be processed, so she'll leave Monday, then return when she has the right to remain."

"Other than your being a settled citizen and proving that you've met her, don't you have to prove you can support her to get a marriage visa, Mister 'must-have-lived-in-Grand-Cayman-to-avoid-paying-taxes-until-now'? You don't have a museum worth touring yet, let alone a job."

"Since she was born here, once she has a British passport and enters the country with it, it ought not to matter. Pemberley earned a small income from rent while it was in trust, in any event."

"You mean thirty years of rent income was sitting in the bank when you inherited Pemberley, plus whatever funds were already there?" Darcy nodded. "But most of it went to pay inheritance taxes and capital gains?" Darcy nodded again. "How much is left?"

"Including Elizabeth's investment? After the taxes were paid, we are left with two hundred thousand pounds."

"Holy fuck, Darcy!" Frank's pint glass slammed on the table. "Why am *I* buying the beer?"

"That is not enough to live on or to maintain Pemberley forever. But, more importantly, you are buying the beer because we're celebrating *my* engagement."

"Then have you had sex with Elizabeth yet?"

"Why do you keep asking?"

"Because it bothers you, and it amuses me to bother you."

"No. There, are you satisfied?"

"I can't imagine you are. Why wait?"

"Aside from the titles of *husband* and *wife* holding significant value to me? Because I can't even set a date for my wedding yet, and no one wants a child born early."

"There are pills for that, and Elizabeth isn't stupid and neither are you, despite how long it took you two to get together. Do you think Gwen and I had no children by luck?"

"What?" Darcy was befuddled, but Frank had seen a stranger in a United jersey from across the taproom and decided to buy him a drink.

"Lizzy, why are you calling?"

So much maternal warmth. "Hi, Mom. How are you?"

"Fine. What is it?"

"I have good news, and I wanted to share it with you." She had never even mentioned a guy she liked to her mother. "When I was in England after my father died, I met someone special. We weren't together then, but things are different now . . ."

"Is it the doctor with the baby? Are you telling me you're gay?"

"I'm not coming out! I met a *man*. We were close friends, and even then we both wanted more, but it, um, it wasn't a good time. I saw him again when I came to visit Charlotte . . . and he asked me to marry him." A smile stretched her lips. "I love him, and I said yes."

The silence extended so long that Elizabeth lifted her phone from her ear to see if they were still connected.

"Mom? I'm getting married, in two months." She counted to pass the time her mother was silent; when she got to ten, she tried again. "I know it sounds sudden, but we've known each other a long time and he's perfect for me. His name is—"

"I don't care! He's nothing to me, and I can guarantee, sooner than you think, you'll be nothing to him. What the hell are you thinking?"

"I'm thinking I'm twenty-six and can make my own decisions, and I'm marrying him because we love each other."

"Are you pregnant?"

Elizabeth swore under her breath. "Thanks for assuming that's why a man would ask me to marry him."

"That's the only reason why, after everything I've taught you and how we struggled after your father left, you might consider saying yes. A casual relationship is one thing, but why *marriage*?"

"Because marriage and commitment have real meaning to both of us. And being without him after I came back from England was why I was so unhappy."

"You were unhappy?"

Elizabeth sighed in frustration. "Yes, Mom! He's clever, and strong-minded, and handsome, and loyal. You can't even begin to understand how much he loves me."

Another long silence. "Is this man coming with you on Monday? I don't need to meet this person."

"You make it sound like it's a punishment to meet my future husband! No, I'm coming back alone, but as soon as my British passport is processed, I'm on a plane back to England for good."

"*You're* the one moving? Are you even qualified to work as an accountant in England? Please tell me you haven't combined bank accounts; that will make things messier when he leaves you."

"I know you think you're helping, but you have to stop. He's not like my father was. I am getting married. His name is Fitzwilliam Darcy, he is twenty-nine, he's never been married, he owns a house here that we are working together to turn into something amazing. If you want to know more, I'll be at Jane's until my passport is processed. Good night."

Elizabeth was still struggling to not cry when Darcy came home. He marched into the parlor, reading something on his phone. "Elizabeth, why did you neglect to—" He stopped short at the sight of her. "What is the matter?" Before she answered, she noticed how modern he acted. No bowing, no asking after her health; he just came into the room and talked to her.

"Nothing that should've surprised me." *When was the last time my mother said "I love you"?* She stood to kiss him hello. "It's a good thing we're having a small wedding because the mother of the bride won't be coming." She threw him a half smile as she fell back onto the sofa.

A line appeared between his brows. "Your mother responded to our engagement as you feared?"

"I never thought she would be that bad. She thinks because my father abandoned her that every man is like him. She didn't even want to know your name!"

"Jane was happy for you when you told her."

"That's because Jane wants to get along with everyone. When she talks to my mother, I'd bet Jane agrees with her that I'm making a mistake. Jane's support is very superficial. My family is awful!" It was little wonder she'd needed to hear Darcy say the words "I love you" before she could believe it.

Darcy sat next to her and held her hand, his thumb stroking the side of her wrist. "My entire family is gone and has been for two hundred years."

Elizabeth sank her head back. "I'm sorry. I sound horrible."

"I mean that we both are without our families, and I, for one, find solace in the new connections I have made and the family I will have with you."

"Ever since I was young, I wanted my own family so I could have the relationships that my parents and sister never gave me."

"Although we may be without family, I suspect that with your lively and social nature you will have us surrounded by friends who will force me into constant exertion."

"What a punishment. Maybe then you'll meet someone who wants to fence or ride and not just watch soccer." She rested her head against his shoulder. "Did Frank give you the names of the Museum Association people?"

Darcy, with less slowness than she expected, forwarded her an email. "There are enough names for you to get started with."

"Me?" Elizabeth looked up from the list of conservators, restorers, project managers, and professional associations Gwen had suggested. "Why me?"

"I can manage three tenants, their land, and their rent, and since I know Pemberley better than anyone, I can oversee its restoration. However, I doubt I could ask the right questions to begin this museum process."

"I think you've proven that you can do anything."

He exhaled a soft laugh. "I know nothing about what would make one qualified to work in a museum or what a business needs in this century to be profitable. You naturally know more than I, and you will be able to learn all that you need faster than I could. I would rather leave this in your capable hands."

"You want me to be in charge of hiring the people who will open Pemberley to the public and managing them?"

"I will not leave it to you alone forever, my dear, but the man who two days ago confused a calculator and a computer is not qualified. You are the one who thought this was where Pemberley's future would lie. I need you, and I have no doubt in your abilities."

She could have told him how much his faith in her meant to her, but decided to tease instead. "So I get to be mistress of Pemberley after all?"

"In some manner."

"Can I get that belt of keys and tools thing Reynolds had?"

"No."

"Do we still have to lock up the tea? Do I get to be in charge of the tea key?"

His eyes narrowed slightly and crinkled into laugh lines at the outer corners. "No." Darcy walked toward the stairs, and Elizabeth followed.

"Mr. Darcy, I need pin money to go shopping. I need to practice the quadrille if the mistress of Pemberley is going to host a ball."

"Are you quite finished?"

"For now." She leaned against the door frame as Darcy kicked off his shoes without untying the laces and charged his phone. "I'll call the people Gwen recommended and start learning, but I'll schedule meetings for after I get back from the States. The advisor I spoke to said since I was born here, it won't take long. They took my biometrics and have the paperwork. If I wasn't worried about you falling under scrutiny, I would try to stay. But since we're doing things by the book, it should take a month."

Darcy sighed and sat on the edge of the bed. She crossed the room to him, and he wrapped his arms around her waist. "Fitzwilliam, it's not as bad as a year and a half apart with no hope of ever seeing you again." He held her tighter. "Besides, with me on the other side of the world, you might read Georgiana's diaries. Think of all the time that's been wasted by me trying to get you into bed."

"You know I would rather have you here." He pulled back to look into her eyes. "Speaking of your attempts to seduce me, why did you neglect to mention that for fifty years a drug to prevent conception has been available to any woman who wants it?"

If she ever made a list of the things Fitzwilliam Darcy was least likely to say, that would be at the top. "I guess I took it for granted. Besides, you wanted to wait until we're married."

"I am astonished that we can decide precisely when we wish to have children. It does explain, to someone born in 1784, the promiscuity of this century."

"You're thinking of the nightclub and Missy King? That's a little harsh, but I get your point. I remember you saying something about not wanting to defile you or me with wandering lust. What does it matter that I didn't think to mention contraception?"

"I said that when I thought I would never see you again, let alone be able to marry you. Moreover, how could I have done that and left you, *and* possibly my child?"

It took the length of one heartbeat for her to process his implication. She shook her head. "I'm happy to wait. I know it's important to you. But I will continue my shameless attempts to defile you with my not-at-all-wandering lust."

"Good," he said, heat deep in his eyes.

May 6, 2013

Being without Elizabeth for thirty-five days and counting was harder to bear than when Darcy assumed he would have to live without her forever, and still worse than the months when he questioned if his elaborate scheme to return to the twenty-first century would succeed.

At least I have steady occupation; Elizabeth is awaiting news that she has permission to remain in England. She has only been able to make phone calls to set matters into motion at Pemberley that she cannot complete until she returns. The interval of waiting and doing little is distressingly long for her.

Darcy walked to the house to oversee the day's efforts. For two weeks, refurbishment work had started modernizing the electrical wires, the heating and cooling, and the plumbing. He would not admit it to Elizabeth, but her absence did leave him more time to contract Pemberley's initial renovations, become better acquainted with his tenants, discuss Pemberley's joining the Historic Houses Association, and finish reading Georgiana's diaries.

The nervous girl of sixteen had become a confident woman. However, Georgiana's wondering over what happened to him cast an air of sadness over her. Expositions on Pemberley's new investments were clouded by worries if he had found the house still standing. Her hopes that Mr. Willers might look on her as more than her employer, if she should speak first, were shaded by wondering if Fitzwilliam had found Elizabeth. Georgiana's amusing anecdotes about her son's scrapes, and her grandson's similarities to her own little boy paralleled her musings on if he had children, or if he was still alive.

Woven throughout her letters was news about loved ones Darcy had left behind. Fitzwilliam never resigned his commission even though he eventually inherited Rosings from their cousin, often joking that the house could have been Darcy's if he had married Anne. Reynolds refused to be pensioned off; she said that wherever Mr. Darcy was, he would not want her to be idle. His friend Bingley wrote to Georgiana every year hoping to hear news of his old friend, long after the stack of letters Darcy left for him ceased to arrive.

Everyone I left lived full lives with families and meaningful employment, but the greatest cloud over those lives was apprehension over me.

"Mr. Darcy!"

Mr. Tasker from Hill Close Farm got out of his car to join him in the quarter-mile walk the rest of the way to the house.

Darcy held out his hand, irritating habit that it was. "Thank you for coming."

"I was curious about what you found, and I've never been in the house. My father used to talk about meeting with Ms. Willers-Darcy in the seventies. As a kid, I used to imagine her as a Miss Havisham, but I think her dedication is the reason Pemberley is in as good a condition as you found it."

"I understand she rarely left Pemberley in the last twenty years of her life, but kept a steady correspondence with the girls whose school occupied the house during the war."

They had to raise their voices to be heard over the work being done near the courtyard. Elizabeth told him to find a place for the textile staff to catalog and evaluate gowns, so he hired another crew to convert the old brew house into a conservation space. It was not until he and Mr. Tasker were inside and past the noisy workers on ladders near the main staircase that they were able to speak in a normal voice.

"This was the steward's office. There was a fire at some point and many records were lost, but I found lease agreements between your family and mine dating to the end of the nineteenth century. After what you mentioned about your daughter's curiosity, I thought she might like to see them."

"Yeah, my kids are interested in family history stuff." He carefully turned the pages. "This one is from 1809."

Darcy saw his own signature next to Davy Tasker's. The agreement had been drawn up in Mr. Willers's precise hand. Darcy stepped away to give Mr. Tasker privacy to view the records, and looked around the room that had once been Mr. Willers's domain. He felt Mr. Willers's presence here more than he did in his steward's former house. It made Darcy reflect on how much he owed to the loyalty of others, and how deeply those people worried for him after he was gone.

"May I borrow these to show my daughter? She's got one of those digital scanners; she'll be careful with them."

Darcy did not know what he meant, although he agreed. "Is your daughter still intent on establishing the home farm at Pemberley?"

"She doesn't want to take over my lease—my older son will—but she's a teacher so she loves the idea of having ponies for kids and tractor rides and school group visits. You won't find anyone better suited."

Darcy thought that showing children how animals lived in a farmyard and allowing them to handle small animals was preposterous, but Elizabeth said it would draw families to Pemberley. They walked to the front of the house and, when they passed the mahogany staircase, Mr. Tasker raised his eyes to take in the space and the workers bustling around them.

"Before I head out, I wanted to tell you that the community is excited by the changes you've brought. It's good for us to have a family at Pemberley. And no one in the neighborhood is going to say no to the tourism money after you open."

"Thank you. The Darcy family has been here a long time, and its legacy is important to me."

"My family's been at Pemberley for a lot longer than *you* have." He laughed, and Darcy refrained from shrugging. "But we're glad you're here now."

"So am I," a soft voice called from behind them.

Both men turned; Elizabeth was smiling in a self-satisfied way. Before Darcy could do more than say her name in delighted astonishment, she came forward, laughing. "I got my passport two days ago and hopped on a plane last night. I wanted to surprise you."

Elizabeth, ignoring the curious looks of his tenant and a dozen workers, came to his side, likely expecting a warmer welcome than he was prepared to give in public. She grinned like a Cheshire cat. She knew he wanted to kiss her, and she saw his frustration because he would not do so in front of anyone else.

"Elizabeth, may I present James Tasker of Hill Close Farm? Mr. Tasker, my fiancée, Miss Bennet."

They shook hands and Mr. Tasker offered his congratulations, and there followed a lengthy chat on where she was from, how was her flight, when was the wedding, what did Hill Close produce, and further inanities. During their conversation, Elizabeth held a gentle grip on his hand and cast him bold looks. The waiting of the past thirty-five days was nothing compared to this.

"Mr. Darcy?" Elizabeth looked at him with mock deference. "If you're finished with Mr. Tasker, maybe we can book an appointment at Bakewell's registry office to give notice of our marriage?"

The workers resumed climbing ladders and tramping past them, and Mr. Tasker left before Darcy felt able to speak. "I missed you exceedingly."

"I missed you." She gave him a lingering look that emboldened him. "I'm tired from traveling and should go to bed. But you're probably busy at Pemberley. You'd rather show me the work that's been done rather than take me home right now?"

No one in his life had ever been so sportive with him. "Certainly; let's start in the library."

Her expression fell. "Oh, okay." Darcy turned away to hide a smile. "I thought we weren't doing anything in the library since that will be one of the rooms kept private for us."

"It is." He gave her a wink, and Elizabeth's expression brightened beautifully.

May 22, 2013

"Your foreman said structurally Pemberley was better than he expected, but they'll wait to start on the first floor until we decide which rooms will be public. I want whoever will be the museum director to help with that."

She looked at Darcy, who was poring over faded yellow documents. He had been nodding along in agreement until now. "Let's get married in two years instead of two weeks, okay?" Silence. "I told the foreman that he would do as well as you, so I'm going to marry him instead."

Darcy looked up. "Did you speak to me?"

Elizabeth swallowed the desire to tease. "It's a good thing my self-esteem is pretty high, because you've ignored everything I said."

"I am sorry; what did you say?"

"I'm more interested in why you keep going over your sister's letters."

"Georgiana was a great success at Pemberley, and she had a loving family. I know she was proud of herself and proud of what she had done with Pemberley. But I fear she was hippish."

"I don't know what that means."

Darcy looked up as if the definition was printed on the ceiling. "A kind of melancholy. Often low-spirited."

"Depressed? You think she was a little depressed? Well, her only child died when he was in his twenties, and her husband, who was likely her closest friend and confidant even before they married, died not long after. Anyone would be low-spirited then."

"But it is pervasive from her first letter in 1813 until her last." Darcy tapped the cover a few times while he stared at it. "I do not feel guilty about leaving the nineteenth century. It was the right choice for us, and Georgiana willingly took on Pemberley, but I regret how she worried."

"If you both didn't know she had the confidence and ability to manage Pemberley, you would never have left, not even for me."

"She flourished, and so did Pemberley. I think she was low-spirited because she never knew what happened to me. I disappeared in front of her eyes, and fanciful imaginings of my future were not enough to counter that no one knew for certain what happened to me."

Elizabeth rested a hand on his arm. "Why don't you go to see her?"

"I told you, I don't regret leaving—"

"I don't mean go forever, but there's no reason you can't take a three-month holiday."

"No, I won't. I am committed to *this* life, our happy life. And everything was carefully put in place to make this happen for us. I would never risk changing Georgiana's life or ours by going back and forth. What if seeing me again changed the way she viewed her role and she lost her confidence? Or what if, by my spending three months there, she made a different choice that undid some action that led to me being able to live the life I have here?"

"One visit might be enough to change Georgiana's outlook for the rest of her life."

He shook his head. "It would be reckless and selfish. These are peoples' lives I would be meddling with, and I did enough of that to get here."

"You're sure?"

"I have no doubt. It is equally as possible that I ruin her future by accident as it is that I bring her contentment. I won't abuse the strange power in Nine Ladies any more than I already have." Darcy noticed her frown and put his arms around her. "You need not worry for me. I am not the sort of person to be made a fuss with and not to make a fuss myself over a trifling matter."

She was happy to fuss over him, and she didn't think it was trifling, but Elizabeth kept her silence. He was always quick in both forming his resolutions and acting on them. But if he wouldn't do something about Georgiana, she would.

June 5, 2013

Darcy paced outside the small Council Chamber in the Bakewell Town Hall, needlessly shooting out his sleeves, tugging on his cuffs, and adjusting the knot in his tie.

"Just be still!" Frank was seated cross-legged with his hands behind his head.

Darcy looked toward the door, sighed, turned on his heel, and walked back down the corridor.

"Why the hell are you pacing?" Frank would not stop talking. "Relax! This is what you've been waiting for."

At long last, Elizabeth walked briskly into the corridor, Gwen and Charlotte behind her, wearing a dress he could not describe in any terms other than "pretty," "short," and "white," flowers he could not describe further than "purple," and the most extraordinary smile on her face that he had ever seen. From far away, he heard Frank mutter, "He looks relaxed now."

After the porter who carried their luggage into their London hotel room left, Darcy tore off his coat and tie and shared a silent look with his new wife. He had never been so bewitched, so impressed, so fascinated by a woman as he was by her. Her confident, expectant expression made his heart race as he walked closer.

He slid his hand into her hair and pulled her against him. "God, you tempt me."

Elizabeth dragged him down until his mouth was on hers, and she plucked open his shirt buttons before tearing it off his shoulders and running her hands across his skin. He nipped at her lower lip with his teeth, and then his tongue met hers until a low hum of pleasure sounded in her throat.

"I looked up what a flyer meant," she said with a knowing smile, slipping off the underwear he often wished she wouldn't wear.

In one swift motion, Darcy lifted her off her feet and backed her against the wall while she wrapped her legs around him. She quickly unfastened his trousers, and then unzipped her wedding gown while he trailed his lips down from her neck, pushing her further up the wall until he captured her breast in his mouth, sucking hard. She moaned his name and let her head drop back after he gathered up her skirts to reach underneath them.

He would have slowed down but Elizabeth began to beg, grinding against him and digging her nails into his shoulder. She wanted him this way, and his blood was on fire at the sounds his wife made; even as her head thumped against the wall when his pace quickened, she pleaded with him to take her harder and faster. Darcy pressed his mouth to hers as her volume increased along with the force of his thrusts, but anyone on the same floor would have heard both of their poorly stifled moans.

They laughed shyly afterward, sharing amused smiles and kisses while untangling themselves and helping each other out of the rest of their clothes before making their way to the bed. The second time was full of whispered endearments and more gentle touches. Darcy held her arms above her head, their fingers tightly laced, and he had loved her with slow thoroughness.

"Did you select this hotel on Brook Street because it existed in 1812?" he asked as he ran his fingers through her hair as she rested her head on his chest. "The townhouse my family leased for generations is down the street." Darcy thought this wedding trip was a waste of time, but the idea of it meant something to Elizabeth.

"I did want something familiar, but who wouldn't want to spend their honeymoon in luxury?"

The ceremony had been short and sincere, yet their small audience thought the occasion was not properly concluded until they watched him kiss Elizabeth. The event had elements he little understood, from kissing his wife in public to her having to put a sixpence in her shoe. The important part, for him, was that Miss Elizabeth Bennet was now Mrs. Darcy.

Thinking of the ceremony reminded Darcy of something. "Who is Audrey Hepburn?"

She sat up in bed to look at him. "She was a British actress; a style and film icon. Why?"

"Before we left Gwen said, 'Doesn't Mrs. Darcy look like Audrey Hepburn in *Funny Face* in that dress?' By the tears in her eyes and Frank's lack of sarcasm, I took it to be a compliment."

Elizabeth turned pink and looked at the gown that was crumpled on the floor near to the door. "If I'm going to wear it when we host a belated reception at Pemberley, I should make sure it doesn't get wrinkled."

"Are you going to add your own clothes to Pemberley's collection? Your wedding gown could be the first."

"Me? The clothing is a Darcy thing."

"Yes it is, Mrs. Darcy." Darcy stared at her a long moment to give Elizabeth the opportunity to remember her new name.

"You think I should?"

He absently assented, distracted by the sheet slipping off of her bare shoulder. She raised her eyebrow and settled into his arms with a grin.

"Fitzwilliam, now that you've experienced so many things in 2013, what's the *best* part about living in this century?" Elizabeth's foot was slowly rubbing along his calf.

"I could not say for certain." Darcy knew very well what she wanted him to say.

She lightly kissed along his jaw. "No ideas? No chamber pot under your bed, maybe? Smooth tarmac roads? Shoes specifically designed for the left and right foot?"

"There are too many. This century is unrecognizable from the one I spent my formative years in."

"You can't name the absolute best thing about living in 2013?" Her hand stopped tracing along his chest and slid lower.

"If I had to choose one thing, dearest Elizabeth? A Double Decker. Maybe a Crunchie, or the chocolate egg with cream inside."

The kissing abruptly stopped and her hand stilled. "Candy? Are you talking about candy?" She pushed away from him with her mouth gaping open in indignation.

The laughter he had tried to repress came out in a torrent of mirth.

With a determined stare that countered the amusement she tried to suppress, Elizabeth moved to lay atop him, her breasts pressed against the muscles of his chest. Soon her lips moving over his and her tongue swirling in his mouth were not enough, and his visceral ache of longing intensified. Before he could ask, beg if need be, she straddled his hips and raised herself onto her knees. He immediately brought his hands to her breasts while she lowered herself onto him.

The sound of his name on her lips, urging him on, was nearly his own undoing. He lifted her by the hips, thrusting with firm strokes that had her reaching for his chest with her fingertips to steady herself. The hard, fast, steady rhythm made his breathing labored, and she braced her knees and rode, eventually crying out and trembling around him.

There was surely no lovelier feeling in any time than this, no sight more beautiful than his wife's head tipped back, her lips slightly parted, her breasts lightly rising and falling.

December 21, 2013
Winter Solstice

"Pemberley is two hundred years out of date, despite the improvements. The clothing on display from even the 1970s is so unlike what women wear today."

"You're out of date too, but you fit in well."

Darcy ignored her teasing as their footsteps echoed while they took a solitary tour of the house. "Will enough people pay to see a Georgian home and Victorian gowns in 2013 for us to remain at Pemberley?"

"I know you trust my judgment, and I don't doubt the educated opinions of the museum, costume, and historic home people impatient to work here. Not to mention the organizations that have given us funds, and the interest we're already generating. Pemberley will have a refined taste from its architecture and furnishings, and the clothes will humanize it. It's not just a stately home that's an example of Regency-era living. As of tomorrow, the Darcy family resides at Pemberley."

The past six months were spent restoring furniture to its original state, recreating furnishings when they couldn't obtain originals, and doing a lot of things involving the conservation of plasterwork and cleaning of oil paintings that Elizabeth did not understand. The gowns were cataloged and being organized into a collection under the direction of an exhibit manager. Pemberley would open to the public in the new year.

She paused in the gallery to look at Darcy's portrait from over two hundred years ago. "Do you think anyone will notice the striking similarity between you and this portrait?"

Darcy didn't even spare it a glance. "No one will notice."

"What makes you sure? You're not even ten years older now than when this was painted. It's *you*."

"Only those who shove themselves onto the notice of others, posting selfies, demanding attention, talking constantly, come under scrutiny. The generality of people now gaze right past what is in front of them."

"You don't think someone might say, 'That is definitely our Mr. Darcy'?"

"No one will assume anything out of the ordinary. It's not difficult for me to move about any longer, and I don't create undue notice, that thing about dinosaurs notwithstanding," he added.

She had seen the flicker of confusion in his eyes as he tried to construe the meaning in that conversation. One of the furniture movers had been looking for a footstool in a room piled with furniture and compared it to a dinosaur dig. *I would never have thought I had to tell him about dinosaurs and their fossils.* There was a tiredness in him after encounters like that. She wanted to comfort him, but pointing out that she saw his vulnerability from being out of place would hurt him more. He was still the master of Pemberley, after all.

Darcy walked to the other side of the gallery where Georgiana's family portrait hung, showing her and Mr. Willers with their son when he was around ten. Darcy looked at his sister, who was both long dead and yet, through Nine Ladies, still alive. Elizabeth slipped her hand into his and looked at Georgiana Willers.

"Read her letters again."

"You've been suggesting that all autumn."

"I know you miss her, and that you feel guilty for causing your friends and family worry."

"Everything else turned out better than I ever had imagined." He squeezed her hand. "I have no regrets. This is where I want to be."

"You should read her letters one more time, though," she encouraged.

"Why would I reread them when, in addition to life with you and constant work at Pemberley to occupy me, I have two hundred years' worth of culture and history to absorb into my knowledge?"

He would never read the diaries if she did not confess. "Fitzwilliam, I changed things."

He dropped her hand and gave her a quizzical look.

"You were right that going back and forth through time is dangerous. It could threaten their future and our life here. But I couldn't live with your feeling guilty, and I love Georgiana too and I didn't want her to be unhappy."

Darcy's face paled. "What have you done?"

"I found an artist to sketch a drawing based on a photo Charlotte took of us on our wedding day. The one of you and me outside, looking at each other and smiling. I wrote to Georgiana that we found each other and that Pemberley is as beautiful now as it was then. And on September 22, when you were away for the weekend with Frank watching the Manchester Derby, I wrapped it in oilcloth that I snuck out of the textile room, wrote Georgiana's name on it, hiked out to Stanton Moor, and threw it into the center of Nine Ladies before the sun went down. I waited until it vanished."

He looked stunned. When he didn't speak, she went on in a nervous ramble. "I didn't give her any details about this century or what we were doing with Pemberley, and I didn't write a thing about her future. I just wanted her to know that you were safe and happy so she wouldn't worry."

She watched as tears brightened his eyes, but he did not shed them.

She wondered if nineteenth-century Darcy would walk to stand by the window until he was in complete control. Instead, he asked quietly, "Do you think she found it?"

She nodded, holding back tears of her own. "I reread her letter from October 1813. She wrote how delighted she was to learn that her brother was married. It's four pages long! There are new letters tucked inside her diaries too. Colonel Fitzwilliam wrote some of them. You'll have to read them to see what changed, but I suspect all it did was make her a little happier than she would have been otherwise."

Darcy cleared his throat, likely using all his willpower to keep the tears in his eyes from falling.

"Thank you."

"You're welcome. I couldn't stand to have any regrets arising from how you left your loved ones to take away from your happiness here."

"I have a woman I love with every part of myself, I have my home, a job worth doing, and people who trust me. I have the hope of a family someday." He gave her a warm look. "I wouldn't have been melancholy or unhappy, but I'm grateful to you all the same." Darcy pressed a firm kiss against her lips and looked around the room with a disbelieving expression. "There is no rational reason Pemberley should still be mine in 2013."

"What does reason have to do with druid stone circles and time travel?" Darcy had no answer. "You cared for this land and its people well when it was yours before, and you'll take care of its future now just as well. Your plan worked; that's why Pemberley is still yours."

"It worked because my sister and her family felt a sense of duty to Pemberley's legacy, and because duty is a powerful force."

"Well, so are *you*. I've never known anyone as determined as you are. And," she lilted, wrapping her arms around his neck and giving him an arch smile, "you mean Pemberley is *ours*. I married you, after all. Marriage in this century means all my stuff is yours and all your stuff is mine."

"I prefer to think of our marriage as a rather lovely intertwining of lives and souls."

"Determined *and* romantic."

EPILOGUE

April 9, 2016

A side from the original principal bedrooms and dressing rooms and, of course, the ballroom, the rest of Pemberley's first floor were converted for private use in such a way as to make it so the Darcy family could live their lives without passing through security or running into a lecture on the transition from cage crinoline to bustles.

Elizabeth set her husband's morning coffee in front of him, and at the sound of the mug hitting the table, he murmured "thank you" from behind one of his daily newspapers.

"You are single-handedly keeping the newspaper industry in business."

"I stare at a screen often enough as it is; if I can get information from another source, I will happily take it."

It was an old argument, and Elizabeth smiled as she checked her email and read the day's news. They had ten minutes of companionable quiet before Darcy cursed. He handed her the paper, pointing to an article on the bottom.

Elizabeth skimmed it. *"Local Derby woman turns life around after years of drug addiction.* Troubled teenage years, heroin use, lost her kid, ten years in jail, got clean, now speaks to schools about not doing drugs. Why am I reading this?"

"Keep reading." His voice was low.

Elizabeth read how when Ms. Leigh was sixteen and living on the streets, she and her boyfriend did not realize their infant was missing until welfare services responded to the grandparents' concerns that they had not seen the child for months. Investigations showed that Ms. Leigh brought the child to drug-filled parties in the woods. Although cleared of harming the child, she served time for child neglect and failing to report a missing person. Ms. Leigh served additional time for drug possession before turning her life around; the baby's father died of a drug overdose. The article concluded with words from Ms. Leigh about her guilt over the loss of her fifteen-month-old daughter and how it fueled her mission to prevent other teenagers from making her mistakes.

Elizabeth set the paper down to see Darcy's pale face. "You think this is Georgiana's mother?"

"It says the daughter was lost when Ms. Leigh was sixteen and she is now thirty-six; she could have lost her daughter in 1995. It explains why we never found missing child articles around the equinox—her parents were too addicted to drugs to know what was going on, and months passed before the child was reported missing. We searched the wrong dates."

"You think this Ms. Leigh was partying on Stanton Moor, and Georgiana crawled into the stone circle?"

Darcy had a pained look on his face. "The timing makes it possible, and the woman has the same nose, smile, and fair hair as Georgiana."

She did look similar to Georgiana's portrait in the gallery. "Fitzwilliam, what should we do?"

Her husband rested his elbows on the table, folded his hands, and pressed his forehead against them. "I don't know, dearest. Her greatest regret is not knowing if her daughter is alive."

"We can't say that her daughter is living two hundred years in the *past*."

"I feel guilty that I know something that might ease her mind, yet if I anonymously write to tell her anything about the life of her missing child, I would distress this woman even more. In the end, nothing can be proven, and she might suffer more than she already has."

Elizabeth gave him a sad smile. "She experienced a terrible loss and made awful choices, and now she's changed her life and is using that experience to help others. Georgiana was cared for, loved, and was happy. I love that you want to help this woman, but not even you can solve everyone's problems."

"What will we do if others appear at Nine Ladies?"

"Georgiana's letters never mentioned anyone appearing or disappearing while she lived at Pemberley. If this started when Stanton Moor was first excavated in the 1780s and people only appeared then from the future, I think it's safe to say no one is going to disappear from the nineteenth century into the seventeenth, or the twenty-third into the twenty-first."

"Even if no one from this time went back after you did, it is possible that someone from 1816 could wander into Nine Ladies and appear in our time."

"We check twice a year and no one has ever appeared."

"Not yet."

She came around the table to kiss Darcy's forehead. "If it happens, we'll deal with it, and we'll help them. You and I are experts." He answered by wrapping an arm around her waist and tugging her into his lap. "I have to run. Charlotte and Mary will be here soon, and I want to meet them so they don't get stopped by a docent who wants to show them plasterwork."

Darcy lifted her to her feet and slapped her lightly on her backside. "I like those," he said, gesturing at her legs. "What are they?"

"Leggings. Jane sent them to me." She shrugged. "The patterns are wild, but she tells me they're popular in the States right now. I'm surprised you like them."

"I like them because when your shirt pushes up, I can see you better in all of your callipygian glory."

Usually she was the one who used perplexing words. "And what does 'callipygian' mean, Mr. Darcy?"

"Look it up." He smiled.

She gave him a long glance, not liking his pretend innocent expression. She grabbed her phone and sounded out the word the best she could, walking toward the door as she typed. She made it as far as their entry hall before she ran back to the kitchen. "Did you just say in Regency-talk that I have a nice ass?"

MARCH 30, 2018

Pemberley's second annual Historical Costume and Textile Conference had twice the attendance of its first. Elizabeth recognized the curator from the Fashion Museum in Bath who talked with the patrons of the School of Historical Dress. A cluster of Costume Society members spoke to reenactors. Attendees wore the historic dress between the late eighteenth to early twentieth centuries. Pemberley was filled with teachers, students, fashion designers, reenactors, costume makers, and museum staff to promote the study, conservation, and construction of historic dress.

Elizabeth loved the conferences, the consulting, and the educational outreach Pemberley did relating to historical dress. If Darcy was more interested in managing their staff and their tenants, she was more interested in the fashion exhibits and which of Pemberley's items had been loaned to which museum somewhere in the world.

Catherine Willers-Darcy's 1940 siren suit was currently at the V&A, Georgiana's 1867 silk taffeta crinoline dress was at the Met, and the 1926 flapper dress was soon to come back from Kyoto. It was satisfying to think that in one hundred years someone from the Musée de la Mode et du Textile in the Louvre might request something she wore.

Elizabeth looked across the crowded ballroom until she found Darcy at the center of a small group. He had wholeheartedly thrown himself into his life here, and there were times she could forget he had been born in 1784 and not 1984. She knew he made every attempt to behave in a manner that was above reproach, to avoid doing anything that might expose him to ridicule. He had even learned to drive a car, at least once he ceased trying to stop by bracing his foot on the gas pedal and pulling back on the wheel while saying "whoa."

She watched her husband talk with Pemberley's own employees. *He'll never be a loquacious man, no matter what century he's in.* He inspired respect, despite his reserve, and his employees had only the best things to say about working for him. While he remembered the details of their lives, Darcy made certain that personal conversations never circled around to him. His staff stayed within the boundaries he prescribed for them, yet they didn't think less of him for knowing little about him.

The director of Past Pleasures's costume department stopped speaking to the pattern maker next to them. "And where did the pattern for your gown come from, Mrs. Darcy?"

Elizabeth was wearing the same gown she had once worn through a time-travel stone circle while she hauled a dying man to erythromycin. "It's been in the family for years; it's a morning gown from 1810. What I know for certain is that it was shortened and taken in because it was designed for someone taller and bustier than I am."

"Are Mr. Darcy's clothes reproductions?"

No, his sister made his shirt in 1812. "Those are original evening dress too. They were found in a trunk when we did renovations to open the house to the public." She imagined Georgiana thought she was doing her brother a favor to leave some of his own clothes, but in his mind, it was a punishment. Darcy detested "dressing up in costume." Elizabeth thought it was because he resented having the clothes he contentedly wore for over twenty-five years reduced to playing dress-up like Mary Lucas.

"I understand that your wedding gown was recently added to the collection."

Elizabeth noticed that her husband, a public history professor engaged to give a lecture, the event's coordinator, and their fashion archivist were now in a heated discussion. Darcy's expression was as black as his evening coat.

"Yeah, it's on the ground floor, along with the George III diamond tiara I wore that belonged to Georgiana Willers's mother, Lady Anne Darcy. Would you please excuse me?"

Elizabeth smoothly made her way through the jovial costumed crowd. When she reached the group, she motioned for them to follow her out of sight of the others and toward the gallery. "Is something the matter?" She looked at Darcy, but the event coordinator answered.

"The model from the historical interpretation company the professor arranged for his lecture tomorrow backed out."

Elizabeth turned to the professor, who was wider than he was tall and wearing reproduction regimentals from the early 1900s. "We can get images to put on the screen. Your lecture doesn't have to change because the model won't be here."

"Mrs. Darcy, the presentation is about the structure of the layers of men's fashion during the early nineteenth century. It complements several other events on the program. Verbal descriptions will not do it justice."

"And of course, our formal collection is only *women's* clothing," their fashion archivist added. Elizabeth realized what was being asked of her husband and why he looked as though, usually a dignified and calm man in public, he were about to flip his lid.

"A demonstration of how the clothes are put on and how they properly fit on the body is what you need for your lecture?"

"Yes."

"Can we get another model with a historically accurate Regency costume here by nine a.m.?" she asked the coordinator, who said he'd had no luck thus far. Elizabeth refrained from asking the portly professor in a Boer War uniform if he had accurate Regency-era clothing he would be willing to take off in front of a crowd. "Keep trying, but if you need someone to model clothes from the early eighteen hundreds to demonstrate how they were designed to fit, Mr. Darcy would be pleased to step in."

Darcy looked so angry with her that he would not cross the street to stomp on her if she was on fire, but Elizabeth gestured for the others to return to the ballroom. To his credit, Darcy kept his silence until he marched her into their private residence.

"What in God's name was that? I once thought I could refuse you nothing, but you cannot mean to put me forward to participate in such an undignified spectacle! It would be the most humiliating picture. I do not scruple to add that it is an insult to propose my involvement in such a scheme."

She held back her smile. Darcy always slipped into his former way of speaking when he was angry. The contractions were dropped, his sentence structure changed, and that haughty expression of superiority came back in full force. *It's adorable.* "The theme is the evolution of clothing design and construction from 1800 to 1900. Clothing in the late Georgian era and how it was made to fit is how they're kickstarting their program. They can't get anyone else at this late notice, and you have your own clothes."

"I hardly know what to say, how to class, or how to regard this offensive request. You must comprehend that the professor intends to discuss the entirety of a gentleman's wardrobe."

"You won't be naked."

"I would nonetheless begin in a state of dishabille that, frankly, madam, I am surprised you would wish anyone other than yourself to witness."

"It's not like you'll be swinging around a pole!"

"I have no notion as to what that means!"

She sighed. "I know, and I love you more for it. Fitzwilliam, we want these people to come back next year."

"You know the participants will not leave or refuse to be involved with Pemberley over one missed lecture whose absence was not our fault."

"But you will impress them, and everyone will talk about how Mr. Darcy saved the day. It will give people a way to talk about you without there being any questions we would have to avoid. All you have to do is stand there." She neglected to remind him he would begin in only a lawn shirt and short drawers, long drawers if he was lucky. "It's not an unreasonable request in modern times."

"You ask too much of me. I am of the opinion that modernity is just an excuse for a lack of manners."

"Think of what you would do for anyone who depended on Pemberley in 1818. If a meadow needed to be drained, or a roof needed to be repaired, or someone needed a position, or if gifts of food or medicine were needed, you wouldn't hesitate because it was your responsibility. This is the same thing; you are helping people who depend on Pemberley."

Darcy closed his eyes, and Elizabeth played her trump card. "You know I love those tight riding breeches you wear with the top boots, and the yellow-and-white waistcoat with the stand collar . . ." She punctuated this statement with a few kisses along his jaw and a light bite on his earlobe.

"I insist on no pictures. The last thing I need is Frank to get a hold of them."

Frank would pay good money to see his friend red-faced standing in front of a crowd in a Regency undershirt and boxers. "I'll tell everyone they can take notes, but they can only take pictures at the end when you're fully dressed."

"Do not insist on my being agreeable."

He still looked miserable; she pecked him on the lips. "Well, *that* would be an unreasonable request."

THAT WAS THE MOST HUMILIATING AND INSULTING TWO HOURS OF MY LIFE. To appear in public in drawers, stockings, and a shirt! To have a stranger—not a trusted valet but a stranger—dress him, and before a crowd, was a near-intolerable indignity. He was not the sort of man to complain about his wife. He would not make Elizabeth the subject of sport or himself an object to be pitied. However, Darcy wished he could have told the gawking crowd whose fault it was that he suffered for their sake.

He stormed into their bedroom, eager to take off the clothes and wear something less conspicuous.

"No, leave the hat on! I love the hat!"

In his pique, Darcy had stormed past Elizabeth without seeing her. He gave her a cold look before taking off the hat and setting it slowly on the chest of drawers. He ignored her pout. "Why are you dressed as though you are about to make morning calls in 1811?"

"The lecture on ladies' clothes in the early nineteenth century that paralleled your topic was earlier. I wanted to commiserate with you."

"No one asked *you* to exhibit half-naked before a crowd and be ogled by a horde of middle-aged men who demanded to take your photograph."

"Only because you have too much love, pride, and delicacy to let me. I was born in 1987; I'm much less inhibited. I watched your show from the back of the room. Those lady costume professionals were swooning in their corsets." She slipped off her spencer jacket and walked closer.

Her flattery would get her nowhere. "I had to wear riding boots, gloves, and a hat in the *ballroom*. My mother would turn over in her grave."

"I like the boots too." After he refused to meet her playfulness, she said, "Did the inaccuracies drive you crazy?"

"That alleged historian was often incorrect. Why are these fashion professionals so concerned with the dates on old Ackerman plates? They cannot believe a style was worn before or after the year it was printed in one magazine!"

"Total morons," she said absently. Elizabeth's attention had moved up from his top boots, and she was now undoing his coat buttons.

"He was wrong about the styles of buttons in use at the time. Simply because there *were* many styles available, it does not follow that they were equally worn by people of fashion. Dorset Wheels and Singletons were worn more often than the others he mentioned."

His coat was pushed off his shoulders, forcefully, and he allowed her to tug it off his arms. "His abuse of the pocket watch was abysmal, Elizabeth. He swung it around by the chain; the chain! No one does that."

"You're going to leave the boots on, right?"

"You're not even listening."

Elizabeth gestured to the hook and eyes on the back of her gown. Darcy shrugged and unhooked them. She turned back to face him and let the gown fall to the floor. He kept his eyes firmly on her face. "No, I am not leaving the boots on. I shall not leave this costume on another second."

"But you know how much I like it. You're just mad about the lecture. Though who knows why because you were the hero of the day."

"I prefer suits now to this." He ran his hand down his waistcoat. "This feels too much like a caricature."

She was determined to have her way. "Either one works for me. I've had enough practice taking off both." Within seconds, she proved her point by untying his cravat and tossing it aside. He tried to hold on to his anger while Elizabeth happily slipped off his waistcoat. He attempted to glare while she struggled to unlace her petticoat that tied in the back. *There is something to be said for zippers.* She had an easier time undoing her stay laces that tied in the front.

"Still mad at me for making you model?" she asked with her fingers tracing the buttons on the fall of his breeches.

"Infuriated. You know I have an unyielding temper." He sat on the edge of the bed. "And for that, I won't leave the boots on." Darcy tried to contain his grin as he made slow work of removing his boots, and his wife made a great show of being disappointed that the boots would come off. "I do not know how I shall forgive you."

"You can't because I haven't asked for forgiveness. I won't apologize for making the most of a situation that got you into breeches and boots."

He couldn't help but smile at her now. He reached out to her, pulling her until she fell into his lap. Darcy tried to kiss her, but she leaned back and whispered, "And I know you love the idea of seducing Miss Bennet out of a dress like this."

He rolled his eyes before lowering his head to kiss her. She breathed him in, tracing her tongue along his bottom lip. He slid his tongue into her mouth and sighed with pleasure when she deepened the kiss and swept her tongue along his. Elizabeth let out a moan at the contact, her hand coming up to thread in his hair. She shifted to straddle his hips, her lips never leaving his as she kissed him feverishly. Darcy crept a hand slowly up over her stomach to her breast, causing her to strain in anticipation. What began with slow, gentle stroking became an insistent grasping in reply to her soft moans. He lifted up her shift and brought a hand under, and then pulled his lips away far enough to murmur, "That's not historically accurate."

"I can't go out without underwear; it's too weird."

He shifted her off of his lap and stood in front of her, pulling his shirt over his head. He gestured with his hand, and Elizabeth slipped off the offending item, now only wearing a nearly transparent shift.

"I'll remember that the next time you ask me to wear these clothes."

She smiled before her tongue invaded his mouth with quick strokes and circles. He felt her breath hitch against his lips as he moved his hands down her body. One hand's nails scraped up from the nape of his neck, keeping their lips pressed closely together, and the other hand's nails raked down his back, driving him wild. His control splintered when her right hand later moved down to what strained to free itself from his clothing. He groaned, the deep sound jarring against what had been until now silent except for soft sighs and low sounds.

"All this because of breeches and a pair of boots?" he breathed into her ear, while he squeezed her breast harder through the thin layer of linen separating them.

"I like you in a suit too," she panted as she unfastened the rest of his buttons. "The first time I saw you wear one to go to that nightclub, I wanted to tear it off of you."

"What did you want that night at Charlotte's? How did you want me?"

She captured his neck in a wild kiss that was all tongue and teeth, tearing another moan from him. Darcy pulled away to look in her eyes. "Tell me, Elizabeth."

Elizabeth breathed faster, her skin flushed pink, her voice shaking. "I loved you, and you were leaving. I wanted to feel the imprint of your mouth and your hands on me, the weight of you against me, pressing into me hard enough so maybe I could still feel you after you were gone forever."

Their last few articles of clothing were torn off and, before she could speak again, Elizabeth was on her back and he was on top of her, his lips hard on hers, his tongue deep in her mouth, and his hands were fierce on her, then beneath her, holding her firm while he thrust deeply into her. She wrapped her legs around his hips, and they loved each other long and hard until they were both panting and broke apart with rapturous cries.

DECEMBER 21, 2018
WINTER SOLSTICE

Darcy had grown accustomed to electric lighting, but florescent bulbs were unnatural, unflattering, and flickered irritatingly. He had been seated in the same chair for long enough to wonder if the unsteady light from the bulb in the corridor could induce an epileptic seizure.

If I suffer a fit and fall to the floor, I would be so lucky if those walking past stepped over me rather than stepped on me.

His elbows rested on his knees, his hands were clasped, and his chin rested upon them. No one said a word to him, but Darcy noticed the raised eyebrows, slight frowns, and surprised looks of the people who passed him as he bored a hole in the doorway across from him with his eyes.

This chair was where he ought to be. No one agreed with him, save Elizabeth. Having been married for five years, he knew by now which of her agreements were ones he could take at face value, which ones he ought to assume the opposite, and which ones required further discussion to ascertain her true feelings. In this case, Darcy was certain he could sit in this chair for the duration.

It is not as though I have been removed from this affair. Darcy shifted his weight in the most uncomfortable chair built in the last two hundred years. He attended every appointment; he read every book; what Elizabeth did, he did; and from what she abstained, so did he likewise. He accepted what the role required of him in this century with eager delight.

That happiness, mingled with a natural sense of terror, was now being replaced by guilt. Another woman glanced his way as she passed and rolled her eyes. Elizabeth said it did not matter what the modern convention was and that he had made enough sacrifices for her sake.

For all the talk of the equality between the sexes, was this not the one sphere in which, naturally, women must rightfully have to themselves? Self-reproach crept into his heart and pushed aside the anxiety and excitement that had, until now, taken over. *She said I could remain here, and I believed her.*

His phone had chimed a dozen times since they arrived. Mrs. Bennet regretted being woken up. Jane would be on a flight after she could get her shifts covered. James Tasker asked if they'd made it in time. Frank asked if he fainted. The rest were well wishes and requests for news when there was any to be had. That was the drawback to his wife being launched, a week early, in the middle of their annual Christmas party for their friends, tenants, and employees.

As far as Elizabeth was concerned, he could stay in this chair, but he knew he ought to be in the room. It was, likely, not an obligation comprehensible to any man born before 1950, but he had never avoided any responsibility his family had need of.

When he knocked and entered, the nurse pursed her lips and said it was time for the doctor and left to find her. Charlotte looked as though she had spent hours plotting his painful murder. Thankfully, he received a stay of execution, and she moved to allow him to come to Elizabeth's bedside and take his wife's hand.

"You look much better than you did when I brought you in three hours ago." Granted, his wife whimpered and breathed more loudly than when he last saw her, but he had suspected screaming and cursing would be more along the lines of what would follow.

"Pethidine, my dear Darcy. You ready to help me breathe my way to serenity?"

"You're not disappointed in me?"

"I always knew you'd change your mind on your own." She smiled briefly, then closed her eyes and exhaled slowly. Darcy was about to say she had more faith in him than he did, but she crushed his hand with a force unknown to man for another thirty seconds before she let go and collapsed. She heaved a weary sigh. "I'm glad you're here."

"So am I. Do you need to break the fingers on my other hand?"

"This is your fault, anyway. It's the least you can do."

"I THOUGHT YOU LIKED THE NAME GEORGIANA," ELIZABETH SAID QUIETLY.

"I do, but people would often pronounce it wrong. She would always be saying 'it's Geor-jayna, not Geor-gi-anna.'"

"Anne, then, for a first name rather than a middle name? Or Catherine?"

Darcy stared into an unfocused set of blue eyes, wondering how long before they turned deep brown to match her parents'. "Now that she's here, I think she ought not to be named for any Darcy. I don't want her to feel obligated to take on Pemberley. It would be unfair for her to feel that she must live up to my sister or my sister's great-granddaughter."

"You forget she's a Darcy. I know from experience that, either by nature or nurture, Darcys are a devoted, family-oriented lot. How would you feel if she wants nothing to do with Pemberley?"

"Pemberley can become a charitable trust, if need be. Its legacy will live on even if no Darcy manages its care, and my daughter can make her own choices. I wish for my family's happiness above all else. I have more pressing things than a house or a museum to consider now." The tiny swaddled bundle gave a wide yawn, and Darcy carefully handed his daughter to his wife.

Elizabeth gazed at her for a long moment. "What about Sandra?"

"I'm not familiar with that name. Cassandra I know, but not Sandra."

"Sandra was Mrs. Reynolds's first name."

He shared a look with her and, not for the first time this long evening, felt the hot pinprick of tears that threatened to fall. "That is perfect." *Sandra Anne Darcy.* Darcy sat on the edge of his wife's bed and kissed her forehead. "Do you remember the name of the artist you commissioned to sketch the wedding picture of us?"

Elizabeth, with drowsy eyes, tilted her head to meet his gaze, smiling softly. When she nodded, he said, "After we return to Pemberley, I have a letter to write to be posted in March. I can think of a few people who might wish to meet the new Miss Darcy."

THE END

JOIN HEATHER'S NEWSLETTER

Receive the *Persuasion*-inspired short story *That Voice* when you sign up for my monthly newsletter. It imagines what might have happened if Captain Wentworth fell on the Cobb instead of Louisa.

Subscribe for sales info and new release updates, exclusive excerpts, contests, and giveaways!

www.heathermollauthor.com

ACKNOWLEDGMENTS

With every book I write I thank the same people, but my debt to them continues to grow. As always, I am so grateful to my friend and editor Sarah Pesce who works tirelessly to make my stories better while cheering me on. Thank you to my friend Cathie Smith for sharing all of the highs and lows of indie publishing with me. I am so appreciative of the A Happy Assembly community and to everyone who was on either #Team1811 or #Team2011. My parents continue to be the reason I believe that I can accomplish anything I set my mind to.

This book would not exist without the unconditional and wholehearted support of my husband and the cheerful encouragement of my son, who proudly tells people that his mom writes, "really good Jane Austen books."

ALSO BY HEATHER MOLL

An Appearance of Goodness
Can a Derbyshire meeting lead to love or will Pemberley be plunged into mystery?

An Affectionate Heart
Are love and affection enough to overcome the pain of grief and anger?

Nine Ladies
How can Darcy and Elizabeth overcome 200 years of differences in this time-travel love story?

Mr Darcy's Valentine
Will an exchange of secret valentines lead to love?

A Hopeful Holiday
Is the holiday season a perfect setting for a second chance at love?

His Choice of a Wife
When a man's honor is at stake, what is he willing to risk for the woman he loves?

Two More Days at Netherfield
How would spending a few extra days in each other's company affect the relationship between Elizabeth Bennet and Mr. Darcy?

The Gentlemen Are Detained
"Will Elizabeth welcome the renewal of our acquaintance or will she draw back from me?"

ABOUT THE AUTHOR

Heather Moll writes romantic variations of Jane Austen's classic novels. She is an avid reader of mysteries and biographies with a masters in information science. She found Jane Austen later than she should have and made up for lost time by devouring her letters and unpublished works, joining JASNA, and spending too much time researching the Regency era. She is the author of *An Appearance of Goodness*, *An Affectionate Heart*, *Nine Ladies*, and *Loving Miss Tilney*. She lives with her husband and son, and struggles to balance all the important things, like whether to buy groceries or stay home and write.

Connect with her on social media or on her blog, and subscribe to her newsletter for updates and free stories.

- facebook.com/HeatherMollAuthor
- twitter.com/HMollAuthor
- instagram.com/HeatherMollAuthor
- goodreads.com/HeatherMoll
- bookbub.com/authors/heather-moll

Made in the USA
Las Vegas, NV
28 September 2023